AM[illegible]EVE

The Accidental Actress

First edition

This book was professionally typeset on Reedsy. Find out more at reedsy.com

"False face must hide what
the false heart doth know"

William Shakespeare, Macbeth

Preface

This book is the 2nd in the Heather Bay Romance series. Although each book can be read in isolation, it's strongly recommended that you read book 1, *The Accidental Impostor*, first, to avoid spoilers.

Heather Bay is a fictional town in the Highlands of Scotland. Below is a map to help you find your way around...

The Two Sisters
Puffin Cove
Darroch Mountains
Thistle Falls
Scarlett
Heather Bay
Lexie
The Torr
Jack
Glenroch
Emerald

Chapter 1

I suppose the first thing you need to know about me is that I'm the villain of this story. The bad guy. Girl. Whatever.

The second thing you need to know is that I absolutely *did not* pour that drink on the guy by the bar on purpose, like he's trying to say I did. He must have just knocked me off-balance while he was trying to grope my ass, is all. At least, that's my story and I'm sticking to it.

(The third thing is that one of those first two things isn't *strictly* true. I'll leave you to work out which one it is...)

"Lexie, we've been through this before. We can't assault the customers. Not even the ones who richly deserve it. You know that."

Summer puts both hands on her hips and gives me what I've come to think of simply as The Look. It's approximately one part exasperation and one part resignation, and it normally means she's about to push her hair back from her forehead, and say, "Oh, *Leeexiiieee*," like she's my mum about to tell me she's not angry, she's just *disappointed*.

Summer is my boss here at Joe's Bar, but she's also my flatmate (Or "roommate" as they say here in California. Those crazy kids.), and my best friend. Well, my *only* friend, really, unless you count my mum, and I'm not even sure my *mum* would count my mum right now — especially considering I haven't spoken to her in almost 12 months — so... yeah. I guess I'm not much of a people person. What can I say?

Anyway, Summer's Australian, and when I asked her if her name was supposed to be a reflection of her sunny personality, she pretended to punch me in the thigh.

I took that as a "no", then. It turns out Summer's not much of a people person either, really. I'm pretty sure that's why we get on so well.

"I swear, Summer, I didn't do it. I would *never*."

I widen my eyes innocently as I look her right in the eye, the very picture of sincerity.

This will work. I see it will, because I'm a practiced liar, having been honing my skills since I was a kid. Also, no one can resist my baby blues when I threaten to turn on the tears, like I am now. I might be the villain, but I *look* like the heroine, all blonde hair and blue eyes, set above a cute little upturned nose. And that's the main thing, isn't it? When you're pretty, you can get away with anything.

Well, *almost* anything.

Just to be sure I get away with this, I allow my bottom lip to wobble slightly as I lower my eyes to the ground. When I raise them again to meet Summer's, they're filled with tears — crying on demand has been my party trick, ever since I was a kid — and my boss sighs in defeat, before shrugging her shoulders and handing me a tray of drinks.

"Oh, *Leeexiieee*," she says, smiling at me despite the lingering doubt I can see in her hazel eyes. "Take these to table 12, will ya? And try to stay out of trouble, Lex. I mean it."

I smirk with satisfaction as I turn away.

Lexie, 1; Creepy guy at the bar, 0.

I win.

I *always* win.

Except when I *don't*, of course.

There *was* one time I didn't win. Just one time, but it's the reason I'm here, really. I don't want to talk about it. It's amazing how often people *ask*, though. Not about how I screwed-up my *entire life,* obviously; that would be a pretty weird conversation starter, really, even by L.A. standards. But they do ask what brought me from the Highlands of Scotland to Hollywood, and I can't exactly tell them the truth, so I mostly just smile sweetly and say I really love that Human League song. You know, the one about working as a waitress in a cocktail bar?

(And, okay, *Joe's* isn't so much a 'cocktail bar' as it is some random dive bar with sticky floors and questionable hygiene standards. No one writes songs about those bars, though, do they?)

People love that answer. It doesn't matter that it's not true; it makes a good story, and that's all most people care about. Trust one who knows.

But as I was saying. I'm not the heroine, and this is not a love-story. How could it be? I'm just a barmaid with a bad attitude, and right now I *really* want to get back in Summer's good books, so I grit my teeth and conjure up a smile as I carry the tray over to the table by the window, stealing a curious glance at the occupants as I set it down.

There are two of them: both men, but otherwise as different as can be. One is older — late fifties, I'd say — with neat gray hair and an immaculate navy suit, which my practiced eye can tell cost more than my rent this month. A silver fox, Summer, would call him. I'd rate him 7/10, but only because I'm not into older men. Otherwise he could be pushing an eight.

The other man, however, is a solid three. Baseball hat crammed over his eyes. Thick black hoodie, even though it's over eighty degrees outside. Saggy shorts. *Pool slides.* One of those terrible, bushy beards guys started wearing a few years back, when everyone suddenly looked like axe murderers.

No, wait: that's unnecessarily rude to axe murderers, isn't it?

As if reading my mind, the man at the table looks up, his eyes meeting mine with an intensity that should really be terrifying given that I was just picturing him on a murderous rampage, except... except his eyes are green flecked with gold, and, even from across the table, I can say beyond doubt that they're most beautiful eyes I've ever seen — and, of course, they're fringed by the kind of thick, dark lashes that are totally wasted on men, and that women will gladly pay a fortune to fake. They don't make up for the beard and the scruffy outfit, obviously — no eyes in the world are *that* nice, let's face it — but they're enough to stop me in my tracks and mentally raise his score to a 3.5. A grudging one, but still.

"Everything okay here, guys?" I say brightly, deliberately looking away to force him to drop his gaze before it gets any more uncomfortable than it already is. "Can I get you anything else?"

"You can get *me* something, smart ass. Like an apology for that little stunt you just pulled for starters."

I roll my eyes as I turn to face the guy from the bar, who's followed me across the room, his jaw set in anger. There's a large wet patch on his crotch from where the drink I "spilled" landed, and, judging by the wedding band I can see on his finger, I'm guessing that stain's going to be pretty hard to explain when he gets home to his wife tonight.

I guess groping the waitress wasn't *such a great idea after all, was it? Who would've thought it?*

"Is there a problem, Sir?"

I straighten my shoulders, trying to make myself look taller. God knows I'm used to dealing with creeps — it kind of comes with that "dive bar" territory, you know? But this one is angrier than most of them, and as he takes a step towards me, I briefly wonder if I should try to reign in my impulses some of the time — at least when it comes to the customers.

I bet there's a 12-step program for that. I should look into it sometime.

"You better believe there's a problem, you stupid Scottish bitch," Drunk Guy says, taking another step closer. "And you know what it is, too."

A couple of flecks of spittle land on my cheek, and I try my best not to gag as I raise my hand to pointedly wipe them off.

I do not *get paid enough to deal with this shit.*

The man is right up in my face now. His breath stinks of beer, and there's something caught between his front teeth. I hover somewhere between justified fear and the totally illogical desire to insult him again, and, before I can figure out which side to land on, an arm reaches out from somewhere behind me and pushes Drunk Guy firmly in the chest, making him stagger back a step.

"Hey, knock it off," says Mr. 3.5, speaking as if this is a perfectly normal conversation to be having with a stranger in a bar. "And watch your language, will you? No one wants to hear that shit."

He moves a sliver closer to me. I really want to look around and see what he's doing, but I don't want to miss Drunk Guy's reaction, so I just stand there, feeling a bit like Princess Leia when Luke and Han finally turn up to rescue her. The difference is, though, that Leia immediately took charge of that situation, like the strong, sassy woman she is, and I'm just sort of *standing here*, feeling a bit stupid, really. And also kind of scared, if I'm honest.

(Oh, and the other difference is that Han Solo wasn't wearing pool slides and a hoodie, obviously. Harrison Ford's career would've taken a totally different trajectory if he had been.)

Drunk Guy stumbles backwards, then rears forward again, squaring up to 3.5 as if he's getting ready to fight him. Behind the bar, Summer whirls around to see what's going on, and I see her reach for the phone, ready to summon Joel, the security guard. Just as she picks it up, though, Drunk Guy has a sudden change of heart.

"Oh," he says, his bushy eyebrows raising in surprise as he looks from 3.5 to me, then back again. "Wow. Sorry, man, I didn't realize."

I look on, confused, as he raises his hands in a gesture of surrender.

"Wow," he says again, his eyes still fixed on 3.5. "No offense, man. I'll get outta your hair. Can I buy you a drink, in fact? Here, lemme buy you a drink..."

He reaches into his pocket and pulls out a wallet, but 3.5 continues to stand there behind me, his body radiating heat onto my back.

"No need. Just leave the lady alone, got it?"

The man behind me hasn't moved since his initial contact with Drunk Guy, but now he steps away and sits back down at the table, leaving me feeling strangely exposed without his comforting presence behind me.

I wish he'd come back — pool slides, weird beard and all.

Drunk Guy raises his hands again before walking backwards, all the way to the front door, which he almost trips over in his attempt to find his way through while still staring at 3.5. As the door finally closes behind me, Summer shoots a questioning look in my direction, which I answer with a quick shrug of the shoulders.

Not me almost starting a fight between two of the customers. Nuh-uh.

"Um, thanks," I say, turning to the table, where 3.5 and Silver Fox have resumed their conversation in hushed voices, the brief altercation already forgotten. "That was really... decent of you. I mean, I could totally have handled it obviously, because I'm a strong, sassy woman. Like Princess Leia. But, you know, *thanks.*"

I actually mean what I'm saying, but I'm not really used to speaking so sincerely — or randomly mentioning Princess Leia — so the words come out a little stiffer than I intended. I plaster on my brightest smile to make up for it, and 3.5 looks up in time to catch the full effect of it.

"You're, you know, *welcome,*" he says, allowing those luminous eyes of his to rest on me for a second. "I hate creeps like that. Hey," he adds, almost as an afterthought. "You're Scottish, right? I noticed the accent."

I nod, hoping he's not going to tell me he's one fifty-third Scottish on his mother's side, or ask me if I know his great-aunt Jeanie, from Shetland. I get that kind of thing a lot. What is it with Americans and their need to be something else all the time? Why can't they just be themselves?

Haha, nice one, Lexie. Like you *can talk.*

Thankfully, though, 3.5 has something else in mind.

"Can you recommend me a whisky?" he asks, swirling his glass in distaste. "A better one than this, I mean? I heard of a new blend called The 39, or something like that. You heard of that one?"

I stand there open-mouthed as the floor of the bar drops sharply away from me, making me reach out and grab the table in front of me for support.

I can recommend him a whisky, all right. My family own a brewery back in Scotland, so you could say that whisky's in our blood. Quite literally, in some cases. It's one of the reasons I went into bar work when I moved here, actually; it's one of the few things I know anything about. Sometimes when I'm serving drinks, all it takes is the slightest whiff of whisky and I'm right back there in Heather Bay, listening to the sea crash on the rocks from my little cottage. And sometimes that memory is so painful that it's all I can do not to burst into tears right there in the middle of the bar. Which would be unusual for me, because I *never* cry. Well, not for real, anyway.

As it happens, the brand 3.5's asking about — The 39 — is brewed in Heather Bay, too, so yes, I *have* heard of it. I really wish I hadn't, though, because, in a roundabout way, the owner of that brand is the reason I'm out here in L.A., serving beer and throwing drinks at customers, rather than back home, where.... well, where I'd be doing much the same thing, actually, only for my Mum's business rather than for someone else's. And even though it's all my fault, and I like it here just fine, I sometimes wish that's exactly what I was doing.

(Not the throwing drinks bit, of course. I hardly ever wish I was doing that.)

But this is my penance. Being here is my punishment for what I did back home, which is why, once I've taken a second to recover from this unexpected collision of my old life and my new one, I straighten up again, and look 3.5 in the eye, smiling as if my heart doesn't feel like it's been ripped right out of my chest, and completely ignoring the nagging pain in my stomach which started up as soon as he mentioned The 39.

"I'm sorry, sir, I've never heard of it," I say, shrugging apologetically, as I pick up his now-empty glass. "I guess it can't be any good."

Oh yeah, that's the other thing you need to know about me and my life here: it's all fake. Everything in L.A. is fake — from the impressive pair of boobs on the woman in the corner of the bar to the lie I just told the man in front of me. And that's fine with me, really, because if none of this is real, that means it can be whatever I want it to be. *I* can be whatever I want to be.

And that's exactly why I like it.

Chapter 2

Do you ever do that thing where you put on some music and pretend you're in the opening scenes of a movie, even though you're actually doing something totally ordinary, like going for a run, say, or loading the dishwasher?

(I'm going to pretend you said yes to that. Otherwise this confession will be *super*-awkward.)

I do that all the time. I'm doing it now, in fact, as Summer and I clear tables and give the floor of the bar a half-hearted swipe with the mop at the end of the night. In real life, I'm a waitress wiping sticky drink residue off a table, my hair pulled back, and my eyes heavy with fatigue. In my mind, though, I'm the star of my own personal movie: the camera framing me perfectly as I stand, Cinderella-like in the middle of the empty bar, the dirty glasses and tacky neon signs acquiring a poignancy that's totally lacking in real life as the music swells around me.

In the movie of my imaginary life, I'm no longer Lexie — Heather Bay exile, and Woman With Only One Friend. No, I'm Alexandra; tragic heroine of some Oscar-nominated tale, the details of which I haven't quite ironed out yet, but it'll be *epic*, I'm sure.

(This version of myself is also at least 4 inches taller than my actual self, and looks a bit like a young Grace Kelly, who Mum — in a rare moment of praise — once said I reminded her of. So if you could imagine me like that from now on, that would be fantastic, thank you.)

"Oh my God, Lexie, you've *got* to come and see this!"

I pause in the act of wiping down my last table as Summer's voice breaks into my silver-screen daydream, making the image in my head shatter like a champagne flute being dropped from a great height.

To be perfectly honest, I don't really care about whatever it is she wants to show me. It's been a long night, and, unfortunately for me, the trouble didn't end when Drunk Guy left the bar, because, rather than heading home — you know, like a *normal* person? — the dickhead stood outside, taking photos through the grimy window, until finally Joel had to threaten to call the police unless he moved on.

He did, of course — I mean, *we* all know Joel's a complete softie, who's probably never raised his *voice* in his life, let alone his fists, but he *is* 6'5", and built like a tank, so people tend not to argue with him if they can possibly help it. Not even drunk ones. I've felt uneasy about the whole thing ever since, though; the same way I do when there's a storm brewing over Heather Bay, and the air feels heavy and loaded, even though you can't see the dark clouds yet.

Why was Drunk Guy taking photos of the bar? And who was he photographing? Was it me? Mr. 3.5? Is he going to come back tomorrow with his arm in a sling, saying one of us assaulted him, and now he's going to sue the bar? Because that's the kind of thing people do over here, and I'm in enough trouble as it is without adding lawyers into the mix.

"Lexie, come on!"

Summer isn't about to give up on this, so I heave a heavy sigh, and give the table I'm cleaning one last flick with my cloth before reluctantly following her over to the window. The bar is empty now, and, with most of the lights switched off, we have a clear view out onto the street beyond. The street which is slick and shiny in the streetlights, covered in...

"Is that *rain*?" I ask, my voice hushed in astonishment. "Is it actually *raining*?"

"It is! Can you believe it?"

Summer opens the blinds a bit wider, and we stand there for a minute or two, watching the light drizzle hit the pavement, like we're Stone Age people worshiping some kind of God.

I may not be from California originally (Hardly anyone is, to be fair), but I've been here long enough now to know that this is something of an *event.* In the time I've been in L.A., I can count on one hand the number of times I've seen it rain. Back in the Highlands, by contrast, I could probably have counted the number of times it *didn't* rain in the same time period. It's no accident that when I walked out on my life in Scotland, I chose somewhere as different as possible to run to; somewhere there wouldn't be memories and reminders hiding around every corner, and ghosts rising out of the damp on the pavement — sorry, the *sidewalk* — to ambush me at every turn.

"Summer, don't!"

I'm so lost in my thoughts that I don't realize my friend is about to open the door until she's already done it, and the smell of rain on concrete is filling my nostrils, almost suffocating me with memory.

"Get a load of that!"

Summer stands by the door for a few seconds, drawing in deep lungfuls of damp air, and I pull myself away from the window and busy myself behind the bar again, before picking up my bag and slinging it over my shoulder.

"You ready?"

I look over at Summer, but she's busy on her phone now, the weather outside forgotten.

"Sorry, darl," she says, finally looking up at me with a grin. "That was Amy, asking if we want to go to that bar with her again. Remember the one we went to last weekend?"

I frown in annoyance.

Amy is our other roommate (Well, *one* of our other roommates. There's also a guy called Ben, apparently, but I've never actually met him, and am secretly convinced the other two are just making him up), and her job in P.R. means she can get us into some of the best places in town. Which would be *amazing*, obviously, except I have a sneaking suspicion that Amy doesn't really *like* me all that much. Summer says I'm imagining it, but she never looks me in the eye when she says it, and, I don't know, there's just something about the way Amy only ever acknowledges me when Summer's there too that makes me not trust her.

Just because you're paranoid, it doesn't mean they're not out to get you.

"You go," I tell Summer, impatiently jiggling my car keys as I wait for her to finish typing her response to Amy. "I just want to go home. And I didn't really like that place, anyway."

Amy. I don't really like Amy *is what I want to say. Because she's a classic, Grade A Mean Girl, and you can trust me on that, because it takes one to know one.*

"Oh, come on, Lexie," Summer says pleadingly. "You said

you loved it. And it's not the same without you. You know we depend on you to make us look better."

I smile weakly. I know she's just trying to be nice, but I'm flattered nonetheless. I'm used to being the Main Character, you see. Back home, I was *always* the Main Character — until, suddenly, I wasn't.

I miss it, actually; what it was like to be Lexie Steele, most popular girl in the High School of Life. It's not like that out here, though. Here in L.A., *everyone* is the Main Character. Or, at least they're trying to be. Out here, I'm not special or interesting. I'm not the prettiest girl in the room, like I always was back in Heather Bay, but I'm not the *worst* girl in the room either, and I'd really like to keep it that way. I promised myself I would — that I'd be good, and try my best to make better decisions from now on. Which is why, as Summer looks up at me pleadingly, I simply heave a sigh of resignation and put my bag back down on the bar.

"Go," I tell her again, waving away her protests. "I can tell you're dying to. I'll close up here for you. It's not like I've got anywhere else I need to be."

"Lexie, you're an angel," Summer tells me, blowing me a kiss as she grabs her coat from the hook behind the bar. "Tell you what, I'll buy you lunch tomorrow to say thank you. How's that sound?"

"You don't have to do that," I start to tell her, but she's already halfway out the door, her phone in her hand as she taps out another message, so I turn my attention back to the task in hand, desperate to be done with this so I can get home.

Fifteen minutes later, I'm locking the bar door behind me, and doing my best to ignore the flutter of nerves in my stomach as I step out onto the rain-slicked street. I love the city during the day, when it's sunny (And it's *always* sunny), but I'm not sure I'll ever get used to it at night. And as I make my way down the street to where I parked my car, I'm starting to regret not just leaving with Summer, like she wanted me to.

What if Drunk Guy is out here waiting for me? What if he wasn't content with taking photos, and now he's going to—

"Aaaargh!"

I'm so keyed-up from all the over-thinking I'm doing that when my foot makes contact with something soft and warm on the pavement — *sidewalk* — the scream that bursts from my throat is so shrill that it doesn't even sound like it belongs to me.

I leap back, instinctively trying to get away from whatever the object is on the ground, while at the same time trying to work out exactly what it is.

Please don't be a dead body, please don't be a dead body, please don't be a dead body.

My heart is pounding with fear, but curiosity gets the better of me, and, when the object fails to react to either my scream or the contact from my foot, I edge forward, risking a closer look.

It *is* a body — I can see that right away. Fortunately, though, it's not a *dead* one. I can see the slight rise and fall of the chest which indicates that this body is very much alive, and the good news continues as I move closer still and establish that, although it's definitely a drunk guy, it's not *the* drunk guy: a.k.a. the asshole from the bar.

At least that's something.

It might not be Drunk Guy — or, indeed, Dead Guy — but, nevertheless, there *is* something vaguely familiar about the shape on the ground before me, and as my eyes flick down to the outstretched feet, clad in an obnoxious pair of pool slides, then back up to the wiry beard, I realize who it is.

It's Mr. 3.5.

And he's passed out in the street in front of the bar.

Shit.

What am I supposed to do now?

I stand there uncertainly, looking down at the body in front of me. I'll admit it: I'm more than a little pissed off. Now that the adrenalin has started to fade and I know I'm not in mortal danger from this man, I'm just plain annoyed with him. I mean, okay, I know he stepped in to defend me from Drunk Guy earlier, and I'm grateful. I really am. But now he's given me a moral dilemma to deal with in return, and I don't do that sort of thing. I don't want the responsibility of this random stranger hanging over me. All I want to do is go home and fall into bed. But, instead, here I am, standing on this rainy street in the dark, feeling like I should be Doing Something to help him.

And I don't want to.

Because I'm the villain, remember? I'm not the Good Samaritan here, and I really resent being cast unwillingly in that role.

A sudden burst of laughter makes me jump again, and I shrink closer to the wall of the building 3.5 is slumped against as a group of young guys walk past, some of them looking back curiously as they go. Now that I'm standing even closer to him, I notice his phone clutched in his outstretched hand. I bet his wallet is in his pocket too, and if someone doesn't *Do Something*, he's going to be waking up tomorrow morning without either of them.

Assuming he wakes up at all, that is. And given the type of

neighborhood this is, I wouldn't count on it.

Oh, for God's sake.

Bending down slightly, I put out my foot and prod him gently in the side with my toe.

That counts as doing something? Right?

There's a loud groan, which makes me jump yet again — *wow, I really am spooked tonight, for some reason* — and he rolls over onto his other side, the phone falling from his hand with an ominous crack.

Uh-oh.

"Hey, wake up," I say, poking him with my toe again. "Please," I add, as an afterthought. Well, I *did* tell myself I was going to try to be good, didn't I?

At first there's no response. Then, with another loud groan, 3.5 rolls over again and throws up extravagantly on my shoes.

Great. Just great. That's where "being good" gets you, Lexie. No good deed unpunished, huh?

Okay, now I'm *really* annoyed.

"Oh, *come on*," I yell, my voice still sounding unnaturally shrill. "You've got to be kidding me?"

"Huh? What?"

The vomiting episode has apparently helped clear Mr. 3.5's head somewhat, and he pushes himself up into a sitting position, staring at me groggily.

"Oh good, you're awake," I say sharply, bending down and picking up his cracked phone, which I put into his hand before he has a chance to protest. "I'll leave you to it, then."

I turn on my heel, intending to walk away, but something stops me. I think... I think it might be my conscience? I can't be *sure* obviously, because I don't hear from it all that often — we're only very slenderly acquainted, really — but I know enough to realize that the nagging feeling of discomfort I'm currently experiencing has nothing to do with the dampness that lingers in the air from the rainfall, and slightly more of a connection to the very hairy man who's currently staring up at me through unfocused eyes.

"Hey, I know you!" he says, sounding absurdly pleased with himself, given that he's almost *literally* lying in a gutter right now. "You're the girl from the bar! The Scottish one! Lady Macbeth!"

"The hell?"

I've been called a lot of things in my life, but "Lady Macbeth" is a new one on me. He must be even drunker than I thought. He did order a *lot* of whisky back in the bar, though. And he kept on going long after the Silver Fox guy he was with had left. Summer had to get Joel to throw him out in the end— and it doesn't look like he got very far, either.

"Yeah, I thought you sounded like Lady Macbeth," he says, slurring so much that I can barely understand him. "I've been thinking about her a lot lately. You know, from the play by—"

'I know who Lady Macbeth is," I snap, losing patience with this bizarre conversation. "I just don't know why I'm talking about her with a random stranger in a dark alley in the middle of the night."

Okay, it's not really an alley, and it's not quite the middle of the night, either. It is, however, an utterly ridiculous conversation to be having right now, and I open my mouth to tell him that, but, before I can speak, he's off again.

"Look like th' innocent flower," Mr 3.5 slurs. *"'But be the snake under't.* Are you the snake or the flower, though, Scottish girl? That's what I'd like to know."

"Serpent," I say irritably. "It's serpent, not snake. If you're going to quote Shakespeare, you should at least get it right. Also, you're drunk."

"I know I am," he says, chuckling almost to himself. "But what are you, though? You didn't answer my question?"

"What I am is sick and tired of this conversation," I tell him bluntly. "I've been on my feet all day. I've been groped by one customer, yelled at by at least two others, and now some drunk guy's quoting Shakespeare — incorrectly, I might add — at me on the street. I'm going home. You should do the same."

This time I *do* turn and start to walk away, and my conscience, I'm pleased to report, doesn't have much to say about it this time. Even it knows better than to mess with me when I'm in this kind of mood.

Mr. 3.5, though, *doesn't.*

"Wait!" he yells, struggling to his feet, and falling right back down again. "Where are you going, Lady Macbeth? You're my muse. You can't just leave me here!"

"Oh, I definitely can," I assure him, looking back over my shoulder. "And I'm not your 'muse' either. You *really* need to go home and sleep it off now, trust me."

"I would if I could," 3.5 mutters, looking around the street as if he's seeing it for the first time. "Where the hell am I, anyway?"

I give an exaggerated sigh, which is purely for his benefit.

"You're outside Joe's," I tell him. "The bar you got blind drunk in? Remember?"

"Yeah, yeah. I remember being at Joe's," he says. He's getting slowly to his feet now, one hand still leaning on the wall for support. I'm fully expecting him to fall flat on his face again, but although he sways slightly, he somehow remains upright.

Well, that's a start.

"So, what happened when you left it?" I ask, curious in spite of myself. "How'd you end up sleeping in the gutter?"

Mr. 3.5 rubs his forehead as if he's trying to extract a memory from it.

"I was waiting for my ride," he says at last, speaking with what sounds like considerable effort. "But then I decided to take a leak." He nods towards the dingy little alley that leads off this street, and I wrinkle my nose in distaste. "And when I got back here..."

He trails off, shrugging.

"You passed out drunk," I finish helpfully. "And now you have no way to get home, am I right?"

"Nope," says 3.5, showing a flash of implausibly white teeth as he grins at me from under his beard. "You're wrong. I *do* have a way to get home." He points at the car key in my hand, which I'm carrying like a weapon, the way women do when they have to walk somewhere alone at night.

"*You* have a car," he says, sounding utterly delighted by this revelation. "*You* can be my ride."

Chapter 3

I have absolutely no idea why I agreed to do it. I mean, I could easily have just put him in an Uber and sent him on his way, couldn't I? And I know he stood up for me against Drunk Guy at the bar, but it's not like he saved my *life*, is it? It wasn't like he was Jack Dawson or something, dying so Rose could live. I don't owe him anything.

Or do I?

For some reason, after a lifetime of near-silence, that pesky conscience of mine decides that now is the perfect time to get chatty. And really quite sassy, too, now you come to mention it.

Not now, conscience. Not now...

The thing is, it's not often someone takes my side on something. It's not *ever*, really. Even when I'm in the right, I'm usually wrong, somehow, which makes it hard for people to want to defend me. Mr. 3.5 *did*, though; and I would never admit it, but I was quite touched by it. It made me almost like him. *Almost*. And in a strictly platonic kind of way, obviously, because, well, *look* at him.

For a few brief moments back in that bar, though, someone was on my side. We were a team: me and the bearded guy in pool slides, whose name I didn't catch. And, okay, it wasn't a big deal, in the great scheme of things. It's not like one day I'll be telling my grand kids how I met the love of my life in Joe's bar, and then he threw up on my shoes. But, even as I'm standing here, on this rain-slicked street in the dark, I can still feel the warmth on my back when he stood behind me. And he might not have saved my life, but it was nice not to feel like I was on my own for once.

Hmmm.

Maybe this is another part of my penance? Maybe this is the kind of thing I need to do, on my path to becoming a Good Person? And that *is* what I'm trying to do right now, isn't it? I want to be good (Not *too* good, though. Like, I don't want to become *boring* or anything like that. Just good enough to be able to go home again, with my head held high. That would be enough for me.), and maybe this is how I'll do it.

I will not, however, do it with good grace. I'm not a saint, after all, so, instead of agreeing immediately, I make a bit of a show of considering it; tapping my feet and wrinkling my brow, before finally huffing with annoyance and tightening my grip on my car key/weapon.

Then I turn on my heel and start walking in the direction of my car.

"Well, come on then," I say over my shoulder as I go. "If you want a lift, you better hurry up."

"A Lyft?" says 3.5, frowning as he stumbles after me. "No, I wanted *you* to drive me. I don't have any cash on me for a Lyft. And I think my phone's broken."

"A ride," I say impatiently. "I'm giving you a *ride*, stupid."

I will never get used to this country and its ways. Like how they call a lift a "ride"and no one seems to own an electric kettle. Weird.

3.5 has caught up with me now, and I feel suddenly awkward

as we reach my beat up little Honda, which was the only thing I could afford when I moved over here. Buying it totally wiped out the small amount of savings I had, but I couldn't do without it — no one walks anywhere here — so me and the car are now friends for life. Or for as long as it takes me to save up to buy something better. Which, to be fair, probably *will* take the rest of my life, given how little I make at the bar, and how much I seem to spend.

"This is your car? Wow, it's tiny. Like you."

Mr. 3.5 doesn't mince his words as he pulls open the passenger door and drops inside, completely missing the glare of outrage I give him.

"Yeah, yeah, I'm short, I get it," I reply tetchily, getting in beside him and inserting the key into the ignition. "I've heard it all from my mother, don't worry. I'm too short for runway modeling, and my boobs aren't big enough for glamour, so I'm just a crushing disappointment all round, really."

I pull out into the road, ignoring the outraged honks that follow my maneuver.

"I... um... I wasn't trying to imply anything," 3.5 says, sounding sheepish. "And I wasn't even looking at your boobs, I swear."

I swallow, feeling suddenly embarrassed by my outburst.

Why did I start talking about my boobs to a guy I'm alone in a car with? What's actually wrong with me?

I shrug my shoulders by way of response, and we drive on in silence for an uncomfortable couple of minutes before I realize I have no idea where I'm going. I've automatically started driving back to the house I share with Summer and Amy (And Invisible Ben, who I still don't believe in) in Burbank, but I'm definitely not about to take this guy home with me, so

I quickly pull over and turn to face him.

"Hey."

Mr. 3.5 seemed pretty lucid when he got into the car, but he's already started to dose off in the few minutes we've been driving, so I have to snap my fingers in front of his face to wake him.

"Oh, hey," he says amiably, as those green eyes flutter open. "How're you doin'? We home yet?"

"No," I snap, exasperated by how laid-back he is about this massive favor I'm doing him. "I don't know where 'home' is for you, remember?"

He looks vaguely puzzled at this, so I heave what must be my 100th deep sigh of the evening before pulling out my phone, opening up Google Maps, and handing it to him.

"Here," I say, getting ready to pull back out into traffic again. "Put your address into that."

It takes all of my concentration to insert my little car into a gap in the traffic (Let's just say L.A. is a far cry from the Highlands) and I don't dare to take my eyes off the road after that, so once we're on our way again, I concentrate on following the soothing tones of the SatNav lady as she tells me where to go, and thank my stars that 3.5 has lapsed back into silence.

Even when he's not talking, though, it's hard to concentrate with his hulking presence right next to me in the small vehicle. It's oddly intimate, somehow, being stuck in a car with someone you don't know, and, as I drive on, I'm painfully aware of how *close* he is. Either my car is even smaller than I thought it was, or he's taking up *way* too much space in it.

I swallow nervously. This probably wasn't my brightest idea, now I come to think of it. Didn't my mother always warn me not to get into cars with strangers? And now, here I am, playing chauffeur to someone whose name I don't even know.

Well, that's a simple enough problem to solve.

"So, what's your—"

"Have you really—"

We both start speaking at the same time, and there's another awkward silence, broken only by the SatNav telling me to take the next left.

It seems to be taking me into the Hills. That can't be right, can it?

"I was going to ask if you've really read Macbeth?" 3.5 says as the car starts to wind its way around the narrow bends that lead up to the Hollywood Hills. "You seemed to know it pretty well when you were quoting it to me back there?"

"Yeah, it turns out waitresses can actually read," I say drily. "Who knew? Guess I'm not just a pretty face after all."

"I didn't say you *were* a pretty face, Lady M," 3.5 shoots back instantly. I allow myself to glance over at him, grudgingly impressed with the speed of the comeback. I've got to hand it to him, he can give as good as he gets. I have to admire that. Even though I'm deeply irritated by it.

"You're not *just* a waitress, though, are you?" he asks after another few beats of silence. "No one out here is ever *just* a waitress. So, what is then? Actress? Singer? Very tiny model with, er, totally normally sized boobs, not that I would know?"

His eyes widen innocently as I turn to look at him.

"Nope, nope, and nope again," I say at last, returning my eyes to the road. "I really *am* just a waitress. Possibly the only one in L.A., actually."

I snap my mouth closed before I can tell him that pouring drinks and looking pretty are *literally* my only skills. And I'm not even all that great at pouring drinks, if I'm honest. When I came to California, I didn't come to make my fortune, or get discovered, like so many of the girls I work with at the bar. No, I just came here to escape. What can I tell you, it...seemed like a good idea at the time?

"So, you're a real waitress," 3.5 is saying now, "But you also like reading Shakespeare in your spare time. Or is it just Macbeth?"

I hesitate, wondering how to answer this.

The truth is, reading is my secret shame. Secret, because my mum thought reading books was a waste of time (And also that I'd get premature lines on my face from frowning in concentration, which is a bad habit of mine), so I used to sneak them into the house under her radar and read them under the covers. And shame because, in High School, everyone thought I was an airhead (a pretty, popular one, but still: an airhead) and I did my best to play up to that image, so they wouldn't realize I was secretly a geek, who read books for fun. Because who *does* that?

I steal another quick look at 3.5, who's waiting patiently for my answer.

I think he *probably does, actually. He quoted that line from Macbeth to me, after all, so I guess he must have read it. Maybe he's a geek too. In which case...*

"I like all kinds of books," I tell him, deciding my secret is probably safe with a man I'll never see again. "I studied Macbeth in high school, which is why I know that line, but I read anything, really. I just love books."

I pause, wondering if I should tell him how I wanted to study literature; how I applied and got accepted for a place at Edinburgh University, and how my mum talked me out of taking it because she wanted me to "learn the ropes", as she put it, at the family distillery instead. How I still think about it every so often; the life I could have led, and how different things might be if I'd followed my heart rather than just doing what my mother told me, like I always have. How books are sometimes the only things that actually feel real to me, and how, when I was growing up, getting lost in one was the only guaranteed way to block out the sound of my mum arguing with whichever boyfriend she was with at the time, in the next room.

Or, worse still, *having sex with them.*

Talk about awkward.

I could tell 3.5 all of that. I'm not going to, though, because, before I can speak, a soft snore from the passenger seat makes me clamp my mouth shut again, embarrassed by all the things I almost confided in a man who's so disinterested that he's already fallen asleep.

"You have reached your destination."

I pull the car to a stop outside a set of impressive wrought-iron gates as the SatNav makes its announcement. We're up in the Hollywood Hills, somewhere high above Sunset, and, by the looks of things, this is *not* the home of the alcohol-soaked body snoring in the seat next to me.

Great. He must have put the wrong address into the SatNav.

"Hey! Wake up!"

Instead of snapping my fingers in his face, I poke 3.5 firmly in the ribs this time, making him jerk awake with a start, his long eyelashes fluttering as he struggles towards consciousness.

"You gave me the wrong address," I tell him, pointing at the gates in front of us. "Look where we are."

Mr. 3.5 blinks once, then his face clears.

"Oh, great," he says. "That didn't take long. I think I must have dozed off."

Then he reaches into his pocket and pulls out something that looks a bit like the remote control for my TV, before pointing it at the gates, which start to slide smoothly open, without so much as a sound.

What the...?

"Is this... is this your house?" I ask, my voice sounding strangely squeaky in the confines of the little car. "*Seriously?*"

"Yeah, well, I mean, it's one of them," 3.5 says, as matter-of-factly as a very drunk man can manage. "This is the one I use most often, though. And it's closest to your bar, too. Are you going to go in?"

For a second, I think he's inviting me into his house — his really fucking *huge* house — and I'm still so surprised to find he actually *owns* this place that I just sit there gaping at him at first, until I realize he's just asking me to pull the car into the driveway.

Clearing my throat in embarrassment, I drive forward, finding myself at the start of a large, circular driveway which curls around the front of a white concrete block of house, all chrome and glass and, well, *money*, basically. This house absolutely *screams* money, and my eyes narrow with suspicion as we crunch to a stop, and I swivel around to face 3.5.

"Wait a minute," I say, as he reaches for the door handle. "You're telling me you actually *own* this place? *You*? Seriously?"

Okay, I could possibly have been a *little* more tactful there. Tact has never been something I'm known for though, and, try as I might, I can't stop my eyes flicking down his body, from his unkempt hair situation to his sloppy slides.

"Um, yeah." For the first time, 3.5 looks ever so slightly rattled. "Where did you *think* I lived, Lady M?"

"How would I know where you live?" I retort instantly. "I just... I just can't imagine it being *here*, somehow."

I nod towards the house, which continues to sit there looking back at us, all elegant and sumptuous, and God, I would do anything to live in a house like this. Literally *anything*.

"Well, it is," says 3.5 shortly. "Thanks for bringing me home. I owe you one."

He puts his hand on the door again, but no use; I'm not letting him get away with this.

"Uh-uh," I say, reaching out and tapping him smartly on the wrist. "Not so fast. I'm not stupid, you know. Are you seriously expecting me to believe that this is *your* house, and that you're not just, I don't know, the *cleaner* or something, trying to pretend it's your house, so I don't realize how tragic your life is?"

(Look, I know it sounds far-fetched, but I know someone who did this *exact* thing back in Heather Bay. I'm not joking. So you'll forgive me for being just a tiny bit suspicious when some guy who looks like he hasn't showered in days tries to tell me he owns a mansion in the Hollywood Hills, you know? It's like they say: *Fool me once, shame on you. Fool me twice, shame on me...*)

"Lady M."

I can't make out much of 3.5's face in the darkness of the car, but I can tell he's not amused.

"Lady M, I promise you, this is my house. Where I live," he says, sounding weary. "And yes, my life is pretty tragic, as it happens, so you got that right. But that doesn't change the fact that This. Is. My. House. And I'm going to go inside and get some sleep now, if it's all right with you."

And, with that, he opens the car door, lurches out...and falls flat on his face on the driveway.

Ouch.

Chapter 4

The house is even more impressive on the inside than it was on the outside.

Not that I would know, mind you. No, as soon as I get 3.5 inside — and I will never know exactly *how* I managed to do that, considering the state he was in — he crashes onto a couch in the entrance hall, and immediately falls asleep, leaving me standing there like one of old Jimmy's prize turnips, wondering what the hell I'm supposed to do now.

I *want* to have a good look round the house, obviously. Oh, come on: who *wouldn't*? This is quite possibly the swankiest house I've ever been in. It's more like a hotel than someone's home, really, and it makes me feel instantly grubby and out of place, like little orphan Annie when she first arrives at Daddy Warbucks' place.

Hey, I wonder if there's one of those walk-in pantries, where all the food is meticulously organized, like in a shop? Because that's my idea of porn, basically (Look, I like things neat, okay?), and now that I've thought about it, I'm just itching to go and find out if it exists.

At the same time, though, I have that pesky new conscience of mine to think of, don't I? My conscience, which keeps piping up to remind me that I'm trying to be good, and that snooping around someone else's house in the middle of the night would be the exact *opposite* of that, really. And also that I'm still not 100% convinced Mr. 3.5 isn't just the cleaner, or gardener, or something, and that the *real* owner isn't about to come downstairs with a gun in his hand, and ask me what I'm doing in his pantry.

What *am* I doing here, though?

Good question. I've been asking *myself* that too, actually.

So far the answer involves me sitting in the vast marble foyer of this house, watching 3.5 snore on the couch he collapsed onto, and turning him onto his side every time he rolls onto his back, so that he doesn't throw up in his sleep and then choke on it.

Nice of me, I know. Quite unlike me, too, to be honest. There's a reason I've never owned any pets — not so much as a gerbil, or a goldfish — and it's that I don't want the responsibility of keeping something other than myself alive.

So how did I somehow manage to become responsible for this hairy stranger, then? And how long do I have to sit here, I wonder, before I can go home and leave him to it?

I have no idea. Fortunately for me, though, Mr. 3.5 hasn't given me much trouble; or not unless you count the obnoxious snoring, and the occasional grunt he keeps giving in his sleep.

He seriously could not be less attractive if he actually tried. And, I mean, I know ugly people can be rich, too, obviously. Mum might have raised me to believe my face was my fortune — as well as being the only thing I had going for me — but I'm not as stupid as I let everyone think I am. I know you don't have to be born beautiful to be successful in life (Look at all of those tech billionaires, for instance.), but there's no denying it *helps*. And 3.5 is... he's...

I frown, trying to think of a nice way to finish that train of thought.

Be good, Lexie. Be good.

"Mphhhh!"

The figure on the sofa lets out a weird, strangled grunt, then rolls onto his back again, and I lean forward, hovering over him as I take him by the shoulders and try to ease him back onto his side.

"Wh... what's happening?"

His eyes snap open, and his arms come up to grab at my waist. I'm not sure if he's trying to pull me closer or push me away, but the movement knocks me off balance and sends me hurtling towards his surprised face as he lies on the couch beneath me. At the last second, my hands come up to break my fall, landing one on each side of 3.5's head.

I'm practically straddling the guy now, my body weight entirely supported by his hands as I lean over him, my hair swinging in his face, and our noses almost touching. We're so close I can smell the sour trace of whisky on his breath, with some kind of musky aftershave lurking underneath it. So close that I can feel the muscles in his legs tense underneath me as he shifts position, making my body tip even further forward,

Could this night possibly *get any worse, I wonder?*

Those emerald eyes of his widen in surprise, and my entire body cringes in anticipation of what's about to happen.

He's going to try to kiss me. I just know it. And, okay, I guess I kind of *am* giving him the impression I might be into that, given my current mortifying position astride his lap, but I'm afraid he's going to be disappointed, because there's absolutely no way I'm going to...

"OUCH!"

Mr. 3.5 moves so fast I don't have a chance to get out of the way, and, before I know what's happening, his forehead makes sudden and dramatic contact with my lips, ricocheting off my face hard enough that I'm sure I'll have a bruise tomorrow.

Well, I guess we can add "terrible kisser" to 3.5's list of crimes, then.

Seriously, though. I've known horses back home who can probably kiss better than that. *Horses.*

"What the actual fuck?" I yelp indignantly, leaping off the sofa and rubbing furiously at my lip. "What do you think you're—"

"Sorry. I'm sorry."

Mr. 3.5 is sitting up on the sofa, with his head in his hands and a greenish tinge to the small amount of skin I can see under that infernal beard.

Well, at least he's apologizing. That's something, I suppose.

"I'm sorry," he says again, finally looking up at me, warily. "But, look, I'm not... I'm not going to sleep with you. I'm very grateful for the ride home and everything, and I'm... I'm really flattered, you know? But it's just not happening, okay?"

"Wh...what?"

It's not often that Lexie Steele finds herself lost for words, but for a second I just stand there gaping at him like he's speaking another language.

Sleep with him? Does he seriously think I *want to sleep with him?*

"I don't know what you're talking about," I say, finally finding my tongue again. "I know you're drunk, but are you actually *insane?*"

"Look, I know what everyone thinks," 3.5 says, holding up a hand as if he's heard all this before. "But they're wrong, okay?

I'm not like that. I don't pick up women in bars. And I don't sleep with people I barely know. I'm sorry."

He makes it to the end of this astonishing little speech before closing his eyes again wearily and slumping back on the sofa, while I continue to stand there with my mouth open and my mind whirring as I try to make sense of what I just heard,

Did I just get rejected by a drunk guy in pool slides? Me, Lexie Steele, three-time winner of the Miss Western Scotland competition, and the Highlands' best-know Junior Pageant Queen? (Well, "best-known" among people who follow child beauty pageants, obviously. Which isn't *that* many people. But still.)

I have never been so insulted in my life.

"Excuse me," I begin hotly, but 3.5 just raises a weary hand and flips onto his back, like a goldfish that's given up on life.

"It's okay," he mumbles through a thick fog of whisky breath. "I get it a lot. I'm used to it."

"Oh, I *seriously* doubt that," I say, looking pointedly at his once-black hoodie, which is now speckled with dots of vomit, from when he threw up on my feet earlier. For a man with so little going for him — well, other than the amazing house, obviously, and I'm *still* not convinced it's really his — he certainly has a high opinion of himself. He must follow a bunch of those "self love" gurus on Instagram, or something. There's just no other explanation, for his bizarre "rejection" of someone who, to be totally blunt, would be out of his league, even if she *had* been coming on to him. Which, just for the record, I definitely *wasn't.*

All I was doing was trying to help him. Trying to make sure he didn't hurt himself in his stupid drunken stupor. Trying to be a good girl, and do the right thing for once, and what do I get in return? A shoe full of vomit, and a giant bruise to my ego. Which, it turns out, isn't *quite* as bulletproof as I like to pretend it is.

No, this is just not acceptable. Not in the slightest.

I consider waking 3.5 up, just so I can tell him that if anyone's going to be rejecting anyone else around here, it's going to be *me*, thank you very much. Or words to that effect. I'm sure I'll come up with something suitably cutting once I get started.

As soon as I get close to him, though, I realize any attempt to wake 3.5 is going to be in vain. He's fallen into a sound sleep, his head lolling back and his eyes tight shut, dark lashes fanned out against his skin. As I watch him, he murmurs something indecipherable, then shifts position on the couch. Now he's facing me, his cheek resting against a cushion, and as I crouch down to make sure he's still breathing, I'm struck by the shape of his lips, which are just visible through that bird's nest beard of his. The beard is an abomination, sure, but the lips under it are full and pouting, smooth and curved up in a slight smile, even in his sleep. They're really quite beautiful, in fact.

Why would you want to hide lips like that under a mess of hair?

I frown as a memory tugs at the corner of my mind, letting go almost as quickly as it came. Those lips remind me of someone, I'm sure. I just can't remember who it is, or where I've seen them.

Have I met this guy somewhere before?

No. I can't have. I'd remember it, I know I would.

I shake my head to release the weird feeling of déjà vu. Whoever it is he reminds me of, I'm unlikely to remember anytime soon, because now that 3.5's safely on his side again, I think I'm done here.

Why should I stick around to babysit a grown adult, anyway? Especially not one who just insulted me?

Making up my mind, I pluck my bag off the marble floor, where I dumped it when we arrived, and rummage in it for my car keys. Behind me on the sofa, 3.5 mutters something else, and I hesitate for just a moment.

Maybe I should wait just a bit longer?

Just a few minutes, say, to make sure he really is okay?

Oh, shut it, conscience. You and I have always gotten along just fine, you know. Why'd you have to start bugging me now?

It's no use, though. My newfound conscience has spoken, and she will not be ignored. She reminds me a bit of my mother, in fact.

I shudder at the thought. Then I heave a sigh of resignation, put my bag back down on the floor, and then sink down beside it, wincing as my butt makes contact with the cold marble tiles.

Just two more minutes. That's all he's getting, then I'm out of here. This "being a good person" thing has gone on for long enough.

Chapter 5

I'm woken three hours later by a sliver of sunlight on my face and the nagging certainty that there's something I've forgotten.

As soon as I try to sit up, and my hand makes contact with the cold floor beneath it, I realize what it is.

Home. I forgot to go home. And now I'm sitting here propped against the wall in Mr. 3.5's imposing — but deeply uncomfortable — foyer, while 3.5 himself sleeps soundly on the sofa opposite me, his eyelashes fluttering slightly as he dreams. Probably about whisky, if his behavior last night is anything to go by.

Did I seriously spend the entire night here? Because Florence Nightingale's got nothing on me, if so. Can I get some kind of medal for this, do you think? Or even just a cup of hot coffee? Because that would be good too, around about now.

I ease myself carefully into a sitting position, wincing as my entire body screams in protest at the movement.

I am not cut out for this "sleeping on floors" business. Not now, and not ever. This guy definitely owes me that cup of coffee — at the very least.

My tongue is welded to the roof of my mouth, and my bladder is about to burst, so, after a quick glance in 3.5's direction, to make sure he's not about to wake up and catch me, I tiptoe cautiously out of the foyer and into the hallway beyond, which is roughly the size of my entire cottage back in Heather Bay.

I know I said I wouldn't snoop, but he can't begrudge me a trip to the bathroom, can he?

Unfortunately for me, though, finding a bathroom is easier said than done.

The first door I try opens into what looks like an office, although I don't linger long enough to find out. The third is a cinema room; like an *actual* cinema room, with plush chairs, and a screen with curtains on each side of it, like in a movie theater. I kid you not.

Okay, now I'm even more convinced that 3.5 is lying to me. Why would he be drinking in a dive bar, and dressing like a broke college student if he could afford a place like this? He wouldn't *be, would he?*

Feeling more uncomfortable by the second, I open door number three and heave a sigh of pure relief when it turns out to be the bathroom I was looking for.

And what a bathroom it is, too. Gold taps. Double sinks. More marble. Giant movie poster featuring Jett Carter in *Islanders* on the wall opposite the toilet... Oh, you know: just your standard, run-of-the-mill Hollywood bathroom, really.

Okay, *not* really. Sure, the decor is probably more or less what you'd expect from a Rich Person bathroom — not that I'd know, of course — but it's not every day you have to take a whizz in front of a movie star, and the fact that this is just a *poster* of one rather than the real thing only makes it very *slightly* less awkward.

I guess 3.5 — or whoever actually owns this house — must be a big Jett Carter fan, then?

The toilet itself is on a little raised platform, which I ascend feeling a bit like Cersei walking up to the Iron Throne. As I sit down, I'm uncomfortably aware of the eyes of the poster opposite, which seem to be looking right at me, with polite interest.

Weird. Just... weird.

Seriously, I know Jett's pretty hot, but you'd have to be a *really* big fan of his movies to want a life-sized photo of him watching you pee, because it's seriously disconcerting. So much so that, although I was desperate to pee when I came in here, I now seem to have a bad case of performance anxiety, which means I just sit there, staring at the image of the most famous man in the world, who stares back at me, his green eyes appearing to take in every inch of my—

Wait.

Green eyes. Ones with tiny flecks of gold in them, set above a perfectly proportioned nose, and full, pouting lips.

Where have I seen that particular combination before?

I tilt my head to one side, staring curiously at the poster as the memory struggles to break the surface. *Islanders* was Jett Carter's first ever movie. I think he was about 21 when he starred in it. I remember bunking off school one afternoon and taking the bus to Fort William to see it with Frankie Allison, and some of the other girls from school. Jett played an up-and-coming football star who got stranded on a desert island on his way to a match, and, oh my God, he was *gorgeous*. So gorgeous, in fact, that I went back on my own that weekend just so I could see it again. And a third time the weekend after that.

His sun-bleached blonde hair. His tanned six-pack, sprinkled with drops of seawater. His emerald eyes, which... no, there it is again. That pin-prick of memory is more insistent than ever, and as I stand up to fasten my jeans, it stabs me so hard that the blood seems to drain from my body.

No.

It can't be.

It just can't *be.*

It *is*, though. I'm almost sure of it. And, as I slowly approach the poster on the wall, my legs trembling slightly from the force of the realization that's just hit me, that certainty grows even stronger.

No no no no no. This cannot *be real.* Surely *it can't be real?*

It's real.

It's very, very real.

It's as real as the man I left sleeping on the sofa in the foyer of his Hollywood mansion just a few short minutes ago. That man is at least 10 years older and about a hundred times more hairy than the one staring back at me from a sunlit beach, which was probably built on a sound stage somewhere near here. But now that I'm looking at him — *really* looking, I mean — the resemblance is unmistakable. I don't know why I didn't see it before.

Why didn't I see it before?

Whatever the reason, now that I've seen it, I can't *un*-see it. Suddenly, it all makes sense. The way the drunk guy in the bar backed away from 3.5, and how he came back later to take photos — of *him*, obviously, not of me — through the window. The house in the hills that 3.5 had a key for. The way he said he was "used to it" when he thought I was coming on to him.

(Which I definitely wasn't, by the way. I just want to be *really* clear about that.)

He's not a broke college student, and he wasn't lying about

being the owner of this house.

He's Jett Carter — the youngest member of the Carter acting dynasty, and one of the most famous men in the world.

And now I'm *definitely* not going to be able to do that pee.

Chapter 6

My hands are trembling so much as I come shooting out of the front door of the house that it takes me a good few seconds to get the key into the ignition of my car, and even longer to get through the double gates, which, in a rare moment of good luck for me, open automatically as I approach them in a panic.

At least one thing's going my way.

My little Honda splutters in protest as I slam my foot down on the accelerator, but it carries me dutifully back down the hill and onto the freeway... where I drive straight into the usual morning traffic jam.

Great.

Just the one *thing going my way, then. It figures.*

By the time I pull into the driveway of the little blue-painted bungalow I share with my roommates, the sun is high in the sky, the air is filled with the distinctive scent of rain-soaked pavements being dried by the morning sun, and I'm almost hysterical with the need to talk to Summer. Or Amy, in a pinch. Or, hell, I'd even settle for Weird Ben right now, because if I don't tell *someone* what just happened to me, I'm going to burst.

If I don't get to the bathroom quickly, though, I really *am* going to burst, so I drop my bag in the entrance to the house, then go thundering along the hall to the bathroom door, which I slam into with a jarring thud, rebounding off it like a tennis ball when, instead of opening, like I expected it to, the door remains shut and locked.

"Fuuuuucckkk," I wail, rubbing my forehead. "Summer, are you in there? I really need to goooooo."

Silence.

"Amy?" I shout, hopping from foot to foot in desperation. "Weird Ben?"

The silence deepens.

Weird Ben, then, it seems.

I... maybe shouldn't have called him that to his face. Or to the door, rather. There's nothing I can do about it now, though, so I turn on my heel and hop-run to Summer's room, which is the only one with its own bathroom.

The room is disappointingly empty — although thankfully, so is its bathroom — as is Amy's, when I try it a few minutes later.

Damn.

Either my roommates got up very early, or they're out very, very late. Either way, I'm on my own here. Well, other than...

I pause for a split second outside Weird Ben's room, but the door is closed, as always, and I might be dying to tell someone my news, but I'm not prepared to actually *die* for it — which I just might if Ben is as weird as our nickname for him would suggest.

"Oh, come *on*," I mutter furiously to myself, stamping my foot like Veruca Salt in Willie Wonka when she doesn't get her own way. "I'm actually going to burst here if I don't tell someone I met Jett Carter!"

Jett Carter.

Jett *freaking* Carter.

I fled home with Jett Carter. I, Lexie Steele, went home with *Jett Carter.* To his house. Where he lives. Jett 'Golden Boy of Hollywood' Carter. And me, Alexandra Louise Steele, Not-So-Golden-Any-More Girl of Heather Bay, Scotland.

Nope, it's no use: no matter how many ways I try to say it, I just can't make it make sense. Probably because — *whisper it* — the story I've been repeating to myself all the way home isn't *totally* accurate, is it?

I didn't really "go home" with Jett Carter, for one thing.

No, I went "home" with Mr. 3.5 — a total loser with a hideous beard, who I'd barely even looked twice at, even though I'd been serving him drinks all evening, and he'd casually rescued me from an aggressive drunk.

There's a lesson in this somewhere, I suppose. Probably that old, hackneyed one about not judging books by their cover. I've been being judged by my "cover" my entire life, though, and it looks like it's had more of an effect on me than I'd really like to admit. I mean, can you blame me for taking one look at that neanderthal beard and instantly dismissing the guy wearing it?

You *do*?

Okay. I guess I deserve that.

What I absolutely do *not* deserve, however, is to come home after meeting my teenage heartthrob and have absolutely no one I can tell a highly dramatized version of the story to.

That's just not fair.

And neither is the fact that, when I head to the kitchen in defeat, I find we're we're totally out of coffee.

"Aaaarrgh! Shitty McShitterson! This is so unfair!"

I want to scream with frustration, but that would just be time I could spend getting myself appropriately caffeinated; so after a quick change of clothes, I sling my bag back over my shoulder and head out the door. I don't have to be at work until this evening, and there's a coffee shop right at the end of this street. I'll grab a coffee, then see if I can track down Summer before I'm due to start. Maybe that way I can start to turn this day around.

Or maybe not.

The coffee shop is unusually crowded for this time of day, and by the time it's my turn, I'm almost frothing at the mouth with impatience. I order my skinny vanilla latte, then take it to a table by the window to drink it while it's still hot. Well, lukewarm. I come to this place because it's close, not because it's good. And also because it's usually pretty quiet.

Not today, though.

Outside, the sidewalk is empty, as usual, but, on the opposite side of the street, I notice a small crowd seems to have gathered. A small, almost exclusively male crowd, most of whom are clutching gigantic, flashing cameras with telescopic lenses, which...

Aha!

Paparazzi!

Shit just got interesting.

Feeling perkier, I glance around the coffee shop with interest, wondering who the paps are hoping to photograph coming out of it. It's not particularly unusual to see photographers — and even the occasional celebrity — in this part of L.A., but, much to my disappointment, I never seem to see anyone interesting. I have an uncanny knack of managing to leave a club or bar minutes before some A-lister or other arrives.

Seriously, I can't even tell you the number of times I've served someone famous at the bar without recognizing them.

(Okay, I can, it's twice. Although one of those times it was a Real Housewife, which doesn't really count.)

And that's without even *mentioning* Jett Carter, who I grudgingly watched sleep for several hours before I realized who he was.

Hollywood is really wasted on me, isn't it?

Today, it seems, is going to be no exception. There are no celebrities inside this coffee shop — not even someone with a scraggly beard hiding a world-famous face. I know, because I look extra-carefully at everyone with facial hair, just to be sure. You better believe I won't be making that mistake *again*.

Disappointed, I turn back to my coffee and my phone.

Summer still hasn't answered me, so I spend a few minutes idly scrolling Instagram (Ada Valentine has been sent yet *another* box of free stuff, I see. God, I *hate* that woman...), before idly opening up TMZ, to see if there are any clues to be found there about who the paparazzi crew on the street opposite me are staking out now. Maybe now that I've met Jett Carter, my celebrity-sightings drought is over, and I'll start seeing them everywhere? Maybe celebrities are like busses, and you just wait forever, before three come along at once?

I scroll past a couple of celebrity breakups, plus a detailed discussion of the *Housewives of Beverly Hills*. I'm just about to give up and put the phone back in my bag when I see something so out of place it's like seeing a unicorn at the supermarket. Or the late Queen standing in line at the ATM.

It's me.

On TMZ.

Or, at least, I *think* it is.

Breathless with sudden tension, I pinch and zoom on the photo in front of me, squinting desperately in the hope that it'll turn out to be some *other* short blonde girl handing a bearded Jett Carter a drink in a bar that looks suspiciously like Joe's.

It... could happen? I guess?

It doesn't, though.

The harder I stare at the pixelated photo, the surer I am that it's me. And the surer I am that it's me, the harder it becomes to breathe through the wave of panic that's currently crashing over me.

Stay calm, Lexie. Stay calm...

The photo has been taken through the slightly grimy window of the bar, so it's not as clear as it could be. It's clear enough, though, for me to recognize my own stupid self, leaning over 3.5's table while he gazes up at me, smiling up at me in a way I don't even remember.

Did 3.5 smile at me like that last night?

And how come I don't remember it, if so?

I know I was just placing yet another tray of drinks in front of him when this shot was taken, but the angle of the photo makes it look like we're almost touching, his eyes level with my bust, which I appear to be almost thrusting into his face.

Oh my God.

My heart hammers painfully in my chest as I glance down at my non-existent boobs, barely able to believe they would betray me like this.

This cannot *be happening. It just* can't *be.*

I blink rapidly, then rub my eyes quickly for good measure, convinced that when I open them again, the photo will be gone, like a mirage in the desert. I was thinking about me and 3.5

— Jett — in the bar last night, and now my brain is trying to convince me I can *see* us, too. I'm... I'm probably going mad! Yes, that's it! I'm just losing my mind, that's all. Which I know isn't *great*, obviously, but which is still preferable to someone taking a really shit photo of me at work, and then sending it to TMZ. *Seriously.*

My hopes rise slightly at the thought that I really could just have imagined all of this, and then instantly crash when I tentatively open my eyes to find that, not only is the photo very much still there, there's a second one right underneath it.

Just when I was thinking things couldn't get worse.

The second photo is worse. Much worse, in fact.

This one's been taken through the wrought-iron gates of Jett's mansion, and shows me standing next to my car in the early hours of this morning, my eyes wild and my hair disheveled as I fumble with the key.

Is... is that seriously *what I look like?*

Horrified, I bring the screen of the phone up to my face, taking in the pale skin and puffy eyes of the woman in the photo; a woman I absolutely refuse to recognize as myself, even though I know the chances of there being two scruffy blondes leaving Jett Carter's house in an ancient Honda this morning must be slimmer than one of Jett's supermodel exes.

And that's pretty damn slim, trust me.

"IS THIS JETT CARTER'S LATEST HOOKUP?" screams the headline of the article accompanying the two photos. "Heart-throb actor spotted TWICE with mystery blonde."

It goes on to breathlessly explain that the "heartthrob" in question was spotted enjoying the company of a "leggy blonde" (That would be me.) at Joe's Bar in Hollywood, hours before the same woman (Me, again) was seen leaving his house, having apparently spent the night there.

Then there's a bunch of snide stuff about all of Jett's ex-girlfriends, coupled with some "witty" observations about how I'm the latest in a long line of one-night stands.

Are you fucking kidding me?

For a second, I'm so offended by the tone of the piece that I almost forget it's not real. Jett and me, I mean. He wasn't "enjoying my company" in the bar (And I *certainly* wasn't enjoying his...), I didn't "spend the night with him" (Well, I *technically* did, I suppose. Just not in the way they're trying to imply.), and there's no way in the hell that I'd consent to be the latest in a long line for *anyone*. Not even Jett Carter.

Not that he's asked me, of course.

Oh, and I'm not really "leggy" either, to be honest, but I'm not going to quibble with that one.

Mum always said my legs were my best feature. She'd be really happy to know TMZ apparently agrees with her.

My mouth dry with shock, I take a gulp of my coffee before clicking on the comments box under the article.

There are 264 comments.

And pretty much all of them are *horrific*.

Within the space of the next five minutes, I quickly learn that I am, in no particular order:

1. Short.
2. Ugly.
3. Like, really, *really* ugly.
4. Not good enough for Jett Carter.
5. Far too old for him.
6. Not nearly as pretty as his other "girlfriends".

7. Like a "snaggle-toothed troll"
8. Just after Jett's money
9. A "stupid, deluded bitch" if I think he'll ever love me.
10. Obviously good in bed, because I have nothing else going for me.
11. Did I mention 'ugly'? Because I'd hate for anyone to forget how hideous I apparently am.

And those are just the *nicer* comments.

The other ones are... are...

Oh God, I think I'm going to be sick. Actually, scratch that, I think I'm going to die.

Getting shakily to my feet, I push back my chair with an ostentatious clatter, which makes everyone in the coffee shop stop what they're doing to look round at me curiously.

Oh, don't mind me; I've just been completely and utterly eviscerated on the Internet. No biggie.

My eyes swimming with tears, I stumble my way to the door of the cafe, desperate to get back to the safety of home, where I can attempt to digest all of this in private. (And also where I can put on some makeup. Because if those photos are what I look like without it then I'm never leaving the house again, I swear to God.)

Before I can reach the door, though, a few things happen simultaneously.

First, someone in the back of the cafe jumps up and starts filming me with a cellphone. Just standing there, arm out, brazenly recording my stumbling path to the door, as if he has every right in the world to invade my privacy. As if I don't even get a say.

Secondly, I see some of the paps across the street peel away from the rest of the group and start to cross the road towards me.

Oh no. I completely forgot about them.

As I push open the heavy door of the cafe, I'm surrounded by the sound of car horns and the click of camera shutters. There's a flash of white light right in my face, and I'm vaguely aware of someone shouting my name. Which makes no sense at all, because how would any of these men even know it?

The flash sends an explosion of stars into my vision, momentarily blinding me. I try to turn round to go back into the relative safety of the shop, only to find my route blocked by Cellphone Guy, who's still holding his phone up, grinning with the look of someone who knows he's going to go viral on TikTok any time now.

I feel a sob of panic work its way into my throat as I spin frantically around, looking desperately for a way out. The shutters continue to click around me, giving the whole scene a surreal, nightmarish quality. The cry is about to burst free. I can feel the hysteria start to take over as I turn frantically around again, this time tripping over the dangling strap of my shoulder bag, which somehow manages to thread itself between my ankles, almost whipping one foot out from under me.

The scream I've been holding onto finally escapes my mouth as I pitch dramatically forward, the pavement coming rushing up to meet me before, all of a sudden, my body jerks to a stop, a pair of strong hands looping themselves under my arms and pulling me upright.

Safe. I'm safe.

Or am I?

No sooner am I upright again, my body pressed hard against

that of my rescuer, I find myself being pushed forward, and then lifted clean off my feet. I can't see whose arms are holding me, but, whoever it is, the small crowd of photographers are intimidated enough to step aside for them as they push their way through the tangle of bodies, to a long black car which sits purring by the side of the road.

A long black car which opens like a trap, one of its door yawning wide in a way that feels more threatening than inviting to me.

Oh, hell to the no. I am not *going in there.*

Too late, I kick back against the person carrying me, struggling desperately against arms that barely even flinch as I rain blows down on them.

"Hey," I yell, finally finding my voice as I reach the car. "Put me down or I'll... I'll..."

But I have no idea what I'm going to do to get out of this situation. And before I can say another word, I'm inside the limo, which screeches away from the kerbside before I can come up with a suitably threatening end to my outburst.

I... think I might be being kidnapped?

And now I'm definitely *going to be sick...*

Chapter 7

"Miss Steele? Would you like some water?"

I raise my head from between my knees, where I've been desperately trying not to throw up, and find myself looking straight into the cool blue eyes of a gray-haired man in an expensive suit, who doesn't look remotely like a kidnapper. He looks like someone's granddad, actually. And also vaguely familiar.

"Silver Fox!" I blurt, my body snapping abruptly upright as I realize where I know him from. "You were in the bar last night with three point... with... ummm... you know."

It's not like me to lose the power of speech, but given that I've just seen myself named on TMZ as Jett Carter's latest "flame", before being bundled unceremoniously into the back of a limo, I'm sure he can forgive me just this once.

"I do know," says Silver Fox, his eyebrows rising slightly as he looks at me appraisingly. "If you don't mind, though, I prefer Asher to — what was it? '*Silver Fox*'?" He speaks the last two words as if they taste bad on his tongue. "Asher Ford," he continues, holding out an elegant hand, which I shake warily, noting how soft his skin feels. "And this is Jett's assistant, Miss Sullivan."

My eyes swivel curiously to his left, where a woman around

my age with a kind face and slightly anxious expression is smiling at me encouragingly.

"Grace," she says warmly, offering me her hand, which I shake a little more enthusiastically, before turning to the third figure in the car — a muscled giant of a man who looks like he's having to bend double in order to squash himself into the seat.

"And I believe you've already met Leroy," says Silver Fox — sorry, but I just can't think of him as anything else now — as the figure in question gives me a cheerful grin, followed by a fist bump.

"Sorry 'bout that back there," says Leroy, nodding in the direction of the coffee shop, which has long since receded behind us. 'I figured picking you up was the fastest way to get you out of there. You hardly weight nothin', in any case."

I return his easy smile, allowing myself to relax slightly. I've no idea what this is about, but these people are obviously connected to Jett, so I'm pretty sure I'm not being kidnapped. Nevertheless, I have *questions*. Lots of questions. Like...

"Where are you taking me?" I ask suspiciously, turning back to Silver Fox, who's tapping something urgently into his phone. "And how do you know my name? Or where I'd be this morning?"

"I know everything about you, Miss Steele," says Silver Fox coolly, not bothering to look up at me. "Or everything worth knowing, at least."

"Okay, you can cut the James Bond villain crap," I tell him, folding my arms across my chest defiantly. "I'm not here for it. And you're not pulling it off, anyway. You need a white cat on your lap if you want to go down the 'evil mastermind' route."

Opposite me, Grace giggles in horrified delight, before clamping her hand over her mouth and glancing wide-eyed at Silver Fox, who looks ever-so-slightly put out as he reaches up to straighten his tie.

"Yes, well," he says stiffly. "As I was saying, it's my job to find out things, and—"

"No, it ain't," says Leroy, slapping him genially on the back and almost pushing him off the slippery leather seat of the limo in the process. "It's your job to make money for Jett and his pa. Tell the lady the truth now."

He grins widely, and Silver clears his throat, annoyed.

"Mr. Ford is Jett's agent," Grace offers, glancing nervously at him. "Well, he's Mr. Carter *Senior's* agent, really, but—"

"I work for both of the Carters," Silver snaps, recovering himself. "Although not normally in this particular, er, *capacity*," it has to be said.

I lean back against the seat, chewing a nail thoughtfully. Everyone knows who Jett's father is, of course. Charles Carter had already won his first Oscar and been nominated for his second by the time his son, Jett, was even born. Legend — and, by "legend" I mean "Shona McLaren, Heather Bay's leading gossip" — has it that Charles missed the first month of Jett's life because he was off on location somewhere, and having an affair with his co-star. True story. Well, *probably*.

With that kind of background, I guess it's no surprise that Jett grew up to follow in his old man's footsteps; in more ways than one, if Shona McLaren's to be believed. And she normally is, to be frank.

What I want to know, however, is what any of this has to do with *me*.

"You didn't tell me where you're taking me," I say, tapping

my foot impatiently as I look at the mismatched trio in front of me; Silver looking frosty, Grace looking anxious, and Leroy looking into the bottom of a bag of Lays chips, which he's produced from a hidden compartment built into the seat next to him. I'm just about to repeat my question when a quick glace out of the car window tells me I don't need to. The huge gates we've just pulled up to are stomach-churningly familiar, as is the glossy frontage of the house behind them.

I'm back at Jett Carter's house.

And I'm not any better prepared than I was the last time I was here.

Chapter 8

Walking into Jett Carter's house for the second time in less than 24 hours feels a bit like the time I tried to sneak into the Heather Bay Bar, even though I was underage at the time, and I knew Big Ian, the landlord, would tell my mum if he caught me.

I'm not worried that Jett Carter's going to *tell my mum* about me being in his house, you understand (although nothing about this situation would surprise me). All the same, as Grace walks me through the now-familiar entrance and down the hall, I realize I'm moving almost *furtively*, as if I know I shouldn't be here, and I'm scared I'm going to get caught.

Grace smiles reassuringly as she opens the door to a vast living room with floor to ceiling windows which look out onto an infinity pool with a view over the city.

I'm a bit disappointed, to be honest. I was really hoping for a look at that giant walk-in pantry I've been imagining. I guess this will have to do, though. I'll just have to settle for this tastefully decorated room, which has a grand piano at one end (Can he even *play* piano? I did not know that.) and some kind of weird sculpture at the other. It looks a bit like a bagel. Which makes me think of the pantry again. There must be one in a place this size? I mean, *surely*?

Dumping my bag on the floor, I walk over to the sculpture and peer through the hole in the center of it. There's a mirror on the wall on the other side, in which I can see my own face reflected back at me, like an evil twin. I stick my tongue out at it, pulling a face — and that's the moment Jett Carter chooses to walk into the room.

He still has the obnoxious beard, but he's changed into a pair of gray sweatpants and a simple t-shirt, both of which look a whole lot better than the "hoodie and saggy shorts" combo he had on yesterday.

Of course, now I know who he is, I *guess* he could have grown the beard for a role. I wrinkle my nose thoughtfully as I consider the possibility. That would make sense, actually. Much more sense than him just making himself look ugly on *purpose*, anyway.

"Is there something on my face?" Jett says, breaking into my thoughts. "It's just, you're staring at me in a way that doesn't really suggest you like what you see."

He takes a seat on the expensive-looking white sofa which dominates one end of the room, his green eyes seeming to burn right into my soul.

I really wish he would stop doing that.

He looks surprisingly alert, given the state he was in last night, and I feel suddenly self-conscious in front of him.

"You're one to talk about staring," I retort, before I can stop myself. "And, yes, there *is* something on your face," I continue, sitting down on an armchair opposite him, and immediately sinking so far into it that my legs are left dangling off the edge, like a toddler's. "*And* your neck. And I wouldn't be surprised if it went all the way down to your chest, too."

A sudden image of Jett Carter's naked torso, as I last seen it in

Ace of Spades, flashes through my mind, unbidden. He played a gambling cowboy in that one, and, honestly, it's surprising just how often cowboys have to take their shirts off. Not that anyone in the audience was complaining, mind you. Especially not me.

I swallow hard, flushing at the memory.

I really need to stop thinking about him as Jett Carter, movie star extraordinaire, and go back to thinking of him as Mr. 3.5 — random hairy dude with whisky breath and no dress sense. It'll be easier for me that way.

Much easier.

"I can assure you, my chest is as smooth as yours is," Jett replies, his eyes flicking quickly down my body to the open neck of my shirt. "Or I assume so, anyway."

I open my mouth to reply to this, but I can still feel the path his eyes traced on my skin. It's as if he actually touched me, rather than just *looking* at me, and it's having a surprising effect on my insides. A Jett Carter effect rather than a 3.5 effect. A very, very dangerous effect, given that he's probably had me brought here to tell me how annoyed he is about the whole "mystery woman" story that's probably all over the internet by now.

Maybe he thinks I started it myself? Or that I want it to be true?

"Did you grow it for a role, then?" I ask bluntly, desperate to take my mind off the news article. "The beard, I mean? Or did you grow it for a dare?"

Jett's eyebrows rise slightly, but his eyes remain locked on mine. I'm *really* starting to hate the way he does that.

"I grew it for me," he says simply. "To hide behind. You'd be surprised what an effective disguise it can be. It's basically my only chance of getting to live a semi-normal life — and even that doesn't often work."

He sounds ever so slightly bitter. Or maybe just sad, actually. I've never been the best at reading people, but even I can tell that this is not a 100% happy man sitting in front of me. Which is hard to believe, really, given who he is.

Imagine having everything you ever wanted, and still not being happy. Would that be better or worse than having none *of the things you think will make you happy, but at least still having the hope that they're out there?*

I shift uncomfortably in my seat. These thoughts are too deep for this particular moment in my life. They're making my head hurt.

"I'm *not* surprised, actually," I confess, looking up at him. "*I* didn't recognize you at all last night. Not until I saw the poster in your bathroom, and..."

I stop, digging my fingernails into my palms as I realize I've just let slip that I went wandering around his house this morning. To my relief, though, Jett just chuckles drily.

"Oh, that," he says, showing a flash of perfect white teeth through his beard. "Yeah, my ex-girlfriend got me that. I think she thought it was funny."

I smile uncertainty at the casual mention of his ex. Which one was it, I wonder? Ada Gilmour? Violet King? Evie Crawford? Willow Fraser? I could go on. The thing is, Jett Carter has had a *lot* of ex-girlfriends, as anyone who's ever flicked through a gossip magazine in the checkout line, or tapped their way through Deux Moi's 'Sunday Spotted' can testify. The man's love life is the stuff of legends. In fact, he's almost as famous for the long list of women he's dated as he is for his acting career. And he's *really* famous for his acting career, trust me.

But none of this is getting me any closer to finding out why he brought me here, so I clear my throat again and do my best to sit upright among the cushions that keep threatening to swallow me.

"So, are you going to tell me why I'm here?" I ask, sounding as dignified as I can manage with my feet dangling off my seat. "Because if it's just so you can thank me for everything I did for you last night, you're welcome, but I think having me followed home was a bit much, don't you?"

"I didn't have you followed," Jett says, frowning. "I sent Leroy round to the bar when I woke up this morning to ask about you. The owner told him where you live. I'd complain about that, by the way, if I were you. They shouldn't be giving out people's addresses to customers. You never know who might turn up."

"You don't say," I mutter under my breath. Before I can say any more, however, the double doors leading to the hallway open, and Silver Fox comes striding in importantly, followed by a harried looking Grace. A lock of hair has escaped her ponytail, and there's a smudge on the lens of her glasses, which she keeps trying to rub at with her sleeve when she thinks no one's looking. She looks like she'd be more at home sitting knitting in front of the TV with a cat on her lap, than playing PA to a Hollywood star, and it makes me like her all the more. Especially when she trips over her own feet on her way across the room, and has to grab frantically at Silver Fox's jacket in order to remain upright, totally ruining his entrance.

I think I love her.

"Ahem." Silver Fox glances from me to Jett, then back again, before taking a seat next to his client. Grace bobs nervously beside him for a second, then follows suit, leaving the three of them lined up opposite me, almost as if they're about to interview me for a job I didn't actually apply for.

I'm suddenly nervous, although I don't know why.

"So, Jett," begins Silver Fox, shuffling the sheaf of papers in his hand, "I assume you've explained our plan to Miss Steele?"

Plan?

What plan?

I lean forward slightly, trying to ignore the frantic hammering of my heart in my chest.

Why does this already sound like something I'm going to hate?

"No, Asher, I haven't," Jett replies, sounding painfully bored. "Because I haven't agreed to it myself, remember? And I'm not going to."

"Now, Jett," the agent begins, speaking like a parent addressing a particularly naughty child. "We've been through this already. You know you need to clean up your image if you want to have even the slightest chance of getting the *Macbeth* role. Duval has already been making it known that he doesn't want your reputation overshadowing his movie, and that was *before* your little escapade with Miss Steele, here."

Huh? His what *with me?*

My eyebrows rise with indignation, but no one notices. After all the trouble they went to get me here, it appears I'm irrelevant to this conversation, so I allow myself to sink back into the cushions and try to follow it as best I can. I know Justin Duval is a director, and the fact that he's rumored to working on a movie version of *Macbeth* at least explains why Jett was quoting the play to me last night — or trying to. As for what, exactly, all of this has to do with me, though, I have absolutely no idea.

"It wasn't an 'escapade', Asher," Jett says with a sigh I can feel all the way across the room. "I got drunk in her bar and she was kind enough to drive me home. That's it. Nothing to see here."

"Kind enough to drive you home, and stupid enough to get photographed doing it," says Asher, favoring me with an icy glare.

I bristle furiously in my seat as I return the frosty look. I know I said I'd rate this guy a 7, but I think I'm going to have to take a point off, just for personality.

You're down to a 6, Silver Fox.

"And now she's all over the news, being described as your latest 'love interest,'" Asher goes on, oblivious to his rapidly dropping rating. "As if you'd date a barmaid."

On second thoughts, make that a 5.

'Excuse me," I say hotly, finding my tongue at last. "I'm sitting right here, you know? I can hear you talking about me. And I might be just a barmaid, but I'm not going to sit here and be insulted."

With that, I struggle awkwardly to my feet, hoping my face isn't as red as it feels right now. My intention is to grab my bag and stalk proudly out of the door, with my head held high, but Jett ruins my big exit by standing up to join me, his height making me feel even smaller in comparison.

"That's enough, Asher," he says wearily, rubbing a hand over his eyes and rumpling his dark hair in the process. "I've already said I won't do it. You can tell my father that when you see him. I know he's the driving force behind this scheme, and I'm sorry, but I'm just not prepared to play along."

Asher's hands tighten on the paper he's holding, and a muscle twitches in his cheek as he tries and fails to hide his frustration. For a moment, I think he's about to become the third person in this room to stand up and prepare to walk out, but, instead, he simply sighs as if he's heard all of this before.

"Your father's just worried about you, Jett, that's all," he says calmly. "As am I. We know how much this role means to you, but we also know you're not going to get it if you keep on like this, being linked to a different woman every week. That might have been okay when you were starring in action movies and werewolf franchises, but it's not going to fly with Justin Duval, and you know it. Which is why you need to clean up your act, like I said. You need to convince people that this latest liaison is the real thing."

He nods in my direction, and everyone turns to look at me, as if I'm on stage or something. *This would all be quite thrilling, really, if it wasn't so mind-bendingly bizarre.*

"You need to show the world that Miss Steele wasn't just another one-night stand, or casual fling," Asher continues, matter-of-factly. "You need to make them think you're in love with her. And you need to start now."

Chapter 9

"I don't want a fake girlfriend, Asher."

Jett's voice is low and steady, but something tells me he's ever so slightly rattled. Which isn't surprising given that what Silver Fox has just suggested is the most ridiculous thing I've ever heard in my life; and I was there when Jimmy McEwan tried to claim his sheep, Edna, could sing, so I'm not unacquainted with the ridiculous, trust me.

This, however, makes Edna's singing seem like a fairly reasonable proposition in comparison.

He wants Jett to pretend he's in love with me?

So he can get a role in Macbeth?

Have I slipped into some kind of alternative universe here?

"You might not *want* one," Asher says smoothly, "But you can't deny you need one. Those photos are all over the news now, and no matter how much you protest, Jett, you gotta admit, the optics aren't good."

He nudges Grace, who obediently holds up an iPad with the photo of me getting into my car filling its screen, and I wince again at the sight of my disheveled hair and shell-shocked appearance.

He's right. "The optics" really aren't *good. I should book a haircut. Or maybe just a full-body makeover.*

"I don't care what it looks like," Jett snaps, losing patience. "My private life has absolutely nothing to do with my acting ability. Nothing. God, I'm so sick of this shit."

He turns and strides over to the window, where he stands staring out at the view, his arms crossed defensively over his chest. I'd actually feel sorry for him, if I wasn't too busy feeling sorry for *myself* for getting mixed up in this madness. And, well, if he wasn't a multi-millionaire Emmy-winning heartthrob, obviously.

"It does as far as Justin Duval is concerned," Asher says, apparently unmoved by this outburst. "He's a family man, Jett. You know that. And he doesn't want your reputation detracting from his movie — which is why you know you have to do this. Come on Jett, think about it. I know your publicist has suggested this kind of thing in the past and you've always said no, but you know *I* wouldn't be suggesting it — and your father wouldn't be suggesting it — if we didn't think it was the only way to get Duval on side. You do want to at least be considered for that role, don't you?"

Jett hesitates. I can practically feel his resolve wavering. I'm going to take that as my cue to leave.

"Okaaay," I say breezily, picking up my bag. "This has been fascinating. It really has. But if you don't mind, I think I'll be off now and let you continue your weird conversation without me."

With that, I give a cheery wave, then turn to leave the room... only to walk straight into the rock-hard chest of Leroy, who's crept into the room surprisingly quietly for a man his size.

"Hey," he says, grinning at me. "How're ya doing? You good?"

I take a step back. He isn't stopping me from leaving, but he *has* spoiled my exit for a second time, and the few seconds it takes me to recover myself gives Silver Fox an opportunity to jump right in there.

"Maybe you two should take some time to talk about this," he says, getting to his feet and gesturing to Grace to follow him. "Smooth out some details. Get to know each other a bit better."

"There's nothing to discuss," says Jett bluntly, without turning around. "I don't want a fake girlfriend. And, even if I did, I don't think she's the right person to do it. I mean, she tried to kiss me last night when I was almost passed out. I just don't need that kind of complication in my life. Get an actress, if you must set me up with someone, not a fan."

"Excuse *me*," I say hotly, drawing myself up to my full height. All 5'4" of it. "I did *not* try to kiss you. I was trying to make sure you didn't choke to death in your sleep. And I am *not* a fan, either, Mr. Bigshot."

Well, not if he keeps on like this, anyway.

At this, Jett finally turns around and looks at me. His hands are thrust into the pockets of his sweatpants, and I can't tell whether he's amused or annoyed, because that stupid beard of his is hiding most of his face.

"I think we're done here," he says quietly, nodding to Leroy, who moves to open the double doors behind me. "Can you drive her home for me, please, Leroy?"

Okaaaay, I guess we're going with 'annoyed' then. Good to know.

"Um, Jett?"

Grace looks up timidly from the sofa, where she's been scrolling through her iPad.

"I'm sorry to interrupt," she says, looking like she wishes

she could just die on the spot. "But there are some new photos on TMZ — and most of the other gossip sites, too. They've also found your Instagram, Lexie," she adds, glancing at me apologetically. "Sorry to be the bearer of bad news."

Jett and I spring forward simultaneously, our heads almost clashing as we both bend over the iPad she's holding.

These photos aren't quite so bad, I'm relieved to see. Well, the ones taken in the coffee shop this morning aren't *great*, to be honest, but at least they've been taken from far enough away that you can't see the dark shadows under my eyes from lack of sleep. The ones from my heavily curated Instagram, however, show me at my very best, and I sneak a sidelong glance at Jett, wondering what he's thinking as he looks at them.

Nothing, would appear to be the answer to that, though. Absolutely nothing.

Jett's expression is inscrutable as he plucks the iPad from Grace's trembling fingers and scrolls past the photos until he gets to the text underneath.

"Shit," he says at last, running an exasperated hand through his hair. "This is worse than I thought. I'm getting absolutely dragged in the comments on this thing. They reckon I'm some kind of sexual predator who picks up women in bars, then kicks them out the next morning."

"Asher says you're not supposed to read the comments," Grace says, blushing. "He says I'm supposed to read them for you, then let him know if there's anything you should be aware of."

"And he should definitely be aware of this," Asher interrupts, holding up his phone. "It's not just TMZ saying it, Jett. It's everyone. I'm sorry, but I don't think you have much of a choice right now. You're going to have to do something fast, before it gets out of hand. We'll let you two talk."

He nods again to Grace, who gets up and scuttles after him as he strides across the room towards the door, which Leroy is still holding open.

"We'll be just down the hall," Asher says, as the three of them leave. "Take as long as you need. Just... not *too* long, okay?"

The door closes behind them, leaving Jett and I alone.

Awkward.

It would be strange enough finding yourself alone with a Hollywood superstar even if you *weren't* supposed to be discussing the possibility of becoming his fake girlfriend, but given that I *have* somehow managed to find myself in this totally bizarre situation, I don't quite know what to do with myself.

"Shall we take a seat?" Jett asks, coming to my rescue.

I hesitate. I really want to go home. But I also really want to stay here and see where this is going to lead. Oh, come *on* — it's Jett Carter, man of my teenage dreams. The least I can do is hear the guy out, right?

"Okay."

He sits back down on the sofa, and this time I take a seat beside him, perching carefully on the very edge of the cushions, so I don't get swallowed up by them.

"So, fake relationship, huh?" I say, desperately wanting to break the silence that falls once we're both seated. "That's actually a thing here, then?"

"Oh, it's a thing alright. You'd be surprised."

Jett's tone is neutral, but I see his lip curl with something like distaste.

"And what exactly would I have to do?" I ask, nibbling nervously at my thumbnail. "Not that I'm going to do it, obviously, just... just out of curiosity? What does being the fake girlfriend of Jett Carter actually involve?"

I'm not lying. I'm *dying* of curiosity here. I'm not *totally* naïve. I've read the gossip pages. I know there are always rumors about celebrity romances; how some of them are just for the publicity, like when two co-stars have a movie to promote, say, and they want to get maximum exposure for it by pretending to be madly in love. *Showmances*, Summer calls them. Or *Fauxmances*, if you prefer.

I've heard about all the faux-show romances. I just didn't for a second ever imagine myself being asked to be *in* one. Although there's not exactly a *huge* demand for fake celebrity romances back in the Scottish Highlands, to be fair.

"Not much," Jett says, shrugging. "A few photos, probably. Maybe we'd go out to dinner or something, make it look like we were on a date. Oh, and you'd get paid, obviously. Asher will fill you in on the details, if you really want to know."

"I'd get *paid*? To go on dates with you? Are you actually serious?"

I feel a hysterical laugh start to work its way up my throat. This is absolutely *insane*. Like, *batshit* insane.

All the same, though, I have to admit, I'm intrigued.

And ever-so-slightly tempted.

I used to have a poster of this guy on my bedroom wall when I was a teenager. His face was briefly my phone's home screen wallpaper. I once asked Mum if I could have a birthday cake with Jett's face on it; and, okay, she just ignored me and got me a Teletubbies cake instead — and I was 17 at the time. But even so. The intent was there. Which means that in my late teens, when Jett's first movie came out, I would have literally *eaten him up on a cake* if I possibly could have.

And now I'm being offered money to *date* him?

"Well, to *pretend* to date me. It wouldn't *actually* be a date, obviously."

Jett's voice breaks into my thoughts, and at first I think he must have somehow read my mind before I remember the question I asked him.

"Okay, so I'd get paid, and you'd get to have a shot at this movie you're into," I say, licking my dry lips. "And that's it? That's the deal? What's the catch?"

"No catch," Jett replies wearily. "Other than the fact that it's completely fucking ridiculous, obviously."

I stand up and walk over to the glass wall opposite, and stand there looking out at the city, my mind whirring.

Getting into a fake relationship would, as Jett says, be "completely fucking ridiculous". That is, indeed, a catch. It's not, however, the *only* catch in this bizarre plan. There is another one: and it's currently sitting on the sofa behind me, looking like it would rather be anywhere else but here.

The catch is Jett Carter — and the fact that, if I go ahead with this, there's a very strong chance of me falling in love with him. Not in his present state, obviously. I'm safe enough from him *now*. But I know what he looks like under that beard. I know what he looks like on the red carpet, in a tuxedo and a bow tie. I know what he looked like in *Wolf*, when he played a sexy werewolf, and the critics all said his career was over, but the fans went absolutely *wild*.

I should probably try not to think about that right now. Or, you know, ever.

I'm worried I'd fall in love with him. That pretending to be his girlfriend would feel real to me, even though it would be fake. Pretend. Not real. Not true. It'd be like that time Emerald Taylor from my hometown pretended to be someone else so she could date the local Laird (Sorry, long story...), only not really, because Emerald actually *did* end up dating the local Laird. And I will definitely *not* end up dating Jett Carter. I'll just pretend to: an idea so alien to me that I can't even begin to get my head around it.

"Is there anything else you want to ask me?" Jett asks, breaking into my thoughts.

I turn and look at him speculatively.

"Yeah," I say at last. "There is."

He raises his eyebrows questioningly.

"Do you have one of those really huge walk-in pantries?" I ask in a rush. "Like Khloe Kardashians? And can I see it, if you do?"

Chapter 10

"And, yeah, that's a shelf for cereal. I guess. I don't really come in here much, to be honest."

Jett and I are standing inside the pantry of my dreams, and it's even better than I imagined it would be. Every kind of pasta under the sun, all neatly arranged in labeled glass jars. A full section just for condiments. So many different types of candy it's like an old-fashioned sweet shop — or the Cracker Barrel Old Country Store.

I *love* it.

"You're seriously interested in this?" Jett asks, scratching his head. "A pantry?"

"Oh God, yes," I breathe, running my hand along one of the shelves. (This one contains a selection of teas and coffees. I want to inhale it.) "I grew up in chaos, basically. Organization is like therapy to me."

Jett looks at me curiously, but before he can comment on this, the pantry door swings open, and Grace's surprised face peeks around it.

"Oh, there you are," she says, trying not to look surprised to find us surrounded by pasta. "Asher asked me to come and find you. He's waiting in the other room."

My stomach somersaults, like it's doing a trick.

"You ready to face the music, Lady M?" Jett asks quietly, as we follow Grace back down the gleaming marble hallway to where Asher's waiting for us. "You worked out what you want to do?"

I shake my head, wishing I hadn't taken Jett's offer to help myself to the candy in the jars back there quite so literally.

"Nope," I say, shrugging. "Got any suggestions for me?"

Jett shakes his head firmly.

"Uh-uh," he says, as we reach the doors to the living room. "The ball's in your court, Alexandra. It's totally up to you."

I swallow nervously. At some point in the next few minutes, I'm going to have to decide whether I want to fake-date Jett Carter.

And I have absolutely no idea what I'm going to say.

* * *

The question is *not*, apparently, whether I want to fake-date Jett Carter.

No, the *real* question I'm facing, it seems, is how much trouble I'm prepared to get into if I *don't*.

It's about 20 minutes after the conversation in the pantry, and things have gone rapidly downhill.

Despite his earlier reluctance, Jett seems to have resigned himself to the fact that we're going to be fake dating. His eyes are closed as he leans back against the sofa, physically present, but emotionally detached from the scene that's unfolding as Asher places the sheaf of papers he's been clutching like they're his firstborn child onto the low coffee table in front of me.

"What's this?" I ask, feigning disinterest. "Your life story?"

"Yours, actually."

My stomach flip-flops with sudden fear as he reaches over and spreads the papers out like a fan on the table.

"We didn't have a lot of time, obviously, but this is everything we were able to find out about you in the last few hours. Want to take a look?"

"Here's an idea," I say, not wanting to give him the satisfaction. "Why don't you just tell me whatever it is you want me to feel worried about, and I'll do my best to look worried about it. How does that work for you?"

I flip my hair over my shoulder in a show of nonchalance, but the truth is, I don't have to try to look worried. I *am* worried. Because, judging by the way he's sitting there with his eyebrows raised like the James Bond villain he clearly dreams of being, Silver Fox has got something on me.

And I have a pretty good idea what it is, too.

"It's the small matter of your visa," says Silver Fox, with a "gotcha" look on his face.

Bingo. Got it in one.

The issue with my visa is that I don't actually have one: and I'm not talking about a credit card here either. I *definitely* have one of those.

No, my good friend Fox here is talking about a work permit, of course. The one I need to work legally here in the U.S. The one I don't have, because... well, because I didn't bother applying for one.

I *meant* to do it. No, really, I did. But, the thing is, when I arrived here, on the same three month tourist visa as everyone else who comes to California for a sunshine break, I didn't plan to stay. I just needed to get away from Heather Bay for a bit. Away from the shocked faces who looked at me like I was something less than human. I wanted to get away from *myself*, really — but I brought myself right along with me, as evidenced by the way I got here and immediately got myself into trouble: not only by outstaying my welcome, but also by getting a job — which definitely wasn't allowed under the terms of that visa.

My tourist visa lasted three months.

At the end of month one, I met Amy, who told me there was a spare room available in the house she was renting.

At the start of month two, I met Summer, who'd just moved in, and who was looking for bar staff to help out at work — cash in hand, no questions.

By month three, I was pretty much settled in, and Heather Bay felt like it was in another *world*, not just another country.

By month four, I was officially over the limit of my tourist visa, but by month five, my head was firmly buried in the sand about it. I knew I should do something to make my stay legal, but I had no idea where to even start, and anyway — who was going to know? I'd done something wrong, sure, but the world hadn't ended. A bunch of men in black suits hadn't come beating down the door, ready to throw me out of the country. I was safe. And, well, also *terrified.* Well, wouldn't *you* be? Just because those men in black hadn't arrived *yet*, it didn't mean they weren't going to — and going by the look on Silver Fox's face right now, I'm guessing he knows exactly where to find them.

Oh. Merde.

"No need to look so worried, Miss Steele," he says pleasantly, surprising me. "No one needs to know about this little...

discrepancy in your paperwork, shall we call it?"

"No?"

My heart leaps with hope, then immediately sinks again as I realize what he's about to say to me.

"Of course not," Fox tells me, with a smile made of ice. "Jett and his father have a lot of contacts, you know. And a lot of money. They can make all of this go away. They just need you to do something for them in return. I'm sure you can guess what it is."

He sweeps a hand over the papers on the table, and, all of a sudden, I understand how perfectly ordinary people can be driven to commit murder.

"What about my job at the bar, though?" I say at last, as a sudden thought strikes me. "I can't just walk out on it and leave them in the lurch, can I? I'm supposed to be working tonight, actually."

I glance at my watch, surprised to see how much time has passed since I've been here. Summer will kill me if I'm late for work again.

"It's okay," Asher says smoothly, "You're obviously not going to be able to go back there if you decide to go ahead with this, but don't worry. We'll speak to Joe. We'll make sure he's compensated for the loss of his best barmaid."

He raises one elegant eyebrow to register his skepticism at the idea of me being someone's "best" anything, but I choose to ignore it.

"Wait. There's a Joe?" I ask incredulously. "A real one? I thought 'Joe's Bar' was just some random name?"

What a day of surprises. Next they'll be telling me Weird Ben, my so-called roommate, is actually an International Man of Mystery. Or that Jett Carter might one day want to date me for real.

I nibble my fingernails thoughtfully, before realizing what I'm doing, and abruptly sitting on my hands to stop myself. "So unladylike, Lexie," I hear Mum say in my head. "No wonder your hands are so ugly when you insist on biting your fingers like a hamster all the time."

Mum.

A shiver runs down the full length of my body as I realize she's probably seen the photos of me and Jett by now. *Everyone* will have. Everyone here. Everyone back home. Everyone who knows me, and everyone who hates me, and all the people who think I'm just a silly girl who ran away in disgrace, and who they'll never hear of again.

Imagine the looks on all their faces if they find out I'm dating the most famous man in the world, though?

Not that I'm going to say yes, obviously.

That would be crazy.

And wrong, in the way that any kind of lie is wrong.

And... quite possibly illegal, if Asher's seriously suggesting Jett's family could somehow pay someone to make my visa problems go away?

No, agreeing to this insane scheme would directly contravene my promise to Be Good, in so many ways that I don't even want to think about counting them.

Then again, I suppose you *could* argue I've broken that promise already, by getting myself into this situation in the first place.

What if this is my way of making it right?

What if this is my golden opportunity to get my life back on track again?

What if this is the thing that allows me to go back home? To crawl out from underneath the dark cloud that descended on me after the events of last summer, and to emerge as a whole new Lexie? A better one? A *normal* one?

I take a deep breath as I look at the three figures on the sofa. Three people I didn't even know until this morning, but who are about to change my life dramatically — although whether for better or for worse is something that still remains to be seen.

"Okay," I say impulsively, "I'll do it. But on one condition."

On the couch, three sets of eyebrows rise simultaneously in surprise.

"He has to shave off the beard," I say, nodding at Jett. "Because there's just no way anyone's going to believe I'd date someone *that* hairy."

Chapter 11

I wake up the next morning in a suite at the Beverly Hilton, and, yup, this is officially the weirdest thing that's ever happened to me.

Weirder even than Edna's singing.

Weirder than the masquerade ball where my life dramatically imploded last summer. (Like I say, it's a loooong story...)

Even weirder than the time Bella McGowan tried to persuade the Community Council to do one of those nude calendars for charity, but Old Jimmy was the only one who was up for it. (That's a long story too, now I come to think of it. I should start writing this stuff down.)

Are you getting that this is weird? Because this, my friends, is *seriously* weird.

Since this time yesterday, I've gained over 80,000 new Instagram followers.

I have a grand total of 53 missed calls on my phone, and twice as many message notifications. Or, at least, I *did* at the point where I decided just to switch the thing off altogether, to avoid the temptation of actually answering it — which I absolutely *cannot* do, on account of the strict non-disclosure agreement I signed last night, promising not to tell a single soul about what's really going on with me and Jett.

Not even Summer.

Not even Mum.

Mum. She'd called at least half a dozen times before I switched my phone off, and I'm willing to bet she's probably on her way to the airport right now, desperate to get herself out here and bask in my reflected glory.

Well, *Jett's* reflected glory.

I glance nervously around the room, almost as if I'm expecting her to step out from behind the curtains, like a magician.

Honestly, I'd put nothing past that woman. Nothing at all.

The suite, though, is totally empty. And, for just a fraction of a second, I don't know whether to feel disappointed or relieved.

Hi, I'm Lexie, and my toxic trait is hoping you'll call me, then refusing to pick up when you do. Please leave a message after the beep...

I *did* listen to one of the messages, though. The very first one, in fact.

"Lexie, darling, call me when you get this," she said, sounding slightly breathless — the excitement, I assume — but otherwise normal. As if it hadn't been almost a year since we last spoke. As if that final conversation hadn't ended with me deciding that driving to the airport and getting on the first available flight (Thank God it was California, and not that place in Alaska where the sun doesn't rise for weeks on end, is all I can say...) was my best option under the circumstances.

There's no trace of that in Mum's breezy little message, though, and I'm strangely deflated as I listen to it. It's not that I expected her to apologize or anything like that. I know that's not her style. But to act like *absolutely nothing happened* is cold, even for her.

Isn't it funny how easy it is for some people to *pretend*?

Not that I can talk, mind you. Mum might have her moments — and, trust me, Mum has a *lot* of moments — but she's not the one who just signed a contract agreeing to a fake relationship with a movie star, is she?

No, that was me. I did that. Of *course* I did. And although I'd love to be able to say I did it because of the whole work visa situation — that my hands were tied and I had absolutely no choice in the matter — the truth is that I did it for her. For Mum. To prove to her that I'm perfectly fine without her in my life; that I've moved on and moved up, and that I don't even care that she hasn't bothered to call me since the day I left Heather Bay.

So there.

How do you like me now, Samantha Steele?

"Helloooo? Lexie, are you in there?"

I'm so busy mentally squaring up to my mother that it takes a few seconds for me to realize someone's banging on the door. I jump up and open it, to find Grace standing there, her arms weighed down with expensive-looking shopping bags.

"Here," she says, tossing them onto the bed. "Take your pick."

I circle the packages like a vulture, peering into each bag in turn, and finding them filled to the brim with stuff. Clothes. Makeup. Expensive skincare products. A small, fluffy teddy bear with the words "I wuff you" embroidered on its tiny t-shirt.

"Whoops, that's mine, sorry," says Grace, turning scarlet as she reaches it. "I must have swept it off my bed along with all the other stuff."

She nods to the bags on the bed.

"These are all PR samples," she says. "Asher had them sent over. I wasn't sure what size you were, or what you'd like, so I just brought a bit of everything."

"So… I get to keep this stuff?" I ask, amazed. "Like, *forever?*"

"And ever," Grace confirms. "Consider it a perk of the job. Like the hotel room."

She goes over to the window and pulls open the curtains, letting the sunlight stream in, and I smile at her uncertainly. The suite is beautiful, don't get me wrong; it's the most luxurious place I've ever stayed in my life, and, under normal circumstances, I'd be reveling in its opulence, while emptying the mini bar.

I'm not here for a break, though. I'm here purely because, by the time I was ready to leave Jett's place yesterday, the paparazzi had already found their way to my front door, and were camped outside it, prompting a flurry of messages from Summer and Amy, all of which I had to ignore, on Asher's strict instructions. When he wasn't looking, though, I snuck my phone out of my bag and sent Summer a quick message.

"*Sorry,*" I wrote, wondering which emoji would be most appropriate for situations where you inadvertently set the paps on your housemates, because of your imaginary boyfriend. "*Can't talk now. Will explain everything soon. Don't worry. X*"

She *will* worry, though. I mean, who *wouldn't*? And the fact that I can't just call her and tell her what's going on is the worst thing about this whole bizarre setup.

"Lexie?" Grace says gently, interrupting my guilt-fest. "Do you want to start getting ready? We have to go and meet Jett."

* * *

Just over an hour later I'm sitting on a wide balcony, which is basically just a glass box hanging off the side of Jett's house, with the entire city spread out below me.

Down below me, I can see someone cleaning the pool, while over to the left, there's a low hum from a strimmer, as someone else works on the immaculate garden.

Now that I've seen the pantry, I wonder what the closets are like? And how I could somehow manage to work that into the conversation I'm about to have?

The thought of talking to Jett again, however, makes my mouth go dry with nerves.

I've no idea why I'm feeling so anxious all of a sudden. It's not like I haven't been here before, after all. It's not like I haven't seen *him* before.

This is my third time in his house. In Heather Bay terms, we're practically married. If we were at home right now, the entire village would be alight with gossip about me and Jett, and Bella McGowan would be wondering if she should bake some cakes with our entwined initials on them.

That might well be happening, mind you. It's not like they don't have the Internet back in the Highlands, much as it surprises my Californian friends to hear it. When I tell people here where I come from, they instantly imagine us all wrapped in our tartan plaids, stealing livestock and fighting Sassennachs. Actually, though, when I left Heather Bay, Jack Buchanan had just opened a swanky new bar, and Shona McLaren was thinking of starting a blog.

"Or maybe I should go with that Tok-Tik thingummy jig,

Lexie?" she said, the last time I saw her. "I hear that's all the rage now. What d'ye think?"

What I think is that, with or without the power of social media behind her, Shona will make sure that everyone in Heather Bay knows that Lexie Steele has somehow managed to bag herself a movie star boyfriend. They'll all think it's real.

I think I'm going to pass out.

"Hey."

While I was staring down at the city, thinking about Heather Bay, Jett has walked out onto the balcony as stealthily as a cat. And when I turn around to face him, I'm so shocked I almost fall flat on my face.

It's Jett Carter.

And, I mean, *obviously* it's Jett Carter. It's not like I was expecting someone *else* to walk through that door and pretend to be my boyfriend.

Since I last saw him, though, he's done as I asked, and has dutifully shaved off the obnoxious beard. Which means that this Jett Carter — the one standing in front of me, with a totally unreadable expression on his face — is the same Jett Carter I know from his movies. It's the same Jett Carter whose poster I used to have on the wall of my teenage bedroom; instantly recognizable, and really quite devastatingly attractive.

Oh, mierda.

This is *really* not good news for me, is it?

The thing is, I've been thinking about this a lot since last night, and I'm more convinced than ever that if I'm going to be this man's fake girlfriend, I *cannot* allow myself to fall for him for real. I just can't afford the heartbreak I know it will cause me when he doesn't love me back. And he won't, will he? Because he's a Hollywood superstar, and I'm just a girl from the Highlands, who works in a dead-end bar and only has one friend. Two if you count Grace, and, actually, I think I *will* count Grace, just to make myself feel a little better about this.

So, two friends — one of whom I'm forbidden from talking to — and one fake boyfriend. Who doesn't seem to want to talk to *me*, if the way he's just pulled out his phone and started scrolling through it is anything to go by.

Okay, so we're back to just the one friend again. I should probably mention this to Grace, just so she knows she's the designated BFF now, whether she wants to be or not.

"Are you okay?"

Jett's stopped looking at his phone and is staring at me again. It's not a particularly friendly stare.

"You're muttering something under your breath," he says pointedly. "Something about your friends. And you look like you can smell something bad."

He raises one arm and sniffs experimentally at his armpit, and I smile in spite of my churning stomach.

"Oh, that's just my face," I assure him, sounding much breezier than I feel. "I have a resting bitch face. It runs in the family."

It's true. My "resting" expression would probably be best described as "pure, undiluted disgust." "Smile, it might never happen," is the thing people say to me most often; and absolutely *hilarious* it is too, I'm sure you'll agree.

"Uh-huh." Jett looks unconvinced, but at least he's not being openly hostile. I'll take that as a win.

"This is kind of awkward, isn't it?" he says, taking the seat opposite mine.

I nod, relieved he said it first.

"Do you want to just, I don't know, pretend it's *not* awkward?" I say. "Just kind of skip the awkward bit, and go straight to the part where we're totally comfortable with each other, just a regular old fake boyfriend and girlfriend, with nothing to prove?"

He considers this, thoughtfully.

"Like acting, you mean?"

I shrug. "I suppose. Isn't that what all of this is about, anyway?"

He smiles slowly, and the effect it has on my insides is really quite disconcerting. If this is how he can make me feel just by smiling, then I think I might be in trouble here.

Like, seriously big trouble.

The kind it's impossible to get out of in one piece.

"I think I can do that," Jett is saying now. "Fake relationships, no. Acting, yes."

"Well, I would hope so," I say, grinning back at him. "Otherwise this whole charade is going to be a bit of waste, really, isn't it?"

Whatever he's about to say to that is lost as the door opens again, and Asher walks out, followed by my new bestie, Grace, and a man I've never seen before. He has a shaved head and several eyebrow piercings, and Asher looks slightly scared of him. I like him already.

Then he goes and spoils it all by opening his mouth.

"Well, this just isn't going to work *at all*," Shaven Head says, throwing his hands in the air dramatically as he strides over to where I'm sitting and peers into my face as if I'm not actually attached to it.

"We need to do something with this," he says, prodding at my hair with distaste. "And... *these.*" He points at my eyebrows and then looks away, as if the very sight of them has offended him.

And here was I thinking I was just about to meet Friend #3.

"Umm, Lexie, this is Jakob," Grace says nervously, her hands twisting anxiously at the necklace she's wearing. "He's a stylist we've asked to come and... to come and... well, *help* you. Not that you *need* help, obviously, it's just that..."

"Oh, she does," Jakob interjects, folding his arms across his chest decisively. "She really, really does."

I pull myself up as straight as I can manage in his infernal chair, and flip my hair over my shoulder haughtily.

"If this is the bit where I get a makeover, and everyone suddenly decides to accept me, I don't think a man in Birkenstocks is best placed to help me with that, thanks," I say acidly, allowing my eyes to sweep my latest nemesis from head to toe.

Jakob gasps in outrage. For a second, we glare at each other, like gladiators about to go into the ring. Then, before either of us can speak, there's a loud sigh, and Jett stands up.

"Enough," he says, looking from Jakob to Asher and back again. "She doesn't need a stylist. She's fine. Her eyebrows are fine. Her hair's fine. Now, can we just get on with this, please, Asher? I have things to do, you know."

I get slowly to my feet, feeling once again deflated. Jakob might have insulted my eyebrows, but Jett has just crushed my spirit completely.

Fine?

He thinks I'm *fine*?

Talk about *insulting*. I thought every man knew that "fine" is the very worst thing you can say to a woman in regards to her appearance. And I know he's not really my boyfriend, but the fact is, I don't want him to think I'm just *fine*. I don't want to *be* just *fine*.

I want to be better than that.

I *will* be better than that.

"Actually," I say, turning back to Jakob, who's now circling the balcony like an angry cat, "Maybe I could use some help after all—"

"Nope," Jett says firmly, interrupting. "No time for that. I'm not sitting around here all day while you preen yourself. Grab your stuff. If we're going to do this, we're going to do it *now*."

Chapter 12

"And what is 'this', exactly? This thing we're going to do?"

Jett and I are in the back of what I'm assuming is the same car that picked me up from the coffee shop yesterday.

Was it seriously just yesterday? Because I think I might be in danger of getting whiplash from how quickly my life has turned itself around here...

Leroy is in the front seat, next to the driver. I'm in the back with a bad attack of nerves and the start of a stress headache. Jett's sitting next to me with his phone, which appears to be the *real* love of his life, given how much time he spends gazing at the thing.

If I thought I had even half a chance with him, I'd be jealous.

"What? Oh, it's our first date," he says, barely even looking up at me. "Asher arranged it. He's had someone put in a call to some of the tame paps he knows, to tip them off. For the photos, you know?"

I nod, as if this is all totally normal to me, but my stomach feels like it's trying to leave my body, and my headache's just kicked it up a notch in response to the words "photos" and "paps".

I knew this was part of the deal, of course. It was all right there in the contract I signed. Jett and I would go out a few times on "dates", so the paps could get some photos of us and everyone would think our relationship was legit. Fine. It's just... I didn't think the first one would happen so *soon*, is all.

"I thought we'd maybe spend a bit of time getting to know each other first," I blurt out, sneaking a sidelong glance at the man next to me, whose profile is so startlingly familiar from all the movies I've seen him in that I still can't quite believe he's sitting here next to me. Or that it took me so long to realize who he was.

Who knew a beard could be such a good disguise?

Jett's eyes flick up to meet mine, and I'm suddenly intensely aware of how incredibly small the back seat of an insanely huge car can feel when there's a movie star sitting on it.

"That's what dates are for, Alexandra," he says matter-of-factly. "For getting to know each other. Is this your first time on a date?"

"It's the first time I've been on a *fake* date, yeah," I shoot back. "So forgive me for not knowing exactly how it's supposed to work. And it's Lexie, by the way. Only my mother calls me Alexandra."

"That was the name on the paperwork Asher had pulled together on you," Jett replies, shrugging. "It's nice. I like it."

He's already looking at his phone again, his limited interest in me and my name completely used up. I'm not done with him yet, though.

"What else did it say?" I ask nonchalantly. "The paperwork, I mean? What did Asher manage to dig up about me?"

I twirl a lock of hair around my finger, doing my best to look like I couldn't care less what Asher has up his sleeve. I do, though. Oh, you better believe I do. Because the issue with me overstaying my work visa might be the worst thing I've worked in the eyes of the *law*, but it's not the worst thing I've done *ever.* And that's what's worrying me.

There's no way a P.I. could find out about that whole business with the distillery, back in Heather Bay, though, could they? Especially not in the few hours they had to do it. And anyway, that was Mum's fault, not mine. I was just an accomplice after the fact. They didn't even press charges in the end, so Jett can't possibly know about it.

Can he?

"Nothing much, as far as I know," he says, without looking up. "Just that you had the wrong visa or something. Why do you ask?"

"Oh, no reason."

I smooth down my hair and try to relax. Then another thought occurs to me.

"Hey," I say, ignoring the exasperated eye-roll I get for interrupting his precious phone time yet again. "Where are we going, anyway? Where does Jett Carter take someone on a first date?"

I feel my mood lift slightly as I wait for his answer. Maybe it'll be somewhere nice. Maybe I'll actually be able to enjoy this?

Then, just as easily as it arrived, my hopeful mood is shattered.

"The Crab Shack," Jett says, finally putting his phone away as the car draws to a halt. "You like seafood, right?"

* * *

It's not that I *don't* like seafood.

Not *exactly*.

I mean, I come from a fishing village in the Highlands of Scotland. If you don't like fish, you starve, basically.

No, it's just crabs I don't like.

The spindly legs. The spiteful little claws. The certain knowledge that, given the opportunity, the mean little bastards would take over the world and make us all their helpless slaves.

Well, okay, not that last bit. I think that's maybe more of a *me* thing than it is a *crab* thing, really. A thing resulting from that time I found a particularly gruesome specimen washed up on Heather Bay beach, and, later that day, Mum told me if I didn't make myself scarce before her new boyfriend came round, the crab would come back to life and peck my eyes out in some kind of gruesome Zombie Crab scenario.

I think I was about five at the time.

Cheers for that, Mum.

After that, the phobia took hold. Then it grew and grew, until it reached the point where I couldn't even look at a photo of a crab — zombie or otherwise — without screaming.

And that brings us fully up to date.

It also brings us to Santa Monica Pier, where I'm apparently going to be coming face-to-face with my sworn enemies. And then eating them.

"No. No way."

I don't even know I'm going to say it out loud until the words are out of my mouth and Jett is pausing in the act of opening the car door to look at me with exasperation.

"Look, I don't want to be here either, Alexandra," he says, speaking as if to a very small child. "But we have to. It's in the contract, remember?"

"Crabs aren't in the contract," I say immediately, relief flooding through me as I spot a possible reprieve . "I would *definitely* remember that."

Jett frowns, and a line appears between his eyes. It somehow manages to make him look even more handsome. I hate him.

"The Crab Shack isn't good enough for you?" he asks bluntly. "Were you hoping to go somewhere fancier?"

"No. Well, yes. I mean—"

I pause, flustered. I wasn't expecting him to fly me to Paris or something, but I *was* hoping for somewhere that didn't come straight out of a horror movie, you know? Literally *anywhere* other than this would've worked for me. Even McDonalds, say. At least a Big Mac doesn't look like *it's* thinking about eating *you*, right?

I can't really tell Jett this, though. One of the many things I've learned in my 30 years — sorry, 25 — on this planet is that, for reasons that are totally incomprehensible to me, Other People just don't see crustaceans as the evil predators they so clearly are. And once they know you're scared of them, they will take that fear, and they will use it against me. Like the time Charlie Lawson snuck a hermit crab into my schoolbag one break time, just to make me cry. Or the way Mum cheerfully led me to believe that all the crabs in the great ocean were only after one thing: Lexie Steele's eyes.

Fear is weakness.

That's another thing I've learned from life. Well, from my mother, to be exact. She was right, though. Maybe not about the eye-pecking zombie crabs, but about the fact that, if you want to protect yourself, you can never tell anyone what you fear.

So I won't.

I'll just let Jett go on believing I'm a superficial airhead who's disappointed in his choice of venue for our first date.

That'll work.

"It's fine," I say stiffly, unbuckling my safety belt. "I love seafood. Who doesn't?"

Jett looks at me, clearly unconvinced.

"Well, as long as you're sure," he says, with the weariness of a man who's been dealing with idiots like me his entire life, and who just wants a break from it all. "Let's get this over with."

Chapter 13

To be fair to me, The Crab Shack *is* a pretty weird place for an A-lister of Jett's caliber to be hanging out. Inside it's "rustic" and "charming", in a way that's designed to look totally authentic, like a genuine old-style seafood shack, but which you just know has been put together by an interior designer who's never seen the sea in their life. There's probably a warehouse in Wisconsin or somewhere filled to the brim with mass-produced fishing nets and sailor's hats, which chain restaurants can buy in bulk.

And that's *without* taking into account the huge lobster tank in the entrance, which I have to close my eyes to get past.

It's a nightmare. I'm just having a nightmare. Soon I'll wake up, and all of this will be over.

I repeat this mantra to myself as Jett leads me through the tightly-packed restaurant to a table in the back, which is tucked away in a corner, but still uncomfortably exposed.

"Sorry, they don't have private rooms here," he says, holding the seat out for me, like a gentleman. "I guess that would've kinda defeated the purpose, though, given that we're here to be photographed."

He frowns as he says it. He has a baseball cap crammed low over his eyes, and his shoulders are hunched defensively as he sits down opposite me. He does *not* look like a man who wants to be photographed. He seems almost as on edge as I am, actually.

Well. Isn't this fun?

"Is that why you picked this place?" I ask, fiddling nervously with the paper napkin in front of me. "So that plenty of people will see us? Because I think it's working, if so."

I might have had my eyes closed as I walked past the lobster tank, but when I opened them again, it was impossible to miss the ripple of excitement that passed through the restaurant as Jett and I were shown to our table. Angelinos as a group are generally too cool to make a fuss over celebrities, but, then again, Jett Carter isn't just any old celebrity, and although no one's been brave enough to approach us, I can practically *sense* all the cellphones that are pointed at our table right now.

Who needs paparazzi when you have Instagram and TikTok?

I shift uncomfortably in my seat, trying to arrange myself in the most photogenic way I can manage. Mum always told me my left side was my best side ("If only your face was more symmetrical, Alexandra," she once sighed. "You'd be really quite stunning."), but it's my right side that's facing the restaurant, and I know that unless I can somehow manage to keep this rictus grin plastered to my face, my resting bitch face will take over, and I'll look like Voldemort, basically.

God, this is stressful.

And we haven't even got to the bit with the crabs yet.

"It's why Asher picked it, yes." Jett is scanning the menu, holding it so it covers his face. "If we'd gone to one of the places I usually hang out, no one would ever have known about. All those places are too private. That's why I like them."

"I do kinda like places like this," though, he says, lowering it just enough for him to look me in the eye. "People don't expect to see me in a place like The Crab Shack, so if they do see me, they assume they've got it wrong, and I'm just a lookalike or something."

"Like hiding in plain sight," I say, nodding. "Clever."

"I think most actors are just hiding in plain sight," Jett says, so quietly that I have to lean closer to hear him. "Maybe that's why we do it. Making a living by pretending to be someone else all the time. It makes it easier to avoid having to be yourself."

Jett's hand comes up to reflexively stroke at his chin, almost as if he thinks the beard is still there, and my fingers pause in the act of anxiously ripping up my napkin. I have a feeling he's just shared something important with me, and I'm not quite sure how to respond to it.

Fortunately for me, though, I don't have to, because, just as I'm opening my mouth to see what kind of nonsense will come spilling out of it, the server appears to take our drinks order, and she's so determined to make sure Jett notices her that she positions herself right in front of me, her ass level with my face. Once she's taken his order, Jett has to call her back to remind her to take mine, too, and let me just tell you that if looks could kill, I'd be as dead as the crabs we're about to eat.

To *try* to eat.

I've been trying my hardest not to look too closely at the tables around us as we sit here, but I know perfectly well I'm in the presence of The Enemy.

ZOMBIECRABSZOMBIECRABSZOMBIECRABS

Maybe it'll be okay, though.

Maybe this is as close as I'll ever have to get to them?

Or... maybe not. Because what are the odds of Jett bringing

me to The Crab Shack and then *not* ordering the crab?

"Um, would you excuse me?" I mutter, standing up so quickly I almost knock the table over. "I just need to use the restroom."

What feels like dozens of pairs of eyes follow me with undisguised interest as I clatter my way across the room to the door on the other side, then follow me all the way back again when that door turns out to lead to the kitchen, and I have to turn on my heel and head back in the direction I just came in.

"Why don't you just order for us both?" I say brightly as I pass our table for a second time. "Just get me a salad. I'm not that hungry, anyway."

Finally, I find the door to the restrooms, heaving a sigh of relief as I slam it closed behind me.

I'm safe. For now.

I'm just going to stay here for five minutes. Okay, six. Seven at the most. Just long enough to pull myself together and prepare to meet my nemesis.

I can do this.

More importantly, I *have* to do this. I signed the contract. And I'm here now. Photos have been taken, receipts have been got. I can't exactly run out on this date now, just because of a stupid phobia that started when I was five years old.

I *will* do this, then. I will. In approximately eight minutes' time.

Okay, *ten*.

How bad can it possibly be, after all?

* * *

As it turns out, it can be bad.

Like, really, *really* bad.

As in, however you're imagining this scenario playing out, multiply it by ten, then do the same again.

It's even worse than the time I "accidentally" set Emerald's dress on fire just before she was about to walk out onto the stage at the Heather Bay Gala Day. That incident only resulted in the town hall burning down. This one involves *crabs*. Lots and lots of *crabs*.

Did I mention it's bad?

I get back to the table exactly 12 minutes after I left it, to find it absolutely covered in crustaceans.

Covered.

"I don't know what you like to eat," says a bored sounding Jett, who's presiding over the table like some hellish Lord of the Underworld or something, "So I just asked them to bring us a bit of everything. Oh," he adds, seeing my horrified expression at last, "I did order you a crab salad, though. That's what you wanted, right?"

Wrong.

That is very much NOT what I wanted. I can't imagine it being what anyone in their right *mind* would want, to be perfectly honest. And while I'm sure a crab salad probably *doesn't* mean a heap of lettuce with lots of evil little claws sticking out of it, I'm not about to hang around to find out, because this is just too much.

There's one huge crab in the center of the table, looking like all of my worst dreams come to life. Or death, as the case may be. Why aren't there more horror movies about crabs, I wonder? Because they'd make the *perfect* monsters, and as my horrified eyes sweep over the table, taking in the multiple smaller monsters dotted around the terrible centerpiece, something in me snaps.

I can't do this.

I just can't.

All of a sudden, I am five years old again, and there's a monster under the bed.

This time, though, I can run.

So that's exactly what I do.

I open my mouth to apologize to Jett for what I'm about to do, but when nothing comes out, I turn, and I run.

I run right across the restaurant, ignoring the camera phones which are now being blatantly held up in my direction, and head straight for the front door, not caring who sees me. I'm vaguely aware of someone following hot on my heels — Jett, I assume — as I reach the front door of the restaurant. I just have to run the gauntlet of the lobster tank and I'll be back to safety, so, without slowing down, I screw my eyes shut and run blindly for the double doors, bursting through them with my hands held out in front of me like weapons, and my face a mask of horror.

And that's the photo the assembled paparazzi get of me and Jett on our first date.

Chapter 14

"This is a disaster. It's a straight-up disaster. It could not have gone worse if we'd planned it. I *told* you we should have hired a real actress."

It's the next morning, we're all assembled in Jett's state-of-the-art kitchen, and I'm way too embarrassed to even *think* about asking to see that amazing pantry again.

(I would still like a look at the master closet, though. I should probably save that for later.)

The photos of me and Jett running out of the restaurant made the front page of all of this morning's papers and briefly crashed Instagram when one of the celebrity gossip accounts got hold of the video version.

I've had to switch off my phone again in a bid to ignore the increasingly frenzied messages from Mum and Summer ("Lexie. Call me," was all Mum said in her most recent voicemail, sounding considerably less breezy than she did in her first one.), and although I haven't *officially* been sacked yet as Jett's fake girlfriend, I've packed my stuff in preparation for the inevitable moment I'm asked to leave the hotel.

(On the plus side, The Crab Shack is apparently booked solid for the next three weeks now, so, despite what Asher would have us believe, I guess it's not a *total* disaster.)

"It's a total disaster," Asher repeats, running an exasperated hand through his silver gray hair as he paces back and forth on the shiny tiles. At the breakfast bar, Grace, Leroy and Jakob sit in a row, their eyes nervously following him as if they're watching a tennis match. (I have no idea why Jakob is here; this really doesn't seem like a moment that anyone's going to need to be "styled" for, but he sidled up to me when he arrived and hissed, "Just FYI, Birkenstocks are *totally* on trend, you know," before stalking off again, so I suspect he's just here to witness my downfall. And who could blame him?)

"We get it Asher, we get it. It wasn't the result you were hoping for. Still, it could have been worse."

Jett is standing over by the window, and hard though it is for me to imagine how things could possibly be worse right now, I'm grateful to him for the intervention. I smile tentatively in his direction, but he's already buried in his phone again, and I end up catching Asher's eye instead.

Whoops.

"Do you seriously think this is *funny*?" he says, stopping his pacing to glare at me. "Do you have any idea what's at stake here? Jett's career, his reputation... his father's career, his father's—"

"Enough, Asher," Jett interrupts. "You've made your point. You don't have to rub it in. And this has literally nothing to do with my father, anyway."

Asher's mouth tightens into a thin line, but he doesn't reply. I sincerely hope Jett will be rewarded in heaven for his kindness in sticking up for me, especially considering that I'm sure he must be just as angry as his agent is right now. When I told him in the car why I'd run out on him like that, he simply nodded tightly, then sat looking out of the window. He didn't explode with anger, the way Asher has, but he hasn't spoken much since then either, so I have no way of knowing what he's thinking.

What are you thinking, Jett?

"Look," he says, pocketing the phone at last. "I'm sure we all have something we're scared of. It's not Alexandra's fault that she happened to be confronted by hers."

Grace nods, eagerly.

"I'm scared of buttons," she offers timidly. "And empty swimming pools. They terrify me."

"Spiders," Leroy admits, looking bashfully. "No creature needs that many legs."

We all look expectantly at Jakob.

"Death," he says. "The inevitable downward spiral towards old age and infirmity. And also harem pants." His mouth twists into a grimace. "There's just no need, is there?"

"Hold up," interjects Leroy. "I want to change my answer to what he said. That's way better."

"Are you scared of your own mortality too, Leroy?" Grace asks, placing a comforting hand on his arm.

"Naw, I mean them baggy pants," says Leroy. "That shit's bad."

"You want to know what I'm scared of?" Asher snaps loudly. "I'm scared of being poor," he goes on, having successfully gotten everyone's attention. "And the rest of you should be, too," he adds. "Because if Jett's out of a job, we're *all* out of a job. And I somehow don't think Justin Duval will be impressed with today's coverage, do you?"

There's a moment's silence during which I have to bite my tongue to stop myself retorting that if Jett has to give up acting, maybe Asher himself should give it a go. He's definitely dramatic enough. This definitely wouldn't be a good time to be drawing attention to myself, though, and I'm still having painful flashbacks to that photo of me running out of the restaurant with my mouth open, mid-scream, so I remain silent, and try my best to retain my balance on the bar stool I'm sitting on, which is one of those revolving ones. This doesn't bode well for me.

"Um, no publicity is bad publicity?" Grace says at last, breaking the silence and earning Asher's wrath in return.

"Nonsense," he barks. "That's just what amateurs say, Grace, you know that. This is terrible publicity. Terrible. *Catastrophic.* And now we need to find a way to fix it. Which, given that we can't get rid of Ms Steele, here, without making Jett look even worse, is going to be a pretty tall order. Suggestions, people. Quickly."

There's another short pause.

"Fix her eyebrows," Jakob says, smirking.

"Maybe we could use this as an opportunity to raise awareness for kabourophobia," Grace says timidly. "That's what you call a phobia of crabs," she adds earnestly. "I looked it up. Maybe Lexie could say she's trying to help other people with the condition. She could start a charity and—"

"I'm thinking we hire a yacht," Asher interrupts her. "Get some photos of the two of them on deck, in their swimwear."

"NO," say Jett and I in unison.

I'm glad there's one thing we agree on, then.

"Okay, Grace, try to find out which events are scheduled for tonight, then," Asher replies, shrugging. "The more public, the better, really."

"No," Jett says again, more quietly this time. "No big crowds, Asher. Not unless we absolutely have to."

He shoots his manager a look, which, to my surprise, instantly makes the other man back down.

"Okay, okay," he says, rubbing the bridge of his nose thoughtfully. "Another restaurant? A better one, this time?"

"Dinner a deux on the beach," Jakob puts in. "But you get, like, a million red roses and arrange them in a massive heart, like when Travis proposed to Kourtney. Jett could give her a diamond necklace or something. Nothing as obvious as a ring, but something almost as good."

Jett and I exchange wordless glances of horror.

"Or we could fly them to Vegas," Grace offers eagerly. "Lexie could post some selfies from the helicopter, then they go round some of the casinos, or go to see a show, maybe, and everyone will wonder if they're *actually* there to get married."

"... because we'll strongly suggest that they are," Asher says, giving her an approving look. "Nice work, Grace. I like it."

Grace turns scarlet with pride, and I slam my hand down on the worktop next to me, sending my stool spinning crazily around, like some kind of strange fairground ride.

"No." I say, swaying woozily as Leroy helps bring me to a stop. "We're not doing any of those things. No offense, Grace—" I look at her apologetically — "But they're just... well, *terrible*, really. I'm sorry, but they are."

"Terrible?" Asher's puzzlement is clearly genuine. "How so?" he asks. "What woman wouldn't want to be treated like a princess for the day, like we're suggesting?"

"Um, quite a few of us?" I reply, feeling a lot less confident now everyone's eyes are on me. And really quite dizzy after my spin on the chair, to be honest. "The thing is," I go on, "These ideas are just the things we're *told* to think are romantic. The things you see in movies and on TV."

Everyone nods, not seeing the problem here.

"And?" Jakob prompts, helping himself to a grape from a bowl so huge I'd assumed the fruit wasn't actually real. "What's your point, caller?"

"My point," I say, not taking the bait, "Is that those things are all very well on TV, but they're not real. And if we do any of them, people will know that. They'll know it's just for show, because movie directors and romance writers might *think* women want flowers and jewels and helicopter trips to Vegas, but that's not what we *really* want. Well, not *all* of us," I hastily amend. "I can only speak for myself here, obviously."

"And what do you *really* want, then, Lady M?"

Jett's tone is as deadpan as ever, but there's a spark of interest in his eyes I haven't seen there before, so, encouraged, I go on.

"I mean, I just want to feel like someone's actually taken the time to get to know me," I say, looking directly at him and ignoring everyone else. "Enough to know what my idea of the perfect date would be, rather than just copying something from the Kardashians or whatever."

Jakob hisses like a cat. Jett, however, is still listening intently. He's put his phone down and everything.

"Okay," he says, coming over to join us at the breakfast bar. "So tell me, then. What's Alexandra Steele's idea of the perfect date?"

I consider this for a moment. My *actual* perfect date would probably involve fish and chips — and definitely no crabs — on Heather Bay beach. Maybe a bottle of cheap wine stuck in the sand, and a fire to warm us up when it started to get cold. That's not exactly L.A. appropriate though — and thinking about it is making me homesick — so I refine it a little.

"Santa Monica pier," I tell him. "Cotton candy. The Ferris wheel. Then, I don't know, maybe a drive up to Griffith."

"The Observatory?" Jett says, surprised. "Why there?"

"I love it there," I say simply. "It was the first place I went when I came here, so it's always felt special to me. You can see the whole city from there. I just... I just like it. I can't explain why."

I can, actually. But the explanation involves being away from home for the first time; finally feeling like I had the opportunity to start over, and be myself, without pressure from Mum, or friends, or anyone else. That explanation feels like it might be a bit much for a kitchen table conversation surrounded by near-strangers, though, so I keep it inside, and offer up the one that makes more sense. Thankfully, Jett seems to buy it.

"I like it too," he says softly. "It's a good place for a date."

I smile at him tentatively. Are we... are we having a *moment* here? Because, if we are, I can tell Asher's about to ruin it, and, sure enough...

"I still like the yacht idea," he says briskly. "I think we should go for that one."

"Nope," says Jett, getting back up. "We're going with her idea." He nods in my direction. "We're going to Griffith."

"And to the pier," I remind him, trying to jump down from the stool, but just sending myself spinning again.

"And the pier," Jett agrees, wearily. "Why not?"

Chapter 15

Santa Monica Pier is yet another disaster.

From the moment we arrive — flanked by Leroy and another bodyguard, who introduces himself as Evan — I can tell Jett's on edge.

"You really don't like the pier much, do you?" I ask awkwardly as we make our way through the crowds on the boardwalk, walking close enough to touch, but not *actually* touching. Because that would be too much, apparently.

"I like the pier fine," he replies through gritted teeth. "It's all the people I don't like."

He has a point. Santa Monica Pier is crowded even at the best of times, but today it feels like half of the city has decided to come here, and now that Jett's revealed himself to be even *less* of a people person than I am, I suspect that's going to be a problem. Especially when the people in question are all gaping openly at us and jostling for space around us until I feel like I'm going to scream.

"Maybe we could go on the Ferris wheel?" I suggest timidly. "At least it would get us out of this crowd?"

"Fine," Jett says tersely, after a short pause, during which he looks like he's thinking about just jumping into the water and escaping that way. "Let's get it over with."

Then he turns on his heel and marches off in the direction of the Ferris wheel, not bothering to wait and see if I'm following.

As romantic moments go, this is right up there with the time I went to get braces on my teeth and threw up all over Mike-the-dentist. At least Mike was *nice* about that, though. Jett, on the other hand, is acting like he's been forced here at gunpoint, and the awkwardness only intensifies as we climb aboard one of the little brightly colored carriages that will take us soaring above Santa Monica. It gets worse still as we begin our ascent.

Who would've thought things could get worse?

The view is glorious, even from a short way up. The boardwalk recedes below us, making the people on the beach below it look like they're in a Gray Malin photo. The coast stretches out on both sides, and I feel like a little kid again, watching the landscape unfurl below us as the ride lifts us higher into the cloudless blue sky.

God, I love funfairs.

Jett, on the other hand... well, not so much, it would appear.

My fake boyfriend sits opposite me, his arms crossed and his body rigid. I can't see his eyes behind the dark glasses he's wearing, but I have a sneaking suspicion they're closed.

Is he actually sleeping *on our date?*

Our fake *date, I mean?*

Even so. I know it's not a real date, but I'm still a real *person* — despite what I know McTavish back home says about me — and the very least he could do would be to have the courtesy to stay awake and talk to me.

Leaning forward, I prod him sharply in the stomach, making the little carriage rock gently in the air.

"What the fuck?"

Jett jumps as if he's been punched, but instead of anger, it's fear I detect in his voice. And also in the way he immediately leans forward, his body huddled over, and his hands gripping the plastic seat until his knuckles turn white.

"Hey," I say, leaning forward myself, until my head is level with his. "Are you okay? It's just—"

"I'm fine," he snaps, not sounding remotely fine. "Just... just don't move, okay? Like, *at all*."

"Are you scared of heights?" I ask as realization dawns. "Seriously?"

I'm about to laugh, then I see the outline of The Crab Shack appear at the end of the pier, and clamp my mouth quickly shut again.

"You were the only one who didn't share your deepest fear," I say, remembering. "Is this it, then? You're scared of heights?"

"It's not my *deepest* fear," Jett says, turning his head cautiously to look up at me. "But yeah. I don't like heights. Especially not really wobbly ones, where you're suspended in a plastic *bucket*. I don't understand why anyone does."

"Because it's fun," I insist, risking a glance above the door of the carriage. "And the views are amazing."

"I'll have to take your word for it."

His skin is slightly green now, and he's still clutching his seat like a lifeline. It makes him seem a bit more *real*, actually. Less Jett Carter, movie star, and more... well, just *Jett*, really. An actual human being, who just so happens to be famous.

This just in: celebrities are people too. Who knew?

Not me, anyway. So far, I've been so in awe of Celebrity Jett that I've almost been afraid to speak to him, knowing we could have absolutely nothing in common. This guy, though — the one with the white knuckles and the 'get me out of here' expression? This guy I can get along with.

"Here," I say, holding out both hands. "I've got you."

He looks up at me suspiciously, then reaches out and takes my hand. His palms are a little too sweaty for it to feel romantic, exactly, but it does feel kind of *nice*. His hands are soft and warm — and, okay, *clammy* — and he holds onto mine as if I'm the only thing keeping him afloat in a stormy sea. Under my t-shirt, my heart speeds up a little.

Oh, no you don't, Lexie. You're not going to fall for him, remember?

"Do you seriously think this is fun?" Jett asks, turning white as the carriage rocks slightly. "You don't feel like you're about to plunge to your death, say?"

"Nope," I reply cheerfully, ignoring the treacherous beating of my stupid heart, which I'll be having strong words with later. "I promise you, no one's going to die. Not on my watch."

"I'll take your word for that too, then," he mutters.

He continues to hold my hand all the way back down, and when we stand up to leave the carriage, and he finally lets me go, I have to remind myself that there's absolutely no reason for me to feel disappointed. It would be stupid of me to think he might have continued to hold my hand after the ride stopped, and absolute madness for me to actually *want* him to.

I am not stupid, and I'm definitely not mad. Which means that what I'm feeling right now can't possibly be disappointment.

Can it?

* * *

By mutual agreement, we decided to leave the pier right after our un-fun ride on the Ferris wheel, and head back to the car for phase two of our "date". By the time the long black limo starts to climb the hill that leads towards Griffith Observatory, the sun is low in the sky, and the city looks golden, spread out below us.

L.A. is an unfashionable city to like, let alone love. You're supposed to hate the crowds, and the traffic and the *expense* of it all. To talk about the concrete jungle, and how everyone is fake, and the city has no soul. And some of that is true, obviously. Like the insane traffic, for instance, and how I could probably buy an actual *castle* back home for what I'd pay for a modest bungalow over here.

But I still love it. I love the perma-sunshine and the beaches. The purple jacarandas and the palm trees that make everything look like a movie set. (And, well, the *malls*. Don't look at me like that, we don't have a whole lot of shopping opportunities in the Highlands, okay?) Most of all, though, I love the way the city looks from the hills at sunset, and I'm really hoping that Jett's going to like *this* view at least a *little* more than he did the one from the Ferris wheel.

Or to at least not hate it. That would be progress.

The parking lot at the observatory is full, but the place isn't crowded the way the pier was, which allows Leroy and Evan to fall behind Jett and I, letting us walk on ahead as if we actually *want* to be together, as opposed to just playing a role so we can be spotted by the photographer Grace contacted this morning, who's been shadowing us all day. So far, he's still keeping discreetly out of sight, so he can get his exclusive without having to fight a dozen other paps for it, but I know he's there, and the knowledge makes this whole experience even more surreal than it would be, anyway.

Which, let's face it, wouldn't be hard.

"Where to, then? Inside or out?"

Jett stops in front of the steps leading up to the building, and I look up at it, taking in the iconic domed roof that's featured in too many movies to count. When I first came here, I felt like I was walking onto a film set, and although I've visited many times since, the feeling's never really gone away.

The building itself is home to the planetarium, but it's the view from the terraces behind it I'm really here for.

"Outside," I answer Jett. "If that's okay with you?"

He nods, and we turn and walk around the side of the building, to where the panorama of the city is waiting for us. The two bodyguards have dropped even further behind now, and although there are a few curious glances from some of our fellow tourists, most of them are too busy taking photos of each other to really notice us. I can almost *feel* some of the tension leave Jett's body.

At the back of the building we find a quiet spot and lean against the wall, looking out. From here, you can see the Hollywood sign nestled into the cliffs, looking out over the endless grid of buildings, with their skyscraper centerpiece. We stand there silently for a minute, just soaking it all in. Or I do, anyway. Jett's expression is as inscrutable as ever. He could be thinking about what he's going to have for dinner, for all I know.

"So, if this is your idea of a perfect date," he says, proving me wrong, "Does that mean you've already done that? Come here on a date, I mean?"

I freeze, still staring out at the view. If he was anyone else, I'd think he was trying to find out if I have a boyfriend. But he's Jett Carter. He must know I don't, or I wouldn't have agreed to a fake relationship with him. And surely he wouldn't care, even if I did?

"Nope," I say lightly. "This is my first. You?"

"Me? God, no," he says, shaking his head firmly. "I don't really 'do' dates. It's hard, what with... well, you know."

He trails off, and I turn to look at him curiously.

"Yeah, I guess it must be hard getting to know someone when you're constantly being watched," I say.

Neither of us have mentioned it, but I'm still very conscious of the photographer who I know must be clicking away somewhere behind us. The thought makes me instantly suck my stomach in and pull my shoulders back. I turn back to the view, moving so stiffly I must look like a shop mannequin come to life.

It must be horrible having to live like this all the time.

"It's not easy," Jett confirms, his voice low. He's leaning on the wall next to me, our shoulders almost touching. "And not just because everything's always being documented by the press," he adds. "It's hard to know who's being genuine with me, and who's just in it for themselves, you know? To get famous by association or whatever. Get their photo on the Internet, and then sell their story. That happens a lot."

I swallow nervously, thinking about the NDA he made me sign.

Is he talking about me right now? Does he think I'm just doing this because I want to be famous and I think I can use him to do it?

All of a sudden, I understand what people mean when they say their blood ran cold. I know this is purely a business arrangement, rather than a fledgling relationship, so it shouldn't really matter what he thinks of me, but it does. It matters. And I don't want him to think I'm using him when I know I'm not.

"I'd hate being famous," I tell him, slightly more clumsily than I'd have liked. "I'd hate not knowing who I could trust."

His beautiful eyes meet mine.

"That's the worst thing about fame," he says, bitterly. "One of the worst things, anyway. Being popular isn't all it's cracked up to be."

"Yeah, I know."

He looks at me in surprise.

How could you possibly know that? his look says. *What would you know about popularity?*

"I'm not *universally* disliked, you know," I say, nudging him indignantly. "I might not be *famous*, but I was pretty popular back in the day. I had a lot of friends. Just... just not many who actually *knew* me."

I falter, feeling shy.

That was a bit over-sharey. *I've obviously been in California too long.*

Jett, however, is nodding his agreement.

"I get that," he says. "That's my life, right there. I guess it has its compensations, though, so I can't really complain."

"Oh, I would," I assure him, laughing softly. "I'd complain all the time. I love a good complaining session, though. It's one of my toxic traits. Or so I've been told."

"Who told you that? Your boyfriend?"

Okay, there's no mistaking it this time. He's definitely fishing for information. I mean, he *has* to be, right? There's no other explanation. And if he's trying to find out if I'm single, then that must mean...

No. No, it can't possibly. You have *to stop this, Lexie.*

I take a deep breath to steady myself before I answer him.

"You don't seriously think I'd have agreed to this... this *thing*... if I had a boyfriend, do you?"

I speak teasingly, surprised by how steady my voice sounds given that my insides currently feel like they're trying to learn the Highland Fling.

"No," Jett says, equally causal. "But there could be someone back home waiting for you, I guess? Or someone you'd *like* to be waiting for you?"

His gold-flecked eyes don't stray from my face. I almost hate him for being so beautiful. It's blatantly unfair. Having this conversation with someone who looks like him makes me feel like I've brought a knife to a gunfight. I should just put my hands up and surrender before he completely disarms me.

"There's no one waiting for me," I say, the hard truth of those words making them difficult to get out. "I'm not... well, I'm not very easy to fall in love with, let's put it that way."

I try to give the statement a definitive, *let's stop talking about this* kind of tone, but Jett isn't done messing with my head just yet, apparently.

"I think it would be very easy to fall in love with you, Lexie," he says, so quietly I think I must have misheard.

Before I can ask him, though — or even work out *how* to ask him — he steps back from the wall, and puts his hands in his pockets, his expression giving nothing away.

"Come on," he calls back to me as he walks away. "Let's go look at the statue."

Chapter 16

The statue Jett's referring to is the disembodied head of James Dean, which sits off to one side of the Observatory, with the Hollywood sign providing the perfect backdrop.

"You seen the movie?" Jett asks, still behaving like he didn't just casually drop the bomb that is the 'L' word into our conversation on the terrace. Well, sort of.

"The movie?"

I blink, confused. Unlike him, I *don't* normally go around telling people how easy it would be to fall in love with them, so you can confuse me for being a little discombobulated, as Bella McGowan from back home would say.

"Rebel Without a Cause?" prompts Jett, his brow creasing in a way that shouldn't be attractive, but which absolutely *is*. "James Dean? Natalie Wood? They filmed a lot of it here?"

"Oh. Yeah. I know. But no, I haven't seen it," I admit, still struggling to get my brain to focus on the conversation I'm currently having, rather than the one Jett's probably already forgotten. "It's a bit before my time."

"It's before mine too," he chuckles, "But I've still seen it at least a dozen times. It's one of the reasons I got into acting, in fact."

"Really? I would've thought you'd have gotten into acting because of your dad?"

He frowns, and the temperature seems to drop a couple of degrees.

"No," he says shortly. "Quite the opposite, actually. Seeing my dad's career — what it did to his family — convinced me I never wanted that for myself. But then I started watching some of the old black and white movies he had stashed away at home, and that was it. I fell in love. *Rebel* was one of them."

I flinch as his last words hit me right in the stomach. It's the second time he's mentioned falling in love in less than ten minutes. Maybe it doesn't mean the same thing to him it means to everyone else? Maybe I'm reading too much into this?

"I can't believe you've never seen it," he's saying now, still circling the statue. "It's an absolute classic."

"So I've heard." I can't help but smile at his enthusiasm. It's like he's fully alive for the first time since I met him. "I'll make sure I try to see it sometime."

"Uh-uh," he says, shaking his head as he finally stops circling. "Not *sometime*, Lexie. That's not good enough. You have to see it *now*."

"Now?" I look around, half-expecting a cinema screen to have popped up since we arrived. "I don't think it'll be showing anywhere, for some reason. The theaters around here tend to show more current movies."

Like the ones with you in them, for instance.

"Well," he says, smiling over at me. "It's a good job I've got the movie at home, then, isn't it?"

* * *

The cinema room back at Jett's place is exactly as I remember it from my search for the bathroom earlier this week, and I have to pretend I've never seen it before when he shows me in and starts fiddling with the huge screen at the front.

I'm confused.

We're supposed to be going to places people will see us. People where the "tame paps" Grace has alerted will take our photos, then send them to the media, so we can be talked about as the loved-up couple we absolutely are not.

But this is just a room in Jett's house. A huge, implausibly luxurious room, granted, but still a private room.

And that's why I'm confused.

We did our bit for the photographers. We went out in public and we allowed ourselves to be photographed. Asher will be thrilled, I'm sure. Or as thrilled as someone without normal human emotions can be, at least.

But now he's brought me back to his house, rather than telling his driver to take me back to the hotel. Now he's dimming the lights, and settling back in one of the velvet seats, while motioning for me to join him. And it's *just* him. And me, of course. And no photographers anywhere.

You can see why I'm confused, right?

I peer curiously around, wondering if there's maybe a pap hiding under one of the seats or something.

"You okay, Lady M?" Jett says from the front of the room. "It's just about to start. You want some popcorn?"

I shake my head wordlessly as I force my legs to take me to

the seat next to him, which I sink into gratefully.

When I told him about my perfect date earlier, I didn't mention a black and white movie in a private cinema. I'm starting to think I should have, though. Because, if this was a *real* date — which I have to keep reminding myself that it definitely is *not* — I'm pretty sure I'd be really enjoying it.

And what's even more confusing is that I think *he* would be, too.

* * *

I spend the duration of Rebel Without a Cause waiting for Jett to give me some kind of hint that this is a real date, and not just a continuation of today's fakery, but by the time the credits roll, and the bowl of popcorn balanced between us has been emptied, I've come to the conclusion that I was wrong.

Not only does he fail to try to hold my hand, or wrap his arm around me, there's no sign that he's even aware of me at all. Not even at the very end, when the tears start dripping off my nose unattractively.

I'm quite glad he didn't look at me at that bit, actually.

"If I had one day when I didn't have to be all confused and I didn't have to feel that I was ashamed of everything. If I felt that I belonged someplace. You know?" mutters Jett, as he gets up to switch the lights back on.

"Yes! I *do* know! I feel like that too," I reply, realizing almost as I say it that he's quoting from the movie.

Jett chuckles lightly.

"I'm glad you liked it, Lady M," he says, grinning delightedly at me. "It's an important part of your movie education. If you like, I can show you some more sometime. I've got all the classics."

I smile back at him, wondering if my body will ever feel normal again, or if I'm just going to have to walk around feeling this weird combination of confused and excited for the rest of my life. Because I feel like that's going to be pretty inconvenient, somehow.

"So."

Jett's holding the door of the room open, but my legs aren't obeying the brain's command to move. I know it must be late by now. I don't expect he's going to ask me to stay, but—

"I, um, guess I better be going, then?"

I try my best not to phrase it like a question, but it comes out that way anyway, and I have a strong urge to kick myself.

"Sure," Jett says pleasantly. "Just give me a second and I'll get my driver to take you back to the hotel."

He disappears into the hallway, and I sag with disappointment before quickly pulling myself together again.

Maybe it's a good thing he's sending me home, like we're just two colleagues or something, who decided to catch a movie together after work. That's all we are, after all. And that's the way it's going to stay. Anything else would be totally unthinkable. And dangerous. And a guaranteed way to stop me in my quest to become a better person who doesn't make stupid mistakes. I know that. I know it perfectly well. So when Jett comes back to tell me the car's outside, he finds me waiting patiently by the front door, my bag over my shoulder, and my smile firmly in place.

"Thanks for the movie," I say, as if I'm always coming round to Hollywood mansions to hang with the stars. "Goodnight."

"Goodnight," he says in return, holding the door for me courteously. If there's a hint of disappointment on his face, then I'm sure I must be imagining it. And if there's the slightest twinge of regret in my heart on the drive back, well, I'll just completely ignore it, I decide.

So that's exactly what I do.

Chapter 17

"Okay. Pap walk. On the beach. This afternoon."

We're back in Jett's living room the next morning, and Asher seems to be speaking a different language.

"Pap walk?" I ask, glancing at Jett with a *help me* look. "What's that, exactly?"

"Oh, it's literally just a walk," says Asher, who's looking pleased with himself after the success of yesterday's "date", which was covered extensively on the Internet, with photos of me and Jett standing looking out at the sunset from Griffith Observatory, our heads almost touching as enjoy what TMZ describe as "a romantic tête-à-tête".

(There were also a few of Jett looking like he's about t throw up on the Ferris wheel, but we're not going to talk about those until Grace manages to get them taken down, apparently.")

"You and Jett go for a walk on the beach," Asher continues, "and we make sure there's someone there to photograph you. It's so simple even you'll be able to do it."

I'm about to say something cheeky in response to this. Then I remember my performance at The Crab Shack, and decide to zip it.

"What do you think, Jett?" says Asher, turning to his client, who's been suspiciously silent during all of this. "Can we do this today? Can you clear your schedule? I think it would be a good idea to capitalize on the coverage we got yesterday. You and Ms. Steele are the couple of the moment right now. Everyone wants to see more of you both. So let's give the people what they want. Whaddya say?"

Jett shrugs, like a man who would rather be locked in a box with midges, but who knows he has very little say in the matter.

"Malibu," he says, by way of response. "We can do it at the Malibu house."

Asher nods triumphantly.

"Excellent idea," he agrees. "We can make it known that you've taken Alexandra to your secluded beach house to help her recover from her...trauma. We'll refer to it as your 'love nest.'"

He looks so pleased with this idea that it seems a shame to bring him down to earth by pointing out that I'm cringing so hard I'm going to have difficulty standing up now. I open my mouth to say it anyway, though, but before I can speak, Asher delivers his death-blow.

"Oh, and one more thing," he says, smiling benignly. "You'll have to kiss."

* * *

"No. Absolutely not. I'm not doing it, and that's all there is to it."

That, however, is *not* all there is to it, because as soon as the words are out of my mouth, I instantly start listing all the reasons why me and Jett kissing for the paparazzi cameras would be a spectacularly bad idea.

"For one thing, it's not in the contract," I begin, ticking the items off on my fingers. "So you can't make me do it, anyway. For two, it's weird. Seriously, though, don't you think it's weird?"

I pause to look at Jett, who's listening to me patiently, with a pained expression on his face.

Asher and co. left the room a few minutes ago, to give Jett and me a chance to talk in private. So far, though, I've been the one doing all the talking, so I figure I should at least give him the chance to agree with me. At least that way we can present a united front when we tell Asher where he can stick his stupid "fake kiss" idea.

"Isn't it, though?" I prompt now. "Isn't the whole idea of kissing someone you barely know, just for the camera, super, duper *weird*?"

I have no idea why I'm blushing. Or why I'm finding it hard to say the word "kiss" in front of him. All I know is that *talking* about kissing Jett Carter is making me *think* about kissing Jett Carter, and that's a road I know I must not go down, no matter how clear the signposts are pointing me in that direction.

Maybe that's why I'm protesting so much about Asher's "staged kiss" idea. And why I can't seem to say anything other than the word "weird".

Jett, however, simply shrugs in answer to my question.

"Not really," he says, surprising me. "Not to me, anyway. I do it all the time."

My eyes widen in astonishment, and he hurries to correct himself.

"Kissing for the cameras, I mean," he clarifies. "It's part of the job, you know? Actors have to kiss each other sometimes. It doesn't mean anything. It's no different from any of the other things you have to pretend to do as an actor. So, no, I guess it's not all that unusual for me, really."

He shrugs again as I consider this. I know his movies almost always have some kind of romance element to them. I've seen him in tons of on-screen kisses over the years; sex scenes, too, for that matter. None of which makes it any less... *weird*... to me.

"I'm not an actress, though," I point out, stating the obvious. "So it might be just a job to *you*, but to me it would be totally—"

"Weird?" He suggests. "Yeah, I got that. Don't worry about it, Lady M," he adds, as if we're talking about the weather, or something equally innocuous. "I get it. You don't want to kiss me, you don't have to. You don't have to do anything you don't want to. It's cool."

I look at him suspiciously.

"You wanna do Rock, Paper, Scissors?" he says. "I win, we kiss; you win, we don't?"

"Wh... what? Are you being serious?"

He grins, making my heart flutter traitorously.

"'Course not," he says. "I'm joking, relax. Just trying to lighten the atmosphere a bit. Like I said, you're in charge, here. I'm not going to ask you to do anything you're not comfortable with."

"But Asher—"

"I'll take care of Asher," he says soothingly. "Just leave it with me. You okay to do the beach walk without the kiss, though? Because I think if we do that, it'll get him off our backs for a while."

"Um, yeah. Sure."

I sit back down, feeling like I've been wrong-footed somehow.

I'm getting exactly what I wanted — and without so much as the slightest hint of an argument.

So why do I feel so deflated?

* * *

"Be honest, you didn't want to kiss me either, did you?"

Jett and I are standing by the edge of the water on Carbon Beach, in Malibu, where Jett just so happens to have a home. Because *of course* he does.

The house in question is directly behind us, tucked between a couple of other multi-million dollar homes, and when I walked into it, it was all I could do not to collapse in hysterical laughter at the sheer ridiculousness of this situation.

Until now, I'd thought Jack Buchanan's house in Heather Bay was the very epitome of wealth. But Carbon Beach makes the banks of Loch Keld, where Jack's mansion is situated, look pretty ordinary, really. As I walk out onto to the golden sand, I'm surrounded by so much money that even though I'm wearing one of the designer outfits I dug out of Grace's shopping bags, and Jakob has grudgingly done my hair and makeup, to make me look like the best possible version of myself, I feel instantly grubby — and very, very fake.

I do not belong here. That much is patently obvious as I turn and look back at the house behind us, where Asher, Grace, and — unaccountably — Jakob, are all lined up on the glass-fronted balcony, watching us as we stroll casually down to the water, looking for all the world like any other ridiculously mismatched couple taking a romantic walk together.

Or, at least, that's the idea.

Jett's doing just fine, of course. Well, he would be, wouldn't he? He's an actor. This kind of thing is as easy as breathing to him. I, on the other hand, must look every bit as awkward as I feel. And now I've just gone and made it even worse with my stupidly needy comment about him not wanting to kiss me.

Why can't I stop fixating on this?

"You okay, Lady M? It's just, you seem a bit on edge, is all."

Ignoring my question, Jett shoots me a concerned look from under the brim of his baseball cap, which is once again crammed firmly down over his eyes.

"I'm fine," I say, sounding anything but. "Absolutely fine!"

Just to prove how very, very fine I am, I nonchalantly toss my hair over one shoulder, somehow managing to knock my sunglasses off in the process. As Jett bends down to fish them out of the shallow water for me, his hat falls off too, getting instantly soaked by the waves.

Asher will be loving *this, for sure.*

"Relax," Jett mutters under his breath, wringing the water out of his cap before slipping it into the pocket of his shorts. "It's just photos, okay? And they're going to be taken from quite far away, so they won't even be particularly good ones, anyway. Trust me, you can't mess this up."

"Oh, I can," I assure him, as we turn and start to walk along the shoreline. "I can mess *anything* up, believe me. It's a special talent of mine."

I glance nervously over my shoulder, wondering where the photographers are. Asher said he'd get Grace to put in a call to one of the agencies, tipping them off that we'd be here. If they took the bait and sent someone to photograph us, though, I can't see them, and the thought that I'm probably being secretly watched right now — other than by Asher and Grace themselves — is making it impossible for me to relax.

"Just act normal," Jett says again, placing a reassuring hand on my arm, which makes me jump in shock at the contact. His hand is warm and soft, and when he takes it away, I can still feel it on my skin.

That can't be a good sign.

"You don't know what you ask of me," I say ruefully, glancing up at him. "'Normal' isn't exactly something I'm known for."

"Me neither," he says, grinning suddenly. "At least that's something we have in common."

"It has to be the only thing," I reply without thinking. "Hollywood, the Highlands... there's just not a whole lot of crossover there, is there?"

It's true. Jett's Malibu beach house might be smaller than his place in the Hills, but it's still worlds away from the little stone cottage I inherited from my grandmother on Heather Bay beach; or, indeed, the house I grew up in, which mum always claimed she was just "too busy" to clean. I spent most of my life trying to help her maintain the charade that we were doing well because of the distillery, while behind the scenes, our lives were just barely held together by credit cards and sheer willpower.

Jett and I might as well be from different worlds, let alone different backgrounds.

"I've never been to Scotland," Jett says thoughtfully. "What's it like?"

I think about this for a moment.

"It's... green," I say at last. "It's very, very green. And cold. And wet. Especially compared to here."

"You're really selling it to me." He chuckles drily. "When can we go?"

I smile weakly, but the truth is, just talking about Scotland is making me homesick.

I really wish I hadn't started this conversation.

"I'm serious," he insists. "It sounds about as different to here as it gets, and, honestly, I could be doing with a change."

"Yeah," I agree blandly. "I can see how this place would get on your nerves after a while. All this sunshine, and luxury, and having to decide which of your houses to sleep in every night... It would get you down, for sure. You'd find yourself desperately wishing you were in Heather Bay, about to choke on a deep-fried Mars bar from the Wildcat Cafe"

"You're making that up," Jett snorts, ignoring my sarcastic jibe. "No way is there a place called The Wildcat Cafe, selling fried whatever-it-was. I'm calling bullshit on that."

"There is," I tell him. 'There's a stuffed wildcat in a glass case above the counter and everything. Just the thing you want to look at over a tasty lunch. Not that you get a tasty lunch in the Wildcat, mind you. Food isn't exactly their specialty."

"Well, that settles it," Jett says, chuckling. "I'm there. I gotta see this place."

We walk on, me still desperately trying to swallow down the bitter taste of sadness that rose up in my throat as soon as I started thinking about home. The irony of Jett and I both wanting to be somewhere other than where we belong isn't lost on me, and the line he quoted from the movie last night comes back to me in a rush.

If I felt that I belonged someplace.

Did he mean it, I wonder? Is that how he really feels? Or is it just another line he learned by heart?

"So, how come you're scared of seeing dead crabs in a restaurant, but you're okay with potentially seeing live ones on the beach?" he asks as I ruminate on this. "Shouldn't you be freaking out around about now?"

"There aren't any live crabs on this kind of beach," I say, indicating the smooth golden sand that rolls out beneath our feet with nowhere to hide. "There are too many people around."

Actually, the beach is fairly quiet. The windows of the houses that crowd around its edges, though, are all watching us like a thousand eyes. It's not just the crabs who'd feel uncomfortable under that level of scrutiny, really,

"They prefer to lurk in rock pools," I go on, trying to ignore the feeling of being watched. "The creepy little bastards. Did you know coconut crabs probably pecked Amelia Earhart to death? Those ones can *climb* and everything. I will never, for the life of me, understand why people aren't more afraid of them."

I'm about to explain the theory about the body washed up on a Pacific island which might have been Earhart when another thought suddenly strikes me.

"Hey," I say, shading my eyes from the sun as I look up at him. "That reminds me: you still haven't told me your deepest fear?"

"I did. It's heights. You saw it with your own eyes."

Jett's response doesn't exactly encourage me to go on, but I plunge right in, anyway.

"No," I correct him. "That's just *a* fear. You specifically said it wasn't your *deepest* fear."

"I'm scared of *you*," Jett replies immediately. "Isn't everyone?"

I smile, but I know he's just stalling; using humor to try to hide what he's really thinking. I know because I do that too.

Takes one to know one, I guess.

Jett doesn't want to tell me what he's afraid of. Which is fair enough, obviously, but it was just a couple of days ago that I was forced to confront my own biggest fear at The Crab Shack, so I'm not letting him off that easily.

"Come on," I say softly, nudging him gently in the ribs. "I told you mine. It's only fair that you tell me yours."

At first I think he's just going to ignore the question, like he did when I clumsily tried to get him to tell me why he didn't insist on going through with the fake kiss. But then he clears his throat as if he's about to make a speech, and I realize he's actually taking this seriously.

Okay, now I feel bad.

"It's okay, you don't have to—" I say hurriedly, but he's already started to speak, so I clamp my stupid mouth shut and listen.

"I'm scared of my dad," he says, so softly I have to strain to hear him above the crash of waves on the shore. "Of disappointing him. Of never being good enough, no matter what I do."

There's a single beat of silence between us as I try to decide what to say to this.

I was expecting him to say he was scared of snakes, or empty swimming pools, say, even if he had to make it up. Instead, though, it would appear he's decided to trust me with something *real*. It's a plot twist I wasn't expecting, and I'm not totally sure how to react to it.

"I know that probably sounds stupid," Jett mumbles, reaching up to rub at his invisible beard.

"No. No, it really doesn't," I say, turning to look up at him and feeling suddenly shy. "I feel the same way about my mum," I admit. "She's terrifying. And she's *not* a world-famous actor. I can't even imagine the pressure I'd get from her if she was. It's bad enough as it is."

"Yeah?"

The dark glasses he's wearing are hiding his eyes, but I can tell Jett's interest is genuine.

"Yeah."

"Well, then, you know how it feels to never be good enough for someone, then," he says matter-of-factly. "I feel like I've been trying to live up to my dad my entire life. Still haven't managed it, though. Starting to think I never will."

"That's why you're doing this, isn't it?" I say, the realization making me stop in my tracks. "This fake dating thing, I mean? It's not because of Justin Duval, or *Macbeth*, or even your reputation, is it? It's about your dad."

I'm so engrossed in the conversation we've been having that I've completely forgotten about the hidden paparazzi with their telephoto lenses. As far as I'm concerned, it's just me and Jett, alone on this beach. And, as it turns out, we seem to have a lot more in common than either of us realized.

"My dad played *Macbeth* when he was my age," Jett says at last. "On stage, not on screen, but still. Won a Tony for it. Hasn't stopped talking about it ever since."

He hesitates for just a moment, and when he starts speaking again, there's a desperation in his voice that I've never heard before.

"If I could just get this role, Alexandra," he says, turning to face me. We've walked far enough now that the house we started from is far behind us, Asher and Grace just tiny specs in the distance.

"If I could just get this role," Jett repeats, raking a hand through his hair. "If I could just persuade Duval to give me a shot at it, it would make all the difference. Because I know I can do it. I know I can. I'd be good at it, too. I just need a chance."

He pulls off his sunglasses to rub his eyes wearily, and when he looks back up, those green-gold eyes of his hit me like a punch to the gut.

He's so beautiful.

And so very, very sad.

"I'm sure you would," I agree, nodding slowly. "I'm sure you'd be great. And I'm sure you'll get the part. I'm certain of it, in fact."

Jett smiles uncertainly.

"Thanks," he says, shrugging. "It's good to know someone's on my side."

"I am on your side," I assure him, taking a tentative step closer through the shallow water we're standing in. "And Jett?"

He looks down at me, his eyes questioning. Even this close, his face is disconcertingly familiar, and almost disturbingly handsome.

"You're good enough," I tell him, feeling my cheeks flush with embarrassment at the very un-Lexie-like utterance that's just fallen from my lips. "You're definitely good enough."

And then I kiss him.

Chapter 18

I'm not sure who's more surprised: me or him.

I was so insistent I wasn't going to do it. I made such a performance out of my refusal to play along that I even managed to convince myself.

And the Academy Award goes to Lexie Steele, for her ground-breaking performance in 'Not Wanting to Kiss Jett Carter.'

But, of course, the truth is, I *did* want to kiss him. Not just because he's gorgeous, and was my first-ever celebrity crush, but because when he opened up to me about his relationship with his dad, I related so hard that before I knew quite what had happened, helping him get that role became the most important thing in my life.

Or at this particular moment of my life, anyway.

I think I might have my conscience to blame for that. *Again.*

I was aiming for a quick peck, really. Just a swift, chaste brush of the lips, that the tabloids would go wild for, but which wouldn't make things too awkward for us once it was over.

That's not what I get, though.

I have to stand on my toes to reach his lips, and, after a half-beat of confusion during which an emotion I can't read flits briefly across his face, Jett realizes what I'm trying to do and comes to my rescue, like the pro he is.

One arm loops around my waist, pulling me close; the other finds its way to my chin, his fingers resting gently on my skin as he tilts my face up to meet his.

Right on cue, my heart starts hammering in my chest, every nerve in my body sparking suddenly into life as the musky scent of him fills my nostrils. I know this isn't real, but it's almost like I've been programmed to respond to his touch, and there's no way to control it. Or like my teenage self has somehow managed to re-inhabit my adult body, just so she can kiss her favorite movie star, and the body in question is responding accordingly.

We haven't even kissed yet, and I already know I'm going to be replaying this moment in my head for the rest of my life. Who cares if we're just acting?

Are we, though?

I have to ask myself that, because when his lips touch mine, it feels pretty real to me.

And also pretty *hot*, if you want to know the truth.

"Put your arms around my neck," Jett murmurs into my hair. "It'll look more realistic that way."

Well, okay, maybe not *that* bit. That was more like getting an instruction from your boss than a request from a lover. It reminds me of the time Bella McGowan made most of the village do the Ice Bucket Challenge, and Old Jimmy McEwan threw the ice *and* the bucket at me when it was my turn.

I still think he did that on purpose.

Nevertheless, I do as Jett asks, looping my arms around his neck, which has the effect of bringing us even closer. His hands are on my waist, his fingers just grazing the sliver of bare skin where my top doesn't quite meet my jeans.

Aaaaand we're back to "hot" again.

Who knew fake dating would involve quite so many emotions?

"That's better," he whispers, his arms tightening around me.

His lips hover above mine for just long enough for it to be absolutely unbearable. Then, just when I don't think I can stand the tension one second longer, he leans in, and suddenly we're kissing like we mean it. His hands are in my hair now, his mouth pressed urgently against mine, as if he's been waiting for this moment his entire life, and, now that it's here, he's going to make the wait feel worth it.

And it *is.*

It definitely is.

As kisses go, it's a 9.5 out of 10. I deduct half a point purely because it doesn't seem right to give full marks to a fake kiss, but honestly, if I didn't know it was fake, there's absolutely no way I'd have guessed it. His lips are warm and soft, and our mouths glide against each other as if we've been doing this forever; deep, passionate kisses that I can't help but think are going to look *amazing* in the photos that are surely being taken of us right now.

Wait: that's kind of weird, isn't it?

I'm confused, though.

Because I know this isn't real, but there's no getting away from the fact that it *feels* real.

Every time I start to pull away, Jett's pulls me back towards him, as if those brief moments of separation are more than he can stand.

They're certainly more than *I* can stand, that much is certain.

The kiss goes on and on; much longer than seems totally appropriate for an entirely staged photo shoot, but not nearly long enough for my inner teenage self, who strongly suspects she might just *die* if it ever has to end.

He really is an excellent actor.

Too good, in fact; because when we finally break apart, and stand there smiling uncertainly at each other as the waves lap at our feet, I feel bereft — like a little girl who's just been told that playtime is over, and it's time to pack away all her toys.

And I really don't want to.

"Um, we should probably head back to the house," Jett says, rubbing his hand bashfully against his chin. "They'll be waiting for us."

"Yup. Got to get back for the debrief," I say, as lightly as I can manage. "We can't keep Asher waiting."

Jett hesitates, and, for a fraction of a second, I wonder if he's going to take my hand, or put his arm around me. Just to make this look more authentic, you know?

Instead, he simply pulls the still-damp baseball cap out of his pocket and pulls it back on, making sure the brim covers his eyes.

"Well."

"Well."

He shrugs his shoulders, and then turns around to walk back to the house, me trailing awkwardly behind him.

"Oh, Lady M?" he says, stopping to look back at me.

"Yeah?"

"I didn't ever say I didn't want to kiss you, by the way," he says over his shoulder. "Just so you know."

That's when I know, beyond doubt, that he's going to break my heart.

And there's not a single thing I can do about it.

Chapter 19

The 'beach kiss' photos are a huge success. Even Asher is grudgingly impressed by my "performance" as he calls it, and, when we got back to the beach house, I thought Grace was going to pass out from excitement.

It's the third time Jett and I have been seen together now, which makes us practically an old married couple in Hollywood terms. I'm being referred to as his "new girlfriend" rather than as his "latest squeeze", and I have 24 voice messages from Mum on my phone, none of which I've plucked up the courage to listen to yet.

Things are going well, in other words.

So why do I feel so *empty*?

It's two days after The Kiss. I'm still living at the hotel, and Jett hasn't called me. Or got *someone else* to call me, even.

Not that I was expecting him to, obviously. Why would he? This is just a business arrangement, right? It doesn't mean anything to him, and I've spent the best part of the last 48 hours trying to convince myself it doesn't mean anything to me, either. It's not like we're *actually* dating, after all. He doesn't owe me a phone call.

He doesn't owe me anything.

Instead of dwelling on The Kiss, then, I do my best to keep myself busy, so I'm not tempted to read whatever's being said about me online. Or to keep checking my messages to see if there's one from him. The problem is, there's just not much to do here when you're a fake girlfriend trying her best not to get into trouble. I'm too scared to leave the hotel in case the paparazzi are out there waiting for me, and although I've sent Summer a couple of brief messages letting her know I'm okay, and will explain everything as soon as I can, the thought of having to lie outright to her makes me refuse her offers to meet up, or even talk on the phone.

All of which means I've spent the last two days hanging out in my hotel room, working my way through the room service menu, and venturing out only to use the gym and pool, although only at the times I think they'll be least busy.

As it turns out, fake-dating a movie star is a lot less glamorous than you might think — which is why, when a knock on the door jolts me awake from my second nap of the day, I'm almost giddy with excitement as I rush to see who it is.

Then I open the door, and all that excitement disappears in a flash.

"Trust me," says Jakob, heaving a couple of giant bags into the room behind him, "I'm as happy to see you as you are to see me. We've got work to do, though." His nose wrinkles in distaste as he takes in the leggings and over-sized t-shirt I haven't bothered to change out of since my trip to the hotel gym. "Quite a lot of work, by the looks of things. Is that *snot* in your hair? I mean, seriously?"

"It's popcorn," I say, tugging impatiently at the offending item. "I fell asleep watching a movie."

One of Jett's movies, actually. Which I was watching purely for research purposes, I swear. Thank God I had the sense to switch it off before I opened the door.

Jakob heaves the world-weary sigh of a man who has been putting up with other people's shit for way too long, before striding across the room and starting to empty the bags he's carrying.

Interested in spite of myself, I step eagerly forward, letting out an involuntary squeal of excitement at the sight of the selection of dresses Jakob is laying reverently on the bed, handling each one as carefully as if it's made of china.

"Wow, check this out," I say, picking up a gold sequined evening dress and holding it up against me. "Where would you even *wear* something like this?"

"I mean... to the Carter Foundation Gala?" Jakob replies, as if this is the stupidest thing he's ever heard. "D'uh!" he adds for good measure.

I frown, watching him pluck another dress out of the pile on the bed and hold it up to the light appraisingly.

I've heard of the Carter Foundation, of course. Jett's parents founded it years ago, and its main aim is to raise money for... orphaned jellyfish? Wigs for bald orangutans? Seven-legged spiders? Okay, so I don't actually know *that* much about the Foundation itself, obviously. I do know *aaall* about its annual fundraising gala, however; mostly because the guest list is basically a Who's Who of Hollywood, and the red carpet fashion is To. Die. For.

Wait.

Why has Jakob brought a selection of dresses that would only be appropriate for an event as swanky as The Carter Foundation Gala to my hotel room? And why is he laying them out on my bed?

"Umm, Jakob?" I venture timidly as he bends down and starts fishing shoe boxes out of another bag. "This might be a stupid question, but—"

"I'm sure it will be," he sniffs, opening one of the boxes to reveal a pair of jewel-encrusted sandals that we both have to take a second to just stare at in awe.

"I'm just wondering," I continue, trying to ignore the knot of anxiety that's twisting my stomach. "What all of these clothes have to do with me? Like, why are they here? With you? Why are *you* here?"

Jakob turns and stares at me, with an *I've heard it all now* expression on his face.

"Because you're going to the ball, Cinderella," he says at last. "And I guess that makes me your fairy Godmother, here to dress you for it."

* * *

"Here, drink this. Just make sure you don't spill any of it on the clothes."

I'm sitting on the edge of the bed, nervously nibbling on my fingernails, while Jakob empties miniature bottles of vodka into a glass for me.

The good news is that the Gala isn't actually happening *tonight*, like I'd assumed it was when Jakob broke the news of my expected attendance to me. No, it's not until tomorrow, which at least means I have a bit of time to get used to the idea of it, as well as to pick out something to wear.

The bad news is that I definitely have to go to it. Which I suppose could also be *good* news, really, depending on how you look at it?

What girl *wouldn't* want to go to one of the biggest red carpet events of the year, after all?

Picture me sheepishly raising my hand right now. My hand with its bitten nails, which almost made Jakob pass out when he caught sight of them.

"I don't really have a good track record with events like this," I tell him now, taking a huge slug of the vodka, then erupting into a coughing fit. "The last ball I went to ended with mountain rescue being called, and my mother almost getting arrested. And don't even get me started on Galas"

"You were at a Gala on a mountain?" Jakob asks, confused. "With your mother?"

"No, not *on* a mountain. And it wasn't the kind of Gala you're thinking of, either..." I start to explain, before stopping and taking another drink instead. "It's a long story," I say, looking up at him apologetically. "Well, *two* long stories, really. Probably best left for another time."

"Let's move you over to the couch," Jakob says, glancing nervously at the dresses, which are still laid out on the bed, waiting to be tried on. "And let's maybe get you some water instead of this."

He takes my glass and goes over to the minibar, while I pull my phone from my pocket and swipe to open it.

"I just would've thought Jett might have told me about this himself," I say, glaring at the phone as if it's somehow at fault. "He could easily have sent me a message, or... Oh."

My 24 voice messages have now crept up to 57, and I have six unanswered calls. My heart leaps at the thought that Jett has been trying to contact me, after all, and then sinks again as I recognize Mum's number.

I guess the beach photos have definitely reached Heather Bay, then.

"Problem? Other than the eyebrows?"

Jakob is standing in front of me, holding out a glass of water, which I reluctantly accept.

"No. Well, yes, I suppose," I say, starting to chew my thumbnail and stopping when he shoots me a murderous look. "It's just my mum," I tell him, sighing. "I haven't spoken to her in a year, but now that she thinks I'm seeing Jett, she suddenly wants to be back in contact. Funny, that."

"Is she pissed about it, do you think?"

Jakob takes a seat beside me, his drama antennae clearly having been triggered by this.

"Nope." I shake my head. "Likely to be the opposite, in fact. She'll be absolutely delighted. She probably wants to come out here and meet him. Get in on the action."

"And you don't want to see her?"

Given the bad start we got off to, Jakob is proving to be a surprisingly good listener. His question, however, is one I'm just not sure how to answer.

"It's complicated," I tell him at last. "Mum is... Mum is... well, she's *a lot*. If she comes over here, she'll want to take over; make it all about her. I don't want to have to deal with that, but even so—"

"She's still your mom?" Jakob smiles sympathetically. "I get that," he says. "Families are complicated. I've never known any that aren't."

"I miss her," I admit, staring at my chewed nails. "But at the same time, I don't want to see her. Is that weird?"

"No weirder than anything else you ever say."

With that return to his usual sass, Jakob gets up and starts fussing over the dresses again, while I sit there mulling over our conversation.

I can't count the number of times I've wished I could call Mum in the last 12 months. Every time I've thought about it, though, I've remembered what she did last summer; how she tried to sabotage another distillery, and how I still haven't forgiven her for it. That's the real reason I'm not picking up any of her calls now; that and the fact that I know beyond doubt that if she didn't think I'd somehow managed to bag myself a famous boyfriend, she wouldn't be calling at all.

As if on cue, my phone chooses that moment to start ringing again, and I glance at the display, expecting to see Mum's number. This time, though, the number is one I don't recognize, other than from the area code, which is from Inverness, the nearest city to Heather Bay.

That's strange. Who'd be calling me from a number in Inverness?

I hesitate for a second, then reject the call. After a few more seconds, I switch the phone to silent, just to be sure.

Whoever it is, they're going to have to wait.

This Cinderella has a ball to prepare for.

Chapter 20

You know that romance movie trope where there's a heroine who's stunningly, jaw-droppingly gorgeous, but she *just doesn't know it* until the power of true love, or some such nonsense, shows her the truth?

Yeah, that's bullshit.

Never happened.

In my experience, beautiful people *know* they're beautiful; if not because of what they see in the mirror, then because of the way people respond to them.

People treat you differently when you're beautiful — or even just pretty. They pay more attention when you talk, smile more, hold doors open for you... You get the picture, I'm sure.

"It's called Pretty Privilege," Summer told me once, when I presented her with this theory. "I read about it somewhere."

I nodded, thoughtfully. The fact is, I grew up pretty, by Heather Bay standards. But the thing I quickly came to realize when I landed in the States was that I was *only* pretty by Heather Bay standards. In L.A., I'm just average; and right now, standing among some of the most famous faces in the world, I feel less even than that.

"Breathe. Just breathe."

CHAPTER 20

Jett and I are posing on the red carpet outside the Los Angeles County Museum of Art, where the Gala is being held, and I think I'm going to die.

No, I mean that literally. All the dresses Jakob produced for me to try on yesterday were sample sized, and I am... *not* sample sized, apparently. Which is why, rather than waste time sending them all back and ordering new ones, Jakob produced a flesh-colored contraption that looked a bit like a surgical stocking, and made me wriggle into it so I could fit into this dress.

And here was I thinking he was starting to warm to me, too.

"It's just shape wear, Lexie," he hissed, his face tomato red as he stood on a chair next to me, desperately trying to haul the girdle thing over my hips. "Everyone wears it."

"Yeah, but can everyone *breathe* in it?" I gasped once it was finally on. "Because I'm not sure I can."

"Just... try not to eat anything from now until tomorrow night," Jakob said uncertainly. "Everyone does that, too. Trust me. Here, have some more vodka."

I trusted him. (And I also drank the vodka, which is another thing I'll be filing under *Things I Regretted in the Morning.*) Which is why I'm standing here next to Jett, having eaten nothing since last night, and feeling like I'm about to either throw up, faint, or both.

So, we're off to an excellent start, then.

"Breathe," says Jett again, speaking out of the corner of his mouth as the cameras flash around us. "Breathe, Alexandra. It's good for you, I promise."

"That's easy for you to say," I whisper, pretending to turn and smile up at him. "You're not the one having your organs mashed together by a corset. Is it just me, or is it *really* hot in here?"

Jett's brow creases in concern, but, before he can answer me, my phone starts buzzing ostentatiously in my handbag — which is shaped like an apple, for some reason — and the concern turns to frustration.

"Maybe you should switch that off," Jett murmurs, reaching over and taking my hand. To anyone looking on — and I'm trying hard not to think about just how many people will be "looking on" when these photos are published — he looks totally relaxed; maybe even slightly bored. The palm that grips mine, however, is ever so slightly sweaty, and as he shifts his weight from one foot to the other, I get the distinct impression that he's not quite as comfortable with this situation as he's trying to pretend he is. Just to test my theory, I give his hand a quick squeeze, and, after a slight pause, he returns the gesture, his eyes still fixed on the crowd of photographers. It's a small thing, really; so small that at first I wonder if I've imagined it. Then he squeezes again, and suddenly I'm breathing a little more easily.

Standing in front of the bank of cameras feels like facing a firing squad, but, just like when he stood up for me in the bar, Jett's presence makes me feel like I just might be able to do this.

Even *with* this infernal corset threatening to squeeze the last breath out of my body.

"Lexie!" one of the photographers closest to the front of the group calls. "Hey, Sexy Lexie! This way, please."

My cheeks flush red as a flash goes off in my eyes.

"Hey," Jett calls, raising a hand in front of my face. "Enough with the names, please. It's Alexandra to you lot."

The photographers laugh and go on clicking, but I'm grateful for the hand Jett places around my waist, pulling me closer, and ignoring the cheers that go up from the crowd at the unexpected PDA from him.

"Come on Jett, give her a kiss," someone shouts. "We know you're good at that."

Jett smiles good-naturedly, but the arm around my waist is suddenly rigid with tension, and, after a few more seconds, he turns and steers me away from them, through the doors of the building behind us to safety.

Or as close to that as you can get among a crowd made up almost entirely of celebrities, I suppose.

As soon as we're out of sight of the cameras, I pull out my phone to switch it off, but it instantly starts ringing again in my hand, and I'm so keyed up with nerves I almost drop it in fright.

It's that number again: the Inverness one I've been ignoring. It's probably just some random acquaintance from back home, wanting to pretend we're besties now that they've seen my photo all over the tabloids. Grace warned me that kind of thing might happen. It's one of the reasons I haven't been listening to my voice mail, or reading any of the messages that keep threatening to blow up my phone. The head-in-sand technique might not be the best idea, all things considered — it's the reason I don't have the appropriate work visa, after all — but it's the one I've always fallen back on, and I can see no reason to change now.

Except Jett.

"Just. Answer. It."

We're standing in a holding area just inside the building, waiting to be shown to our table, and if I thought Jett seemed slightly on edge before, the way his eyes are scanning the room now confirms it.

"Please just answer it," he repeats, his tone pleading as he turns to glance at me. "My parents will be here any minute. I really want this to go smoothly."

"Okay, okay."

I don't know why the thought of answering this call is making me feel sick to my stomach, but I know it's not just the too-tight shapewear that's to blame for the way my breath seems to be running out as I raise the phone to my ear and press the answer button.

"Hello?"

"Oh, hello, is that Alexandra Steele? Lexie? Och, I'm glad I managed to catch you at last."

The voice on the other end of the line is slightly crackly and sounds like it's coming from very far away. There's no mistaking the Scottish accent of the woman speaking, though, and I realize I'm gripping the phone almost tightly enough to break it as I wait to hear what she says next.

"My name's Mary McNamee," she says gently. "I'm a nurse at the Raigmore Hospital in Inverness. I'm calling about your mum."

* * *

"Is everything okay? It's just, you look a bit weird, if you don't mind me saying. Was it the phone call? Has something happened?"

Jett and I are seated next to each other at an elaborately

dressed table in the center of the room. The place card on the seat next to me says 'Charles Carter' and I'm assuming the one next to it is for his wife, Gabriella — Jett's mum — so to say that I'm feeling out of my league here would be the understatement of the century.

"Jett. Glad to see you made it on time. I take it this is the girl we hired?"

Actually, on second thoughts, make that the millennium.

Jett jumps to his feet at the sound of his father's voice and shakes him by the hand, before going to give his mother a kiss on the cheek.

Up close, Charles Carter is smaller than he looks on the screen, but he's every bit as handsome — and absolutely *terrifying.* He has the kind of natural presence about him that makes it very easy to understand both the level of success he's achieved, and the way that everyone who approaches our table does so with an almost apologetic air, as if they know they're not worthy of being in this man's presence, and are expecting to be sent away again at any second.

His wife, meanwhile, looks exactly like the former model she is, with high cheekbones and an expression which suggests she can smell something bad.

From what I can gather, *I* seem to be the 'something bad'.

"But Jett, darling, who is this girl?" she says, barely glancing in my direction, her Italian accent still noticeable even after all the years she's been living in the States. "Whatever happened to our lovely Violet?"

I glance up at Jett curiously. Violet King was his first girlfriend — or the first famous one, anyway. They met on the set of *Islanders*, and were together for a few years before Jett went abruptly off the rails and became a serial heart-breaker.

Everyone says it was the pain of the break-up that did it. Well, all the gossip sites say that. And Shona McLaren, obviously, but that goes without saying.

"Now, Gabby, we've been through this," Charles Carter says, taking his seat and placing a napkin on his knee with a flourish. "Violet left him, remember? This is the new girl. The one Asher found for us. I told you this already. Did you take too many Xanax again?"

He has one of those mid-Atlantic accents that old movie stars used to use. I'm having a really hard time trying to wrap my head around the fact that he's actually *real* and sitting next to me.

"Oh, yes," says Jett's mother vaguely, taking her seat on his other side. Jett glances at me apologetically as he sits down too, and I shiver in spite of the warmth of the room. I can't help but notice that although the two senior Carters have been taking *about* me, neither one of them has bothered to speak *to* me.

It's as if they've taken one look at me and immediately seen right through the glossy facade I try to project to the *real* Lexie underneath. The one who *isn't* actually more than just a pretty face, and who therefore isn't really worthy of much notice, anyway.

Okay, now I feel like shit.

I guess it's true what they say about being careful what you wish for.

If you'd asked me just a few weeks ago, I'd have said I'd have given anything to be here right now; at a glamorous, red-carpet event, surrounded by A-listers, and with People Magazine's Sexiest Man Alive as my date. Literally *anything*.

Now that I'm actually here, though, I would have to admit

that I'm kind of *hating* it.

This is a plot-twist I wasn't really expecting. I've always sold myself as a bit of a party girl. 'Sexy Lexie' isn't just what the photographers outside have called me — it's basically the image I've been trying to present to the world for as long as I can remember. Hot Girl Lexie. Good Time Girl Lexie. Destined for Great Things Lexie. I've played that part for so long now I've actually made myself believe it.

Deep down, though, I just... I'd rather be at home, reading a really good book, you know? With my hair in a messy bun, and wearing an over-sized sweatshirt and an ancient pair of leggings. Maybe with a cat or something for company.

Note to self: buy a cat.

Instead though, here I am, sitting ramrod-straight at the table, and nibbling politely on a piece of asparagus, because God knows, that's all my shapewear is going to allow me to fit in. Well, that and the champagne I've been guzzling in a bid to steady my nerves and give myself something to do with my hands.

Jett and his dad spend the entire meal having an in-depth conversation about acting over the top of my head (both literally and figuratively), while Gabriella pointedly ignores everyone at the table, except Asher, who's sitting on her left side, and surreptitiously checking his phone under the table.

I'm sitting between two of the most famous men in the world, and I feel completely invisible.

And then there's that phone call from Scotland nagging away at the back of my mind.

I'm trying my best not to think about that, either.

I *will* think about it, of course. Just... not *now*. Not when I have so many other things to think about first. Like the fear that this corset thing is *literally* going to kill me, for instance, and whether that really is Violet King whose glossy hair I can see on the other side of the room.

Picking up my champagne glass, I gulp down what's left of the liquid inside it, feeling it go straight to my head.

"Lexie. Jett. We need to talk. Urgently."

I'm so busy straining to look at the woman I think might be Jett's best-known ex-girlfriend that I didn't notice Asher leave his seat. Now, though, he's crouched down between me and Jett, his phone in his hand and his brow furrowed.

Uh-oh.

"Not now, Asher," Charles Carter interrupts, leaning over me as if I'm not there. "The speeches are just about to start. Whatever this is will need to wait."

Asher opens his mouth to object, but clearly thinks better of it. Standing up, he hands me his phone, which is open to some website or other.

"Read that," he says bluntly as he turns to go back to his seat. "Then come and find me once this is over so we can figure out what to do about it."

Chapter 21

THE HEATHER BAY GAZETTE
— your leading source of Highland News
FROM THE HIGHLANDS TO HOLLYWOOD - BUT HAS JETT CARTER'S LATEST SQUEEZE FORGOTTEN WHERE SHE CAME FROM?
by celebrity correspondent Scarlett Scott

Her daughter Lexie may be living the high life in Hollywood, but for Heather Bay's Samantha Steele (49), reality is very different.

"I just want to speak to my baby one last time," Samantha said, speaking exclusively to The Heather Bay Gazette from her hospital bed. "It's been so long since I heard from her. I'm just worried that it's going to be too late."

Fire-raiser Lexie Steele (33), who left her Heather Bay cottage last summer under mysterious circumstances, has been hitting the headlines in Hollywood, thanks to her highly publicized romance with actor Jett Carter. But her mother claims the former admin assistant at the family's distillery hasn't been in touch with her since she left the country without explanation.

"Not so much as a phone call," Samantha said, wiping her eyes. "I've never met Jett. I didn't even know Lexie knew him until I saw

the photos of them together. I've reached out to her so many times, but she never answers my calls. It's like she just doesn't care."

And for Samantha, who was admitted to Raigmore Hospital in Inverness early last week, time could be running out to get in touch with her delinquent daughter.

"I don't know how much time I have left," she told this reporter, looking lovingly at the photo of Lexie she keeps by her bed. "I just want to see her one more time. To tell her how much I love her, even though she's broken my heart."

It's unknown how long Lexie has been seeing Carter (33), who is the son of Academy Award Winner Charles Carter, and who rose to fame at the age of 19, with his critically acclaimed role in the blockbuster Islanders. *Sources close to the star, however, claim the actor is "super serious" about his Scots-born girlfriend, and that wedding bells could be on the horizon for the pair.*

"Jett is ready to settle down," said the source, who declined to be named. "He's keen to put his wild days behind him and start a family. And Lexie is the one he wants to do it with."

"My only wish now is to live long enough to see my girl get married to the love of her life," says Samantha Steele, sadly. "But if Lexie won't speak to me, I can't make her. She has so much now that I suppose I can't blame her for not wanting to be bothered with her mum. I'm just sad that she seems to have forgotten where she came from. She wasn't raised like that."

Jett finishes reading the article then looks up at me, his expression inscrutable.

We're crammed into a toilet cubicle together, the phone held between us while the party continues outside the door. As soon as I saw the headline on Asher's phone — and the byline — I knew I had to get out of that room so I could read it in private.

Unfortunately for me, though, when I whispered to Jett that I was feeling sick, he insisted on accompanying me. Which is why he got to read Scarlett Scott's complete destruction of my character at the same time I did.

The Gazette has really gone downhill since I left the Highlands.

"I'm not 33," I say defensively. "I'm 25. Okay, 26. And three-quarters. Scarlett's just written that because she hates me. And mum isn't 49, either. She *wishes* she was 49."

I laugh hollowly, as if the thought of mum having had me at 16 is the biggest takeaway from this article.

"I know you're 30, Alexandra," Jett says, frowning. "It was in the paperwork from the P.I. Asher hired."

"Oh. Okay. But that's still three years less than she's trying to claim," I say, jabbing my finger at the screen. "That's outrageous. Can I sue her, I wonder? Is it just me, or is it really hot in here?"

I'm deflecting here, of course. I'm not going to sue Scarlett Scott for casually adding 3 years to my age. I'll just never forgive her for it, is all. Right now, though, all I want to do is distract Jett from all the other things she's said about me.

It's not working, though.

"So, is this true?" he says, scrolling back through the article, which is illustrated with a photo of mum looking sad in what looks like a hospital bed, next to one of the shots of Jett and I fake-kissing on the beach. They do look pretty good, I have to admit. "Is your mom really sick?"

"Well, she's got her hair and makeup done, and she's wearing a silk negligee rather than a hospital gown," I tell him, tugging at my dress in an attempt to relieve the stranglehold it has on my stomach. "So I *think* she's fine. Can we go back to the party now? Your dad will be wondering where we are?"

The line between his eyes deepens when I mention his dad, but Jett doesn't budge.

"Or we could just stay in this bathroom all night," I sigh, leaning back against the wall in a bid to find a position that's easier to breathe in. "Up to you."

"Why does it describe you as a 'fire-raiser'?" he asks, puzzled. "Who is this Scarlett, anyway? She can't be a real journalist, surely?"

"Oh, she is," I assure him. "She used to be a food and drinks writer, but it looks like she's switched to fiction writing these days. And, 'latest squeeze'? I mean, seriously? Why do people keep calling me that? Who even says that in real life? As for 'celebrity corespondent', the Gazette has literally *one* 'correspondent' and she's it. I don't know who she thinks she is, seriously."

"And the fire thing?" Jett's expression is stony. I don't think he really cares much about Scarlett's writing credentials, somehow. "That's kind of a weird thing to make up about someone, don't you think?"

"I'm... um... I'm feisty?" I say, shrugging. "Look, I don't know. From the way this is written, though, I'm guessing Scarlett's considering a career writing thrillers or something? 'Mysterious circumstances', my ass! And calling me an 'admin assistant?' I was practically running that place, and she knows it. I gave her a guided tour once and everything."

I don't say anything about all the stuff from the mystery "source". That bit about Jett wanting to settle down. I know it's made up. I suspect Grace is probably the "source" in question, and she's just done her job and tried to add to the narrative we've created about Jett being a family man deep down.

It would be interesting if it was true, though.

"This really sounds like your mom is dying, though," Jett insists, rubbing nervously at the stubble that's starting to appear on his chin. "Aren't you worried? I can't believe you don't seem more worried."

"I'm not," I sigh, realizing he's not going to drop this. "She's fine. I told you. The nurse at the hospital told me she'd be fine."

"That was the phone call you got earlier?"

I nod.

"So, what's wrong with her, then?"

Jett looks at me, the gold flecks in his eyes standing out under the artificial light.

"I've no idea," I admit. "The nurse wouldn't tell me. She said mum had specifically asked her not to, and they have to respect her wishes. Patient confidentiality and all that. She did tell me she's not dying, though, and I believe her. Look, mum is a drama queen. I honestly wouldn't be surprised if she was just pretending to have something wrong with her, for the attention. This stupid article has just confirmed that for me. It's fake, Jett. Everything she says is fake. So don't worry about it."

I pause, tugging again at the fabric of my dress to try to loosen the shape wear underneath. I actually *am* starting to feel a bit sick now. Is it too early to go home, I wonder? Or do I have to see this stupid Gala out to the bitter end?

"Okay. Well, as long as you're sure."

Jett doesn't sound particularly convinced by my explanation, but from the way his eyes keep flicking to the door, I can tell he's done thinking about it. He's been on edge all evening, and even though I get the distinct impression that he doesn't want to be here any more than I do, he's so keen to play the dutiful son that Scarlett Scott's stupid little article is the very last thing he needs.

Or that I need, for that matter.

"Ready?"

He twists the lock to open the bathroom door, and I nod reluctantly, before a wave of nausea makes panic rise up in my throat.

"Actually, on second thoughts, maybe you should just go on ahead," I tell him, taking as deep a breath as my tight dress will allow. "I'm still feeling a bit sick. I think I need some air."

"Wait, you're actually feeling sick?" Jett replies, his eyes widening in surprise. "I thought you just made that up so you could get out of there and read that story?"

"I did," I mutter through gritted teeth. "But now I'm feeling sick for real. I guess that's what I get for lying."

'Yeah, I don't think that's how it works, somehow," says Jett wryly. "Think of all the things actors would have to go through if it was."

He looks from me to the door, then back again, clearly caught between the desire to get the hell out of here, and the knowledge that he can't just leave me here when I'm sick without looking like an asshole.

"Come on," he says at last, holding out a hand. "I'll take you outside to get some air, then we really need to get back to my folks, okay?"

The eyes that look into mine are filled with anxiety, and I feel a rush of sympathy for him.

Poor guy. All he wants is to make his dad proud of him, and now here he is, locked in a bathroom with a fake girlfriend about to throw up on him at any second because her underwear's too tight.

As the absurdity of the situation hits me, I give a snort of laughter, which makes Jett jump in surprise.

"What are we laughing at?" he asks, smiling warily as my shoulders shake uncontrollably.

"This..." I gasp, holding my sides as I try to get a hold of the rapidly mounting hysteria. "Us. This whole situation. It's... I mean, it's not even remotely funny..."

"It isn't," he agrees.

"But it's just... it's just..."

It's just one of those times when, once you start laughing, you can't seem to stop yourself, is what I'm trying to say. One of those times when you end up laughing *at your own laughter* rather than whatever it was that started it in the first place. A kind of hysteria which, once it infects you, is impossible to shake off.

I want to say this, but as I look up at him, my eyes streaming with tears of laughter, I realize I don't have to. Jett's mouth curves up in a slow smile, and then, all of a sudden, he's laughing along with me, both of us bent almost double in the tiny stall as we laugh like two people who *aren't* just pretending to like each other. Like we're actually having *fun*. We laugh and we laugh, and for just a moment, it feels like we're a team: like there's a *we* instead of just a *me* and a *him*, and like this feeling could, quite possibly, last forever.

But, of course, it doesn't.

The laughter stops almost as suddenly as it started, and, before I know quite what happened, we're just two near-strangers again, squeezed into a bathroom stall, with one of us having to try very, very hard not to throw up on the other.

"Oh my God, I *really* need some air now," I wheeze at last, fanning myself with one hand. "Or to take this dress off so I can actually breathe."

Jett's eyebrows rise at that, but he refuses to take the bait, and simply clears his throat awkwardly before offering me his arm.

"Come on," he says, pushing the door open. "We'll go out the back way. There shouldn't be any photographers out there."

I nod wordlessly as I follow him out of the bathroom and down the corridor, feeling like I'm having an out-of-body experience. Everything is way too loud, and far too bright. Colors swim in and out of my peripheral vision, and I'm drifting in and out of them, reaching out to grab the back of Jett's tuxedo jacket to steady myself as we go.

In retrospect, three glasses of champagne on an empty stomach probably wasn't the best plan I've ever had.

"Here," Jett's saying as we come to a stop in front of a closed door. His voice seems to be coming from very far away, but when he opens the door, the rush of cool night air on my face is such a relief that I push in front of him, desperate to be somewhere I can breathe more easily.

"Lexie! Jett! Over here!"

The explosion of light and sound hits me like a smack in the face. Camera flashes go off all around me, making me raise my hand to my eyes to protect them from the sudden glare.

So I guess there were *photographers waiting back here after all, then. Fantastic.*

"Lexie, is there anything you want to say to your mom?" one of the photographers calls, his voice ringing out above the rest. "Any response to her interview?"

Her interview? With the Heather Bay Gazette? Has that really made it all the way to L.A. already?

I blink stupidly in the lights, trying to work out what to say. Before I can speak, though, I feel Jett's hand on my elbow, holding me steady as he steps up beside me and pulls me close.

"We're obviously very concerned about Lexie's mom's health," he says smoothly. "We're making plans to fly out and see her this week, in fact. It's our main priority. Now, if you'll excuse us..."

He puts his arm around my shoulder, and tries to steer me back towards the building, but I'm so horrified by what he's just said that I simply stand there, as if I've been turned to stone.

"You...you're not serious?" I croak, ignoring the photographers still jostling for attention behind us. "We're not *actually* going to Scotland, are we?"

This is just part of the act. It has *to be. He's just saying it because it's what people would expect him to say if his girlfriend's mother was taken ill. And if the girlfriend was real, and the mother wasn't a straight-up-liar, obviously.*

I gaze up at him pleadingly, doing my best to put every ounce of my desperation not to go to Scotland into that look. My acting is obviously not that good, though, because Jett simply takes both of my hands in his and looks down at me with a sincerity that no one but me would ever doubt.

"Of course we are, Alexandra," he says, just loud enough for everyone around us to hear. "I'd do anything for you, you know. Anything at all."

He looks tenderly into my eyes, one hand coming up to brush the hair from my face as he smiles down at me.

It's the last thing I see before the world goes black.

Chapter 22

I wake with a fierce pounding in my head, which it takes me a few seconds to realize is actually coming from the door of my hotel room.

"Lexie, I know you're in there," yells a familiar voice, with an Australian accent. "So you better let me in or I'll... well, I dunno what I'll do, actually," Summer trails off. "This place is *insane*, Lexie. Let me in before they throw me out."

I stumble out of bed, realizing too late that my eyelashes are welded together with last night's mascara, and walking straight into the door, almost knocking myself out.

I really need to stop walking into doors like this.

"Lexie," shrieks Summer. "You let me in right now or I'm calling your mum."

I scrabble frantically at the door, opening it to find Summer standing in the hallway, looking like she's about to start a fight with the wall.

"You have no idea how hard it was for me to get into this place," she says without preamble as she pushes her way past me into the room. "It's like bloody Alcatraz or something."

"You're telling me," I reply, sitting down gingerly on the bed, my head still throbbing. "It's started to feel a bit like a prison, to be honest. How did you know I was here, anyway?"

"Aww, my heart bleeds for you, being stuck in a dump like this," Summer says, rolling her eyes. "And I saw the same way everyone else knew: by reading about it on the Internet. Seriously, Lexie, what the actual fuck?"

Her eyes are wide circles of indignation, and she looks like she can't quite decide whether she's hurt or just concerned.

"God, Summer, I'm sorry," I groan, rubbing my aching temples. "I can explain, I promise."

I stop, remembering the NDA I signed promising not to tell another living soul about my arrangement with Jett.

Can I explain? Am I even allowed to?

I groan again, as memories from last night come flooding back. Right before he dropped me off at the hotel, I told Jett the deal was off: that I couldn't handle the lies any more — and I *definitely* couldn't handle the thought of flying back to Scotland to continue the charade there — so I was officially calling it off.

I don't remember what he said in reply to that. I'm not sure he said anything, actually, from the moment we got back into the car — me having been thoroughly checked over first by a doctor, who helpfully confirmed that my underwear was too tight — until the terse goodnight outside my room. He insisted on making sure I got back okay, but made it clear he didn't want to stick around... and, of course, I can't tell Summer any of this, because I have no idea whether the NDA still applies now that I've decided I don't want to do this anymore.

"Um, I'm waiting, Sexy Lexie?"

Summer's still watching me, her leg jiggling back and forth with impatience.

I really want to tell her the truth. I know I can't risk getting into any more trouble than I am already, though, so I decide to go for the easiest option I can think of.

"I had to sign a non-disclosure," I tell her, putting my hands over my eyes and peeking through my fingers at her. "So I actually *can't* explain. Please don't be mad."

"Fuuuck," Summer says, her eyes widening even more. "That's wild. I've heard of celebs doing stuff like that," she adds, getting up and crossing the room to rummage through the mini bar. "Like, making their girlfriends sign NDAs so they can't spill all their dirty little secrets if they break up."

She comes back to the bed holding a tub of Pringles, which she pops open.

"I'm not his girlfriend," I say quickly, still hiding behind my hands.

At least that's true.

"Sure, sure," Summer nods, stuffing a stack of crisps into her mouth. "It's just casual. I get it. But look at this place."

She gazes around the room, her face a picture of awe. "He must think a lot of you, Lex. Like, a *lot*. So, what's he like? I'm going to be needing aaaall the details here, just so you know."

Summer goes back to munching on her snack, and I look uncomfortably down at my hands.

"He... he's nice?" I venture at last. "He has this really cool pantry in his house. Like Khloe Kardashian's, only more *manly*." It's the only thing I can think of, but thankfully Summer is used to me by now.

"I can't believe you're seeing *Jett Carter*," she squeals, punching me in the arm. "This is just wild. You should've seen Amy's face when she saw the photos! Oh my God, it was hilarious!"

"Has it been bad?" I ask cautiously, not sure I want to know the answer to this. "The coverage, I mean? I haven't looked.

They advised me not to."

Summer bites her lip and looks away, finding something really interesting to look at on the other side of the room.

"I mean, I probably wouldn't bother Googling yourself," she says at last, popping the last Pringle into her mouth. "And definitely don't go onto Twitter, whatever you do. That would be a really bad idea."

"I won't."

"I tell you one thing, though," Summer says, brightening. "The bar's never been busier. All of these people coming in all of a sudden, all hoping to bump into Jett. Joe's made up about it. Oh! And you'll never believe it, Lex, but it even got Weird Ben out of his room. Some journalist came round asking to interview us all, and Weird B was right there, asking more questions than the journo. Wild."

"Seriously? You got to see Weird Ben? I kind of wish I'd been there for that."

"We did." Summer licks the salt off her fingers, grinning. "He was surprisingly normal looking, actually. English. Blonde. Not bad looking, in a very *clean* kind of way. It was a bit of an anti-climax, really. He asked loads of questions about you, though. Where are you from, what do you do there, who are your friends... It was like he thought *he* was the journalist. Maybe he's going to try to write a tell-all book or something. 'Living With Lexie'. 'Staying With Steele. I could go on."

"Please don't," I say, grinning. "He wouldn't have much to tell, anyway. He's never even met me."

"You'll probably be surprised by the number of people who come out of the woodwork now that you're... well, semi-famous," Summer says, suddenly serious. "Amy was chatting away to that journo like you two were besties, and we all know you wouldn't even piss on each other if you were on fire."

I wince at the mention of fire. I guess that's always going to be a bit of a sore spot.

"I've already found that out the hard way," I tell her, unscrewing the water bottle I keep by the bed and taking a grateful gulp. "Although I should probably have guessed that Mum would be the very first to come crawling."

"Shit," Summer says, clamping her hand over her mouth. "Sorry, Lex, I meant to ask. How is she? I saw the article, obviously. You're looking pretty good for 33, by the way."

"Shut it." I glare at her until she can't hold her laugh in any longer.

"Sorry," she says again, getting a hold of herself. "I know I shouldn't be laughing. Your poor Mum. Is it true that you're going to Scotland to see her?"

I hesitate.

"Yes. I mean no. I don't know."

I start nibbling on my thumbnail as Summer raises her eyebrows.

"Well, glad we cleared that up," she says. "Love how decisive you're being about this."

"God, Summer, it's a complete mess," I groan, putting my head in my hands. "Mum's fine, though. I can say that for certain."

This is true, as it happens. I called the hospital again last night, as soon as I got back to the hotel, and the nurse told me Mum wasn't even close to being as ill as the article in the Gazette made her sound. She sounded pretty pissed about it, actually.

"So, are you going to Scotland? You and Jett?"

"Honestly? I don't know. I don't even know if I'm going to

see him again after last night?"

Summer gives me The Look.

"Ohhhh, Lexxxiieeee," she sighs. "Why would you not see him again? It's Jett Carter, for fuck's sake."

Her eyes light up.

"If you don't want him, can I have him?" she asks excitedly.

I pluck a pillow off the bed and throw it at her.

"It's ... look, it's complicated, Summer," I tell her, once she's stopped shrieking at me. "I really wish I could tell you more, but I can't. I'm really sorry."

"The NDA," she nods. "I get it."

She looks at me speculatively, chewing her bottom lip, the way she does when she's worried.

"Are you okay, Lex?" she asks, unexpectedly. "It's just this whole thing—" She looks around the hotel room again. "I mean, it's amazing, don't get me wrong," she goes on. "And I'm so happy for you, seriously. We all are. Well, maybe not Amy. But you know what I mean."

I nod, taking another swig of my water.

"Are *you* happy, though?" Summer asks, watching me. "Because, if you don't mind me saying, you don't really look like a girl who just started dating Jett Carter. And I'm not talking about the fact that you have mascara all over your face. Oh, you have mascara all over you face, by the way," she adds. "Rough night, huh?"

"Yeah, something like that."

I stare back at her, wondering how much I can tell her without getting myself into trouble.

"I'm fine, Summer," I say eventually. "Everything's just a bit weird right now. You know, with Mum."

And with the fact I'm lying to everyone. Even you.

Summer looks unconvinced, but she seems to accept this. She spends the next thirty minutes chattering on about Jett and how crazy it is that *he* turned out to be the bearded guy she had to throw out of the bar a few nights ago.

"And I didn't even recognize him," she says for what has to be the 10th time since she arrived. "I just can't get over it, Lex. Imagine if you'd come with me and Amy that night instead of locking up on your own? You probably wouldn't be sitting here now."

I open my mouth to reply to this, but, before I can speak, my phone pings with a message, and I glance at the screen to see the name I've been hoping for, but which now sends my stomach spiraling.

It's Jett.

"*We need to talk*," his message says. "*I'll send a car.*"

That's it. Eight words, nothing else. Not even an emoji or two to help me work out whether he wants to talk like two good pals who had themselves a fine old time in a bathroom cubicle the previous night and need to fill each other in on what actually happened, or whether we need to *talk*-talk. Like an A-list movie star, say, and the woman who's pretending to be his girlfriend.

"Is that him?" Summer says eagerly, leaning forward. "Is that Jett? Oh my God, Lexie, I can't believe this. You're so lucky."

She starts jumping up and down on the bed, before stopping to high five me, as if I've won the jackpot. As she's leaving, though, she pulls me in for a hug — which is unlike her, because we're not really huggers — then looks at me searchingly.

"Promise me you'll look after yourself, Lexie?" she says, uncharacteristically serious. "And tell Jett that if he hurts you, he'll have me to deal with, okay? I'm not joking."

"Oh stop it," I say lightly, waving her away. "I'm a big girl, Summer. I can look after myself."

Up until now, that's always been true. As my friend's footsteps fade away though, I'm suddenly not so sure.

Chapter 23

"Well, I guess you got me back for throwing up on you that time."

Jett and I are sitting by the pool at his house, with a pile of magazines like *Us Weekly* and the *National Enquirer* spread out on the table in front of us.

I'm deliberately not looking at them. I don't have to see the evidence to know that Scarlett's article in the Gazette didn't stay in *just* the Gazette. No, in the time it took for Asher to get a Google alert about it — and for me and Jett to have a laughing fit in a public bathroom — that article had gone all the way around the world, syndicated by all the major tabloids and surpassed in popularity only by the follow-up story, which contained Jett's promise to fly me to Scotland immediately, accompanied by a series of photos of me appearing to collapse into his arms in gratitude.

It would be fair to say that this whole fake-dating thing is not going well for me.

Or for anyone, really.

"I'm fired, aren't I?" I say bluntly, fiddling with the mug of coffee that's been placed in front of me, but which I'm still too hungover to drink. "I mean, I know you can't really fire me, because I already quit, but that's why you brought me here, isn't it? Just tell me. It's okay, I can take it."

"What are you talking about? Of course you're not getting fired — or quitting, for that matter. Can you even imagine how bad it would make me look if you disappeared now? People would think I'd dumped you right when your mother's at death's door, and then things would be even worse for me than they are now."

Jett leans back in his seat, glaring at me in a way that's the exact opposite of how he looked at me yesterday. That was in front of the cameras, though. Now it's just me and him — well, and Asher, who thinks we can't see him hiding behind the curtain in the French windows behind us — and it's becoming increasingly obvious that the "Mr. Considerate" act he put on last night really *was* just for show.

"Okay, I get it," I mutter sullenly. "You can't afford any more damage to your precious reputation, which is the only thing that matters to you. Are you trying to channel Asher right now, by the way? Because you're doing a great job, if so."

I'm deliberately trying to provoke him now. I know that. I'm doing it because I want the Jett of last night to come back. The one who laughed with me about absolutely nothing, and then told me he'd do anything for me. I want to believe *that* Jett was the real one, and this one, with his baseball hat crammed over his eyes, and his lips pouting sulkily, is the act.

I *want* to believe that. Who wouldn't? The thing is, though, I'm not that stupid. I know it's not true. That's the whole point, really. We're creating a narrative that isn't true, and if I have any sense at all, I'll just treat it like the job it is, and not let myself get emotionally attached to the man in front of me, whose character keeps changing, as if he's doing his best to remind me that I don't know him at all.

Which I don't.

Before Jett can respond to my sarcasm, there's a flurry of movement in my peripheral vision, and Asher steps out from behind the curtain, as if he's about to do a magic trick.

"This doesn't have to be quite as much of a disaster as it seems," he says, taking a seat at the table next to us, and speaking only to Jett, as if I'm not even there. I'm getting used to that.

"On the plus side," he goes on, "Miss Steele's little fainting act has definitely helped her claw back some of the sympathy she lost with the whole 'abandoned mother' article."

He shoots me an appraising look.

"Well played," he says, speaking as if the words are being pulled out of him against his will. "Very well played."

"I wasn't playing, I really did faint—" I begin indignantly, but Asher keeps on talking, ignoring the interruption.

"The problem we have now," he continues, helping himself to my untouched cup of coffee, "Is that, having told the world's media you're taking her to Scotland, you're going to have to follow through with that. Or you'll look like an asshole, quite frankly."

My heart sinks. And if the look on his face is anything to go by, Jett's does too.

I can't go back to Scotland. I just can't. It would be one thing if Mum was *actually* ill, of course. But she isn't. I know she isn't. The hospital told me as much last night. She's just trying to manipulate me yet again. It's what she does. What she's always done. And if I keep on letting her get away with it, it will never, ever end.

"Yeah, I really don't want to go—"

"Going to Scotland isn't necessarily a bad thing either, though," steamroller Asher continues, talking over the top of me. He's quite like mum himself, actually. I should introduce them. If I ever see her again, that is.

"Think about it, Jett," he's saying now, his eyes shining with sudden enthusiasm. "Think about why you're doing this. Think about *Macbeth*."

"The Scottish Play," Jett says slowly. His eyes are still hidden by the peak of his cap, but some of the tension has left his voice, and he's sitting a little straighter in his seat. "About the Scottish King. And if I went to Scotland —"

" — you'd be able to convince Duval you're taking this seriously," Asher finishes for him. "Show him how much the role means to you."

"I could do some research," Jett says, nodding. "Treat it like a work trip."

"I'm not sure what kind of 'research' you think you're going to be able to do for *Macbeth* in Heather Bay," I snort. "This is going to blow your mind, but things have actually moved on a bit since the 11th century, even in the Highlands. Like, there are no witches offering prophecies on the road into the village, you know?"

Well, not unless you count Shona McLaren, obviously. And most people do, to be fair.

"No witches? Are you sure about that?"

Jett looks me in the eye for the first time since I got here this morning, and I have to force myself to hold his gaze and not look away.

"I'm not stupid, Lady M," he says bluntly. "I know there

won't be witches prancing around the Highlands. But I want this role. And if going to Scotland can help me convince Duval that I'm the right person for it, then I'm sorry, but I'm going to go to Scotland."

There's a tense silence, broken only by the sound of Asher noisily slurping his coffee. I know from Grace that Justin Duval has so far failed to buy into this idea we've been trying to create of Jett as a loyal boyfriend and future family man. The rest of the world might be willing to believe his love for me has made him want to settle down, but Duval still won't even consider him for the part — and I somehow doubt my recent antics will have done much to change his mind.

Okay, now I feel guilty.

I'm supposed to be helping him, but I'm just making his life more difficult instead. Leave it to Lexie to mess things up.

"I could really do with your help here, Lady M," Jett says, leaning forward so he can stare at me even more intensely. "I'm going to need a tour guide, you know. Someone to show me where all the best — what was it? Deep fried Mars Bars? — are."

He smiles, and I feel my resolve start to waver. I know how this ends. He smiles, I capitulate. It's very unlike me — normally when someone asks me to do something, I'll go out of my way to do the opposite. But that's the kind of effect Jett Carter has on me, and I suspect he knows that. It's the kind of effect he has on *everyone*, after all. I'm not special. I am, however, currently his best chance of getting this role, and that means I'm not totally powerless.

I can say no to this plan.

I can stand my ground and not let Jett sweet-talk me into something I know will only cause more trouble.

He needs me right now more than I need him. What's he going to do if I say no, after all? He's just admitted he can't fire me without losing face; and it's not like he can force me onto an airplane against my will, is it?

The ball's completely in my court, in other words. And now I'm going to pick it up and run with it.

"I'm sorry, Jett," I say firmly, pushing my chair back and standing up. "But the answer's no. I won't be going to Scotland. I can't. You don't know what you're asking of me, and if you did you wouldn't even ask."

"So tell me, then," he says, exasperated. "Tell me what's so bad about going home for you. I can help you. I *want* to help you, Alexandra. You just have to let me."

"That's the thing, though," I say sadly. "You can't help me with this. You can't make it any easier for me to go back home and face everyone there. You can't make them forgive me for the things I've done. This is my problem, and I'm the one who has to fix it."

I turn to leave, but before I can take more than a few steps, he's right there behind me, reaching for my arm and spinning me around to face him.

"Oh, yeah?" he says, his eyes blazing. "And how are you going to do that, Lady M? Because I might not know what your problems are, but I do know one thing, and that's that you're not doing anything to try to fix them."

Behind us, Asher's phone starts ringing (His ringtone is 'Wannabe' by The Spice Girls. I file that piece of information away so I can use it against him later.), and he glares at it as if it's personally offended him, before standing up and striding off to answer it, leaving Jett and I alone.

"Well?" he says, as the door closes behind his agent. "I'm

right, aren't I? You're not even trying to solve your problems, whatever they are. You're just hiding from them. Working in some dive bar. Living in a share house. Jumping every time your phone rings, in case it's Mommy Dearest. Is that really how you want to live your life, Lady M? Is it?"

His hand is still on my arm, and I shake it off as if it burns.

How dare he judge me like that? And how dare he be right about me?

My instinct is to fight back — to defend myself, and maybe throw a few insults in his direction, too, to pay him back for how small he's just made me feel. That's what I'd normally do. When I open my mouth to speak, though, I find all the fight has gone out of me.

It's actually quite liberating, realizing I don't have to fight back all the time. That I can just do what I'm doing now, which is to shrug my shoulders and admit that he's right.

"No, of course it isn't," I say, my voice sounding a little less steady than it did in my head. "No more than you want to live your life for your father, anyway. Because that's what you're doing too, isn't it? I guess we're both the same in that respect. Neither one of us is living the life we want, and neither one of us can do anything about it."

Jett steps back as if he's been slapped.

"You don't know anything about me and my father," he says shortly. "You don't know anything about this world and how it works."

"No, I don't." I nod tearfully. "And that's why I can't help you with this. I'm not the right person to do it. I have absolutely no idea what I'm doing. I just keep getting it wrong and making things worse. You should have picked someone else. You should have picked one of those actresses or models you usually date. At least that would've been more believable than you dating a complete fuck-up like me."

I sniff loudly, trying to hold back the tears that are threatening to come. I am *not* a pretty crier. It's one of the reasons I never do it.

"I don't think you're a fuck-up, Lexie."

Jett steps back towards me.

"I am, though," I insist, digging my nails into the palms of my hands. "Trust me, you don't even know the half of it. If I went to Scotland with you, I wouldn't exactly be welcomed back with open arms. I'd just make things worse. That's why you should pick someone else to do this. I don't think 'Fake Girlfriend" is going to make it onto my resume, somehow."

"But I don't want to pick someone else," Jett says simply. "I pick *you*, Lexie. I trust *you*. And I want to go to Scotland with you. You. No one else."

I am not going to cry.

I am not going to cry.

"I meant what I said, by the way," he goes on when I don't respond, smiling that stomach-flipping smile of his again. "I can help you. With your mom, I mean. We can get her whatever medical treatment she needs. Or I can just, you know, be there for you when you see her. Because I get the feeling that's not going to be easy for you, and I'm good with little old ladies. They like me. What can I say?"

Okay, I am possibly *going to cry. Just a* little *bit.*

"Mum's not a little old lady," I tell him, sniffing to hide the emotion in my voice. "Or not like any you've ever met. She'll probably try to hit on you, actually."

Jett's grin widens.

"Even better," he chuckles. "She'll be putty in my hands,

then. Um, just joking. I'll behave myself, I promise. I'm... I'm not actually like that, you know. I'm not how they make me look in the tabloids. That's not really me."

He rubs his chin, suddenly bashful. I have a powerful urge to put my arms around him and hug him; to kiss his beautiful face and tell him it's okay — that I believe him.

I'm just not *totally* sure I do, is the only problem.

"So what *are* you really like, then?" I ask instead. "If you're not the hell-raising playboy everyone thinks you are, who are you?"

Jett looks up in surprise.

"That's kind of a deep question for 11 o'clock in the morning, don't you think?"

"You're right," I agree solemnly. "It's more of a 3 a.m. kind of question. Remind me to ask it again later."

He grins, and the tension between us is gone, as if it never existed.

"Seriously, though," he says, reaching out and taking my hands in his. "We'll do this together. You look after me, I'll look after you. Do we have a deal?"

I should say no to this.

I *want* to say no to this. It would be the best thing to do. The sensible thing. The thing with the least chance of me ending up with my heart broken — by either Mum, or Jett, or both.

Instead, though, I do what I always do in situations like this. The wrong thing. The dangerous thing. The quite possibly *insane* thing.

I say yes.

Chapter 24

"Pacing won't get us there any faster, you know."

We're approximately four hours into our flight to Scotland, and so far the main thing I've learned about private air travel is that once the novelty of being surrounded by so much luxury wears off — which took quite a while, to be fair — you're still basically just trapped in a tin can, with nothing to do but think about what's going to happen when you land.

I really don't want to think about what's going to happen when we land.

"I don't *want* to get there any faster," I tell Jett, throwing myself back down in the seat beside him. "I don't want to get there *at all*, remember?"

He nods without looking up from the script he's reading on his iPad.

"And why is that again?" he says pointedly. "Remind me."

I clamp my mouth shut stubbornly. Other than what I've already said about Mum, and how manipulative she can be, I haven't told Jett anything about Scotland, and why I left, and I intend to keep it that way until... well, until we get to Heather Bay, I suppose, where everyone knows everyone else, and nothing stays secret for long.

Awesome.

I chew my thumbnail nervously as I stare out of the airplane window. The orderly grids of L.A. have long since given way to deserts that seemed to go on forever, before merging into the green and blue of the Eastern seaboard. Before long, we'll be out over the Atlantic, and then we'll be home.

Only I'm not really sure I can call it that anymore.

As I twist impatiently in my seat, Jett heaves a resigned sigh, and puts the iPad down.

"Tell me a story about Lexie," he says, turning to face me. "We should probably get to know each other a bit better if we're going to convince the folks who know you that this is for real. And it's not like there's anything else to do."

I nod uncertainly as I glance around the cabin, which is empty but for the two of us. I had assumed that Asher — or at least Grace — would be accompanying us on this trip, but, much to my surprise, Jett insisted we go it alone, without even Leroy as security.

"I know the whole point of this trip is to be seen together in Scotland," he said when Asher tried to insist on coming with us. "But I don't want to turn up with an entourage. I'd rather not turn this into any more of a media circus than it already is, if it's all the same to you, Asher."

Asher had no choice but to capitulate. Which means it's just me and my fake boyfriend, Jett. Who's completely right when he says we should probably get to know a little more about each other if we're going to have the slightest hope of convincing the good people of Heather Bay that we're together.

So, no pressure, then.

"There's really not much to tell," I say, shrugging. "I'm pretty ordinary, really."

Jett's eyebrows raise in disbelief.

"Oh, I know that's not true," he says flirtatiously.

I hate the way he does that. Flirting wasn't part of the deal. It's an unfair advantage that I keep finding myself blindsided by: like yesterday, when he managed to talk me into this trip by pretending to care about me.

But he doesn't. He's just acting, like he always is, and I'm the sucker who falls for it every time.

"Whoa, that's a Lady Macbeth look, if ever I saw one," he says now, referring to the scowl that stole over my face at the thought of my how gullible I've been. "*Something wicked this way comes*, indeed."

He's been quoting lines from Macbeth ever since we took off. He really is taking this seriously. I just hope Justin Duval is impressed. I'd hate to think I'm putting myself through this for nothing.

"Unless you're hoping to be cast as one of the witches, you're learning the wrong lines," I point out, hoping to change the subject. "And that line's about Macbeth, not his wife."

"Oh, I'm not learning lines," he says smugly. "I know the whole thing off by heart already. I'm just reading it for fun now. And you're deflecting. You do that a lot, I've noticed. So, come on, Lady M, tell me a story about you. Something you've never told anyone before. Tell me something you did when you were a kid."

I look out the window as I consider this.

"When I was a little girl," I say at last, "My mum used to enter me in pageants."

"Beauty pageants? Lexie Steele was a child beauty queen?"

"I'll try not to be offended by how surprised you are about that," I say dryly. "But yes, beauty pageants. I did loads of them; even won a few, actually."

"Fun though it is to think of little Lexie all done up like a doll, this doesn't sound like something no one else knows about," Jett points out. "Stick to the assignment, Lady M."

"I'm getting to that part," I insist. My hands twist nervously on my lap. This isn't exactly a "take it to the grave" kind of secret, but Jett's listening so intently, like what I'm about to say is of the utmost importance to him, that it's just a little unnerving.

I wonder if he learned that in acting class?

"So, the truth is, the pageants were really my mum's thing, not mine," I tell him, resisting the urge to start chewing my nail again. "I mean, sure, I liked the attention I got when I won something. But Mum liked it even more, so I mostly just went along with it to keep her happy. She was great when she was happy. Fun, affectionate..."

I trail off, remembering the times when Mum was happy with me. How she'd get out the old rusty convertible she used to keep in the garage — the one she said used to belonged to my Dad — and we'd go for a ride in it, with the top down, and the heater going full blast. How it would feel like the sun coming out after a rainstorm — and how quickly it could go back in again.

"And when she wasn't happy?"

I look up at Jett in surprise, wondering if I said all of that out loud by mistake. His eyes are still fixed on mine, and there's an understanding in them I'm sure I must be imagining until I remember the things he's told me about his father.

Maybe not.

"When she wasn't happy, it was very different," I say slowly. "Very different. And it got to the point where I just couldn't deal with it anymore. The mood swings. The anger. It felt like her happiness was totally dependent on my ability to win some stupid beauty pageant, and I just... I started to hate having that responsibility all the time. I started to *really* hate it."

"How old were you?" Jett asks softly.

I think for a second.

"About ten? Eleven maybe? I don't think I'd started high school yet, so definitely not more than that. I'd have a pageant every weekend, basically — or a rehearsal for one. And every Friday night, I'd get sick to my stomach, thinking about what would happen if I didn't win it. If I wasn't good enough for her. It literally started to make me ill. Like, throwing up in the car on the way there — that kind of thing."

"She didn't... hit you, did she?"

Jett's mouth has settled into a straight line. This is probably not the fun conversation he was expecting this to be.

"No, nothing like that," I assure him hurriedly. "She never physically hurt me. She'd just sort of *withdraw* from me. And when you're ten years old, that really hurts, you know?"

"That hurts at any age," Jett says shortly. "Your mom sounds like a narcissist."

I nod wordlessly. You don't need to be a psychiatrist to see it, but it's strange — and oddly reassuring — to hear someone say it out loud. It makes me feel less like it's all my own fault; which, deep down, I've always suspected it is.

"So, what did you do? How did you put a stop to the pageant stuff?"

I straighten my shoulders, allowing myself to relax as I finally get to the main part of my story.

"I cut my hair," I tell him, grinning. "Totally butchered it. I looked like Worzel Gummidge — that's like a weird scarecrow guy — by the time I was done. And I did it the night before a pageant, so there was no time to get it fixed, either."

Jett's eyes widen in shock.

"Shiiiit," he says, sounding impressed. "I have no idea what Worzel Whateveryousaid is, but that's a boss move right there. What did your mom say, though?"

"Oh, she was furious, obviously." I gloss over this part as casually as I can, not wanting to think about the fallout from that particular little stunt of mine. "But I told her I'd just been trying to make myself look prettier, and she believed me. She wasn't happy." *Understatement of the century.* "I wasn't either, to be honest. I loved my long hair, and even after the hairdresser tried to neaten it up, I still looked horrific. But I never had to enter another pageant after that, and that was good enough for me."

"The hair must have grown back, though?"

"Oh yeah, it did. But it took a while, and Mum had this wild idea that only girls with princess hair could be pretty, so she didn't see the point in pursuing the pageant thing after that. I think she kind of wrote me off, really."

I flick my hair out of my eyes, as if I'm completely unaffected by this. I don't think Jett's convinced, though, somehow. He takes a few moments to speak, but when he does, his voice is gentle, as if he's worried I might break.

"So you basically sabotaged yourself because of your mother," he says softly. "I can't imagine many girls doing something like that."

"Just call me Rapunzel," I say, as nonchalantly as I can manage. "That's me."

"Seriously, though." Jett's not going to let this drop. "Most of the women I meet are so invested in their appearance that they'd probably rather die than do something to ruin it. Not that you'd have ruined it," he adds quickly. "I mean, I'm sure you still looked lovely and—"

"I looked like a scarecrow," I say, laughing. "And I *did* want to die over it at first, so don't give me too much credit here. It was a moment of madness. I regretted it as soon as I made the first cut, but it was too late by that point. I had to see it through."

"Well, I take my hat off to you, Lady M," he says, reaching up and tipping his ever-present baseball cap at me. "You've definitely got balls. I have to give you that."

"I bet you're wishing you'd just suggested we play Never Have I Ever or something," I reply, my cheeks hot. "That all got a bit dark. Sorry."

"Don't be sorry," Jett says firmly. "I asked because I wanted to know. We can save the drinking games for another time."

"Or we could do it now," I suggest, nodding towards the bar at the other end of the plane. "You owe me a story in return, you know. A story about Jett. One no one else knows."

He hesitates for just a moment.

"Another time, maybe," he says, picking his iPad back up. "I might have exaggerated slightly about how well I know this play. I should probably—"

He gestured vaguely to the script, and my heart sinks with disappointment. It felt good to tell someone about Mum, and what it was like for me growing up. More than that, it felt good to tell *him* — because, for some reason, he seemed to understand. But when I told him all of that, I'd assumed he'd tell me something in return. That we were starting to get to know each other, like he'd said we would. And now that he's made it clear the conversation is over, I can't help but wonder if it was all just "research" for him; like this trip to the land of *Macbeth.*

Is his interest in me genuine, or is he just learning me the way he learns his lines?

And how am I ever supposed to know the difference?

Chapter 25

We land in Scotland to mist and rain. It's basically like the clouds we flew through when we started our descent just continued all the way to the ground, so instead of the majestic mountains and shimmering lochs Jett was hoping for, all we see on the way down is a blanket of white.

So far, so Scotland.

"Are the seasons the other way around here?" Jett asks, peering out of the aircraft window as it taxis to a halt at a little private airfield that I didn't even know existed. "I thought you had to go south before that happened?"

"No, they're the same," I tell him, feeling my stomach clench with renewed anxiety now I'm officially back on home soil. "This is summer. If it was winter there'd be snow and ice as well as mist and rain. Or sunshine and frost. Or maybe all of those at once. We have a saying here that if you don't like the weather, you just have to wait for 15 minutes, and it'll change."

Sure enough, by the time we're pulling out of the airport — in a chauffeur-driven car with blacked out widows that's going to look totally out of place on the streets of Heather Bay — the sun has started to burn through the mist, making rainbows briefly shimmer over the road before disappearing almost before you can see them.

"Wow," says Jett, pressing his nose against the glass like a little kid. "This sure is pretty."

"Just wait," I tell him as the car makes its way north. "Just wait."

A few miles up the road, there's a memorial to the commandos who died in the Second World War. It stands on a hill, looking out towards the Nevis mountain range, and on a day like today, it looks like it's floating in the clouds. It's the perfect spot to see Scotland from for the first time, and as the car approaches it, I have an idea.

"Can you just pull in here for a second, please?" I ask the driver, leaning forward. "I just really want Jett to see this."

The car pulls into a space in the car park, and I jump out and run up the steps to the memorial, calling to Jett to follow me.

"Holy shit," he says when he catches up to me. "This is amazing."

I stand back and watch him as he turns around on the spot, looking first at the memorial itself, with its floral tributes around the base, and then out towards the mountains, which are looking particularly magnificent now that the sun's shining on them.

I don't know why I want him to like it. It's not as if it matters. It's not like either of us is going to be staying here for long; and it's definitely not like I can take any credit at all for the majestic beauty of these mountains. But even so, I feel a surge of pride as Jett turns to look back at me, his mouth a round 'O' of wonder at the views before him.

I'm home.

I'm actually home.

And it doesn't feel nearly as strange as I thought it would.

Until, all of a sudden, it does.

"Oh, my God! Is that *Jett Carter*?"

I'd barely even noticed the tour bus that pulled up as Jett and I walked up to the monument, but as its doors open and it starts to disgorge a sea of camera-wielding passengers, I realize we're in trouble.

"It is! Oh my God, it's seriously him!"

The girl running up the steps towards us has an American accent, and a phone held out in front of her, which she's using to film as she runs. Within seconds, at least five more people are following her, and, before I know quite what's happening, Jett and I are surrounded, cameras thrust into our faces, and blood pounding in my ears as people jostle for space, some of them blatantly trying to push me out of the way in their determination to get to Jett.

It takes less than five seconds for the lonely monument on the hill to be transformed into the scene of a battle. It's Jett against the tourists — or the female tourists, anyway, who seem absolutely determined to take a piece of him home with them. I'm totally forgotten as they push and shove towards him, and my heart contracts with pity as I see him surrounded by cameras, his green eyes filled with fear as he looks frantically around for a way out of the melee.

"This is a memorial, you know," I yell above the sound of screaming. "Have a bit of respect, would you?"

My words, however, fall on deaf ears. Everything is forgotten in the rush to get close to Jett Carter, and my indignation quickly turns to fear as I see hands reaching out to him, pulling at his jacket, while lipsticked mouths smile hysterically into phone cameras.

There might not be three witches standing waiting for us on the road to Heather Bay, but we've certainly found our toil and trouble. And I can't help feeling like it's all my fault.

"Hey, let him go! Leave him alone!"

The crowd of women has completely forgotten about me now, but as I try to push my way through them, Jett's eyes find me and his hand reaches out towards me.

"Are you okay?" he mouths, still reaching for me. "Lexie, are you okay?"

That's all it takes.

"Get off him," I yell, finally finding my voice and grabbing the woman closest to me by the back of the jacket. "Leave him alone, all of you!"

Or I will fight every last one of you. All 5'4" of me.

Anger briefly gives me strength, and I somehow manage to pull the woman to one side, before plowing determinedly forward to tackle the next one — who spins around in fright, whacking me hard on the side of the face with her elbow in the process.

"Ow!" Stars explode in my peripheral vision, and the horizon lurches awkwardly in front of me before settling back into place.

"Whoops!" the woman giggles, not sounding remotely sorry. "Didn't see you there."

Then she turns back towards Jett and I lean forward, putting my hands on my knees to steady myself as my cheek throbs in pain.

"Hey!" Jett roars, his voice cutting across the babble. "That's enough. Let me through."

I glance up just in time to see him push his way towards me, his hands held in front of his face to protect it — whether from the women, or from their cameras, I'm not sure.

"Lexie, are you okay? Here, let me look at you," he says as he takes my chin in his hand to angle it up towards him.

"Hmmm, that's going to be one hell of a black eye," he says, ignoring the cameras which have started to click around us again, and speaking as if we're the only two people on this hill. "Come on. Let's get you back to the car."

He puts an arm around my shoulder and turns me around, steering me firmly towards the car, whose driver looks up from his phone as we approach.

"Sorry, Mr. Carter," he says sheepishly, jumping out to hold the door for us. "I didn't expect you back so soon."

"It's fine," Jett mutters through gritted teeth. "Let's just get out of here."

In the middle of the crowd, he was as steady and as brave as any other Hollywood hero coming to the rescue of his girl. As soon as the door closes behind him, though, he collapses back on the seat, looking pale.

He hates this. He really, really hates it.

I watch him silently as the car pulls out of its parking spot and back onto the road north. Jett's eyes are closed now, as if to avoid the conversation he knows is coming.

I don't know why I didn't realize before, back in L.A., but although Jett might put on a convincing act, I'm starting to be able to see through it. Or I think I am. The beard, the baseball hat, the agitation outside the event we went to together, and the way he talked about hiding in plain sight...

His life scares him. All of this terrifies him.

I guess it's not surprising, really. It scares me, too. But I'm the lucky one here. I can walk away whenever I feel like it. He's kind of stuck with it. It's not like you can un-famous yourself, after all. Even if he never made another movie — or, well, dated another model — he'd still be Jett Carter. He'd still be the famous son of an equally famous father, and he still wouldn't be able to spend two minutes looking at the view without a crowd of witches appearing to ruin it for him.

"Sorry," I whisper, reaching out and touching the hand that lies next to mine on the leather car seat. "I'm really sorry."

Jett's eyes snap open, and when he turns them on me, I'm relieved to see there's no trace of fear in them any more. He's back to being himself. Whoever that is.

"What are you sorry for, Lady M?" he asks mildly. He doesn't move his hand away from mine, though, I notice, and I close my fingers around it softly.

"Sorry about all of that," I say, nodding back in the direction of the monument that's now disappeared from view. "I wouldn't have stopped there if I'd know that bus was going to pull up right after us. It wasn't exactly the welcome to Scotland I'd have wanted for you. It was a bit of a mess, actually."

"It was a bit of a mess," Jett agrees, his eyes still fixed on my face. "You're the one who got hurt, though," he adds, pulling his hand out from under mine, then raising it to gently touch the redness under my eye, which I can tell has already started to swell. "So I'm the one who should be saying sorry."

His hand is soft against my skin. It feels nice. And I know I shouldn't, but it feels *so* nice that I allow myself to rest my cheek against his palm for just a second, letting the warmth of his touch seep through me.

"That was quite some fight you put up back there," he says, pulling away and leaving me bereft. "I thought you were going to take on all of those women single-handedly."

"I think I was," I admit, closing my eyes as I remember

the indignation that took over when I saw the way they were clawing at him. As if they owned him. As if he wasn't even a real person, just some kind of *thing* for them to touch.

As if he wasn't mine.

But, of course, he's *not* mine, is he?

Not really. So I clear my throat and try to bring myself back to reality.

"I honestly don't know *what* I was thinking," I tell him. "It just... it just really pissed me off, the way they were acting. It was kind of scary, really."

I glance up, wondering if he'll take that as his cue to tell me how he really felt about it. Instead, he just looks out of the window for a while before answering.

"Yeah, it's a trip all right," he says mildly. "Welcome to my world."

"Thanks. And thanks for rescuing me," I tell him. "I thought you were going to take them all on, too."

We grin at each other, almost shyly. It's a moment that feels one hundred percent real. It's almost worth getting elbowed in the face for. *Almost.*

"Heather Bay, 5 miles," Jett says, breaking the silence that's fallen on us both as he reads the road sign that's just flashed past. "Also, 'Bàgh Fraoich', whatever that means."

His attempt at the Gaelic is so terrible I start to laugh, but it only takes a few minutes for the nerves to take hold again, and suddenly I'm feeling sick to my stomach again.

Five miles to Heather Bay.

Five miles until home.

Five miles until *Mum* — and all the other people I thought I'd never have to face again.

"Quick. What's my middle name?" I say, desperately,

turning to Jett as the panic threatens to engulf me.

The lines beside his eyes deepen with amusement.

"Did that woman hit you harder than I realized, Lady M?" he asks. "Do we need to get you a doctor?"

"It's not funny," I insist. "Come on, Jett, we're nearly there. We have to rehearse. People are going to expect us to know each other. To *really* know each other, I mean."

"I hardly think people are going to be stopping me in the street to ask me your middle name, or when your birthday is, Lexie," he says, still looking amused.

"What *is* my birthday?" I fire back. "You should probably know that, shouldn't you? I know yours is June 15th, which makes you a Gemini. Or is it Taurus? But I can't remember—"

"Alexandra Louise Steele," he says, sounding very much like a man who's good-naturedly humoring an idiot. "Born April 12th. Year never to be mentioned. 5'4", unless you're wearing heels, which you almost always do, because you're self-conscious about your height, even though you don't need to be. You dye your hair a brighter shade of blonde than it is naturally, because you've got it into your head that it's not good enough the way it is. You don't have any brothers or sisters, but you do have a second-cousin called Alfie, who you think is 'all right'. You're terrified of crabs, but really like horses. You've read all the classics, but you have a soft spot for mystery novels. You do yoga every day and never eat sugar. You bite your nails when you're nervous, which is often."

He pauses to look pointedly at my fingers, which are currently hovering near my mouth. I snatch them away hurriedly, then sit on them for good measure.

"You like to act tough," Jett goes on, "But you're not really. You want people to like you, but you pretend you don't care, so you don't get hurt. You don't have a favorite color, and you think that's a stupid question, anyway. Is that enough, do you think, or should I go on?"

I stare at him, surprised into silence. I've only told him about half of that stuff. The rest he's just noticed for himself, and I have no idea what to say to it; mostly because I had no idea he was observing me that closely.

Is that another actor trick, I wonder? Study people so you can imitate them later? Or was he listening because he cares*?*

"It *is* a stupid question," I say at last. "Who has a favorite *color*? Why would you even waste time thinking about something like that? It's just so... *banal.* Knowing someone's favorite color doesn't tell you anything about them at all. It's just—"

"Blue," Jett says, interrupting me.

"What?" I blink up at him, confused.

"My favorite color is blue. And I'm a Gemini: not that I believe any of that shit, obviously."

"No, me neither. I don't know why I even mentioned it. Just trying to be prepared, I guess."

Silence falls as the car winds its way through the glen that takes us to Heather Bay, on the coast. In a few minutes, we'll be able to see the top of Westward Tor, peeking up from its position next to the Loch, and then we'll turn a corner and the town will be laid out before us. I know this road so well I could navigate it in my sleep. But this is the first time I've driven down it as an outsider, and the closer we get, the harder it becomes to concentrate on anything other than the butterflies that appear to be fighting their way out of my stomach.

"There is one thing I wanted to ask you," Jett says, breaking into my reverie. "Something I just realized I don't know, and

I probably should."

"Yeah? If it's about my favorite book or movie or song, then I don't have those either," I say, still concentrating on those butterflies. "I can never understand how other people *do*. If someone tells me they have a favorite book, I'm instantly suspicious of them, actually. I mean, how weird is that? Imagine being able to pick just *one* book, out of all the books in the world? That's crazy to me. Isn't that crazy?"

I'm babbling now, and I know it. And Jett obviously knows it too, because he ignores everything I just said, and fixes me with those eyes of his.

"Your father," he says simply. "What about him? You've told me a lot — well, a *bit*, I guess — about your mom, but nothing about your dad. I should probably know a bit about him too, don't you think?"

There's a loud whooshing noise, and it takes me a few seconds to work out that it's the blood rushing in my ears. I close my eyes and take a deep breath, trying to steady my stomach before I answer him.

"If you knew that, you'd know more than me," I say, opening them again. We're over the crest of the hill now. I can see the waters of Loch Keld glittering in the weak sunlight. I want to tell Jett to look at it too, but he's still looking intently at me, his brow furrowed with concern.

"Really?" he says quietly. "You don't know anything about your dad? Nothing at all?"

"Just that he was a loser who walked out on us before I was even born," I say lightly, twisting my hands nervously in my lap. "Oh, and he drove a convertible. An MGB GT. I still have it, actually. That's all I have, though. Mum refused to tell me anything else about him. I'm not sure she knew much herself, to be honest. So, hey, on the plus side, that's one less person you have to learn about."

I laugh without humor. Jett must be wondering what the hell he's gotten himself into here. The more I tell him about myself, the less I seem to know; and the more messed-up it makes me feel. He didn't sign up for any of this. All he wanted was someone pretty to hang off his arm for a few weeks before he gets the part he's after. Instead, he's got the mess that is me.

He looks at me like I'm a puzzle he has to solve. Before he can speak, though, the window separating us from the driver slides down.

"We're here, Mr. Carter," the man in front says. "Where would you like me to take you?"

I look out of the window. The car is traveling slowly down Heather Bay High Street, with its row of pastel-colored shops. As we stop at the lights, I recognize Bella McGowan coming out of the post office, wearing a pair of purple Doc Martens and a bright red beanie, even though it's summer. She climbs onto a rickety old bicycle that's leaning against the wall — she's pretty agile for someone in their 80s, I have to admit — then pulls out into the road, glancing curiously at our car as she passes it.

I instinctively duck down, not trusting the tinted windows to keep me hidden from anyone else who happens to walk past.

I am really not ready for this.

I am not ready to be home, or to face these people.

There is, however, nothing to be done about it, so I straighten up again with a sigh, and point straight ahead, through the front widow of the car.

"That way," I tell the driver. "My house is that way."

Chapter 26

The cottage looks exactly as it did when I left it, sitting pink and pretty in its spot on the promontory, staring out to sea as it's been doing for the last 100 years or so.

Sure, the roses in the garden and around the door are a little more unruly than usual, but it's otherwise the same, and it's so strange to think of it, sitting here waiting for me all this time, that my eyes are suddenly suspiciously damp.

Hi house. I've missed you.

"Well, this is it," I say, as Jett gets out of the car behind me and stops to look around him, stretching after the long journey.

I push open the gate and am just about to usher him through it when a familiar figure rounds the corner and makes its way towards us. Well, two figures, rather. Old Jimmy, the farmer, and Edna. His pet sheep. Who has a bright pink leash attached to a collar around her neck, and who's walking along beside Jimmy as if she's a very woolly dog.

"What's that sheep doing in the street?" Jett blurts out, staring at the twosome in astonishment.

"Well, she got banned fae the bus, didn't she?" Jimmy replies, looking annoyed. "How d'ye expect her to get fae place to place, if no' on the street?"

He sniffs loudly, then marches past us both, Edna trotting obediently behind him. The entire interaction took less than thirty seconds from start to finish, but now that we've been spotted, I know the news of my return will be all over the village in less than half that time.

Let's just hope Jimmy isn't well-versed enough in pop culture to have recognized the man with me as Jett Carter.

"I liked ye in yon cowboy movie," Jimmy shouts back at us over his shoulder. "I didnae like the yin wi' the spaceships, though. Nae offense."

Well, that's one hope dashed, then. Fabulous.

"Shall we?" I gesture awkwardly towards the open gate as the driver wheels our suitcases towards it. "It might be a good idea to get inside as quickly as we can."

Jett nods, his eyes still following Jimmy and Edna down the street. I'm pretty sure he didn't understand a word Jimmy said. I just don't know if that's a good thing or a bad thing.

"This is nice," he says, following me into the house, which smells heart-wrenchingly familiar in that way houses have of reverting to their natural selves when they're left empty. You don't really notice it when you're living there, but every house has its own distinct scent that's only really obvious to strangers — or to you, when you've been away for a while — and as I walk into the hallway, I realize my house smells like my grandmother's perfume mixed with the faint tang of furniture polish.

I've really missed it.

"Where d'you want me to put this stuff?" Jett asks, interrupting my thoughts.

He's still standing in the hallway beside his bags, looking

absurdly large and somehow very, very American in the Scottish-sized space he's found himself in.

This has to be the most surreal experience of my life. Having Jett Carter — Jett freaking Carter — standing in the chintzy surroundings of the tiny cottage I inherited from my grandmother, and haven't updated much since she died, is like one of those strange dreams where you're in a place you've known your whole life, but in which everything looks different. If Past Lexie had known she'd one day stand in this hallway and watch her biggest ever celebrity crush wander into the living room and look curiously at the photos on the mantelpiece, she'd probably have died of excitement on the spot.

All Current Lexie can do, however, is point awkwardly to the stairs, wondering if the spare bed is made up, and what kind of state she left in the bathroom in.

As far as Past Lexie would be concerned, Current Lexie would probably be a bit of a disappointment. Current Lexie, however, has very different problems from the ones Past Lexie might have imagined, and, right now, all Current Lexie can think about is how the news of her return is going to go down once Jimmy McEwan puts the word out — and what her mother's going to say when she finally comes face-to-face with her again after her 12 months in exile.

Oh, and also how soon might be too soon to get some sleep; because, wow, am I tired, all of a sudden.

"The bedrooms are upstairs," I tell Jett, wondering how I should break it to him that the two attic bedrooms and tiny bathroom are literally *all* that's upstairs. He's already seen both the kitchen and living room, which make up the downstairs of the cottage, and, given the kind of accommodation he's used to, I have a feeling this place isn't going to quite meet his expectations.

He makes no comment, however, as he picks up his bags and carries them up to the spare bedroom, before returning for mine, like a true gentleman.

Jett places my bags on the floor next to the bed, then we stand there uncertainly, neither one of us knowing quite what to do next.

"Do you want to go to bed?" he asks abruptly.

Okay, that's *a plot twist I wasn't expecting here.*

"Wh-what?"

I blink up at him, completely lost for words for once in my life.

"To, um, sleep, I mean," Jett clarifies, as he realizes what I'm thinking. "In, you know, our separate rooms. I'm exhausted after that flight, aren't you?"

"Yes! Yes I am! I'm so, so tired! Yes, let's go to... sleep! Let's do that!"

I stride quickly across the room and close the curtains in a bid to hide my face, which is scarlet with embarrassment.

It was completely obvious that he wasn't asking me to go to bed with him. *Why on* earth *did I think he was?*

Turning back around, I walk straight into Jett as I attempt to cross the room again, then we do an awkward little dance as we try to pass each other in the cramped space. I always knew the cottage was small, but you don't realize just *how* small a space is until you try to share it with a Hollywood megastar you've just humiliated yourself in front of, do you?

"Well, good night, then," I chirp brightly as Jett leaves the room, closing the door tactfully — and firmly, I can't help but notice — behind him. I think it's technically still morning, actually, judging by the way the light is falling against the closed curtains, but as I throw myself face-first onto the bed, I realize I wasn't lying when I told Jett I was tired.

All this jet-setting really takes it out of a girl. Or maybe it's just the anxiety.

I can't be bothered taking my makeup off or getting into my PJs, so, instead, I just wriggle out of my jeans without leaving the bed, and kick them onto the floor. Then I sigh deeply and get up to put them in the wardrobe, knowing I'll never be able to get to sleep with them lying there. I know Emerald Taylor, who used to clean this house for me, has probably told everyone I'm a slob, but that's just because she got me at a bad time. And also because I deliberately left the place in a mess when she came round to clean it.

I should probably apologize to Emerald for making her job harder last year.

I should probably apologize to Emerald for a lot of things, really.

With that thought in my head, I climb wearily back into bed in just my t-shirt and underwear, and pull the covers over my head. I fall asleep within minutes, and, when I sleep, I dream that Emerald turns up at the house with Jakob, and the two of them go through my wardrobe, only to find Jett hiding in the back. When I wake up, I think the insistent banging I can hear is coming from the wardrobe, then I realize it's the front door, and jump out of bed, running my fingers frantically through my hair as I rush downstairs to open it.

"Hi Lexie. Great outfit. Love that on you."

Scarlett Scott is standing on my doorstep, her lips painted as red as her name, and her dark hair framing her pale face, and making her look like Snow White. Actually, though, Scarlett is more like the Wicked Witch, and that article she wrote about me in the *Gazette* proves it.

"How are you, Lexie?," she says, smiling as if we're a couple of old friends who've just happened to bump into each other on the street, as opposed to the sworn enemies we really are. Or that *I* am to her, anyway. To be fair, Scarlett probably doesn't know how much I hate her. She barely even knows me at all, really. She'd only just arrived in town when everything went down last summer, and Emerald was the one who tried to steal her identity — well, sort of — not me. So unless she's decided to take Emerald's side on the whole "burning down the town hall" thing, she doesn't have a dog in this fight.

"So," she says, smiling sweetly at me. "Set anyone's dress on fire recently, by any chance, or have you been too busy for that?"

I guess it's fair to say that Scarlett took Emerald's side, then.

"I'm great, thanks," I say, returning her fake smile. "And how about you, Scarlett? Taken up fiction writing, I see? Good for you, it must be nice to have a little hobby now that you're not working for a real magazine any more. Heather Bay must be a real disappointment compared to London, though."

Before she moved here, Scarlett was a food and drinks writer. It's how I met her, actually. She was sent up here to write some articles about whisky, and Mum persuaded me to try to "woo her", as she put it. To convince her to write about the distillery, as part of a big PR drive she was relying on me to pull off.

Unfortunately for Mum, though, the only articles Scarlett ever wrote about our family distillery ended up being about Mum herself, and how she'd tried to sabotage our closest rivals in order to steal their business. And she wrote those for the Heather Bay Gazette, not the London-based magazine she used to work for, and which might have had slightly less impact on us.

I was long gone by then, though. I only know all of this because I follow Scarlett on Instagram, and she's always banging on about how much happier she is, having moved to the Highlands and started working for the Gazette. "Slow living," she calls it. There's absolutely nothing slow, however, about the speed with which she's turned up on my doorstep this morning; or the way she's looking over my shoulder and down the hall, her eyes scanning ruthlessly for any sign of Jett.

Well, she can forget that.

"Anyway," I say breezily when she completely ignores my comment. "This has been lovely, Scarlett, but I've got things to do, so if you don't mind—"

I slam the door in her face before I can finish my sentence, allowing myself a smirk of satisfaction at her surprised look as the door closes.

"Lexie? I just have a few questions?"

The letterbox flaps open, and Scarlett's face appears behind it, as she yells at me through the gap.

"I wanted to know if you're planning on seeing your poor mother while you're here?" she shouts. "Is that *why* you're here? And is it true that Jett Carter is with you? Because I have two eyewitnesses willing to go on record as having seen him, and—"

"Edna doesn't count as an eyewitness, Scarlett," I yell back at her through the open letterbox, "And my mum isn't 'poor'. She's making it up and you know it. I can't believe you're encouraging her. It's so manipulative. Now, if you'll excuse me, I just really want to get back to bed."

"With Jett?" Scarlett asks eagerly. "Is he really here, then?"

"Get off my property, Scarlett," I snap, losing what little patience I have for this conversation. "Or I'll call the police. I mean it. I have my phone in my hand. I'm dialing now. Look."

I hold my phone up to the gap in the door, so she can see I mean business here.

"Lexie, it's Wednesday," Scarlett says patiently. "Young Dougie has a half day on a Wednesday. You know that."

Shit. I forgot about the stupid half-day-on-a-Wednesday thing. And also that it was Wednesday. Jet-lag really is a bitch, isn't it? And so is Scarlett Scott, for that matter.

"It's still morning," though, I counter, turning the phone round to look at the time on the display. "It's... it's 4:30pm. Wow, I must have been in bed all day."

I shake the offending phone, as if that'll somehow turn back time.

It's not morning. It's not even a different day. It's still the day we arrived in Heather Bay; which means Scarlett must have been even quicker off the mark than I realized.

Scarlett tilts her head to one side sympathetically as she peers through the letterbox again.

"Oh, poor thing," she says, thoroughly enjoying herself. "Look at you, not even knowing what day it is. Why don't I come in and make you a nice cup of coffee, then the two of us can sit down and have a good old chinwag? What do you say?"

"I say you must be insane if you think I'm going to talk to you after what you wrote about me, Scarlett," I hiss back at her, incensed. "You work for the Heather Bay Gazette, Scarlett, not TMZ. Everyone must think you're totally delusional, running around like you're Lois Lane or something."

"Oh no, everyone's much too busy talking about you to worry their heads about me, Lexie," Scarlett laughs, unperturbed. "And the Gazette's being getting a lot of attention lately. Everyone wants to know about the place Jett Carter's new girlfriend came from. And wow, do I have a lot to tell them!"

Okay, that's it.

"Get the hell off my land, Scarlett," I shout, sounding a lot like Old Jimmy McEwan the farmer as I wrench open the door and run at her. Scarlett blinks once in surprise, then, without missing a beat, she gives a smile of satisfaction as she raises her phone and starts clicking away merrily.

"Lexie? What's going on?"

I turn to see Jett standing in the open doorway of the house, rubbing his eyes blearily. Like me, he obviously didn't bother getting fully undressed before he fell asleep, which, in his case, means he's wearing the same pair of sweatpants he wore to travel in, and... nothing else. Just his bare chest. His very toned, muscular bare chest... which I barely even register, because that's the moment I remember *I'm* still in my t-shirt and knickers — and with a bad case of bedhead, for good measure.

We look like we've both just tumbled out of bed — which we have done — having been interrupted in the throes of passion; which we most definitely *haven't.*

Naturally, then, that's the angle Scarlett decides to run with when the photos she's taken appear on the Gazette's website, just over an hour later.

She's a fast worker, I'll give her that.

And now there's absolutely no doubt that everyone knows I'm back.

Chapter 27

Hollywood Star Flees to Highland Love Nest
Exclusive by Showbiz Reporter Scarlett Scott

"We've been in bed all day," purred a disheveled looking Lexie Steele, who returned to Heather Bay early on Wednesday morning, along with her new beau, Hollywood icon Jett Carter.

Sexy Lexie, as she's been dubbed by the press, refused to answer questions about the reason for her visit, saying she was eager to get back to her famous lover. The Heather Bay native, however, had some choice words about the town, which she said was "a disappointment", and about her ailing mother, Samantha, who Lexie (35) described as "manipulative".

There was no comment from 'Ace of Spades' star Jett Carter, who sources claim is in Scotland purely to support his girlfriend, who he's allegedly devoted to.

"I saw the pair o' them going into yon Lexie's cottage," local farmer Jimmy McEwan told the Gazette. "Right lovey-dovey they were. Carter was fair taken with my sheep, Edna."

* * *

"I swear to God, I will fucking kill her."

It's the next morning. Jett and I are sitting at the kitchen table, drinking coffee with the curtains closed, to protect us from the lenses of the assembled paparazzi, who apparently descended on Heather Bay overnight. The Travelodge just outside the village must be doing a roaring trade thanks to us.

"She's added another two years to my age," I go on furiously. "And I see her job title's been upgraded from 'celebrity correspondent' to 'showbiz reporter'. I mean, the Gazette only has two members of staff, and one of them's Scarlett's cousin. Who does she think's being taken in by this rubbish?"

"Pretty much everybody, by the looks of things," says Jett without looking up from his phone, which he's been staring at for the past twenty minutes now. "Those pictures she took of us are everywhere. Asher's going nuts. And Jakob wants you to call him urgently. Something about your underwear not being 'on brand', if that means anything to you?"

I flush, remembering my non-existent outfit of yesterday morning, and how careful Jett had been to keep his eyes firmly above my neck when we'd made it back into the house after our encounter with Scarlett. Not that it mattered, given that the photos were all over the internet an hour later, mind you.

I swallow noisily. I've done a lot of stupid things in my life, but, until now, I've at least had the luxury of doing all of them — well, most of them — in private. Now that I'm with Jett, though, everything I do is immediately placed under the magnifying glass of the world's media. And we all know what happens when the sun hits a magnifying glass.

"What's this woman's deal, anyway?" Jett asks, finally putting down his phone. "Why does she hate you so much?"

I shrug.

"She's just a terrible journalist," I tell him, refusing to meet his eyes. "She wasn't good enough for the magazine she used to write for, and she only got the job at The Gazette because her cousin's the editor. She obviously doesn't know what she's doing."

"Obviously," Jett agrees. "But I have a feeling there's a bit more to it than that, somehow. Like it's something more personal than just her doing her job badly. So come on, Lady M: spill."

I take a long sip of my coffee, trying to buy myself some time.

"It's not just Scarlett," I say at last, staring into my drink. "There's... well, there's quite a lot of people here who don't like me much. I'm not exactly Miss Popularity, let's put it that way."

"Uh-uh. And why's that?"

"Dunno."

I shrug, lifting the mug to my lips. I know I sound childish, but I don't know what else to say, really. How do I condense everything that happened last year — not to mention what I did to Emerald when we were younger — into something Jett could understand? How do I spin me dropping my cigarette onto Emerald's dress, and it burning the town hall down as a result, into the kind of 'accident' he might have some small amount of sympathy for, and not the moment of sheer, self-destructive madness it actually was?

How do I convince him I'm a good person deep down, in other words, when I know perfectly well I'm not?

Jett stares at me for a long moment, then gets up and pours himself another cup of coffee, ducking his head instinctively to avoid the low beams on the kitchen ceiling.

"Look, you don't have to tell me if you don't want to," he says, without turning round. "But I'm going to have to tell Asher something. Because he's not happy. He's saying if you knew this journalist had some kind of vendetta against you, you should have told us straight-up, before signing the contract. He has a point, you know."

"I *didn't* know she had a vendetta against me," I protest indignantly. "I didn't even know the Gazette would be interested in publishing the kind of rubbish she's been writing. When I lived here, it was all stories about cats stuck up trees and what time the community council would be meeting. They've obviously decided to branch out a bit since Scarlett started writing for them. That's not my fault, though. She's probably just hoping to make a name for herself, so she can get a job on one of the tabloids or something. And you have to admit, you being here is the biggest thing to happen in Heather Bay since—"

Since I burned down the village hall and let Emerald take the blame for it.

I can't tell Jett that, though, can I?

I allow my sentence to trail off. Even if I was prepared to be honest with Jett, there's no point. He doesn't actually care what kind of history Scarlett and I have, or why she might think it's fair game to totally ruin me in the pages of the Heather Bay Gazette. All he cares about is his own reputation, and what Asher's going to say when he sees the latest coverage. All Asher cares about is the money Jett will make for him if he gets this role. And as for me, well, no one really cares much about me at all, do they?

I cough loudly to hide the sob that rises up in my throat.

"You want a coffee?" Jett asks, oblivious to my distress.

"I'm making another pot."

"Another one? You must be really jetlagged."

"It's not jetlag," he says irritably. "I didn't sleep well."

"Was it the bed?" I ask, worried. "I know it must seem tiny after what you're used to. What you're probably used to, I mean. I obviously haven't seen your bed. Not that I *should* have, of course, I just mean—"

Jett silences me with a glance.

"It's not the bed," he says, taking another swig of his coffee. "I just don't sleep well. I never have."

"Okay," I reply, not knowing what else to say to that. "So, other than mainlining coffee, what's the plan for today? Pap walk? Photo call? I promise I'll make sure I'm more appropriately dressed this time, whatever it is."

"Hospital visit," says Jett, draining his mug and immediately refilling it. "We came here to see your mom, Lexie, and that's exactly what we're going to do."

* * *

The hospital mum's been taken to is in Inverness. We're driven there by the same driver who picked us up at the airport yesterday, and this time there's no conversation between me and Jett in the car. Not even a half-hearted chat about our favorite foods, or what animal we'd be if we had to choose one.

(Which is a shame, because that's one question I can actually answer. I'd be a unicorn. Partly because they're so beautiful that people can't help but love them, but mostly because they *don't actually exist*, and that would solve a lot of my problems right now.)

Instead of attempting to make awkward conversation, we sit in stony silence; Jett glued to his phone, me staring out of the window at the passing scenery, and hoping the thick layer of foundation I've applied will be enough to cover the black eye I woke up with this morning.

We had to push our way past the gaggle of photographers outside the house when we left, and when we pull up at the hospital — which is a huge, 1970s concrete affair, not the cute little country cottage I know Jett was expecting — there's another group already there waiting for us. I know this is part of the deal. Scarlett's latest article might have alerted them to our presence here a little earlier than expected, but the paps stationed outside the hospital were probably sent there after a tip-off from Asher or Grace, who'll be expecting me to play the role of the dutiful daughter rushing to her ailing mother's bedside, with her loving partner by her side. That, as Jett pointed out earlier this morning, is why we're here, after all.

Now that we *are* here, though, all I want to be is quite literally *anywhere else.*

"Ready?" Jett asks, looking at me for the first time since we stood together in the kitchen this morning.

I swallow nervously.

"Not really," I admit. "I'm feeling a bit sick, actually."

"Well, at least if you faint again, you're in the right place for it this time," Jett says grimly. He still isn't smiling, but at least he's talking to me again. I guess that's something.

"Look, Lexie," he says, as the driver appears to open the car door for him. "It'll be okay, yeah? I'll look after you. Just follow my lead."

Before I can reply to tell him it's not the world's media I'm worried about facing, it's my own mother, he opens the car door, and disappears into the light of a thousand flash bulbs. Okay, maybe just a dozen. It may as well be a thousand, though, because by the time the driver's appeared to open my door for me, they're all shouting and cat-calling at the same time, and I'm grateful for the protective arm Jett puts around me as he leads me past them, and through the main doors of the hospital, which the paps have obviously been refused entry to.

"There you go," he says, removing his arm as soon as we're out of reach of the lenses. "That was easy, wasn't it?"

"That wasn't the bit I was worried about," I mutter, looking around the reception, wondering where I'm supposed to go. I don't even know what ward Mum's in. Or what the visiting hours are. In all honesty, I've been so distracted by Scarlett — and, well, by *Jett* — that I haven't really thought much about Mum's illness at all. Which I know makes me sound like the worst daughter in the world — an assessment I'm sure Mum herself would agree with — but, in my defense, the nurse I spoke to about her on the phone was very clear that it wasn't anything serious.

"I wish I could tell you more, love," she'd said kindly last time I called. "But I'm not allowed. I've got to know your mum quite well, though, since she's been here —" She'd paused here, in a way that made me feel like she was trying to tell me something deeper than her actual words. "—and what I *can* tell you is that if I were you, I wouldn't be too worried. If you know what I mean."

I *did* know what she meant. Or, at least, I *thought* I did. I was sure she was telling me mum was at it again, manufacturing drama for the sake of getting attention. Now that I'm here, in the sterile surroundings of an actual *hospital*, though, I'm suddenly not so sure.

What if she really is ill?

What if she's dying?

What if she's been telling the truth for once in her life, and I've been blithely going about my business, assuming it was all another one of her lies?

What if I really am *the worst daughter in all the world?*

"Alexandra? Lexie?"

The voice that puts a cork in my downward spiral is the one I remember from that phone call, and I turn to see a pleasant-faced woman of about my own age (My *actual* age, I mean. Not the one Scarlett Scott keeps making up on the spot for me.) smiling in that tactful way some medical professionals have. The one that's supposed to be comforting, but which always makes me think they're about to tell me I have two weeks to live.

Did I mention I don't really like hospitals much?

"I thought that must be you," the nurse says, glancing at Jett, before turning her attention back to me. "I recognized you from your photos. The ones your mum keeps beside her bed," she quickly adds, seeing the look of horror on my face. "I'm Mary McNamee. It's nice to meet you, lovely."

I smile back, instantly liking her. Unlike the hospital receptionist, who's gawking at us unapologetically from behind her desk, or the man who was so busy staring that he ended up going through the revolving doors three times, Mary McNamee doesn't seem remotely phased by Jett, and, as she shows us up to the ward, she continues to address all of her comments about Mum to me.

I think this is the first time someone's treated me as a person in my own right since this whole charade started.

The hospital is warren-like inside, and the long corridors and artificial lights do little to quell my nerves. Despite the size of the place, it's almost eerily empty, and I find myself wishing I'd worn something other than the heeled boots, which I chose to make myself look taller next to Jett, but which click a noisy tattoo on the scarred linoleum floor, almost as if they're announcing our arrival.

"We put your mum in a private room, because she was getting quite a bit of attention," the nurse tells me, stopping at last outside one of the many doors in the seemingly endless corridor we're marching down. "I don't think she was very pleased to be on her own, to be honest, but oh well."

She gives me a quick wink, and I decide my first impression was right: I like this woman. And she definitely has the measure of mum all right.

"Visiting hours don't start for another hour," Mary says, pushing the door open, "But we thought it was probably best to make an exception, under the circumstances, so you can have some privacy. And here she is!"

She says the last words as she steps into the room, speaking brightly, the way people do to very elderly people.

Mum will hate that.

"You've got some visitors, Samantha," she says, addressing the figure in the bed, who's still hidden by the door of the room. "I'll leave to have a chat with them."

"Good luck," she whispers to me, putting her hand briefly on my arm as she reappears. "I'll be just down the hall if you need anything."

I hesitate outside the room, my legs too heavy to move. Then Jett gives me a gentle push from behind.

"You got this, Lady M," he says, so softly only I can hear him. "Go get 'em."

And so I go.

And there she is.

Mum is sitting up in bed, her blonde hair piled on top of her head, and with a full-face of makeup, complete with an extravagant set of false eyelashes, one of which is slightly crooked. She's wearing a silk dressing down with marabou-trimmed sleeves, and I can tell instantly that she's pretending to be Joan Collins in an episode of *Dynasty.*

She looks absolutely fine. Borderline Barbara Cartland, sure, but health-wise, *fine.*

I feel some of the tension leave my shoulders. She *is* fine. Surely she's fine? Which means I'm maybe *not* the worst daughter in the world after all.

"Lexie, darling."

Mum reaches out a hand to me. Her fingernails are painted bright red, and she's speaking in a weird, cut-glass accent I've never heard her use in my life.

She's definitely been watching Dynasty on her phone while she's been stuck in hospital.

Not knowing what else to do, I shuffle forward obediently and take the hand that's offered to me, before bending down to kiss her on the cheek, and landing on the pillow behind her instead when Mum ducks quickly out of the way, presumably to protect her carefully applied makeup.

No problems with the old reflexes, then.

My jaw tightens with tension as I step back, watching as Mum turns her Bambi-lashed eyes on Jett, who seems to shrink backwards under her gaze.

"And this must be Jett," she says simperingly. "How I've

longed to meet you, my beautiful boy."

Beautiful boy? 'Longed to meet you'? I stifle a giggle. She's really gone all-in with this act she's putting on for us. I wonder if she's been practicing?

"Come and give your future mother-in-law a kiss," she says, holding out her arms to Jett.

"Mum!" I hiss, horrified. "He's not your future son-in-law! We're not even—"

Jett glares at me silently, then steps forward to kiss Mum on the cheek (She doesn't flinch away from *him*, I notice...).

"It's lovely to meet you at last, Mrs. Steele," he says, his voice oozing sincerity. "Or may I call you Samantha?"

"You can call me Sam," Mum simpers, batting her false eyelashes at him. "All of my closest friends do."

I snort. Unless things have changed dramatically since I left the Bay, Mum doesn't *have* any close friends. She's even less popular than I am.

"Mum tried to get me to call her Sam too, once," I tell Jett. "So people wouldn't realize she was old enough to be my mum."

The two of them turn identical 'annoyed' looks on me.

Play nice, says Jett's. *Or you'll mess this whole thing up again.*

Why must you always disappoint me? says Mum's.

Suitably crushed, I allow myself to drop down into the single chair in the room. Jett's sitting on the edge of the bed now, Mum's hands held in both of his as he chats as easily to her as if he's known her forever.

He's charming her the way he charmed me. The way he charms everyone. Only I seem to realize the charm isn't real. He's just acting, like he always is. Mum is, too. The only genuine thing in this room, in fact, is my growing sense of outrage at the fact that I've traveled all this way, and gone through so much anxiety over it, just for the sake of two people who wouldn't even notice if I got up and left the room.

For a split second, I consider doing exactly that. Then I decide on a different path.

"So, what's wrong with you, then?" I ask bluntly, breaking into Jett's story about all the things "we" will do with Mum when she comes to visit "us" in California.

Fake, fake, fake.

"Excuse me?"

Mum raises her eyebrows as far as she's able to after all the Botox she's had over the years, and looks at me as if I've broken some important rule of etiquette.

"Why are you here?" I clarify. "In the hospital. Telling journalists — well, Scarlett — you're at death's door and you want to see me one last time. Remember that?"

"Lexie—" Jett starts warningly, but Mum simply waves her hand in a regal fashion, as if she's brushing the question aside.

"Oh, you know how it is, Alexandra," she says vaguely. "*Women's troubles.*"

"Women's troubles?" I frown. "What do you mean?"

Mum sighs, martyr-like, then looks pointedly down at her chest, which is hidden from view beneath the folds of her dressing gown.

The hospital temperature is sub-tropical, but my whole body goes cold.

Is she really ill after all?

"Is it... is it...?"

I can't quite bring myself to say the word. Beside the bed, Jett looks pale.

Please don't let it be what I think it is.

"Well, not all of us are happy to be as flat as... well, *you*, Alexandra," Mum says, looking pointedly at my chest. "So I decided to do something about it. But they got infected, so they brought me in here to give me antibiotics."

I feel like I'm having an out-of-body experience. I can almost *feel* the outrage on my own face.

"Are you... are you telling me you're in here for a *boob job*?" I ask incredulously. "Are you shitting me right now?"

"No, of *course* not, Alexandra," Mum snaps impatiently. "Don't be ridiculous. They don't *do* boob jobs on the NHS. I had to go private. But, like I said, the implants got infected, so—"

"That's it, I'm done here."

I stand up and march towards the door, not caring whether Jett decides to follow me. I need to get out of this room. I need to get away from my mother. I need to be on my own, so I can process this, and the very *last* thing I need is—

"Scarlett."

I throw open the door, only to find Heather Bay's answer to Perez Hilton standing on the other side, her hand raised as if she's about to knock, although it's equally possible that she's just been standing there with her ear pressed to the door. Behind her stands a man with a giant camera slung around his neck, and behind *him* is Mary McNamee, frantically mouthing the words "I'm sorry," at me.

"Oh, Lexie, there you are." Scarlett smiles like a woman who knows she's won as she brushes past me. "That's great. We can get photos of all of you together."

"Photos? What do you mean?"

Scarlett raises her hands and pantomimes the act of someone using a camera.

"Photos, Lexie," she explains kindly. "They're a digital likeness of someone. Or, in this case, three someones. Hi, I'm Scarlett," she exclaims, offering her hand to Jett, who shakes it much more eagerly than is really necessary given that this woman has just become my mortal enemy. "I've been chatting to your assistant, Grace? It's so nice to meet you. I'm a big fan."

"Oh, didn't he tell you?" she asks, her green eyes widening with faux-innocence as she turns back to me. "Seeing as the Gazette was the paper that broke the story of your Mum's condition, Jett's people thought it would be a good idea for us to be the ones to cover your big reunion. It'll be syndicated to all the nationals, of course, but we'll have the exclusive. I'm surprised they didn't tell you."

I'm not.

Jett's the only person who *could* have told me, and he's barely spoken to me all morning, so it's not really surprising to find out I'm the last one to know about his intention to involve my newest nemesis, Scarlett Scott, in his plans for the day. I look over at him, but he doesn't meet my eye. He's still all cozied up with Mum, and as Scarlett joins the pair of them, throwing her head back to laugh at something Jett says to her, I feel suddenly murderous towards all of them.

I wish I hadn't agreed to this. Not the whole 'fake-relationship' thing, not the trip back to Scotland, and certainly not this visit to the hospital.

I wish I hadn't met Jett Carter at all, in fact. And as the photographer Scarlett's brought with her raises his camera and starts organizing us all into a 'happy family' group shot, which Jett has to reluctantly pull himself away from his conversation with Scarlett to join, I have a suspicion the feeling is probably mutual.

Chapter 28

"We need to get some security. Is there someone you can talk to about that?"

We're back in the kitchen of my cottage, and it's the first time Jett's spoken to me since we left the hospital after our visit with Mum. It figures he would just be asking me to do something for him.

"Let me see," I say, pretending to scroll through the contacts on my phone. "Which of my other celebrity friends could I ask about that one? Oh wait, I don't actually *have* any other celebrity friends, silly me!"

I slap myself on the forehead and watch as Jett's eyebrows come together in a frown. He's been standing by the kitchen window for the past ten minutes, peering through the curtains while I sip coffee at the table, trying to avoid the impulse to read whatever the gossip sites are saying about us today.

What a weird situation to find myself in.

"You must know *someone* who could do it?" Jett persists. "Like, isn't there a cop or someone who'd be willing to do a bit of extra work on the side?"

I snigger at the thought of Young Dougie, Heather Bay's one and only policeman, doing any work *at all*, let alone "on the side", as Jett puts it.

"If he's young, surely he's got some friends who'd be interested?" Jett says when I tell him I don't think Dougie would be up for a spot of protection work.

"Oh, Dougie isn't young," I explain, relieved we're at least talking again. "He must be pretty close to retirement age, actually. He wouldn't be much use against a crowd of your crazy fans."

"Then why do you call him Young Dougie?"

"Because if we didn't, everyone would think we were talking about *Old* Dougie, his dad," I explain. "And that would just be confusing, wouldn't it?"

Jet nods, looking nonplussed.

"Anyway," he says, turning back to the window. "We're going to have to do something. This is getting ridiculous."

I stand up and go to join him at the window, which looks out across the sloping garden to the beach below. It's suspiciously crowded, especially considering it hasn't stopped raining all morning, and I have a funny feeling the reason for that is standing right next to me. We're sitting in this room rather than the living room because the living room looks out onto the street, which is still lined with paparazzi, plus a growing number of Jett Carter fans, who are standing outside my gate, clutching movie posters with Jett's face on them, which they're hoping he'll sign.

When we got back after our trip to the hospital, it took us a good 20 minutes to get past them, and one of them called me a "gold-digging bitch", so I guess I can see his point about the security, really. It would be nice to be able to leave the house without getting mobbed. Or, you know, *insulted*. Or to be able to go to sleep without worrying that one of the women outside will try to skin me and wear me, just so they can take my place.

From the way some of them are behaving, I wouldn't put it past them.

If only they knew the truth.

"I really didn't think it would be like this here," Jett mutters, starting to pace again. "I'd have brought Leroy at the very least if I'd known."

I don't really know what to say to that. It seems obvious to me that he's going to get mobbed wherever he goes, here included. I guess he's used to living in the type of houses that have huge gates at the front and grounds so large no one can get anywhere near you. That or he really *did* think everyone in the Highlands was going to be riding around on their horses and carts, too busy foraging for nuts and berries and fighting the English to worry about any random movie stars who might turn up. Because that's a possibility too, let's be honest.

"It's not like there's anywhere we need to go, anyway," I point out. "We've done what we came here to do. We've seen Mum, had the photos taken, done the interview. What is there to stay for?"

I watch him carefully as I wait for his answer. Now that the media have had their pound of flesh from us, I'm really hoping we can get out of Heather Bay and go back to L.A., so I can... I'll figure that out what I get there, I suppose. *If* I get there.

Jett, however, has other ideas.

"What do you mean?" he says, frowning again. "We still have tons of things to do here. I need to do some research for the movie, remember? So there's Glamis Castle for one thing." (He pronounces it as 'Glam-is' rather than "Glams." I don't bother to correct him. "Then there's a tree somewhere near here," he goes on, warming to his theme. "The Birnam Oak. It was around in Shakespeare's time, and Birnam wood is mentioned in Macbeth, so I'd like to go visit it. And I was hoping to see a haggis too, at some point."

"Birnam is nowhere near here," I point out, trying not to laugh at the 'haggis' comment. "It's not even in the Highlands. And I don't see how looking at a stupid tree is going to help you get a role in Macbeth, anyway."

"Macbeth shall never vanquished be, until Great Birnam wood to high Dunsinane hill Shall come against him," says Jett, in a fairly credible attempt at a Scottish accent. "Birnam Wood is still there, Lexie. Or some of it is, anyway. I want to see it. Steep myself in the history of the place. And anyway, I like trees. You don't like trees?"

"They're okay," I shrug. "I'm more of an indoor girl, to be honest."

"Well, that's a shame," Jett says, still squinting through the crack in the curtains. "I love being in nature. I get so claustrophobic being surrounded by people all the time."

He tugs at the neck of his sweatshirt as if he's trying to get more air, and I remember the moment at the Commando Monument when I realized how anxious he was in the crowd. He must be absolutely hating being trapped in this tiny cottage, with people on every side of it, and all of them wanting something from him.

"Fine," I say, picking up my phone. "Tell me where you want to go first, and I'll see what I can do about security. Bear in mind that Glamis and Birnam are quite a long drive from here, though. It might be best to leave those until tomorrow."

"No worries," says Jett. He thinks for a minute. "Hey, I know where we can go," he says, his eyes lighting up. "Remember that distillery I told you about? The 39, I think it's called? It's near here, isn't it? They do tours, apparently; I remember reading an article about it. And there's a restaurant by a lake. Let's go there."

I freeze in the act of opening up the contacts app on my phone.

The 39 is the distillery Mum tried to sabotage last year, when she realized it was probably going to put ours out of business. It's owned by Jack Buchanan, who just so happens to be dating Emerald Taylor. The same Emerald Taylor whose dress I set on fire moments before she was about to go on stage as Heather Bay's Gala Queen, over a decade ago. The same dress which Emerald pulled off in fright, and which went on to burn down the town hall. The town hall which... look, you get the picture, right?

Emerald spent the next ten years in London, thinking she was the one who'd been responsible for the fire, and that everybody hated her because of it. When she finally found out it was all my fault, she ran up Westward Tor in the dark and almost died. She's always been very dramatic, Emerald. Oh, and she hates me, of course. I mean, she must do, right? *I* hate me for everything I did — why wouldn't she?

And if I were to bump into her at The 39, I'm pretty sure all hell would break loose.

Naturally, then, that's exactly where Jett has set his sights on going.

"Look, here's that article I was telling you about," he says, holding out his phone, and showing me a photo of the restaurant at The 39 at sunset. "Pretty, isn't it?"

I take the phone and scroll quickly through the article. The byline is Scarlett Scott's, but I happen to know it was actually Emerald who wrote this. You can tell because there's no mention of "love nests" and everyone's ages are correct in it.

"Looks a bit dull, really," I tell Jett, handing back the phone.

"You're kidding?" he says incredulously. "Look at it. It's right next to a loch."

(He says "lotch". I let him.)

"And they serve haggis!" he goes on, looking delighted. "Oh, we're definitely going. Come on, Lexie, let's do it. You must want to get away from all of this, too?"

He gestures at the closed curtains, then looks at me with a sad expression and puppy dog eyes. He's completely irresistible, much to my disgust.

"Rock, Paper, Scissors?" he suggests, with a devilish grin.

I sigh in defeat.

"Okay, okay," I tell him. "Best of three?"

We play three games of Rock, Paper, Scissors. And even though I win every time, once we're done, I get up and fetch my bag.

"Come on, then," I say, rifling through it for my phone. "Looks like we're going to The 39."

Chapter 29

As it turns out, it's harder than you might think to find someone willing to be a bodyguard at short notice in the Highlands.

Which is why Jett and I are currently walking up the steps to The 39's lochside restaurant with Alfonso McTavish in front of us.

"Comin' through, folks. That's it, if ye could just a' get out of the way, that would be grand," McTavish says importantly, holding out his hand to block the view of a pair of startled looking pensioners who are exiting the restaurant as we arrive.

"And nae photos, please," McTavish warns them sternly, making the woman's eyes widen in fright. "I've got ma eyes on ye, ye ken."

"Are you sure this guy's a bodyguard?" Jett whispers suspiciously as the old couple scuttle apologetically past us.

"No, he's a farmer," I tell him. "Sorry. He was the only person I could find at the last minute. And he said he needed the cash."

The truth is that McTavish was the only person who actually answered my call, and he says he only did it because he'd deleted my number from his contacts, so he didn't realize it was me.

Oh yeah, he hates me too, just in case it wasn't obvious. He's one of Emerald's best friends: he was never going to be Team Lexie on the whole 'Town Hall' issue, was he? But it's true that he did need the money, and once I'd doubled Jett's suggested fee, then added a bit more to it, he grudgingly agreed to help us out.

And now it seems he's decided to really throw himself into the role.

"Right," he says now, turning back to us both, and showing a set of implausibly white teeth, which I happen to know are the handiwork of Mike-the-dentist, McTavish having knocked out the originals during the fire at the town hall. "Here we are."

He pushes open the door at the top of the stair, and we follow him into the restaurant, my heart hammering wildly in my chest as we cross the room to a table by the window that's been reserved for us.

I was half expecting the place to fall silent as I entered the room; for the music to stop, and for the ensuing silence to be broken only by the cry of "witch" that would immediately be taken up by the entire crowd.

Actually, though, nothing happens.

The music keeps on playing. The world doesn't stop. And, other than a few curious glances, most of the other diners don't even look up from their meals as they pass us.

It's a bit of an anti-climax, really. If it wasn't such a relief to have made it all the way across the room without seeing Emerald, I'd probably be disappointed. As it is, though, I sink gratefully into the chair Jett holds out for me, and hide quickly behind the menu as he sits down opposite me. McTavish looks around and then, spotting a vacant table, goes over and grabs one of its chairs, which he holds triumphantly aloft as he carries it back to us like a trophy, before sitting down on it to join us.

"Right then," he says, rubbing his hands together gleefully. "What are we a' having?"

"Ummm—"

"Errrr—"

Jett and I exchange confused looks, as I frantically wrack my brain, trying to remember exactly what I said to McTavish on the phone earlier, and what part of it he's managed to translate as an invitation to join us for dinner.

He has, though. I open my mouth to object as he takes the menu out of my hands, then close it again, seeing Jett shrug in my direction.

Might as well go with it, his expression says, and I swallow down the disappointment that it's not going to be just the two of us.

It's not like it's a real date, after all. It's not like he cares that it's not exactly romantic having McTavish sitting between us, like some kind of old-fashioned chaperone. And anyway, I guess it could be worse. At least Emerald and Jack aren't here.

"Lexie?"

I look up from the fingernail I've been nibbling to see Emerald and Jack standing there, almost as if I've somehow managed to conjure them up just by thinking about them.

And now my hell is complete.

"Oh! Umm, hi!"

I sit there blinking up at them both, not knowing what to say.

"Good thanks, how are you?" stutters Emerald, who can always be relied upon to make an already awkward situation even worse. Her long red hair is slightly tangled, as usual, and her pale skin is bright red with embarrassment. Even so, she's still a solid 9, at least, as well as being so much taller than me that she instantly makes me feel like I'm at a disadvantage; which I suppose I am, really, given that I'm standing in her boyfriend's restaurant, and I have very good reason to believe I'm not welcome here.

Instead of instantly having me thrown out, though, Jack simply slips his hand into Emerald's and gives it a quick squeeze, as if to reassure her. His handsome face is set in a frown, but, then again, that's pretty typical for him too, so I try my best not to read too much into it.

"We saw your name on the booking," Jack says, when Emerald fails to follow up her awkward opening gambit with any further attempts at conversation. "We were.... surprised."

I bet they were. The last time they saw me, Emerald was exposing Mum as the person who'd tried to ruin Jack's business, and simultaneously realizing it was my fault she'd inadvertently burned down the town hall as a teenager. It was... well; it was quite a night for her, really.

"Umm, yeah, that was me," I reply unnecessarily. "I hope it's okay—"

I trail off uncomfortably, looking at Emerald, who stares back at me, looking like she's just seconds away from turning and running out of the room. Which she possibly is, knowing her.

I hope it's okay that I'm standing here in your boyfriend's distillery after my mother tried to sabotage it, is what I want to say. *I hope it's okay that I came back here after you found out I'm the reason you had to leave all those years ago. I hope you can forgive me for that, even though I know I don't deserve it.*

I don't actually *say* any of that, of course. I'm too much of a coward. I just *think* it. And plan to excuse myself as soon as I possibly can, and make a run for it while everyone thinks I'm in the bathroom or something.

"Hey, Jack Buchanan, right?" Jett interrupts, standing up and coming to my rescue. "I saw your photo in an article I read about this place," he goes on, coming round the table and offering Jack his hand. "Jett Carter. Really pleased to meet you. This place is amazing."

Jack shakes Jett's hand, looking slightly shell-shocked. Emerald looks like she's about to cry, although I'm not totally sure whether that's because of me or Jett, who does tend to have that effect on women, I've noticed. McTavish, meanwhile, has cheerfully worked his way through the contents of the bread basket on the table, and is looking around for someone to replace it for him.

Of all the ways I'd imagined my return to Heather Bay going down, this is not it.

"Would you like to join us?" Jett's asking them now, just in case this whole situation wasn't weird enough already. "I'd love to hear about the whisky you make here. I've heard it's quite something."

"Oh, it is, it is," Jack replies, recovering himself. "It has quite an interesting back story, too, actually—"

And, just like that, I find myself sitting next to Emerald Taylor, having dinner with her, Jack, McTavish and Jett Carter.

And here was I thinking things just couldn't get *any weirder right now.*

"How's your mum?" Emerald asks quietly, once we've all ordered our starters, and Jack's had a bottle of wine, plus one of his latest whiskys, sent to the table. "I saw the photos of the two of you online."

"Oh, right. The Gazette."

"Naw, Shona's started an Instagram," says McTavish, who's opted out of the conversation Jett and Jack are having about whisky in order to eavesdrop on me and Emerald instead. "And a TikTok. She gets everywhere, so she does. She's got 133 followers, although at least six o' them are Old Jimmy, we think. He couldnae figure out how it all worked, so he ended up wi' multiple accounts. It's good for Shona's 'engagement', though, apparently."

"What's he saying?" Jett interrupts, turning to me. "I don't understand what he's saying. Is he speaking Gaelic? Is that what this is?"

"I was just saying," McTavish shouts, having overheard this, "That Old Jimmy has six Instagram accounts. Although one o' them's Edna's, tae be fair."

Mctavish is going for the "loud and slow" method of speaking to foreigners, which basically means he's treating Jett like he's hard of hearing, rather than just American.

Well, would you look at that? Things did *manage to get weirder, after all.*

"And will Edna be joining us, too?" Jett asks politely. I'm guessing 'Edna' was the only word he actually understood in all that.

"Och, dinnae be daft, ye great galoot," chortles McTavish. "Edna's a vegetarian. This is a seafood restaurant."

I want to point out that Edna is also a sheep — the same sheep we saw outside my house, in fact — but Jett's looking confused enough already, and McTavish has already lost interest in the conversation, preferring to bicker with Jack instead over whether The 39 can accurately be described as a seafood restaurant when, as Jack points out, it serves a wide variety of dishes.

Welcome to Heather Bay, Jett.

"Your mum?" Emerald prompts gently, once the starters are delivered to the table and conversation resumes once more. "She was looking well, considering—?"

"She is well," I say, pushing my salad around the plate without enthusiasm. It's so like Emerald to ask me about Mum. Anyone else would be more interested in me and Jett and our supposed romance, but Emerald's always been a bit *intense*, for want of a better word, and right now her brow is furrowed with concern.

"You know what Mum's like," I tell her, giving up on the salad and putting my fork down in defeat. "She just does things for the attention. There's absolutely nothing wrong with her, Emerald. It was just her way of getting me to come back here."

I turn to face her, forcing myself to look her in the eyes at last. The table is far too small for all of us, and we're all so crammed together that I have to twist round in my seat to do it. When I'm finally facing her, we're so close I'm glad I chose the salad rather than the garlic mushrooms.

"And you didn't want to come back," Emerald says, nodding slowly. "Because you didn't think anyone here would want to see you."

She speaks as someone who's been here before; which, of course, she has. When Emerald came back to Heather Bay last year, everyone still thought she was the one who was responsible for the 'town hall' fiasco. Ironically enough, she knows exactly how I'm feeling right now. (Well, fake boyfriend aside, obviously. I don't imagine there can be too many people who know how *that* feels.) She's probably the only person in the world who does. I just wish I wasn't the reason for her comprehensive knowledge of what it feels like to be the town pariah.

"I don't blame people for not wanting to see me," I say carefully, twisting my napkin in my hands. "It's no more than I deserve, really. I wouldn't want to see me either, after... well, after what I did."

It's the closest I've come to an apology and, right now, it's the closest I *can* come. It's not that I don't want to say more. I do. More than anything, in fact. But when I try, the words seem to stick in my throat, and I feel like an actress playing a role — badly.

Emerald is still watching me, pity sketched all over her face. I wish she wouldn't do that. I wish she wouldn't feel sorry for me. I wish she wouldn't be *nice* to me. Because I don't deserve it, do I?

"Anyway, I'm here now," I say, a little too brightly. "The prodigal daughter returns. Sexy Lexie, that's me!"

I pick up my wineglass and discover it's empty. Emerald silently reaches for the bottle and refills both of our glasses.

"You know no one here takes those articles seriously, don't you?" she says, after a moment's silence, which is broken by McTavish snorting loudly at something Jett's just said to him. "The ones Scarlett's been writing about you? I don't think you should take them too personally, okay? It's just... well, it's just *Scarlett*, really. She doesn't mean anything by it."

I raise my eyebrows skeptically. Considering that Emerald spent part of last year pretending to *be* Scarlett, I guess I shouldn't be too surprised that she's defending her now. Well, sort of.

"So you're telling me people *don't* think I'm a cold-hearted bitch, then?" I joke, in a feeble attempt to shake off the weird atmosphere that's hanging over the table.

"I *dae* think that," McTavish pipes up helpfully. "So does Mike-the-dentist. I went tae see him last week and he was sayin'—"

"McTavish!" Emerald silences him with a look, then turns back to me, her face flushed.

"Most people here know your mum well enough to... well, you know what I mean," she says, looking at Jack for help, but finding him too deeply embroiled in his conversation with Jett to notice her pleading look.

"Scarlett's still fairly new to town," she goes on. "She's still finding her way, I suppose. But, like I was saying, I don't think you should take it too personally. No one here hates you. Well, other than Mike-the-dentist, apparently."

"And Doreen fae the post office," adds McTavish, who appears to have the ability to listen to two conversations simultaneously. "She says ye're probably just after Jett Carter's money."

"McTavish!"

This time, Emerald's shriek of embarrassment alerts Jett, who looks up from the glass of whisky Jack's just handed him enquiringly.

"Lexie's never asked me for a penny," he says easily, swilling the liquid around the glass. "She's the least materialistic person I know, actually," he adds. "And the kindest, too. You can tell Doreen that next time you see her, if you like."

He speaks softly and pleasantly, but with so much authority that not even McTavish dares to challenge him.

"Thank you," I mouth silently across the table to Jett, who

raises his glass to me in return. In the silence that follows, Emerald shifts uneasily in her seat, and I can tell she's trying to think of something to say — Emerald has never been able to resist breaking an awkward silence awkwardly — but before she can speak, there's a high-pitched squeal from across the room, and a tall, wiry man with bleached blonde hair practically throws himself at Jett.

"Oh my God," he shrieks, "I can't believe it's you! Can I have your autograph? Or, actually, no, wait, let's take a selfie. Here, Emerald, you do it, will you?"

He passes his phone to Emerald, who looks like she's about to die of embarrassment.

"I'll have one with Sexy Lexie next," the newcomer says, pointing at me across the table. "I'm Brian, by the way. From the bank?"

I look at him blankly.

"Is that supposed to mean something to me?" I ask Emerald, who seems to be the only one who knows what's going on here.

"Um, Brian and I got to know each other last year," Emerald mumbles.

"When Emerald was trying to find out what happened to that bastard ex of hers, Ben," Brian confirms, nodding.

"Lexie doesn't want to hear about Ben," Emerald says, blushing. "I wish you'd stop going on about him, Brian. That's all in the past now. Anyway," she goes on, smiling as Jack reaches over to take her hand, "After that, Brian decided to come to Heather Bay for a holiday—"

"Well, I'd heard so much about it I had to see the place for myself," Brian interrupts. "And I liked it so much I just decided to stay. I've been here ever since. Emerald!" he snaps, exasperated. "The photo!"

Jett smiles dutifully as Emerald snaps away. Then Brian swoops down on me, and I do my best to stretch my mouth into a grin too. When the photos are done, McTavish produces another chair as if by magic, and Brian (from the bank, as he tells me again) squeezes himself in between me and Emerald, so she has to lean behind him to continue our conversation.

"I'm just saying," she tells me, leaning on the back of Brian's chair, "That you shouldn't just assume everyone agrees with what's been appearing in the paper. And, well, on Shona's Instagram. I know you're probably feeling like everyone's against you right now, and I know what that feels like, trust me."

She pauses to take a swig of her wine and exchange glances with Jack, who, although obviously enjoying his chat with Jett, keeps looking over at her to make sure she's okay.

I wish I had someone who would do that for me.

"But people here don't bear grudges," Emerald goes on, smiling over at her boyfriend. "And you were always popular, Lexie. It's not like everyone's going to suddenly start hating you overnight, is it?"

I consider this as I fiddle with my napkin. It's true that I was popular in high school — and after. But that's only because no one really knew me. I learned really young how to make people like me by pretending to be the kind of person people liked. But that wasn't really me, was it? It was no more real than the role I'm playing now, as Jett's girlfriend, and I feel horribly guilty that Emerald — who, by rights, shouldn't even be *talking* to me right now — is being so nice to me when all I've ever been to her is fake.

"What about you, though?" I ask, suddenly shy. "Do you hate me, Emerald? Because I would, if I were you. I'd hate me for what I did to you at the Gala Day. I *do* hate me, actually. And I'm not going to ask you to forgive me for it, because I know it was unforgivable. But I do want you to know that I'm sorry. *Really* sorry."

I say the last part in a rush, with my eyes still firmly on the napkin. Saying it is easier than I'd thought it would be, though — and once it's out there, I feel immeasurably lighter, as if the words have been weighing me down, and now I'm finally free of them.

"I don't hate you," Emerald says, after a short pause. "I mean, I *did* for a while, I'm not going to lie. I kept hoping a piano would fall out of a window and land on you. Or that the wind would blow really hard and mess up your hair."

I can hear, rather than see, the smile in her voice, and when I finally bring myself to look at her, I'm relieved to see she's joking. Or at least I think she is.

"Oh, come on, Lexie," she says, grinning. "I'm the last person who can afford to hold a grudge around here. It's not like I've never done anything I've regretted, is it?"

She exchanges another smile with Jack, who I can tell has been listening carefully to all of this, even though he still appears to be engrossed in Brian and McTavish's attempt to convince Jett that the haggis is a real creature.

"But my mum. The distillery—"

"You're not your mum, Lexie," Emerald says firmly. "You really need to get that into your head. You're not her, and her mistakes aren't yours. You're your own person."

She sounds like a motivational Instagram quote. One with swirly letters, superimposed on a photo of a sunset or something. But she's right. And by the time the night finally comes to an end and Jett and Jack start arguing over Jack's refusal to let Jett pay the bill, I discover I'm feeling a lot better all of a sudden.

"It's on the house," Jack insists, shaking Jett warmly by the hand. "It's been a pleasure."

"Once Shona finds out ye were here, the place'll be packed anyway," McTavish says cheerfully. "She'll put the word out."

"Och, Shona'll ken already," says Brian, who already seems to know almost as much about Heather Bay as Shona herself. "Shona kens everything."

We all nod solemnly at this (with the exception of Jett, who still has no idea what Brian and McTavish are saying most of the time).

"Well," says Emerald, coming over to me. "It's been—"

"Weird?" I finish for her, helpfully.

"A bit weird," she agrees. "But also... nice? I hope?"

"It's been lovely," I tell her sincerely. "Thank you, Emerald. For... well, you know."

For a second, I think she's going to try to hug me. But, instead, she just nods.

"You're welcome," she says, taking Jack by the hand. "I'll see you around, Lexie. Take care of yourself."

"See you around," I echo, as they walk away, leaving me standing there on my own, until Jett appears behind me.

"That went well," he says, looking pleased. "I think they seemed convinced, don't you?"

At first I think he's talking about my apology, then I realize he's talking about us, and our fake relationship.

Oh, right. That.

A shiver runs down my spine as we follow McTavish out of the now-empty restaurant. I've finally managed to apologize to Emerald — and she's accepted it. So why do I still feel like

I'm doing something wrong?

Chapter 30

"Let's take this car today."

It's the morning after our dinner at The 39, and Jett and I are standing in the old shed I use as a garage, looking at the tiny orange convertible that Jett's just pulled the dust sheet off, like he's a magician doing a trick.

"This was your dad's car, right?" he goes on, leaning forward to peer through the window. "I remember you talking about it."

'Talking about it' isn't really how I'd describe the fleeting mention I'd made of the MG, so I'm impressed he even remembered. I keep forgetting how closely Jett observes things; how you think he isn't paying the slightest bit of attention to you, but he's actually studying your every move. It's disconcerting — but also quite flattering, I guess. It's nice to feel like someone cares enough to remember something I only mentioned in passing a few days ago; even when you know that's not *actually* the case.

"Yeah, this was his," I tell him now, running my hand along the car's still shiny paintwork. "Or according to Mum, anyway. She threatened to get rid of it so many times when I was a kid, but she never did. I don't know. Maybe she liked the reminder of him? Who knows? Anyway, she let me bring it here when

I moved out. I had it restored a few years ago, but it's been sitting here for over a year now. I'd be surprised if you can even get it to start."

"Well, let's see."

Jett takes the keys from me and gets into the driver's seat, looking absurdly large in the little car. It takes a few attempts, but eventually the engine splutters reluctantly to life, and Jett looks up at me, beaming.

"It's a real beauty," he says, running a finger over the walnut dash. "Your Pop had good taste."

"Mum would love to hear you say that," I tell him. "I've got no idea whether or not it's true, though."

Jett's green eyes fix on mine, making me feel like I'm about to be interrogated.

"If you have the car, surely there must be some way to find out who owned it?" he says carefully. "Registration documents, something like that?"

I shake my head.

"The car was registered to Mum when I got it," I say, grateful for the dim light of the shed, which I'm hoping will hide any bitterness in my expression. "She said he gave it to her, but it might always have been hers, for all I know. I only have her word for it that it belonged to my dad first. And Mum's word... well, it's not always worth much, let's put it that way."

I turn away, pretending to polish one of the bumpers with the sleeve of my sweater. The fact is that Mum had a lot of different boyfriends when I was younger. She always claimed to be madly in love with them, but none of them seemed to stick around for long, and I've no reason to suppose her relationship with my father was any different. She always told me this car was his, but there's no way to know for sure. And while I'd like to think she knows exactly who he was — or who he *is*, even — and has some really excellent reason to keep that knowledge to herself, the more likely scenario is that *she* doesn't know either.

Which is why the subject of my absent father isn't something I like to think about very much, or for very long. And why I'm really starting to wish I hadn't brought Jett out here this morning.

"I could hire a P.I.," he's saying now, as he gets out of the car. "The guy Asher uses could probably do it. I bet he could track him down for you in no time, and we could—"

"It's fine," I cut in, my tone sharper than I intended. "Really," I add, more softly. "I appreciate the thought, but I just... I just don't need to know. Whoever my dad is, I've managed just fine without him for my entire life. I don't need him in it now. I don't need anyone in my life who doesn't want to be in it."

Especially not someone who apparently made that decision without even meeting me.

"Sure thing, Lady M," Jett says easily. "It's up to you. Offer's there if you change your mind, though."

"Thanks. I won't. But thanks."

I know I probably sound ungrateful, but I just want him to drop this subject now, so I don't have to think about it any longer.

"Are you sure you want to take this car today?" I ask, changing the subject. "Because I can't guarantee it won't break down halfway there if we do. And there's not a lot of room in it, especially if you want to take McTavish."

I smile to myself, trying to imagine McTavish crammed into the tiny back seat of the MG.

"Maybe we'd be better just calling the firm you've been using?" I suggest, turning to Jett. "It'll be much easier. And safer, too."

"Nah, I want to take this," he insists, tossing the keys in the air and catching them again. "I'm sick of being driven around everywhere. It just attracts more attention."

"Yeah, whereas we'll be totally inconspicuous in a bright orange convertible," I deadpan. "No one will give us a second glance, for sure."

"Trust me," Jett insists. "It'll be fun. I think we'll leave McTavish out of this one, though. I'm not sure this thing's big enough for three adults, somehow — even when one's as small as you."

I stick my tongue out in response to his teasing, relieved by the change of topic.

Maybe Jett's right. Maybe a road trip will be fun. Maybe it'll be just what I need to help me forget about Mum, and Emerald, and all the other things that've been on my mind since I came back here.

"Okay," says Jett, pulling his phone out of his pocket. "Just give me a second so I can arrange for Scarlett to meet us there with her photographer."

Or, on second thoughts, maybe not.

* * *

It takes us almost three hours to drive to Birnam, where the tree Jett wants to see is, and Jett sings the entire way. Literally the entire way.

It starts with Dolly Parton's 'Jolene', which happens to be playing on the radio as we leave Heather Bay (after a few false starts as Jett, who's insisted on driving, gets used to the unfamiliar stick shift), then progresses through a varied selection of tracks, ranging from The Eagles to The Spice Girls, and pretty much everything in between.

"Do you just somehow know every song ever made?" I ask in amazement, as the opening chords to 'Summer of '69 strike up, and Jett immediately joins in.

"I love music," he says, shrugging. "I listen to it constantly back home. It's like a form of therapy for me. I listen to music when I want to change my mood, or take my mind off something that's worrying me. Doesn't everyone?"

"I didn't know that," I reply, slightly shamefaced. I still barely even know this man sitting next to me. I've been so wrapped up in my own problems that I haven't really stopped to think about him, or what might be worrying him, as he puts it.

"And do you want to change your mood now?" I ask, looking over at him. He's wearing a pair of dark glasses and a close-fitting t-shirt, and he insisted on putting the top down on the car, so the wind is blowing through his hair, which is miraculously free of the ever-present baseball cap for once. He looks like he's starring in a movie about some kind of lovable rogue who's on the run from the law. It's almost unbearably sexy. So much so that I almost forget I asked a question until he answers it.

"Nah, I'm good," he says, grinning over at me. "How about you, Lady M? You heard anything more from your mom?"

I stiffen, instinctively on guard at the mention of Mum. As it happens, I have had a few messages from her; mostly asking if Jett and I can come and pick her up when she gets out of hospital after the miraculous recovery she seems to have had. I haven't answered any of them yet. I will, of course. I just need to clear a bit of space in my head first; which is one of the reasons this trip with Jett seems like an even better idea the more I think about it.

"No," I tell him, surprising myself with how smoothly the lie comes out of my mouth. "Nothing at all. Oh my God, I love this song!"

I don't *really*, as it happens. It's *Don't Stop Believin'*, and I associate it with too many drunken nights out in my youth. But I crank up the volume on the radio anyway, and Jett and I sing along, all the way to the little town of Birnam, where the rain starts to fall as soon as we pull into a parking space.

Awesome.

"So, where's this tree?" I ask, wishing I'd worn something a bit sore substantial than the pair of strappy sandals that seemed like a good idea in this morning's sunshine. "Is it close?"

"No idea," says Jett cheerfully. "Scarlett should know, though. Look, there she is."

I twist around in my seat, and, sure enough, there's Scarlett, smiling and batting her eyelashes as she waves at us from under an umbrella. She's in full 'Wicked Witch' mode, wearing a bright red trench coat that matches her name and her lipstick, and I find myself uncharitably hoping she slips and falls into a puddle or something.

By the pricking of my thumbs, something wicked this way comes.

Jett gets out of the car and goes to meet her, with me trailing along grudgingly behind. By the time I reach them, Scarlett's already offered him a space under her umbrella, and I'm left to share with the newspaper's photographer, who doesn't utter a single word as we trudge along a path and into the forest that skirts the edges of the village.

"Sorry, Lexie," Scarlett shouts back at me as the paved footpath gives way to a muddy trail. "You might want to wait there for us, if you don't want to get your feet wet."

"Oh, no you don't," I mutter, earning a look a silent approval from the photographer. I bet he's about as sick of Scarlett Scott as I am right now. "You're not getting rid of me that easily."

I grit my teeth as I squelch my way through the forest, my sandals soaked through within seconds. Scarlett yells that the tree isn't too far from the town itself, but by the time we reach it, I'm freezing cold, soaking wet, and thoroughly annoyed.

All this for a freaking tree.

Still, it's quite a nice tree, I suppose. If you like that kind of thing.

Trying to show some interest, I take a step closer to it, and bend down to examine the sign in front of it, which Jett and Scarlett have stopped in front of.

"*It's not me,*" says the sign. "*I'm a sycamore.*"

Great. Even the trees are fucking with me now.

"Isn't that hilarious?" says Jett, who appears to be having the time of his life here in this moldy old forest.

"Hilarious," I agree grimly. "Just... hilarious."

We walk on for a few minutes before reaching another giant tree.

"*Not me either,*" says the sign in front of this one, making Scarlett squeal with fake laughter.

Surely no one can be that *excited by a tree?*

A few more minutes of squelching, however, finally brings us to our target.

"The Birnam Oak — a living relic of Birnam Wood," Scarlett says dramatically, pretending she didn't just read that off the sign.

"Is... is that *it*?" I blurt, unable to stop myself. "That's what we drove three hours to see? It's... a *tree*?"

Jett and Scarlett look at me pityingly.

"It is, Lexie," Jett solemnly. "It's a tree. But what a tree it is! Just look at it."

I look at it dutifully, even taking the time to step all around it. It's very tall, I'll give it that. But there's an old can of Irn Bru at the base of it, and a droplet of water trickling down my neck, which I guess is kind of killing the moment for me, somehow.

"I'm sorry, but I'm just seeing a tree," I say, shrugging as I return to Jett. "If I'd known, I could've shown you thousands of them back home."

"Lexie, Lexie," he replies, coming to stand beside me. "This is not 'just' a tree, trust me. Come here."

Taking me by the hand, he leads me down the small hill that takes us to the base of the tree.

"Do this," he instructs, placing both of my hands against the trunk.

I do as he says, feeling ever so slightly stupid, but enjoying the way he's leaning in behind me, his body close to mine and the smattering of stubble that's started to appear on his face again grazing the skin on my cheek. The rain doesn't reach us under the canopy of leaves, but I can hear it falling, making it feel oddly cosy standing here next to the giant oak.

"Feel that," Jett says, placing his hands over mine and making my heart start to do funny things inside my chest. "That's history, Lexie, right under your skin. Think of all the things this tree has seen. All the things that have happened while it's been standing right here, in this wood. It's magical, isn't it?"

He's standing behind me, his arms reaching around my body to touch the tree trunk as he leans in over my shoulder. If I turned my head even slightly, our lips would be almost touching, and the impulse to do exactly that is so powerful I have to press my palms hard against the tree trunk to stop myself.

It's definitely not just history that's getting under my skin right now.

"It is," I say, my voice sounding like it's coming from very far away. "It's absolutely magical."

It is, too. Although, don't tell Jett, but it's not actually the *tree* I'm talking about.

Before I can think better of it, I turn around until my back's pressed against the tree trunk. Jett still has an arm on either side of me, but now we're face to face, and I'm starting to think that agreeing to come and see this tree could just be the best decision I've ever made.

"So it's not 'just a tree' then, huh?" says Jett, apparently totally unperturbed to find me close enough to... well, *kiss*, really. *Kiss* is the word that popped into my head as soon as I turned to face him, and it continues to hover over the two of us as we stand there, almost nose-to-nose, with the soft pitter-patter of the rain above us lending the illusion of complete privacy. "You like it?"

"I *love* it," I assure him, still not even remotely talking about the Birnam Oak. "I love this tree. Consider me a fan. Sign me up to its newsletter."

Jett's lips part as he smiles. There's absolutely no reason for us to still be standing here in the rain. And yet here we stand, under the protective branches of The Best Tree in All the Land, with the word *kiss* still hovering between us, and getting larger by the second. It's so big now, and so obvious, that it's impossible to ignore it, or pretend it isn't there. It would be stupid to even try, really, and as Jett leans closer, his eyes locked onto mine, I can't help thinking he's noticed it too.

Kiss.

It's all I can think about now. Gone is the rough bark of the tree against my back, and the smell of the rain on the ground. Gone is the muddy ground under my feet, and the chill in the air that I complained about all the way here. All there is now is me and Jett—

"Perfect," says Scarlett's voice from somewhere nearby. "That's fantastic guys. Our readers will love these shots."

Oh, and Scarlett, of course. Damn. I'd almost forgotten about her.

She's still there, though: her and her silent photographer, standing up on the hill next to the oak tree, the photographer snapping away as if he's David Bailey or something.

"Um, you can stop now, though," she adds, sounding ever so slightly petulant. "We're done."

"You might be," says Jett, straightening up and leaving me feeling like someone (Scarlett) just stole my favorite toy. "I'm not."

He turns on the spot, taking in the forest around us. The rain has thinned to a drizzle now, and I can see tiny droplets of water caught on his eyelashes.

"Isn't it crazy to think this was here in Shakespeare's time?" he says, looking up at the oak tree. "I wonder if he ever saw it? I read that he did come here at one time."

"Yeah, I think he did," I agree, not wanting to crush him completely by pointing out that the Birnam Oak would've been a hell of a lot smaller back then, so even if Will Shakespeare did pass this way, it probably wouldn't have called out to him the way it does to Jett.

"I know it probably sounds nuts," Jett says now, "But I can imagine Macbeth and his witches meeting in these woods."

"I think I see one of the witches now," I mutter under my breath, looking over my shoulder to where Scarlett's standing waiting for us.

"Huh?" Luckily for me, Jett didn't quite catch my snide comment; he's too busy imagining himself back in the days when Scotland still had kings, and prophecies — and well, okay, witches.

"Are you ready to go—" I begin, but he isn't listening. He's still staring up at the Birnam Oak, apparently transfixed.

"*Tomorrow, and tomorrow, and tomorrow,*" he says, sounding totally unlike himself. *"Creeps in this petty pace from day to day / To the last syllable of recorded time."*

I hold my breath, not wanting to ruin the moment as he goes on, all the way through Macbeth's famous monologue; his tale filled with sound and fury, which Jett recites with such passion that if I didn't know better, I'd think it was *his* wife who had died, not Macbeth's.

If Justin Duval could just see him right now, he'd probably offer him the job on the spot.

As soon as the thought enters my mind, I know exactly what I have to do.

Pulling my phone out of my bag, I open up the camera and turn to Jett, who's still standing there, muttering some of the lines from the rest of the scene.

"Do me a favor?" I say, smiling as winningly as I can. "Could you do that again? Exactly the way you did it before?"

I'm half expecting him to object, but instead he just smiles that heart-stopping smile of his.

"Anything for you, Lady M," he says. "Anything at all."

Chapter 31

By the time we get back to the car, the rain, which I'd thought was easing up, has started up again with renewed vigor, and we're all soaked to the skin.

That's not the worst thing about the drive home, though.

No, the *worst* thing about the drive home is Scarlett Scott, who follows us back to the car, waving cheerfully to the photographer as he gets into his own vehicle, having still failed to utter a single word to any of us.

"Can we help you with something, Scarlett?" I ask, somehow resisting the impulse to just tell her to leave us the hell alone now that she's got her stupid photos.

"Oh, didn't Jett tell you?" she replies, feigning surprise. "I'm coming with you. Sam has another job to get to, so Jett very kindly offered me a lift home, seeing as you two are going that way, anyway."

I try but fail to hold back a scowl at this unwelcome piece of news. I'd been hoping Jett and I might go for a nice, cozy lunch somewhere. I'd pictured us curled up by a log fire in some country pub or other, where we could maybe continue the scene we started under the Birnam Oak.

Scarlett Scott definitely wasn't part of that picture, but she's determined to be part of this one, and, much to my disgust,

Jett seems perfectly happy for her to be here, too.

I guess he's not as keen on being alone with me as I am with him. Does that mean he *wasn't* thinking about kissing me earlier? Or was he just acting, like he always is? I was so wrapped up in the moment that I'd completely forgotten Scarlett and her camera. Jett was the one who arranged for them to be there, though, so it would make sense that he was aware of them the whole time. It would make sense that he was just putting on a show for the photos. It would make sense that I would fall for it, yet again.

I pull my sunglasses out of my handbag and slip them on, even though it's still raining.

I'm not going to *cry*. I just need something to hide behind, that's all. Something to protect me from Scarlett's curious glances, and Jett's indifference. Although I suspect it'll probably take more than just a pair of sunglasses to protect me from *that*.

"Isn't this nice?" says Scarlett smugly from the back seat, where she's sitting with her knees up somewhere under her chin, thanks to the non-existent legroom. "Now we can all really get to know each other."

* * *

When Jett insisted on driving to Birnam, I said I'd drive us back: an offer I now vehemently regret, given that it leaves Jett and Scarlett free to chat, while I focus on the road.

I don't think I've ever hated anyone quite as much as I hate

Scarlett Scott.

Other than maybe Jett Carter. Because right now I... don't *hate* Jet, obviously. I could never actually *hate* him. I'm just *confused* by him, I guess. Confused by the way he blows hot and cold all the time. The way one minute he can be gazing into my eyes, as if I'm the only person in the world who's ever mattered to him, and the next minute he's twisting around in his seat to talk to the First Witch back there, like I don't even exist.

I feel a bit like a chauffeur as the car winds its way through Perthshire and back into the Highlands. Just the hired help — which I suppose I am, really. Scarlett, meanwhile, is having the time of her life, sitting there basking in the rays of Jett's undivided attention. And who can blame her? I just hope she's clever enough to realize he's acting most of the time.

Don't make the same mistake I did, Scarlett.

Don't let yourself believe he's actually into you.

The drive to Birnam took approximately three hours. The drive home takes approximately *forever*, and by the time we're finally cresting the hill above the town, and driving down towards the main street, the sun has started to sink into the sea, which is spread out in front of us, like a painting. I'm absolutely starving. There's no way I'm going to mention that in front of Scarlett, though, just in case Jett suggests she joins us for dinner, so I say nothing, and try to ignore the rumbling of my stomach as I drop her off at her house, then turn and head for home, feeling suddenly self-conscious now that it's just me and Jett again.

Every time I find myself alone with him, it feels like the first time. Like I'm still the silly little schoolgirl who went to watch him in his first movie, and felt jealous of every woman he was photographed with.

I really wish he didn't make me feel like this.

I wish he wasn't so damn attractive to me.

I wish—

"Hey, has someone broken into your house?"

Jett's voice jolts me abruptly out of my self-pity spiral. The cottage has just come into view at the end of the road we're driving down, and, to my horror, I see the door is wide open.

"Shit," Jett says we pull into the driveway. "I knew we should've had some security here. Even having that McTavish guy outside would've been better than nothing."

My hands are trembling as I pull the handbrake up and turn off the engine. I can't believe someone has been inside my house, and I'm almost too afraid to go in myself and see what kind of damage they've done.

"It must have been one of those crazy fans of yours," I say, getting reluctantly out of the car. "They've been hanging around for days now. I guess it was just a matter of time before one of them tried to get in. They're probably waiting in your bed or—"

I put my thumbnail in my mouth and start biting it, not wanting to think about what one of Jett's fans could be getting up to in my house right now.

"Should we call the police before we go in?" I wonder aloud, but before Jett can answer, there's a movement in the doorway, and the "intruder" steps out onto the path.

It's not a crazed Jett Carter fan, determined to get me out of the way so they can have him to himself.

No, it's much, much worse than that.

It's Mum.

Chapter 32

The Wildcat Cafe looks exactly the same as it did the last time I was here. Mind you, it's probably looked exactly the same for the past *fifty* years; the checkerboard floor and sticky Formica tables have been here for as long as I can remember, and it's impossible to tell whether the 50s-style booths are ironically retro or just... well, really *old*.

The only difference between this visit to the Cafe and my last one, then, is the fact that this time I'm here with Jett and Mum. Oh, and McTavish, who's stationed himself at the door, to stop anyone from coming in to disturb our privacy.

(This was against the express instructions of Ronnie and Brenda, the Wildcat's owners, by the way. But McTavish has already allowed Old Jimmy in, quickly followed by Bella McGowan and Tam, who drives the village bus, and that's more people than you'd normally find in The Wildcat, so I don't suppose they can complain, really. "Och, these are your pals, Lexie, they're no' going tae bother ye," McTavish said, by way of explanation, completely ignoring the fact that Jimmy and Edna have been openly staring at us ever since they arrived, and Tam's asked Jett if he can take a selfie with him twice now.)

When we got back to the cottage to find Mum waiting for us,

having been discharged from the hospital and made her own way home, I was all for just giving up on this day and going straight to bed. Before I could announce this intention, though, my stomach betrayed me with a particularly loud grumble, and there was nothing in the house to eat, so here we are.

"What's a macaroni pie?" Jett's asking now, holding the menu as if it's an important historical artifact. "Does that come deep fried, too?"

"It's macaroni," says Brenda, who is as obviously unimpressed by her celebrity guest as she is by everyone else who has the temerity to try to eat at her restaurant. "In a pie. And we dinnae have any left."

"Deep fried pizza?" asks Jett, undaunted.

"Sold out."

"Okay, what about the fish?"

"Nane."

"That means none," I start to explain, but, judging by the look on his face, I guess Jett's already gathered that.

"Look, we have haggis suppers, or we have chips n' cheese," says Brenda, in the tone of a woman who thinks this should be blatantly obvious, and is surprised she's even having to say it out loud. "What's it to be?"

"Three haggis suppers, please," I interject, wanting to hurry this along. "Thanks, Brenda."

Brenda laboriously writes our order down in her notepad, before turning to face the counter at the back of the shop, over which the stuffed wildcat that gave this place its name still hangs in a dusty glass case.

"THREE HAGGIS SUPPERS, RONNIE," she bellows "And hurry up wi' it, will ye?"

Jett blinks in astonishment as Brenda retreats.

"Are you sure you should be eating that, Lexie?" Mum asks, casting a meaningful look at my figure. "You know how carbs go straight to your thighs, and if you're going to keep having your picture in the paper—"

"Lexie's thighs are perfect the way they are," Jett interjects pleasantly, smiling across the table at her, as if my thighs are a perfectly normal dinnertime conversation. "She can eat whatever she likes. She always looks good to me."

Mum and I stare at him in astonishment.

Did he really just say that?

And, more importantly, did he mean *it?*

"Well, of course she does, Jett," Mum says, recovering herself. "Her legs are her best feature. Always have been. I'm just trying to help, that's all. You never know when one of those photographers is going to pop up, do you?"

She looks eagerly around the restaurant, and is rewarded with a toothless grin from Old Jimmy, who's turned his chair round to face us, as if he's watching a play.

"NO PHOTOS," McTavish shouts from the door of the shop. "I'M WARNING YE ALL."

I sigh. This has been a *very* long day.

"I still don't understand why you came to my place from the hospital?" I say, turning to Mum. "Wouldn't you be more comfortable at yours?"

"Och, no, Lexie," says Mum, her fake accent slipping slightly. "It's been sitting empty the whole time I've been in hospital. There's nothing in the fridge. And the doctor said I shouldn't be left on my own until I've fully recovered, anyway."

"There's nothing in my fridge either," I point out, wishing I didn't sound quite so argumentative, but somehow unable to stop myself. "And you look pretty much recovered to me."

"Lexie, I could keel over at any second," Mum says, fanning herself dramatically. "And you wouldn't want your poor mum coming out of hospital to an empty house when she's been so ill, would you?" she adds, her eyes wide. "All cold and dusty and unloved."

As it happens, "cold, dusty and unloved" is a pretty good description of Mum's place all the time, not just when she's in hospital. "Add in "messy and chaotic", and you have the perfect picture of my childhood home. No wonder I grew up a neat freak.

"It's going to need a good clean before I go back to it," Mum goes on. "I was thinking of hiring Frankie Allison's firm. You know the one Emerald Taylor works for? Wouldn't it be hilarious to get Emerald round to do the cleaning? That would take her down a peg or two."

"No, don't do that," I say hurriedly. "I'll... I'll come round and clean it for you. Just don't ask Emerald, okay?"

"That's my girl," Mum says, patting my hand fondly. "I knew I could count on my Lexie to help me out. And the three of us will be nice and cosy at your place while I'm waiting. Won't we, Jett darling??"

She beams over at Jett, who smiles warmly back, as if she hasn't just thrown a hand-grenade into the whole fake-relationship thing we've got going on here.

The cottage only has two bedrooms. He knows that. He *must* know that, surely? Two bedrooms means two beds, and if Mum's in one of them...

"You know you're more than welcome to stay with us, Sam," he says, the very picture of charm. "We're happy to have you. And we wouldn't dream of letting you go home on your own so soon after your operation. Would we Lexie?"

He looks at me with such innocence that, for a second, I start to wonder if he maybe thinks the cottage has some kind of secret extra wing or something that I've just kept very well hidden.

"No, of course not," I mutter. "Of course we wouldn't."

"Aye, she would," interjects Jimmy, who's been following the conversation closely. "She's a sly yin, that Lexie. She'll be wantin' to be on her ain wi' her man there."

"Now, Jimmy," tuts Bella McGowan, whose hearing is remarkably sharp considering her age. "Leave them alone. It's none of our business."

"That's right. Thanks, Bella," I say, grateful for the unexpected support.

"And anyway," Bella goes on, as if I haven't spoken. "It's not like Samantha will be in the same room as Alexandra and Jett here. She'll have one room, and they'll share the other. So they'll have plenty of opportunity for 'alone time,' won't they?"

Everyone in the room turns to look at me, as if this is a serious question, and the sleeping arrangements at the cottage are everyone's business. Thankfully, Brenda chooses this moment to lumber back into the room and slap three plates of haggis and chips on the table in front of us, handily bringing the conversation to a close.

Bella words ring in my ears the entire time we're eating, though, and I continue to think about them as we pay the bill, which Jett insists on picking up for everyone in the cafe, seeing as they all might as well have been there for us. "You're a very decent young man," Bella says approvingly, as she thanks him. "Not a patch on Harry Styles, looks wise, of course, but still:

you've done well for yourself there, Alexandra." She gives me a stern look, which I interpret as "*Not that you deserve it*", then we're out of the door, and back onto the street outside, which feels comparatively private after the restaurant we've just left.

We really need to find someone other than McTavish to work as security.

I continue thinking about the bedroom situation all the way home. Bella was right. If Mum's going to be staying with us, Jett and I will have to share a room, or risk exposing the lie of our relationship altogether.

And I know what option *I* prefer.

"Let's just tell Mum the truth," I say, pulling Jett aside as we enter the cottage. "It'll be easier. Then we won't have to sleep together. Which would be terrible. Obviously."

"You think?" Jett waggles his eyebrows at me suggestively. "I bet it wouldn't. I mean, none of the other women I've dated have complained, so—"

"*Sleep* together," I hiss, my face burning. "Sleep, Jett. As in... well, *sleeping*. When you're not awake?"

"Yeah, I know what sleep is, thanks, Lady M," he grins, refusing to see the seriousness of the situation.

"Would you please just listen to me?" I plead, pulling him into the kitchen and pulling the door closed behind me. "Just putting the kettle on," I shout through to Mum in the living room. "Be with you in a minute."

I turn to Jett.

"We could just tell her the truth about us," I suggest, speaking more calmly now. "That way she'll go home, and we each get a bed for the night. We can trust her. She won't tell anyone."

Even as I say it, I know I'm not being honest. I'd *like* to think

I could trust Mum with the revelation that Jett and I are just pretending to be together. Whether I can or not, though, is a different story altogether.

"You sure about that?" Jett says, quietly. He leans against the kitchen counter, suddenly serious. "Because absolutely nothing you've said to me so far leads me to think I can trust your mother, Lexie. Quite the opposite, in fact. We're talking about the same woman who called the local rag and told them she was dying, right?"

I'm so ashamed I can barely bring myself to nod. Looks like he *hasn't* been totally taken in by Mum after all.

"We can't tell her," Jett says. He walks over and puts his hands on my shoulders, his eyes burning into mine. "We just can't. Can you even imagine how it would look if people found out I'd hired someone to pretend to be my girlfriend? Seriously, can you?"

"It... it would be pretty bad," I whisper. "Really bad. I get that."

Jett stares at me, as if he's trying to read my mind.

"I need to know I can trust you, Lexie," he says slowly. "I need to know you're not going to tell anyone about this. About us. And it's not just because of the role. It's because of you."

I blink, surprised.

"Me? I don't understand?"

"Look, I know I've only been here a couple of days," he says, still holding me so I can't step away from him. "But I can see how hard it's been on you, being here. I can see how much you want these people to like you, or to forgive you, or whatever it is you're looking for. And, whatever that is, I can see that you're not going to get it if everyone finds out this was all just an act. Because, the thing is, Lexie, I'd get through it. It would be a few bad headlines, maybe some jokes at my expense at awards ceremonies, but that would be it. I'd go back to L.A., and I'd be fine. It's not like I've ever cared that much what people think of me anyway. But you..."

He lowers his head until he's looking me right in the eye.

"You care what people think about you," he says softly. "I know you like to pretend not to, but I know you better than that. I know you do. And I know that this story would follow you around forever. Especially here, in a place where everyone knows everyone else. It would be much worse for you than whatever it was that happened at the Gala thing."

"Gala," I say, automatically correcting his pronunciation. "It was a Gala Day. And I dropped a cigarette on Emerald, which set her dress on fire. I did it on purpose, Jett. I mean, I didn't mean to hurt her, or to... well, to burn down the hall, which is what happened. I just thought she'd stamp it right out and she'd be fine, but her dress would look shit. Which isn't much better, I know, but Mum was so angry that Emerald got to be the Gala Queen instead of me, and I just, I just—"

I just don't know what else to say, because there's nothing I can *say now. There's nothing I can do to make any of this better. And there never will be.*

"I understand if you hate me," I tell him. "Everyone else does." I try to pull away. But Jett's hands are still on my shoulders, his eyes are still fixed on mine, and he's still standing there, looking at me as if I haven't just confessed to being the worst person in the world.

"When I was 21, I told my best friend his audition had been canceled so I could go instead of him," he tells me. "And I didn't even get the role, either. He's never forgiven me for it."

"That's... not nearly as bad as what I did," I sniff, trying to sound normal.

"Maybe not." Jett shrugs. "The point is that everyone makes mistakes, Lexie. And, okay, maybe yours is worse than mine, I don't know. But I can't judge you for it. I would judge you if you weren't sorry for it, sure. But I know you are. I know you're fundamentally a good person who's done some things she regrets. You just need to believe that yourself."

I chew my bottom lip nervously, not knowing what to say to that. If I didn't know better, I'd think he cared about me. *Really* cared, I mean. But I *do* know better.

Don't I?

"Anyway, that's why we can't tell your mom about us," Jett says, abruptly pulling away from me. "I don't want you to be hurt by this. That's the last thing I want. And I know it's a mess," he goes on, raking his hand through his hair in frustration. "It's a complete fucking mess that we should never have agreed to it in the first place. But we did, and now we have to see it through. Please, Lexie."

He turns to me with something like anguish on his face.

"I don't care about my stupid *reputation.*" He says the last word as if it leaves a bad taste in his mouth. "I don't even care about getting the role any more. If I'm meant to get it, I'll get it, and if I have to pretend to be someone I'm not to get it, then I don't even want it, anyway. I just care about not making your life here any harder than already is. But I can't make sure of that unless you help me. Do you understand?"

He stands there under the glare of the ugly electric light bulb, and I am absolutely, 100% sure he's being honest with me. This is the real Jett Carter: the one hardly anyone ever gets to see. The one I'll do quite literally anything for.

"I understand, Jett," I tell him, crossing the room and

putting my arms around him impulsively. "I understand," I say into his t-shirt. "And thank you."

He just stands there at first, and then I feel his arms come up around my shoulders, wrapping me in *him*.

"Why are you thanking me?" he whispers into my hair.

"For caring about how I feel," I mumble, my face still buried in his chest. "For not hating me for what I just told you. For wanting to help me. I know I don't deserve it."

"Hey, that's enough of the self-pitying talk," Jett says firmly. "The Lexie I know is tougher than that. And she deserves to have someone who cares about her. She deserves to have everything she wants."

We stand there for several long seconds, Jett's arms still holding me close as I struggle to bite back the words that are on the tip of my tongue:

What if what I want is you?

I could say it. I could. I could just blurt it out, and if he was horrified by it, I could just pretend I was joking.

I could do that.

Before I can do anything, though, there's a loud cough from the other side of the door, which swings open to reveal Mum, who grins broadly when she sees us standing with our arms around each other.

"Whoops," she says, giggling. "Sorry, I didn't mean to disturb you two lovebirds. I was just coming to find out if you have any wine in the house, Lexie? I thought we could open a bottle to celebrate me being back?"

"Sure," I mutter, disengaging myself from Jett and going to open the fridge. "Here, "I say, handing her a bottle. "Glasses are in the cupboard."

Mum smiles as she takes the wine from me, but there's a

look in her eyes that I can't quite translate. A look that makes me feel anxious, like a cloud's gone over the sun.

Just how long was she standing there, on the other side of that door?

And what exactly did she hear?

Chapter 33

It's the night that never seems to end.

One bottle of wine quickly turns into two, and every time I think Mum's surely going to get up and go to bed, she starts telling another story, and so the evening drags on.

Jett snuck upstairs at one point during the evening to move his stuff out of the spare room and into mine, but I can't stop worrying in case he's left something behind that will tell Mum that's where he's been sleeping — and don't even get me started about how I feel about having to sleep next to him all night.

After our conversation earlier, though, I can see there's no other option, so once Mum's finally retired for the night, I quickly tidy up downstairs while Jett uses the only bathroom in the house. By the time I emerge from it myself, wearing an over-sized t-shirt with 'My Friend Went to Heather Bay And All I Got Was This Stupid T-Shirt' on the front (Mum's idea of a joke, a few Christmases ago) and an anxious expression that I can't seem to wipe off my face, he's already tucked up in my double bed, with a pillow placed in the middle of it, to form a barrier between us.

"I know you're not exactly keen on the idea of bed sharing," he says, grinning up at me from the book he's picked up from my bedside table. "So I thought this might reassure you that I'm not going to try to jump you during the night."

"That's very thoughtful of you," I tell him, standing awkwardly by the bed. "You're a true gentleman. You're on the wrong side of the bed, though. That's my side. I always sleep on the right."

"Well, whaddya know, *I* always sleep on the right too," says Jett, feigning astonishment. "What are the odds? I guess we have something in common after all."

I pick up the pillow and throw it at him.

"It's a good job we're not a real couple," I tell him primly. "We'd never get any sleep if we were."

"There definitely wouldn't be much sleep going on," he says suggestively, looking me up and down. "Nice... gown. Is that what that is?"

"It's a t-shirt," I point out. "And I wish you'd stop doing that, by the way."

"Doing what?"

"The *flirting*. It's... it's inappropriate."

Jett's brow creases.

"Sorry," he says, giving me his puppy-dog eyed look. "I don't think I even know I'm doing it."

"Yeah, I can tell."

I sigh dramatically, to hide my disappointment. I wanted him to say he was flirting because he meant it. Because he wanted to. But he doesn't, and I watch as he gets out of bed and shuffles around to the other side, carefully replacing the pillow barrier first.

"The least I can do," he says, getting back in and pulling the duvet up to his chin. It's too late, though. I've already seen the plain boxers he's wearing with his t-shirt (Which is a much better fit on him than mine is on me), and it's not exactly an image that's going to make it any easier for me to get to sleep. Again, though, it's not like I have a choice here, so I switch off the light and get into bed, settling gratefully into the warm patch he's left behind.

"Tell me a story about Lexie," Jett says, rolling onto his side once I'm lying down. "One that doesn't involve burning things down, maybe."

"Nuh-uh," I tell him firmly. "I've told you plenty about me. It's your turn now. Tell me a story about Jett. One no one else knows."

"I can't tell you that," he replies, his tone teasing. "Then you'd know all my secrets."

"You can trust me with them," I say into the darkness. "And anyway, the secrets you tell late at night don't count; just like the calories you eat standing up, or the glass of wine you drink on Christmas morning. They're allowed."

There's a silence so long I wonder if he's fallen asleep.

"All of those things count, Lexie," he says at last. "You can't make something not count just because you don't want to think about it."

He sounds sad. I didn't want to make him sad.

"It's okay," I whisper, suppressing the urge to reach out and comfort him. "You don't have to tell me anything you don't want to."

"There is something I want to tell you," he says, his voice low. It's so dark in the little room that I can only see the outline of his profile as he stares up at the ceiling. I have a feeling that if I say anything at all right now, it'll ruin the moment, and make him withdraw back into himself, so instead I say nothing, and just lie there on my side, watching him in the darkness, my body tense with the anticipation of what he's about to tell me.

"All the girls you've seen me with," he says. "The ones I date."

I nod, forgetting he can't see me. I'm aware of his lengthy dating history. Everyone is. It's the reason we got into this fake-dating arrangement in the first place; to convince people that he doesn't see women as disposable. That not all of them are just one-night stands to him.

"They're not really... I'm not really..."

"They're not real?" I hazard a guess, forgetting my resolution not to interrupt him. "They were all just fake relationships, too?"

"No," he says, annoyed. "Believe it or not, you're my first ever fake girlfriend, Lexie. This is as weird to me as it is to you."

"Good to know. I guess. So, what, then?"

"The relationships were real," he goes on, his voice so quiet now I can barely hear him. "Or as real as it gets when you have absolutely nothing in common, I suppose. Other than that you're both insanely hot, obviously."

I snort, amused. Even in a middle-of-the-night confession, he's still aware enough of his audience — me, in this case — to want to make them smile.

"None of them have been serious, is what I'm trying to say," he goes on, more seriously now. "Because none of them have ever really known me. I've never let them get close enough to. That's why none of them have lasted."

He pauses, as if he's gathering his thoughts, before he goes on.

"I met my first girlfriend on a movie set when I was 19," he tells me in a rush. "And I thought I was in love with her. I really did. I thought we'd be together forever. That somehow *we* would be the lucky ones who'd met as teenagers, and who would stay together for the rest of our lives. Because that was what I wanted. What I still want, really. Something real. Something solid. Something that lasts forever."

Violet. He's talking about Violet King, his most famous ex. And I thought I'd hated her before, but wow, do I ever hate her now.

"Then I found out she was hooking up with my best friend," Jett says bitterly.

"Wait. The one whose audition you ruined?"

"Yup. The very one."

His voice is still steady, but there's an anger so palpable in it that I could almost reach out and touch it. My mind, meanwhile, is racing. If the 'best friend' he's talking about is Ethan Curtis, who everyone says owes his entire career to his early friendship with Jett, then this is some pretty juicy gossip he's sharing, and although I'm still seething with jealously over Violet, and what he just said about her, I'm flattered he obviously trusts me enough to tell me it.

"After that, I kind of went off the rails," he goes on. "I felt so stupid for believing Violet had loved me. And I felt like if what I'd had with her wasn't real, then nothing could be. I couldn't trust anyone. But my dad kept on trying to set me up with people. He thought it would be good for me to be part of some kind of power couple, you know what I mean?"

I absolutely don't, but I nod anyway.

"He's always put so much pressure on me," he goes on. "Just like your mom does with you. And I went along with it, because I wanted him to be proud of me, sure, but also because

I kept thinking that maybe there was someone out there who would be the one for me, and that if I could just find her, I'd be okay. I'd be happy."

There's another long pause, during which I shift a little closer towards him, wondering if I dare reach out to him. Because I want to. I really want to. And not just because I saw what he looked like in his boxers, but because I want to be the one to make him happy. And even if I can't, I still want to make sure he's at least *okay*.

Before I can move, though, Jett starts talking again.

"I guess you know the rest." I feel, rather than see, his shrug of resignation. "Lots of women, lots of dates, lots of crazy rumors and manufactured stories. Lots of lies, in other words."

He shrugs again.

"Hey, don't feel bad for me, Lady M," he says, sounding more like his old self. "I have a nice life. I have a job I love. I can't really complain about the way things have worked out. Here, let me get out my tiny violin. "

He laughs softly. I tell he's already wondering if he's said too much, and I'm anxious to reassure him.

"You're allowed to wish things were different, you know," I tell him, pushing the pillow between us out of the way so I can prop myself up on one elbow and look at him. "You're allowed to have regrets."

By now, my eyes have adjusted to the dark, and I can see his glinting back at me. With the pillow barrier gone, I'm suddenly very aware of just how small a standard double bed really is.

"That's the thing, though," he replies, propping himself up so he's mirroring my position. "I don't. Not really. I know Violet wasn't really the one for me. If she was, she wouldn't have cheated on me. And I wouldn't ever want to be with someone I couldn't trust. So I don't really have *regrets*, as such. I do sometimes wish my life was different, though. I mean, I really liked going to Birnam with you today," he says, sounding bashful. " I had a lot of fun. And I liked The Wildcat, too. I wish I could do stuff like that more often."

"No one likes The Wildcat," I correct him. "You don't have to pretend for me."

"I don't pretend for you," he says softly. "I always tell you the truth. And I like it here. I like the people. Even that guy with the sheep."

"Okay, now I *know* you're lying. I bet you're going to try to tell me you like the weather, too."

I pull the covers up over my shoulders to prove my point. It might be summer, but that doesn't mean it's warm here in the Highlands, and while we've been talking, the rain has started up again outside.

"You cold, Lady M?" Jett says, his voice suddenly much closer in the darkness. Before I can react, he reaches out and pulls me towards him, until my body's nestled against his, my head in the crook of his neck.

"That better?" He uses his other hand to arrange the duvet over us both, and I nod, not quite trusting myself to speak. From my current position, I can hear his heart thudding beneath the thin material of his t-shirt — slow and steady, unlike mine, which started to race as soon as he touched me.

I really hope he can't feel it.

I feel his breath on my hair as his arm tightens around my shoulder, pulling me closer, and I have to force myself to relax and pretend this is just a nice, friendly hug. Just two people trying to keep warm, that's all. Nothing more to it than that;

and even though my body currently feels like it's about to snap in two from all the tension, I'm sure Jett's feeling totally relaxed... isn't he?

"I don't actually mind the weather," he says sleepily, confirming my suspicions. "It's nice listening to the rain against the window. Relaxing."

"Yeah. I guess it is," I whisper back, feeling anything but relaxed.

As his breathing slows, I allow my hand to sneak out across his chest, hugging him closer as I try to figure out how I'm feeling right now. Disappointment over the way he fell asleep without trying to make a move on me fights with the relief that he didn't put me in the position of having to work out how to respond if he had done. Because I know I'm attracted to him — that much is pretty obvious. But I also know that getting involved with Jett Carter would be the kind of mistake that could only end one way: with me getting my heart broken.

Of all the things Jett confided in me tonight, the thing that resonated the most was when he told me what he was looking for.

Something real. Something solid. Something that lasts forever.

No matter how much I wish it was, I know this isn't real. He's kind, and he's gentle, and I believe he wouldn't intentionally do anything to hurt me. But I also believe that, for all he said about having no regrets, he's probably still in love with Violet King, who is beautiful, and famous, and everything I'm not. He might not trust her... but that doesn't mean he doesn't love her, anyway. If anyone understands that, it's me.

I'd have liked it if he'd made some kind of move on me tonight. I can't deny it. But if this is the best I can hope for — lying here beside him in the dark, with our hearts beating in tandem, and the rain on the window lulling us both to sleep — then that's going to have to be good enough.

And, let's face it, "good enough" with Jett Carter is more than anything I'd ever hoped for, anyway.

So I swallow back my disappointment as I tighten my arm around his waist and snuggle closer into his neck.

We stay like that all night.

Chapter 34

"That was literally the best night's sleep I've had in years," Jett murmurs into my hair when I open my eyes the next morning. "You're like some kind of sleep-inducing drug. Or maybe a teddy bear or something."

Before I can figure out how to reply to that, there's a loud buzzing sound from the bedside table, and I almost fall out of bed as Jett reaches over me to grab his phone.

"Yeah?" he says into it, slumping back against the pillows as I get up and pull on my dressing gown. "Oh, hey, Asher. What's up? What time is it over there? You must be up in the middle of the night."

I head to the bathroom to clean my teeth and give him some privacy, and when I come back into the room, he's standing at the window, trying to pull a pair of joggers on with one hand, while holding his phone in the other.

"I know," he says into the phone. "I know. I can't believe it either. Well, I guess I'll see you tomorrow, then. Or maybe that's today, your time?"

My heart drops like a stone. He's leaving? Already? I hastily arrange my face into a neutral expression to try to hide the disappointment as he ends the call and turns to face me, his eyes shining.

"You are not going to believe this," he says, striding across the room towards me. "It's Duval — he wants to see me! He called Asher and asked him to set up a meeting. I'm leaving today. Well, as soon as Grace can arrange it, anyway."

And then he picks me up by the waist, spins me around, and kisses me, full on the lips.

It's so unexpected that, for once, I don't have time to overthink my reactions. Instead, I just kiss him back, looping my arms around his neck as if I have every right to, and allowing myself to sink into this delicious, never-to-be repeated moment when Jett's kissing me because he *wants* to, not because there are cameras around.

I know this will never happen again — he's just told me he's going to be leaving today, after all — so I kiss him as if it's both the first and the last time, and after a fraction of a second's hesitation, when he might have pulled away, Jett kisses me right back. He's still holding me by the waist, balancing me easily in his arms, and I wrap my legs around his body, pulling myself closer. I probably look ridiculous, but for once in my life I don't actually care what I look like; if this is the last time I'm going to see him, I'm going to make sure this is the kind of kiss I remember for the rest of my life. And it is; it really is. It's a movie-style kiss, except it's even better than that because it's *real.* There's absolutely no mistaking it — and even though I'm still wearing my ratty old dressing gown, and I'm sure my mouth must taste like the toothpaste I just used, it's absolutely perfect.

Or, at least, it is until Mum steps in to ruin it.

"Whoops! Sorry, didn't mean to interrupt!"

Jett and I pull abruptly apart at the sound of her voice, and I slide sheepishly down from his embrace, turning around to see her leaning in the doorway, watching us with a look I can't quite fathom on her face. Jealousy? Pride? Something else? Who knows?

"Mum," I snap, pulling my dressing gown around myself. "What are you doing creeping around like that?"

"Oh, I wasn't 'creeping', darling," says Mum brightly. "I just came up to ask if you want me to make us all some breakfast. The door was open."

I snort in disbelief. As if Mum, who's been on a diet for as long as I've been alive, would know how to cook anything more adventurous than toast.

"We'll be down in a second," I tell her, not daring to look at Jett. "Or I will, anyway. Jett has to pack. He has to fly home today."

"Um, we both have to pack," Jett interjects from behind me. "You're coming with me, aren't you?"

"Huh?" I spin round to face him. "Me? But I thought... You just said you had to go?"

"Oh, come on," he grins, looking completely unfazed by what just happened between us. "You didn't think I'd go back without my girl, did you? How would I sleep without you?"

He winks, then turns to Mum.

"I'll take some breakfast, thanks, Sam," he says, patting his stomach. "I'm in a very good mood this morning."

He grins again, but Mum's looking over his shoulder at me.

"You're leaving?" she says, using her own accent instead of the weird, affected one she's been adopting since I got back. "But you just got here, Lexie. I thought you'd stay for longer. We've barely even had a chance to talk."

"We were talking for hours last night, Mum," I point out, feeling suddenly guilty. If I didn't know better, I'd think she was actually going to miss me. "And it's not like you're never going to see me again, is it?"

"Well, I don't know that, do I?" she snaps, sounding more like her old self again. "The last time you left, I didn't even know where you were. For a year, Lexie. A whole year. Imagine not seeing your child for a *year*. Not knowing where they are, whether they're alive or dead, or—"

"You knew perfectly well I was alive, Mum," I tell her firmly, glancing warily at Jett, who's pretending to look at his phone. "I messaged you a few times, remember?"

"Oh, 'a few times'," Mum says, her voice rising. "And you thought that was good enough, did you? To just message me 'a few times' and not even tell me where you were? Do you think that's how a good daughter treats her mother? Well, do you?"

"Enough, Mum," I hiss, finally losing my cool. "Don't try to tell me how 'good' daughters behave. We both know you've never thought I was 'good' enough. At anything, really, let alone being your daughter. Not that you were ever much of a mother to me, mind you. Remember all the times you asked me to stay with friends because your boyfriend — I forget which one — was coming round and you didn't want him to know you were old enough to have a teenage daughter? Or how you always wanted me to go on a diet so I could win your precious beauty contests? And while I'm on the subject, remember what you did to Jack's distillery last year? Remember that? Are you really not going to mention it? Are you seriously going to just keep pretending it's not your fault that I left?"

I'm crying now, tears flowing freely down my cheeks. I had no idea I was going to say all of that. I never have before. I've always just bitten my tongue, like the good girl Mum swears

I've never actually been, and walked away before the anger could burst out of me. But I guess it's been building up all this time. Building up and getting ready to explode, and now that it has, I feel... kind of empty, really. Like I've just kicked something defenseless; which is ridiculous, really, because Mum is anything *but* defenseless.

All the same, as she stands there staring at me in shock, her bottom lip quivering, I find myself wanting to reach out and comfort her for what I just said. Wanting to apologize, like I usually do when Mum does something wrong. Wanting to tell her I didn't mean it, when, actually, I think I did.

And, for once in my life, I'm not going to try to take it back.

"Well, if that's how you feel," she says at last, folding her arms defensively across her chest. "I won't try to make you stay. I must say, I'm disappointed in you, though, Alexandra. I know I haven't been perfect as a mother, but I've done my best, and for you to be casting up all of my past 'crimes' like this is just... it's just unkind."

Her voice wobbles, and she puts one hand on the door frame, as if to steady herself.

"And now to leave me like this, when I'm just out of hospital," she goes on, warming to her theme. "Well. I just don't know how you can be so cruel. I don't know how you can—"

"Okay, that's enough."

Mum blinks in surprise as Jett steps in front of me, almost as if he's trying to shield me from the words that are coming out of her mouth.

"But I—"

"Enough, Sam," he repeats firmly. "We've heard enough. I don't want to hear any more of this bullshit from you. You don't get to talk to her like that, you hear me?"

Mum's mouth opens and closes like a goldfish and she looks from Jett to me, then back again. It would almost be amusing if my heart wasn't about to leap right out of my chest from sheer adrenalin.

"Lexie—" Mum starts, turning to me, but Jett holds up a hand to stop her.

"Uh-uh," he tells her, his voice hard. "Don't even think about it. If you want to have any kind of relationship with your daughter in future, Samantha, you'll either apologize to her right now for everything you just said, or you'll turn around and you'll get the hell out of her house. Your choice."

Mum just gapes at him, her face white with shock. I don't think anyone's ever stood up to her like that. I know for sure that no one's ever stood up for *me* like that, and it's all I can do not to throw my arms around him in gratitude.

Thank you, thank you, thank you.

"Okay," Jett says easily, when a few more seconds have passed and Mum's still standing there speechless. "I can see you need a bit of time to think about that one. Come on, Lexie, let's go downstairs. I'll make you a coffee."

"No," I tell him firmly, shaking off the hand he offers me. "No, let's just pack our stuff and go. I want to get out of here. Please, Jett?"

I look up at him pleadingly, and, after a second, he nods, his green eyes fixed on mine.

"Sure, Lady M," he says, as if we're discussing something totally innocuous, like what we're going to have for breakfast. "Let's do that."

He crosses the room and pulls my suitcase down from the top of the wardrobe, where I stashed it when I arrived, and I walk over to it on legs that don't feel quite like they belong to me and open it up. By the time I turn back around to take some of my clothes out of the dresser, the open doorway is empty once more.

I guess she decided to get the hell out, then.

* * *

Jett and I don't talk as we move around the room, methodically packing our stuff. I don't know whether his silence is him being tactful, and letting me process my conversation with Mum, or if he's just feeling awkward about our kiss now that he's had the chance to think about it, but, either way, I'm grateful for the space he's giving me. I really want to thank him for what he just did for me, but right now I don't have the words; and, even if I did, I'm not sure I could get them out without crying.

It's not even 9 a.m., and this has already been one of the weirdest — and most emotional — days of my life. And that's up against quite a bit of competition.

"I'll take this downstairs for you," Jett says, breaking the silence as he picks up the suitcase for me. "It'll be okay, Lexie," he adds, turning to look back at me as he leaves the room. "We'll figure it out. I promise."

I smile weakly in response. He's being so sweet. Surely he can't be faking that?

As he disappears down the stairs with the suitcase, I pause and take a last glance around the room, wondering if I'll ever see it again. Before I can leave it, though, a movement at one of the windows catches my eye, and I stop to look out, blinking in surprise as I see Mum standing in the garden, gesturing wildly as she chats animatedly to a woman whose face I can't quite see. After a few seconds, though, Mum turns and walks away, and the woman she was talking to looks directly up at the window I'm standing at, and I find myself ducking out of sight before she can see me.

It's Scarlett Scott.

Talking to my mother, outside my house.

What was that I told Jett about there being no witches in Heather Bay?

Chapter 35

The chauffeur firm we used to pick us up from the airport is fully booked, and none of the taxi companies I try instead can send someone round at short notice, so I do the only thing I can think of, under the circumstances: I call McTavish.

"Aye, I'll take ye to the airport," he says immediately. "I dinnae ken why ye didnae just phone me in the first place. I drive an Uber, ye ken."

I had no idea we even *had* Uber here in the Highlands, but, sure enough, when McTavish pulls up outside the house in his ancient Volvo, 15 minutes later, I see a piece of cardboard taped to the back window with the word 'Uber' scrawled on it with a sharpie.

Mum mentioned he'd been trying to make some extra money during our wine-fuelled chat last night. I guess this is how he's been doing it.

"Do you want to talk about what just happened?" Jett asks in a low voice as we pull away from the cottage.

"What's that" asks McTavish immediately, looking at us in the rear-view mirror. "What just happened?"

"Nothing," I say quickly, glancing warningly at Jett. "Absolutely nothing. Thanks for picking us up, McTavish. I really appreciate it."

Jett shrugs and pulls out his phone and McTavish turns his attention back to the road, leaving me free to lean my head against the window and watch as Heather Bay slips past us, with its pastel-painted houses, its cluttered souvenir shops, and its cute little cafes.

I'm going to miss it.

I know I didn't want to come back here, but now that I've seen it again, I can't help wishing I'd had more time to show Jett around; maybe take him cold-water swimming in the loch, or buy ice cream cones and sit on the beach together. We could even have gone hiking together, and found some of those trees he's so keen on.

It would've been nice.

Stop it, Lexie.

I steal a sidelong look at Jett, who's buried in his phone again, as usual. The problem is, all of those things I've been imagining us doing together are the kind of things you do with your partner, not the guy you have a weird-ass business arrangement with. And, as of right now, that's still all this is. Or, as far as I know, anyway.

Jett hasn't mentioned the kiss, just like I haven't mentioned the argument with Mum. McTavish's larger-than-life presence in the front of the car means we're unlikely to start talking about either of those topics now, so instead I just roll them around in my head, worrying at them like a kitten with a ball of wool.

Did he kiss me because he's into me, or was it just a spur-of-the-moment thing, because he was so elated by the news he'd just had from Asher?

Did he say those things to Mum because he couldn't stand seeing me hurt, or would he have done the same for anyone?

And where is Mum, anyway? Where did she go after her conversation with Scarlett at the gate? What were they talking about? Why do I have a horrible feeling about all of this in the pit of my stomach right now?

Round and round the thoughts go in my head, my mind jumping from one worry to the next, and then right back to the start again. By the time the car pulls in to the little private airfield we flew into just a few days ago, I've bitten my fingernails almost to the quick, and I'm no further forward with any of the questions that are tormenting me.

"Emerald told me ye apologized to her for what ye did," McTavish says as he pulls our suitcases out of the car for us. "I thought that was decent o' ye. Unexpected, mind, but decent."

I smile weakly.

"It was the least I could do," I tell him. "The very least. And I really am sorry, McTavish. I just wish there was something I could do to make up for it all. I wish—"

I stop short as all the emotion of this weird morning catches up with me at once, making my eyes sting with sudden tears.

"You take care o' yerself, Lexie," McTavish says, his blue eyes filled with concern as he hands me my bag. "Oh, and if ye could get that Violet King's autograph for me, that would be grand," he says, winking. "Or her phone number, even. Well, see ye, Lexie. It was nice to meet ye, Jett. Mr. Carter, I mean."

He shakes hands cheerfully with Jett, whose mouth has settled into a thin line at the mention of Violet's name.

"I haven't said anything to him about you and Violet," I try to reassure him as we walk into the airport's tiny terminal. "It's just a coincidence, him mentioning her right then."

Jett nods tightly, not looking at me. He must know I

wouldn't tell anyone what he confided in me about Violet cheating on him. I mean, even if I'd wanted to, it's hard to imagine when I'd have found the time, what with all the drama that's been going on. All the same, though, the mood between us has shifted imperceptibly.

The silence between us in the car — and in my room, while we packed our stuff — was natural; comfortable, even. The one that descends as we enter the airport, though, and hand over our passports to the man who comes forward to meet us, is altogether different. All of a sudden, the man next to me feels like a stranger again, and my stomach clenches with anxiety as we sit down on a sofa in the waiting area, and he immediately resumes whatever it is he's been typing into his phone all the way here.

I know I said I didn't want to talk, but this is getting ridiculous.

"Miss Steele?"

I look up from my increasingly frantic thoughts to find the airport employee who took our passports standing in front of me with an apologetic look on his face.

"Yes? Is there something wrong?"

Something in his expression tells me the answer to that question is going to be yes, but it still comes as a shock when he says it.

"I'm afraid your visa for the U.S.A. is no longer valid," he says, handing the passport back to me. "I'm sure it's just some kind of misunderstanding, but I'm really sorry, we're not going to be able to let you board until it's sorted out."

* * *

The next few minutes pass in a blur.

Jett argues with someone on the phone, while airport staff hover anxiously around us, offering glasses of water and other things that would be completely useless. I don't need a glass of water, or a nice, comfortable seat. I just need to know what's going on, and why I'm being told I'm not welcome in the United States any more, when the issue with my visa was supposed to have been long-since fixed by Jett's lawyers.

And it *was* fixed, I'm sure of it. Asher told me it would be, and I have no reason to doubt him... and yet, here I am. *Doubting* him. Doubting *everyone*, actually. I'm even starting to doubt Jett, who's still speaking animatedly to whoever's on the other end of the phone, his voice too low for me to hear his side of the conversation.

What's going on? Why won't he tell me what's happening?

"I don't understand," I say for what has to be the one hundredth time so far, turning to the man who seems to be in charge. "I know I'd overstayed my visa by... well, by a little bit. But that was all sorted out. I didn't have any problems on the way here."

"Well, no, you wouldn't have, Miss," he says apologetically. "You're a U.K. citizen. Your passport is valid for here. It's the other end that seems to have the issue."

"Am I... am I going to be arrested?" I ask, looking around in horror, as if armed police might be lurking around every corner.

"Oh, no." He laughs nervously. "At least, I wouldn't think so, anyway."

He frowns, and my heart tries to escape my body through my mouth.

"Normally you'd just be banned from entering the U.S. for

a period of time," the man goes on, clearly trying to sound reassuring. "But, like you say, I'm sure it'll all be worked out. Look, your... companion's... off the phone now."

He takes a tactful step back, looking relieved to be out of the firing line, and I turn round to see Jett striding towards me, his jaw set.

He looks furious.

Something tells me this is not *going to be good news.*

"Jett, what's going on?" I ask, jumping in before he can speak. "I thought the visa thing had been dealt with? Asher said—"

"Yeah, that deal's off," Jett says abruptly. "Things have changed. But I'm sure you know that, don't you?"

He stops in front of me, his eyes blazing. I've never seen him so angry. And it looks like I'm the target of it.

"Wh-what do you mean? I don't understand?"

"Don't treat me like a fool, Lexie," he snaps. "I don't want to hear it. You know what you did. I don't have anything more to say to you. Like I said, the deal's off."

He bends down to pick up his bag, which is lying on the floor between us, then slings it over his shoulder as I stand there gaping at him, momentarily stunned into silence.

"Jett," I say, finally finding my voice as I rush forward to grab him by the arm. "What are you talking about? I have no idea what you're talking about, I swear. Please, Jett, you have to believe me."

"Lexie, I wouldn't believe you if you told me your name," he says, looking weary. He shakes my arm roughly off and turns away, before almost instantly spinning back around to face me.

"I trusted you, Lexie," he says, leaning in so no one else can hear him. "I let you into my life. I told you things I've never told anyone else, because I thought you understood. I thought we were the same. But we're not the same."

He's standing so close that I can practically feel the anger radiating off him in waves. His voice is low and controlled, but there's no mistaking the fury that lies beneath it.

"We're not the same, Lexie," he goes on, "Because I would never have let you down like that. I would never have betrayed your trust. I really hope it was worth whatever you got paid for it. I guess you really were the serpent all along, huh?"

This time when he turns away, I know he's not coming back.

"Jett," I call desperately after him, but all that comes out is a squeak. It's like one of those nightmares where you're screaming for help, but no one can hear you. Right now, I know Jett can hear me, which means he's deliberately ignoring me as he strides off towards the door that leads to his waiting plane, with me running after him, not caring how stupid I must look.

"Jett!" I sob, "Please wait. Please, you have to tell me what I'm supposed to have done. I don't understand— "

I'm shouting louder now, but he waits until he reaches the door before he looks back.

"Is that right?" he says sarcastically as he pushes the door open. "Why don't you ask your friend Scarlett, then? She seems to know it all, doesn't she?"

The door slams shut behind him.

He's gone.

And, just as I knew it would be, back when I first met him, my heart is broken.

Chapter 36

Romance or Showmance? What's really going on between Jett Carter and Lexie Steele?
By Senior Reporter, Scarlett Scott

It looks like the perfect romance: but looks can be deceiving, and rumor has it that things between Hollywood heartthrob Jett Carter, and his Scottish sweetheart, Lexie Steele, might not be all that they seem.

"Jett's relationship with Lexie is totally fake," a source close to the star said, speaking exclusively to the Gazette this week. "He doesn't love her. He barely even knows her, in fact. He's in Scotland to rehearse for a new movie role and she's been helping him with it, but it's nothing more than that. They have separate rooms, separate lives. She's basically just an employee."

Carter and Steele started dating just a few weeks ago, and appeared to have a whirlwind romance, with dinner dates, red-carpet appearances, and romantic walks along the beach. Jett even introduced the Heather Bay born beauty to his parents (Oscar winner Charles Carter, and his wife Gabriella) at an event in L.A. last month, and was said to be so smitten with the distillery heiress that he was ready to settle down with her.

"That's not true either," our source said this week. "Jett will

never settle down. It's not in his nature. He's a commitment-phobe, who's been secretly messaging his ex the entire time he's supposedly been seeing Lexie. She's the only one he's ever loved. All of his other girlfriends were just women his dad wanted him to be seen with, for the sake of his career, and Lexie's no different."

Jett and Lexie are currently staying in Heather Bay, to look after the latter's ailing mother, Samantha. Neither could be reached for comment at the time this article went to press.

By the time McTavish arrives to pick me up from the airport, I've read the article on the *Gazette's* website at least five times, and have finally managed to stop sobbing, although my cheeks are still wet with tears, and every time I reach up to wipe them away, my hand comes back black with mascara.

I must look an absolute state, but McTavish tactfully refrains from comment as he takes the suitcase he unloaded from his car less than an hour ago, and puts it back into the boot.

"Dinnae worry, I didnae have far to come," he says kindly when I start to apologize for making him come all the way back for me. "I stopped at Greggs in Fort William tae get a sausage roll. That's where I was when ye phoned. Here, you can have it. Ye look like ye need it more than me."

He hands me a soggy paper bag, waving away my protests as he gets back into the driver's seat. After a moment's hesitation, I open the passenger door and get in beside him. No point riding in the back when there's just the two of us in the car now, is there?

"Ach, it's a bad business, right enough," McTavish says once we're back on the road to Heather Bay and I've finished reading Scarlett's article aloud to him. "Scarlett shouldnae be spreading gossip like that. It isnae exactly news, is it?"

"It isn't exactly 'gossip' either," I say glumly, unwrapping the sausage roll and taking a bite. It's actually quite good. "Jett's not my boyfriend, McTavish. And he probably *is* still in love with his ex."

I think about how much time Jett spends on his phone, and remember what Scarlett's anonymous "source" said about how he'd been messaging someone else the entire time we'd supposedly been together.

"He's *definitely* still in love with his ex," I correct myself. "He's sure as hell not in love with me, that's for sure."

If I had to come clean to anyone I know, I'm glad it was McTavish. Anyone else might have yelled at me for lying to them, or refused to speak to me for the rest of the journey. McTavish, on the other hand, just keeps on driving, and although his knuckles tighten slightly on the steering wheel, his eyes remain firmly on the road.

Well, he always was a very safe driver, I suppose.

"I have to hand it to ye, Lexie," he says at last, his tone light. "There's never a dull moment wi' ye, is there?"

"Not really," I admit, shamefacedly. "I wish there was. I didn't do it to try to trick anyone," I tell him hurriedly. "It was a business arrangement, really. I did it because I wanted to help him. I really want him to get that role, McTavish. He deserves it. He should get it."

"Aw the same," says McTavish firmly, "Scarlett still shouldnae be writing stuff like that about ye. It's nobody's business but yer ain."

"I think she might be softening towards me, actually," I tell him, scanning the article yet again. "At least she didn't lie about my age this time. And she called me a 'distillery heiress' rather than just an 'admin assistant' like last time. Oh, and a "beauty" too. That was... nice of her. I guess."

"A distillery heiress?" McTavish glances over at me, his eyebrows raised.

"I'd rather focus on the 'Heather Bay beauty' bit, to be honest, but yeah, that's what she said. And, I mean, she's not *wrong*, is she? I am *technically* an heiress, in that I'll inherit the distillery from Mum one day. It's just... What? What is it? Why are you looking at me like that?"

McTavish has a strange look on his face. At first I think he's just looking at the remains of the Greggs sausage roll, which I've wolfed down without even realizing I was doing it, but then he turns red and looks back at the road, and I get a strong sense that he knows something.

"Okay, out with it, McTavish," I sigh, scrunching the paper bag I'm holding into a ball. "You obviously know something I don't, so you might as well tell me. It's not like my life can get any worse right now, is it?"

It's true. The entire time we've been in the car, my body's gone rigid every time I've heard a plane flying overhead. The chances of me spotting the one that's taking Jett away from me are slim to none, obviously, but that doesn't change the fact that it's happening. Right now, he's getting into a plane — or maybe he's already in it — and leaving me. And he's never coming back.

"Just tell me," I mutter, digging my fingernails into my palms to stop myself from bursting into tears again. "At least it'll distract me from... you know. *This*."

I gesture vaguely around me, hoping McTavish gets the gist.

"I think ye should speak to yer mam, Lexie," he says gently. "It isnae ma place."

"Oh, don't worry, I'll be speaking to her alright," I reply bitterly. "Just as soon as I can track her down. I'll be asking her why she told Scarlett about me and Jett, for one thing. Although I very much doubt she'll have an answer good enough for me."

"Yer mam knew? And she told Scarlett, ye think?"

"She must have done. It's the only explanation. I'm sure she heard me and Jett talking last night — and she was definitely talking to Scarlett this morning."

I frown, confused. I know that's what must have happened, but it wouldn't have given Mum much time to pass on the news, and even less for Scarlett to write up her article and get it onto the website. Not that it would've taken long to write that trash, mind you.

But then, how did Mum know about Jett talking to Violet? I didn't even know that myself?

I shake my head to try to clear it. The details aren't important. I know Mum did this. She's the one who's ruined my chances with Jett, and worst of all, she's done it by making him think he couldn't trust me — that I'd let him down.

I will never, ever forgive her for that.

"Aye, ye could be right," McTavish is saying. "She's a wild card, is Samantha. There's one thing ye're wrong about, though. Or as far as I can tell, anyway."

"Oh? And what's that?"

"Ye're wrong tae say he doesnae love ye."

It's strange to hear McTavish, of all people, talking about love, but his tone is matter-of-fact, with no hint of embarrassment.

"I've seen the way he looks at ye," he goes on. "And the way ye look at him, for that matter. That's no' the way folk look at each other when they just have a — what did ye call it? A business arrangement? Dinnae get me started."

He snorts with laughter, and I feel the tears rush into my eyes. I don't always cry when someone's cruel to me, but just a few words of kindness and I'm suddenly a leaky tap.

"Ye're lying, Lexie," McTavish tells me, as he takes the turning that will lead us back to Heather Bay. "Yer arse is oot the windae."

"Hey!" I cut in indignantly. "I've told you the absolute truth, McTavish, I swear. I don't have any reason to lie to you now the truth's all over the Internet. And I don't know what that last bit means, but that's not true either. I expect."

"It means ye're lying," he repeats firmly. "No tae me, ya great galoot: tae yerself. Ye're lying when ye keep tellin' yerself ye were just trying to help him get his role. Ye did it because ye love the guy. It's as plain as the nose on Old Jimmy's face. And that's quite a hooter oor man has there."

He's right.

He's absolutely right.

Not about Old Jimmy and his nose — well, actually, he's right about that too. Jimmy does have quite the nose on him, really.

But he's even more right about me, and how I feel about Jett. Because I love him. I can see that now. I don't just fancy him, or want to help him get the role, and I'd have signed the contract even if I hadn't needed a way out of my visa situation.

I actually love him.

And I'm realizing it at the exact moment he's leaving me.

Chapter 37

Mum's sitting at the kitchen table when I let myself back into the cottage, feeling like I've been gone for weeks, rather than just the few hours it's taken for Jett to comprehensively ruin my life.

Her hair's pulled back into a ponytail, and, without her usual layer of makeup, she looks her age for the first time I can remember.

"Lexie? What are you doing here? I thought you were going back to America with Jett?"

"I was," I say shortly, dropping my keys onto the table and collapsing into the chair opposite her. "But then Jett saw the article in the *Gazette* about us, and, funnily enough, he decided he didn't want me around anymore."

I don't mention the small issue of me being banned from entering the United States for the foreseeable. That's the very least of my worries right now.

"What are you doing here, anyway?" I ask, when Mum makes no comment to this. "I thought you'd be out spending the money you made from selling the story to Scarlett. How much did you get, by the way?"

Mum stares up at me, the shadows under her eyes highlighted by the electric light.

"Money?" she says, sounding confused. "What money? Why would Scarlett give me money?"

"Oh, come on, Mum, don't give me that."

I want to yell at her; to stamp my feet and scream and make the kind of scene I know she'd probably enjoy — she's always been all about the drama — but I'm suddenly exhausted. All I've been doing is sitting in a car, but I'm so wrung-out with all the emotion I've been going through that I could quite happily lay my head on the table and sleep.

"The story, Mum," I say irritably. "The one in the Gazette? About me and Jett and our fake relationship? The one you gave Scarlett this morning? Is this ringing any bells with you?"

"Don't be ridiculous, Lexie," she says, sounding more like her old self. "The Heather Bay Gazette doesn't have the money to pay people for stories. It's a weekly free-sheet, not The Daily Mail."

She reaches into her handbag and pulls out a pack of cigarettes, and I look on in astonishment as she lights one. She hasn't smoked for years. I wonder what role she's trying to play *now*?

"I did speak to Scarlett this morning, as it happens," she says, taking a deep drag and then blowing out a perfect smoke ring. "But not to tell her anything about you, Lexie. Quite the opposite, in fact."

"What do you mean?"

I know I shouldn't engage with her right now. I know better than to trust a single word that comes out of her mouth, but still. I have to know. I have to know why she did it. I have to know how she knew. And, most of all, I have to know whether it was true what she said about Jett and Violet still being in touch.

I lean back in my seat, watching warily as she takes another puff of her cigarette.

"Scarlett already knew about you and Jett when she came round this morning," Mum says at last. "I don't know how, but she did. She'd already written the article, but she needed to speak to you or Jett to get you to confirm it. I'm not sure she even really believed it herself, if I'm honest. She was... strange."

"Scarlett's always strange," I interrupt. "So, what did you tell her?"

"I told her you weren't here," she says, looking me in the eye. "That you'd gone out for the day and I didn't know when you'd be back. And I told her it wasn't true, what she was saying. I told her I'd seen you together with my own eyes, just like she had, and that what I'd seen was a young couple who were completely and utterly in love."

"And why did you tell her that?" I ask, surprised that she thinks I'm buying this for a single second.

"Well, because it's true, of course," she says immediately, looking surprised to be asked. "Isn't it?"

"Oh, come on Mum, you know it isn't," I wail, putting my head in my hands. "Would you just drop the act for once in your life? I know you know. I know you heard me and Jett in the kitchen last night. And I know you told Scarlett about it. What I don't know is why you can't just admit it? Why not be honest for once? You never know, you might like it."

"Lexie, are you telling me Scarlett's article was true?" Mum says, leaning across the table to look at me. "Are you serious? You and Jett were just... faking it?"

She looks so shocked that she almost has me convinced. Almost.

"Acting, Mum. We were acting." My head drops back into my hands, suddenly too heavy for me to hold it up any longer. "It's what he does, remember?"

And what I do too now, apparently.

"Well, I'll be." Mum straightens up, her mouth still hanging open in surprise. "Wait. How much did you get paid?" she asks, her eyes narrowing. "Was it a lot? Because there's something I need to—"

"Are you actually telling me you didn't know?" I burst out, looking up at her. "You must have known."

Mum shakes her head.

"I honestly didn't," she says, getting up and flicking her cigarette butt into the sink. I resist the impulse to get up and clear it away. I want to hear what she has to say.

"I did try to listen at the door last night," she says, looking slightly shamefaced. "But I couldn't hear anything, Lexie," she goes on eagerly. "You were speaking too quietly, and then when I opened the door, you were all over each other, and I thought... Well, I thought you really liked him. I thought he really liked you. And then this morning, in your room... Are you honestly telling me none of that was real?"

I shrug. I know it was real for me, but I have no idea what it meant to Jett. And thanks to Scarlett and her stupid article, I never will.

"I should've got you acting lessons when you were a kid," Mum says thoughtfully. "It might have been a better investment than the pageant stuff. That never really worked out, did it?"

She looks at me for confirmation, then looks away again, embarrassed.

"Not that it matters, obviously," she says awkwardly. "I

was always very proud of you, Lexie. You know that, don't you? You were such a pretty little thing."

"Well, that's the main thing, isn't it?" I reply bitterly. "As long as everything looks good on the outside, who cares if it's secretly falling apart?"

"That's not what I meant."

If I didn't know better, I'd think she was about to cry. Instead, she just walks over to the fridge and gets out what's left of last night's wine, which she pours into two glasses, before handing me one.

Smoking and *drinking. It looks like shit's about to get serious.*

"It's not what I meant," she repeats, sitting back down opposite me. "You were always pretty, Lexie — you still are — but you were also so *good.* Always helping around the house, making sure everything ran smoothly. I never had to tell you to tidy your room, or do your homework. It's like you were the adult and I was the child some of the time."

"*Some* of the time? Er, try *all* the time," I can't resist pointing out.

"Okay, all the time, then. You looked after me. I didn't... I didn't do a great job of looking after you, and I'm sorry for that. No, really, I am."

Mum pauses, seeing the doubt on my face.

"I know you won't believe this," she says with a hollow laugh, "But I really did try, you know. After your dad... after what happened with him, I didn't really cope very well. I was very young, you know. Very scared. And then I was on my own with a baby I had no idea how to look after, and... well, I guess I just got lucky that the baby was you, and you always seemed to know how to look after yourself."

"I didn't 'just know'," I mutter, taking a gulp of my wine. "I had to figure it out, the same way I had to figure out everything else. It's not like I was just *born* like that."

I'm arguing with her, but, if I'm totally honest, my heart's not really in it. Because she's done it again, hasn't she? She's somehow managed to make me feel sorry for her. And even though I know she's probably just trying to manipulate me again, part of me really wants to believe her.

"I know," she says sadly. "I know that, Lexie. Like I say, I was lucky — not just because you were so strong, and so capable, but because you were *you*, and I wouldn't have changed you for anything. But I didn't always show you that, and I'm sorry. I mean that. And, whatever you think of me, I want you to know it wasn't me who gave Scarlett that story. I wouldn't do that."

I watch her suspiciously as she picks up her glass and drains it. I can normally tell when Mum's lying, but this time I'm struggling. This time, it feels like she could be telling the truth. Or is that just wishful thinking on my part?

"You did give her the story about you being in hospital," I challenge her, my voice quivering. "The one about me being a terrible daughter for not rushing to your bedside."

Mum raises her hands as if in surrender.

"Guilty as charged," she says, with something approaching her usual spark. "I did do that. But only because I felt like I'd run out of options. I'd been calling and calling, and you'd never once answered. It felt like the only way to get your attention. Scarlett told me it would be sensitively done. But I think she got a bit carried away, really. Well, we both did. Look, what can I say?" she adds defensively. "It was exciting. I felt like a celebrity. I liked it."

Now that's the Mum I know and... well, love, I guess. Because, in spite of everything, she's still my mum. And I might not be stupid enough to think she' s learned her lesson, and that everything's going to be different from now on, but I believe her when she says she didn't tell Scarlett about me and Jett. She's not a good enough actress, to be blunt. The same Mum who pulled that ham-fisted "Joan Collins" act in the hospital wouldn't be capable of faking the kind of emotion she's displaying now. *I'm* the one who can cry on demand, after all: not her.

"Fine," I say, relenting at last. "I believe it wasn't you. But then, who was it?"

"I don't know," says Mum, who clearly doesn't care much either, now that she knows she's off the hook herself. "Maybe she made it up?"

"No." I shake my head. "I don't think even Scarlett would stoop quite that low. And anyway, she got it right, didn't she? Which means she has to have heard it from *someone*."

I start picking at my nails in agitation, and Mum reaches over the table and puts her hand on mine to stop me.

"Lexie," she says, still holding my hand. "There's something else I have to tell you. I think we're going to need another drink first, though."

I get up with a sigh, and get another bottle of wine, which I pour into our glasses. I'm not even nervous any more. I don't know what she's going to tell me, but, whatever it is, it can't possibly make me feel worse than I did when Jett walked away from me this morning, so I pour the wine, then I sit back down and wait to hear what she's got to say.

"It's the distillery," Mum says, as soon as we're both seated again. "I don't really know how to tell you this, Lexie, but we have to sell the distillery. It's making too much of a loss now.

The publicity it got after that whole business last year—"

"What, when you paid someone to sabotage The 39, you mean?" I say, my temper flaring again as I remember the scene last summer when the truth finally came out. "That business?"

"I don't know what you want me to say," she wails, putting her hands over her face. "I know it was a terrible thing to do. I can't defend it. But I was desperate, Lexie. I was absolutely desperate. We were losing so much money. I was about to lose the house. We were going to lose *everything*, and I didn't know what to do."

"God, Mum," I sigh. "There must have been *so many things* you could have done other than that. Someone could have been seriously hurt. Jack almost *was*."

"That wasn't supposed to happen," she mutters sullenly. "I was assured no one would be hurt. I would never have gone through with it if I'd thought for a second that anyone could be hurt. You have to believe me. I would do anything to make up for it. I swear, Lexie, I would. Anything at all. I just don't know what I *can* do. All I know is that we can't go on like this."

I sip my drink slowly.

"Here's what you do," I tell her, putting the glass down. "You sell the distillery to Jack. Or you give him first refusal, at least. You give him a fair price for it — just enough to cover your expenses, nothing more."

Mum nods reluctantly. I can tell she's not 100% on board with this plan, but she's not exactly in a position to say no, so I forge on.

"I have some money from... from my job with Jett," I say. "That'll tide us over for a while. And in the meantime, I guess I'll start looking for a job. You too."

She nods again, even more reluctantly this time. What an excellent evening this is turning out to be.

"Oh," I add, "And you start therapy. A.S.A.P. Non-negotiable. You get some help, and you get it soon. Understood?"

"Understood," Mum says in a small voice. "I will do better, Lexie. I know I can do better."

"Good."

I pick up my glass again wearily. I know there's so much more to say — so much more we need to talk about. But that fleeting mention of Jett's name has made my heart hurt so much again that it's back to being all I can think of. Earlier today, after he left, I'd made up my mind to send all the money I've been paid so far straight back to him. I haven't touched any of it. It never felt right to spend it, somehow, and it definitely doesn't feel right to keep it, given the way everything's ended.

It doesn't look like I have much of a choice, though.

I'm no longer a distillery heiress, as Scarlett put it. I'm not anything, really. I'm not even a fake girlfriend anymore, and instead of feeling relieved that I don't have to keep up the act, all I feel is sad that I'm never going to be able to tell Jett my side of the story, or to prove to him that I really didn't betray his trust.

I pick up my phone and open the messages app. There's nothing from him. I sent him a short message after I read Scarlett's article, telling him I knew nothing about it, but the words sounded hollow, even to me, and I wouldn't blame him if he doesn't even bother to read it, let alone reply to it.

I wouldn't blame him at all.

"I'm going to bed," I announce, pushing myself up from the

table and taking my glass over to the sink. "I know it's still early, but I'm exhausted. It's been a long day. I'll think about all of this tomorrow."

"That's the spirit," Mum says cheerfully, pouring herself another glass of wine. "Tomorrow is another day."

"I suppose."

I hover awkwardly in the doorway, wondering how to wind this conversation up. I feel like we should maybe hug or something. That's what would happen if this was a movie.

But my life isn't a movie.

And that's never been more apparent than it is now.

Chapter 38

I wake up the next morning to gray skies, and no messages from Jett.

There is, however, a huge number of people standing outside my house, and, instead of the usual Jett Carter fans, who disappeared as soon as the news broke that he'd left town, the huge cameras they're all clutching are a sure sign that the paparazzi have found their way back to Heather Bay.

Fantastic. Now I can't even leave the house without having my photo taken.

Not that I particularly want to leave the house, mind you. My 'early night' ended up being just an excuse to cry myself to sleep, and now that the floodgates have opened, I can't seem to figure out how to slam them shut again.

I guess I'm going to have to give up my claim of being the woman who never cries, then.

I had intended to get Mum to call Jack Buchanan this morning to talk to him about the possibility of him buying us out of the distillery, but I'm feeling so low I end up just lurking in my room, peeking out of the window every now and then to see if the photographers are still there. Which they always, always are.

After a couple of hours, the front door opens, and Mum

totters out in a pair of high heels and approaches the paps. I watch in horror as she appears to address them for a few minutes, to the accompaniment of a lot of shouted questions, then I see Scarlett peel away from the rest of the group — presumably heading back to the office to file whatever story she's going to make up next.

Mum strikes a few poses on the footpath, then turns and comes back into the house, where I meet her in the hallway.

"What are you doing?" I hiss, as if the photographers might somehow hear me. "What did they want?"

That's a stupid question, obviously. I know they want to follow up on the "fake relationship" story, and probably to paint me as a real-life Lady Macbeth, getting Jett into trouble with my scheming ways. And judging by the look on Mum's face, I'm right.

"Oh, you know," she says vaguely, examining her reflection in the hall mirror. "They wanted to talk to you about Jett. I gave them a good telling off, though," she adds, looking at me for approval. "Told them to stop tormenting you, and let you grieve in peace."

"Grieve?" I wail. "You told them I was grieving? Mum!"

"Well, you are, aren't you?" she shrugs. "You're grieving your relationship. I understand, sweetheart. Oh, here, I almost forgot: Scarlett asked me to give you this."

She reaches into her pocked and hands me a folded up piece of paper that's been ripped out of a notebook. "Call me," it says. "I can help." Then there's a number which I assume is Scarlett's, and which I take a small amount of satisfaction in tossing straight into the bin.

There. That'll show her.

Once that's done, though, I'm at a loss. I have no job, no

friends... no real life to speak of. I could call Summer, I suppose. Now that the truth's come out about me and Jett, I guess there's nothing stopping me. But it'll still be the middle of the night in L.A., and...

I squeeze my eyes shut tight to stop the thoughts that come rushing in about L.A., where Jett will surely be by now. I wonder what he's doing? Did he go straight to bed, to sleep off the jet-lag? Or is he lying awake, unable to sleep? Is he thinking about me, or is he texting Violet, telling her he's back home, and he can't wait to see her? Maybe she's even with him. Maybe—

"Lexie!"

Mum snaps her fingers in my face to get my attention, and I open my eyes again to find her standing in front of me, holding Scarlett's note, which she's fished out of the bin.

"Maybe you should call her?" she says, as if this is a totally reasonable suggestion. "See what she has to say? She was ever so nice to me when I was in hospital, you know. She even came to see me a couple of times. Not to interview me, you understand. She just said she thought I could use the company. I think she was a bit lonely, actually. I think—"

"I'm not phoning her, Mum," I interrupt, handing back the note. "Scarlett's ruined my entire life. You must see that? Because of her, Jett thinks he can't trust me. He thinks I was just using him for the money, or to get famous or whatever."

"Well, you're certainly famous now," Mum says brightly, completely missing the point. "Everyone will know the name Lexie Steele after this. You've really put Heather Bay on the map."

"Yeah, and I don't expect anyone's going to be thanking me for that," I mutter as she wanders off to the kitchen, leaving the phone number on the hall table. "It turns out fame's not all it's cracked up to be."

I turn to go back upstairs. Before I do, though, I take Scarlett's note and put it back into the bin, where it belongs.

And that's where it'll stay.

* * *

The next morning, the note is still where I left it, but it doesn't matter, because Scarlett herself is at the front door, lifting up the letterbox to peer through it as she calls my name.

"Lexie," she yells down the hallway. "Please, can you let me in? I just want to talk to you. I can help you. I can let you tell your side of the story."

I crept out of my room when I heard her at the door, and now I'm sitting crouched at the top of the stairs, but I leap up at her words and go thundering down them, pulling up the letterbox on my side, and screaming at her to leave me alone.

"As if I would trust you to tell my side of anything, Scarlett," I sob, unable to stop myself. "You can't even get my age right. And all you care about is creating more drama, anyway. Just leave me alone. I don't need your 'help'."

There's a silence, then her eyes appear again, framed by the letterbox.

"I'm sorry about the age thing," she says contritely. "I was just being a bitch. But I was being serious when I said I wanted to help. I don't know if you've seen any of the articles about you yet, but—"

I slam the letterbox closed on my side. I finally succumbed

to the lure of the Internet last night. I couldn't resist it. I wanted to know what they were saying about me, but, most of all, I wanted to know what they were saying about Jett. Like where he is, for instance. Or *how* he is. And I know it's not like DeuxMoi will be able to give me any unique insight into his state of mind, but if there are any pap photos of him that've been taken in the last couple of days, I'll know just by looking at him. Even in the short time I've known him, I've learned every one of his mannerisms. I know the way he raises his shoulders and pulls his cap down over his eyes when he's feeling anxious. I know the way his whole face changes when he's happy. I know him so well that it seems incredible to me that, from now on, he's only going to be a picture on a screen to me. Nothing more than that.

And, as of this morning, not *even* that, apparently.

There are no new photos of Jett online. No news stories. No unconfirmed sightings posted on the Instagram fan sites. Even Shona's Instagram just has a random photo of an alpaca, and nothing about Jett or me. It's like he's just disappeared. Meanwhile, though, there are plenty of stories about us both; some of which have been illustrated by photos of me and McTavish — who's described by the tabloids as my "new love interest" — arriving back at the house after our round trip to the airport that day: me with my mascara in thick streaks down my face, and McTavish clutching a fresh sausage roll, which he insisted on stopping at Greggs for after I ate the first one.

There's also a lot of hate.

I thought I knew what it felt like to be publicly shamed when Emerald told the entire town it was me who'd set her dress on fire last year. But that incident now seems pretty benign, really, compared to the hell that's raining down on me now. I'm a gold-digger, apparently. A scheming, Machiavellian fame-whore. I am the worst of all possible worsts, according to everyone on Twitter. (Oh, and I also have "legs like a garden gnome" apparently. So that's another thing to add to my list of troubles.)

So, yeah, I've seen the news, thanks, Scarlett. And I definitely don't want to play any further part in it, so once I've closed the stupid letterbox for the last time, I crawl back upstairs and lie on my bed, staring hopelessly at the ceiling until the doorbell rings again.

And again, and again.

"Go away, Scarlett," I scream from the top of the stairs. "Or I'll call the police. I mean it."

There's a long pause, then a woman's voice comes from the other side of the door.

"It's Wednesday, Lexie," she says apologetically. "You know Young Dougie has a half day on a Wednesday."

It's Emerald.

* * *

Emerald perches on the edge of my bed while I lie curled up in the fetal position on my side.

"Sorry," I say, as she looks around the room, which I haven't bothered to tidy; a sure sign of my rapidly declining mental state. "It's a bit of a mess in here. Do you want a coffee or something? Because you can help yourself. You know where everything is."

I'm trying my best to be welcoming here — and, well, to avoid having to go and make the drinks myself, because I just don't have the energy for it — but Emerald freezes at what she assumes is a reference to last year, when she briefly worked as my cleaner, and I want to kick myself in frustration.

Can I seriously not get anything *right?*

"It's okay," she says, smiling uncertainly. "I won't stay long. I just thought I'd pop round to see how you're doing. I... well, I've been reading the news, obviously. I figured you could probably use a friend."

"Are we friends?" I ask, sounding much more suspicious than I meant to. "Even after... The Thing?"

"Well, we weren't exactly friends *before* The Thing, were we?" Emerald points out reasonably. "But, look, people were nice to me when I came back here last year. I thought someone should do the same for you. Pay it forward, you know?"

"But I was an absolute *bitch* to you, Emerald," I sniff, pushing myself into an upright position so I can see her better. "I literally set you on *fire*. Why would you even want to be in the same *room* as me, let alone try to be my *friend*?"

"Because you need a friend," she says simply. "And all of that ... The Thing... was a long time ago. I don't know about you, but I like to think people can change. I know I have. I haven't stolen anyone's identity for *ages*, for instance."

She grins, and I surprise myself by smiling back at her. It kind of hurts, actually. I guess my mouth isn't used to forcing itself into that particular shape these days.

"I meant it when I said I was sorry," I tell her, looking her in the eye. "I know it maybe didn't sound like it. I'm not very good at this. But I've been wanting to say it since it happened. It's the biggest regret of my life, honestly. I say that as someone who's currently the Main Character on Twitter, so that's not nothing, trust me."

"Really?" Emerald asks. "Your biggest regret isn't Jett?"

I pause.

"I'm not sure what I could have done differently with Jett," I admit. "That's the thing. I know what I did to you. I know it was wrong. But I didn't tell anyone about me and Jett. I didn't tell Scarlett, no matter what everyone thinks."

"Oh, I know that," she says, surprising me. "I meant it in the sense of regretting you didn't tell him how you felt about him," she goes on. "Because you did really love him, didn't you? Anyone could see that. Or have I got it wrong? Oh God, have I?"

She puts her hands over her face in mortification, and I rush to reassure her.

"No, you haven't," I admit. "I do love him. And I should have told him. You're right about that. But how did you know it wasn't me who gave Scarlett the story? Everyone else thinks I did."

"Scarlett told me," Emerald says, her eyes wide. "She didn't tell me who it really was," she adds, hurriedly. "She has to protect her source, you know? But she did say it definitely wasn't you. She's been telling everyone that."

I sit there on the bed, dumbfounded.

Scarlett knows who the "source" was. Of course she does.

Which means that Scarlett actually *can* clear my name with Jett.

"I need to call her," I say abruptly, jumping up from the bed. "I need to talk to Scarlett. Thank you, Emerald. Thank you for telling me this. Thank you for coming here."

I lean over and hug her impulsively, and, after a moment's

hesitation, she hugs me back.

"I better go," she says awkwardly as she pulls away. "Jack's waiting for me."

"Oh! Speaking of Jack," I say, remembering. "I need you to give him a message from me. Well, from Mum, really. It's actually more of a proposition —"

* * *

As soon as Emerald leaves, I fish Scarlett's note out of the bin, thanking God for Mum's poor housekeeping skills, which mean she hasn't bothered to empty it while I've been hiding out in my room. When I call the number, though, it just goes straight to voicemail, so I call back and leave her a message, then, just to be sure she gets it, I type out a quick text.

> *It's Lexie. Please call me. Or just come round. It's urgent.*

After that, I don't know what to do with myself. The burst of adrenalin that gave me the energy to call Scarlett disappeared as soon as I realized she wasn't going to pick up, so I go back upstairs, and throw myself back onto the bed again, to mope.

I'm so tired of myself right now. I wish I could just wrap myself up and put myself away in a drawer for a while — maybe rediscover myself in a few months' time, lurking in my mothballs, and a little bit musty with time. Maybe then I'd shake myself out and brush myself down, and the me I'd discover would seem new again. I'd slip myself back on the way you slip on a favorite old sweater — the one you always looked good in, which you haven't worn for months — and it's as good as buying new clothes. I'd like to buy a new me. Or a new life, maybe. Either would do.

Instead, I pull the covers over my head and let myself drift off to sleep. I'm woken what feels like a long time later by the sound of someone banging on the door, and I jump out of bed and race downstairs to open it before Mum can get there.

"Scarlett, at last," I say, pulling the door open and blinking as the light streams in. It must be morning, then. I guess I slept right through the night. "I was starting to think you weren't going to turn up."

"Sorry," says a familiar voice that definitely isn't the one I'm expecting. "I got here as fast as I could."

I look up, rubbing my eyes to make sure I'm not imagining it.

It's not Scarlett.

It's Jett.

Chapter 39

Flashbulbs explode in my face as I stand there on the doorstep, too surprised to speak.

"Um, are you going to invite me in?" Jett says, glancing over his shoulder to where the paps are going wild, all shouting over the top of one another and struggling for space.

"That depends," I say cautiously. "Are you going to give me a chance to tell you my side of the story? Or are you just going to break my heart again?"

"I'm here, aren't I?" he replies softly. "Do you think I'd have come all this way just to break your heart? It's not exactly a short flight."

"Um, no. I guess not."

I have absolutely no idea why I'm standing here talking about his flight rather than just throwing myself into his arms and hoping he'll be okay with that. God knows, every time I've imagined this scenario — and I've had a *lot* of time to imagine almost this exact scenario while I've been lying on my bed feeling sorry for myself — that's how it's gone down.

Mind you, every time I've imagined this, it's also been snowing, for some reason — which would be unusual even for Scotland at this time of year. And then he's kissed me in the falling snow, both of us wearing cute little bobble hats, and all the people who are randomly standing around watching us have started cheering. Which is actually the ending of one of those daytime movies Mum loves so much, now I come to think if it. And, as I know all too well, real life is *not* like the movies, is it?

No, it's not. And I can tell you that with some authority, because, as it turns out, now that the man I've been dreaming about actually *is* standing on my doorstep, all I can seem to do is gape at him, in a way I'm sure is going to look really unattractive when the inevitable paparazzi photos come out. I bet Scarlett's wracking her brains for a suitably cutting image caption already.

"Lexie, are you going to let me in?" Jett prompts, glancing over his shoulder again. "Because I'd really rather not do this on the doorstep, if it's all the same to you."

Do what, though?

"Um, yes. Yes, of course. Come in."

His words break me out of my trance, and I step back to let him inside. There's just time for me to notice the long black car parked outside the house (I guess Jett didn't have to rely on McTavish's Uber service this time, then...), and a splash of color which has to be Scarlett in her red trench coat, then we're standing awkwardly in the hallway, which seemed to be a perfectly normal size when I ran downstairs, but which has now somehow shrunk to Alice-in-Wonderland proportions, leaving Jett and I standing almost toe-to-toe.

"Lexie, is that—"

Mum bursts through the kitchen door in a waft of perfume I recognize as mine, stopping in her tracks when she sees Jett and I standing there.

"Oh!" she says, her eyes widening in surprise. Then, "Ohhhh," she adds, smiling widely as she steps back into the kitchen, slamming the door closed behind her.

I turn to show Jett into the living room, but the large window makes it feel like a fishbowl, providing a perfect view for the assembled photographers, who're still poised outside, presumably waiting to photograph Jett again on his way back to the car.

"Shall we just...?" I gesture towards the stairs, and Jett nodds, standing back to allow me to go first, before following me up the short flight of stairs to my room, which still mirrors my state of mind at the moment, in the sense that it's a jumbled mess. I hastily pull the covers up on the unmade bed, in the hope that Jett will think it's like that because I just woke up, as opposed to it being because I've pretty much been living in it since he left. Of course, the fact that I've been sleeping in my clothes, and still have flakes of yesterday's mascara under my eyes probably tells a tale all of its own, and, as soon as I realize that, I give up my attempt to tidy the room and simply sit down on the edge of the bed to await my fate.

After a second, Jett takes a seat in the chair opposite me, dropping the bag he's carrying onto the floor, and rubbing his eyes wearily. His face looks tired, and, now that I'm looking at him more closely, I notice he doesn't seem to have shaved since I last saw him. It could just be the jet-lag, I suppose, but something in his eyes tells me it's more than that, and I can't help but hope that it's something to do with me.

Something *good* to do with me, I mean.

"How did your meeting go?" I ask, after a moment's silence. "The one with Justin Duval?"

Jett's face lights up.

"It was great, actually," he said. "Really great. I think he's going to give me the role. It's not 100% in the bag, but I have a good feeling about it."

"So he wasn't put off by... by the story?"

This time I don't feel the need to clarify what I'm talking about. Fortunately for me, Jett grins in response.

"Nope," he says. "Didn't even mention it. I don't think he cares as much about my private life as we were led to believe. Mind you, I guess it could also have been something to do with this..."

He pulls his phone out of his pocket and fiddles with it for a second before holding it up so I can see the screen. On it, the video I took of him at the Birnam Oak that day, doing the "Out, brief candle," speech from Macbeth starts playing. He lets it run for a moment longer, before hitting the stop button.

"You wouldn't happen to know anything about that, would you?" he says easily, putting the phone back into his pocket. "How he got it, I mean?"

"From Grace, I would imagine," I reply, feigning innocence. "Didn't he tell you?"

"He did tell me he got it — or his people got it, rather — from Grace, as a matter of fact."

I search his face, and am relieved to find only amusement in his eyes. "But how did Grace happen upon a video of me in Scotland? That's what I'm wondering."

"Okay, you got me." I hold my hands up in a position of surrender. "I sent it to her as soon as I finished filming it; asked her if she could find a way to get it to Duval. I had to do it, Jett," I tell him, leaning forward. "You were just so *good*. He had to see it. I knew if he saw it, he'd want to at least see you. And hey — I was right."

"You were right." He nods. "Thank you."

"You don't have to thank me," I tell him, shrugging. "All I did was forward someone a video. It's not a big deal."

"It is to me."

His face is serious as he holds my gaze.

"It's a big deal to me, Lexie," he says again. "It's a big deal that you believed in me. And that you did this for me, without expecting anything in return. No one ever does that for me. No one does things for me without expecting something back. But you did. And you didn't even tell me, so you could take the credit for it. So thank you."

Okay, now he's making me blush.

"You're welcome," I reply, a little more stiffly than I intended. "But..."

"But what? Tell me?"

"I did it because I believed in you," I say, my fingers twisting nervously at the fringe on the blanket that's lying on my bed. "You're right about that. But you didn't believe in me, did you? When you found out someone had leaked the story about our... our arrangement... you assumed it was me? I don't know how you could have thought that. I don't know why you couldn't trust me."

"I thought it was probably your mom, actually," he says, shamefaced. "But yeah, I assumed she'd have gotten it from you. That you'd told her what was going on, even though I'd asked you not to. And I was wrong. I know that now."

"How, though?" I stop playing with the blanket to look up at him, my eyes full of tears that I'm absolutely determined not to shed. "How do you know? What changed in the last..." I glance at my watch. I have no idea how long it's been since that morning at the airport. I just know it feels like forever, and yesterday, both at the same time. "The last... however long it's been."

Jett's hand comes up to rub at his eyes again. Before he can answer, though, there's a loud pinging noise from the phone in his pocket, and he pulls it out, glances at it and frowns, before putting it away again.

"Scarlett," he says, looking back at me. "Scarlett somehow managed to get a hold of Asher's number, and she kept on calling until she finally got through to Grace. She told her it wasn't you — or your mom, for that matter — who leaked the story. But it didn't matter by that point, because I already knew."

"But... how?"

"I just did." It's his turn to shrug now. "It wasn't because I'd seen the video by that point, or because of Scarlett. I just knew. I think I always knew you wouldn't do that. I just couldn't admit it to myself. Telling myself you'd betrayed me—" He grins. "Sorry. That's such a dramatic word, but it's how I felt. Telling myself you'd 'betrayed' me; that you'd just been in it for the money, or the fame, or whatever." He trails off. "Well, it was easier than admitting the truth," he says at last, not looking at me.

"And what's that? What's the truth, Jett?'

"That I had completely and utterly fallen for you. And I was absolutely terrified by it, because I didn't know if you felt the same."

He says this so matter-of-factly that it takes a moment for the words to sink in, and, when they do, it takes my whirring brain another few moments to work out how to respond.

Did he really just say he'd fallen for me? And, more importantly, did he mean it?

"How could you have not known, though?" I manage at last. "How could you not have noticed I felt the same?"

Jett's smile lights up his entire face.

"You did?" he asks shyly.

"Of course I did, idiot!" I resit the impulse to pick up a pillow and throw it at him. "*How* did you not know?"

"Because you're always so... spiky, I guess," he sighs. "Like you're determined not to let anyone get close to you because you're scared they're going to hurt you. Which is understandable," he adds hastily, seeing the look on my face. "But it's just... you're not like anyone else I know, Lexie. Or anyone I've ever met. You never wanted to kiss me, or even be seen with me, really. And when you found out you were going to have to sleep in the same bed as me, you were so horrified. It was like it was your worst nightmare or something."

"I was horrified because I was crazy about you," I blurt, not caring anymore how stupid I must sound. "And I was worried I'd make a complete fool of myself by making it totally obvious when you just weren't into me. Can you imagine having to spend the entire night lying next to someone you've got the hots for, but who doesn't want to know? It's like a form of torture."

"I don't have to imagine it, Lexie," he says seriously. "That's what I was doing too, remember?"

"You fell asleep," I almost shriek. "How can you say you had the hots for me when I was *right there—*"

"—in your little Heather Bay t-shirt," he interjects. "I liked that a lot. Didn't I say that at the time? I thought I said that?"

"You said it to make fun of me," I insist. "Then you fell asleep."

Jett's phone pings again, and this time when he glances at

the screen, he doesn't bother to put it back in his pocket.

"I wasn't sleeping," he says, returning his attention to me. "I was just pretending. I was trying to be a gentleman, like you said. Let you take the lead, and give me some kind of... I don't know, some kind of sign that you wanted more. But you didn't."

He gives me his dejected puppy look, and I'm not sure whether I want to laugh at him or kiss him.

No, scratch that. I want to kiss him. I definitely *want to kiss him.*

"I didn't," I tell him sternly, "Because I was waiting for you to make the first move."

"I *did* make the first move. I put my arm around you. That was it. That was my move."

"Well, putting my arm around your waist was mine."

Stalemate.

We sit there, eyeing each other warily from our respective sides of the room.

PING! says Jett's phone again, piping up at exactly the wrong moment. I have never hated a piece of technology as much as I currently hate that bloody phone.

"You said you had the hots for me," Jett says, grinning. "You said that."

"You said it too," I shoot back, sticking my tongue out like a child.

"I did. And I meant it. And that's why, as soon as I got to L.A., I knew I was going to have to turn around and come right back. So I called Duval and got him to move our meeting forward, and then, as soon as it was done, I got back on that plane."

He says this as casually as if he's telling me he got to the bus into town, as opposed to flying halfway around the world and back again, in less than 48 hours. But this is *huge*. It's enormous, in fact. So big that I can barely fit it into my head to make sense of it; this weird and wonderful fact that *Jett likes me*. So much that he flew all the way back here just to tell me, even though he must have known the house would still be under siege from the paparazzi who still believe I was only with him because I was under contract.

Thanks for that, Scarlett.

Scarlett.

The thought of her triggers a sudden feeling of unease; a reminder that there's still one thing that hasn't been resolved yet.

"Wait," I say, frowning. "If it wasn't me or Mum who sold the story to Scarlett — which it definitely *wasn't* — then who was it? How did she know?"

I look around the room, half-expecting Scarlett herself to step out from behind the curtains, or slide out from under the bed and reveal she's been watching us this whole time. Jett's eyes, however, never leave my face, and when I finish my inspection of the room and turn back to him, there's a look in them that makes a shiver run down my spine.

He knows. He knows who it was. He knows who it is that hates me enough to want to completely ruin me.

"Tell me," I whisper, my voice croaky. "Tell me, Jett. I need to know."

He clears his throat before he speaks, as if he's preparing to make a big speech, like the one I recorded him doing from Macbeth. When it comes, though, it takes just one word to shatter all my hopes.

"Violet," he says quietly, still looking me in the eye. "It was Violet. And I know, because she told me."

Chapter 40

And there it is: Violet King, Jett's most significant ex-girlfriend, rising up before me like Banquo's ghost, here to remind me that I'm not out of the woods quite yet.

It figures.

"Violet?" I say in a small voice. "She told Scarlett about... about us? But how did she know? Did you tell her?"

I think of that line in Scarlett's article; the one about Jett still being in contact with one of his exes. I'd assumed it was Violet, of course — if it was even true. And now it seems that it was.

As if on cue, the phone pings again, and my heart plummets.

"Is that her now?" I demand, hating the neediness in my tone, but not knowing how to stop it. "Is that Violet? Tell me the truth, Jett. I need to know."

Jett rubs at his eyes again, then picks up the phone and sets it to silent.

"Yeah," he says, looking at me directly. "It's not what it looks like, Lexie, I swear."

"Right. So what is it, then?" I fold my arms over my chest defensively. I can't believe that just a few minutes ago I was thinking about kissing him. Thinking I might mean something to him. And now...

"Did you tell her about us?" I go on when he doesn't reply. "Is that how she knew? Because you told her during one of the cozy little chats you've apparently been having?"

"Not exactly," he says, avoiding my gaze. "But I think I probably said enough for her to figure it out. I'm sorry. I know how it looks. I know—"

"So it's true?" I ask, interrupting him. "You and Violet? You're still in touch with her? Are you still... Are you...?"

I can't quite bring myself to finish my sentence. My entire body is trembling, and I'm not sure whether it's from rage or shock. I just know I want to get away from this room — from *him* — so I can think more clearly about all of this. About how one minute I was sure he was going to tell me he loved me, and the next he's pulling the ground out from under me by telling me he's still in touch with his ex.

"No, Lexie. God, no." Jett stands up, reaching for me, but I'm faster, and, before he can move, I'm standing at the bedroom door, ready to run. Just like I always do when things don't work out the way I wanted them to.

But no. Not this time. This time I'm going to stay. This time, I'm going to get some answers.

"Why are you really here, Jett?" I ask, my hand on the door handle. My voice is so steady it surprises me. Maybe I'm a better actress than I thought I was.

"I'm here to tell you the truth," he says desperately. "I'm not in love with Violet, Lexie. I swear to you, I'm not. Look, it's true that she's been messaging me lately. *She's* been messaging *me*, though. Not the other way around. I promise you, I feel absolutely nothing for her. That's all in the past. The distant past. It's done."

"For you, maybe," I say, still using that weirdly calm tone. "Obviously not for her if she's still contacting you."

"No, obviously not." He runs a hand through his hair in exasperation. "Although, honestly, she might say she wants us to get back together, but I'm not sure I believe her. I'm pretty sure she wants the Lady Macbeth role, and she thinks being with me again would be a good way to get it."

"Right. If you say so."

I don't care about Violet and her career aspirations. All I care about is Jett — and whether or not *he* cares about *me*.

"I do say so." His eyes are blazing as he crosses the room to stand in front of me. "There's nothing going on between me and Violet, Lexie," he insists. "Absolutely nothing."

On his knee, the phone lights up with a message alert. It doesn't ping this time, but I can see the screen — and I can read the name that's written on it.

VIOLET.

Suddenly, I've had enough.

With a sob that feels like it's coming right from my very soul, I turn and run down the stairs, Jett close behind me. I'm vaguely aware of him calling my name, but all I can think about is how stupid I've been, thinking I could compete with someone like Violet King, three-time winner of Maxim's *World's Sexiest Woman* award. Me, Lexie Steele. Who user5634 on Instagram once described as, "a living Troll doll with thighs that could crush a city".

I fling open the front door and find myself staring at Scarlett, who's standing on the doorstep, her hand raised as if she's about to knock. Behind her, there's a sudden roar from the assembled paparazzi, who seem to have doubled in number since the last time I saw them.

"Lexie, is it true that you were just with Jett for the money?" one of them shouts. "Or do you fancy yourself as an actress, too?"

"Um, don't feel like you have to answer that," says Scarlett, who has the grace to look ever so slightly shamefaced about the level of chaos she's unleashed here. "Just go back inside. I'll try to persuade them to go."

My legs shaking with nerves, I start to close the door, but then a flashbulb goes off in my face, and something inside me snaps.

"I'm not an actress," I sob, pushing Scarlett aside and flinching as the cameras go off in unison. "I've never been an actress — well, other than accidentally."

My trembling legs somehow carry me down the path toward the crowd of photographers, moving almost as if they have a mind of their own. Halfway there, I have a change of heart and almost turn back, then I spot McTavish at the back of the crowd, a bemused expression on his face and a sausage roll in his hand. Somehow, the sight of him gives me courage.

"I didn't do it for money, either," I say, squaring my shoulders and raising my chin defiantly. "I'm not interested in Jett's money. I never was. And I know it must be really easy to look at someone like me and think you know me, but you don't. None of you know me. Well, except McTavish," I amend, seeing his blonde head bob up above the crowd. "He kind of does. But other than him, none of you have the slightest clue about my life, or about Jett's," I go on, my voice stronger now. "You don't know us. So you can keep trying to paint me as the villain if you like. Just because you say it, it doesn't mean it's true."

A hush has fallen over the crowd. Microphones are raised

in my direction, cameras whirring silently, all waiting for whatever I'm going to say next. Which is awkward, really, because I have absolutely *no freaking idea* what I'm going to say next.

"So why *did* you do it?" prompts Scarlett helpfully, from somewhere off to the side. "Why were you with Jett, if it wasn't about money?"

"Isn't it obvious?" My voice comes out somewhere between a wail and a sob. I really hope the sound on those cameras isn't great. "I did it because I love him. That's it."

"And I love her too," says a voice from behind me. "That's all any of you need to know."

I turn round so quickly my head spins. Jett has followed me out of the house and is standing behind me. I have no idea how long he's been standing there, or how much he heard. What I do know for sure is that he's looking at me as if I'm the only person here — and if he's hating every second of being out here in public, in the full glare of the media spotlight, there's absolutely no sign of it.

"Come with me?" he asks, those familiar green eyes of his still fixed on mine as he holds out his hand to me, completely ignoring the cameras around us. "Come for a walk?"

A walk?

This seems like a pretty weird time to be thinking about exercise, really. But ever since I heard the words "I love her," come out of Jett Carter's mouth, that's all I've been able to think about. The words are so large they seem to hang in the air above us as I wordlessly take the hand Jett offers me, and let him lead me back down the path, past the front door of the house, where Mum stands gaping in the doorway, and down the sloping garden to the rough seagrass border that separates it from the beach.

The words are still there as we stop, the wind tearing at our hair and clothes as we stand there silently, neither of us knowing what to say.

Back at the house, the paps are still clicking away. One or two of them have snuck through the open gate, and are wriggling commando-style towards us, presumably hoping we won't notice them. Scarlett is nowhere to be seen. (McTavish is still enjoying his sausage roll, though, so at least someone's happy.)

"Do you want to go back inside?" I ask, suddenly realizing how much he must be hating this, standing out here on the very edge of this exposed beach, where anyone who walks by can see us. "So they can't get any more photos?"

"I don't care about the photos, Lexie," he sighs, reaching out to brush the hair the wind has blown back into my eyes, away from my face. "I don't care what anyone thinks about me. I just care about you. That's it. Just you."

I look up, and into his eyes, and I want to believe him. I want that more than I've ever wanted anything in my life. But the photographers have almost reached us now. I can hear the frantic click-click of the shutters as they capture every precious moment of this conversation, and, as much as I hate them for it, I know that, without them, Jett and I wouldn't be standing here at all.

Can something that started as a lie really become the truth?

Is it possible that I was the heroine of this story all along?

"I don't know what's real anymore," I admit tearfully, trying to pull away. But, before I can move, Jett reaches out and turns me around, so his body is shielding mine, and blocking the photographer's view.

"This is real," he tells me, taking my chin gently in his hands. "I am. We are."

It isn't snowing — or even raining, which would be almost as good — and neither of us is wearing a cute little bobble hat. But when Jett finally kisses me, there is indeed a cheer from the crowd behind us — or from McTavish, at least, who lets out a loud whoop, and almost drops his sausage roll in the process.

Not that I notice any of that, of course. I'm too busy concentrating on Jett, and the way his lips feel against mine; his arms wrapped tightly around me, as if he's never going to let me go.

"So, whaddya say," he grins, when we finally pull apart. "Are we going to give this thing a go? A proper one, this time?"

"Are you asking me to be your girlfriend, Jett?" I say, smiling up at him. "Your real one?"

"I am." He leans forward and kisses me lightly on the tip of the nose.

"Will I... will I have to sign a non-disclosure again? Or promise to—"

"You don't have to sign anything," he cuts in. "And the only thing you have to promise to do is love me. That's it."

"I think I can manage that. I think I can love you. I know it, in fact — because I already do."

It's a pretty clumsy way to tell someone you love them, all things considered. But I'm new to this. A complete amateur, in fact. Fortunately for me, though, Jett comes to my rescue.

"Well, that's sure good to know," he says softly. "Because I love you too, Lexie. And it would've been a bit awkward if you hadn't said it too."

"I'm going to say it a lot from now on," I tell him shyly.

"Just so you know."

"I'm going to say it too," he replies, his eyes twinkling. "I think I might say it in private next time, though, if it's okay with you?"

He glances over his shoulder, to where the photographers are all jostling for space, some of them now inside the garden in their bid to get the best shot of us both.

"Come on," Jett says, taking me by the hand. We run together back up the garden to the back door of the house, which is thankfully unlocked. As soon as we're inside, away from the prying camera lenses, Jett pulls me back into his arms.

"This isn't for the cameras," he tells me, his green eyes never leaving mine. "This one's just for us. You and me."

Then he kisses me again. And it might not be the first time, but it definitely feels like the start of something real.

It feels like the start of us.

EPILOGUE

Heather Bay Gazette
FUNDING BOOST FOR THE HIGHLANDS AS HOLLYWOOD MOVIE TO START PRODUCTION SOON
by Finn McNeil, Editor

It was good news for the Highlands this week with the announcement that Justin Duval's hotly anticipated movie adaptation of Macbeth will be filmed in the area. Several locations in Glencoe and on the Isle of Skye have already been earmarked for the production, which will star Hollywood icon Jett Carter in the title role. Casting for the remaining roles, including that of Lady Macbeth, has yet to be completed, with several actresses said to be under consideration for the role of Macbeth's wife.

Although Heather Bay itself will not feature in the movie, it's rumored that the ruins of Cowle Castle, on the town's Loch Keld, will be used as Macbeth's home — with the help of some CGI to restore the building to its former glory.

"It's a huge boost for the Highlands, and for Heather Bay in particular," said retired headteacher Bella McGowan, chair of Heather Bay's community council. "We've already seen an increase in tourists to the area thanks to Jett Carter's visits this year, and if he stays in town during filming, it should create a huge buzz around the place."

Other residents, however, are not so happy.

"It scares the beasts, havin' aw these extra folk tramping through the fields lookin' for film stars," said local farmer Jimmy McEwan. "They leave aw their rubbish lyin' around, and the chippie's always runnin' oot o' deep fried Mars Bars now. I dinnae like it."

Justin Duval, who describes the project as "his life's work", however, is insistent that the movie must be filmed in Scotland.

"Macbeth is the Scottish Play," a spokesperson for the French-born director told the Gazette. "Scotland is the only place it should be filmed. Also, Jett Carter said he wouldn't do it unless we filmed it there, so there was that, too."

Details have yet to be finalized, but inside sources say the movie could begin filming as early as this winter. The Gazette will be on hand for further updates.

* * *

SPOTTED: Jett Carter and Lexie Steele at the Wildcat Cafe, ordering macaroni pies. Yon Lexie looked right pleased wi' herself. Rumor has it she's up tae high doh wi' worry about who's going to be playing Lady Macbeth, though. Right enough, I wouldnae trust that Jett further than I could throw him.

XOXO,

@heatherbaygossip

* * *

Tinseltown Insider

IS JETT CARTER SWAPPING HOLLYWOOD FOR THE HIGHLANDS?

As Jett Carter and girlfriend Lexie Steele were spotted shopping for a new home in the Scottish Highlands this week, friends of the actor have been questioning whether they'll ever see the actor again.

"Jett hasn't been home since he was cast in Macbeth," said a close friend of the star, who declined to be named. "He's barely been in touch with any of us. It's like Lexie has cast a spell over him or something, and now he just does whatever she says."

According to agent Asher Ford, however, who's represented Carter since he broke onto the scene at 19, in his first movie, *Islanders*, says there's another explanation for the actor's continued absence.

"Jett loves being in Scotland," he told the *Insider*. "Not only is he getting the opportunity to really steep himself in the language and culture of the place while he prepares for what could be the biggest role of his life, he also appreciates the peace and quiet of the Highlands. People don't bother him in Heather Bay; he's treated just like anyone else there, and it's been a refreshing change for him."

Whatever the reason for Carter's extended stay in Scotland, one thing is clear: as Macbeth prepares to enter production, with filming taking place largely on location in the Highlands, his Californian friends probably shouldn't expect to see him anytime soon.

* * *

SPOTTED: Lexie Steele wearing what looks like a ring on her engagement finger!

XOXO

@heatherbaygossip

UPDATE: Nevermind, it was just a hair band. And it was on her wrist, not her finger. And actually, now that I look closer, I think it was mibbe somebody else?

XOXO

@heatherbaygossip

ANOTHER UPDATE: Ma money's on her getting a real engagement ring soon, though. Dinnae forget, ye heard it here first...

XOXO

@heatherbaygossip

Thank you

Thank you for reading my second novel.
I really hope you enjoyed it and can take a few minutes out of your day to leave a review on Amazon!

Want to know what happens next?

In Spring 2023, you can follow Scarlett in her pursuit of love (and a missing Ada Valentine).

About the Author

Amber Eve is a Scottish author who's best known for her blog (ForeverAmber.co.uk), and her Heather Bay Romance series, of which this book is Part 2. You can read more from Amber at the links below:

You can connect with me on:

- https://foreveramber.co.uk
- https://twitter.com/foreveramber
- https://www.facebook.com/foreveramberUK
- https://www.instagram.com/foreveramber

Subscribe to my newsletter:

- https://mailchi.mp/cb43d14786a9/book-alerts

Also by Amber Eve

The Accidental Impostor

When Emerald Taylor is forced to return to the Highland home town she left in disgrace over a decade ago, her main aim is to stay out of trouble.

But trouble has a way of finding Emerald, and when she impulsively tries on someone else's dress, only to be caught in the act by the handsome new Laird, there's only one thing she can do: lie.

She's only an *accidental* impostor —but the risk to her heart is very, very real; and meeting Jack Buchanan could just be Emerald's biggest mistake yet.

The Accidental Investigator — coming Spring 2023

Moving to the Scottish Highlands isn't quite what Scarlett Scott expected it to be. And when local influencer Ava Valentine goes missing, things start to get even more complicated; especially when the dour new village policeman gets involved.

For Scarlett and Dylan, it's hate at first sight. But can they work together to find Ada? And can enemies ever really become friends... or more?

Printed in Great Britain
by Amazon

18521501R00202